CONSEQUENCES

JULIETTE A H CAVENDISH

ISBN Paperback: 9780648853084

ISBN Ebook: 9780648853008

www.juliettecavendish.com.au

For those who needed to be loved and weren't.

CONTENTS

ONE

SAPPHIRES AND RECTANGLES

Catherine spotted the small bookshop behind the sandwich bar at Paddington Station. It would serve as a potential refuge from the swirling crowd, armed police and suitcases that were swarming around her. It had been a while since she had travelled anywhere by train, mainly due to having been in Covid lockdowns for an eternity, and the scene in front of her was brewing a massive tension headache. She looked around, feeling like an extra in an action movie. There were numerous police with fingers hovering over triggers, ready to shoot invisible terrorists, and cameras following her every move. She looked at the moving mass of people and suitcases. Surely this was too many for an enclosed space of this size?

She hoped that a few minutes of solace amongst the quiet of a bookstore might help to restore her chakras, now out of alignment and begging for peace. They were temperamental at the best of times, a result of having to reside with an anxious disposition gene. She lugged her bulging suitcase through the doors to the shop, where it promptly blocked the

1

non-fiction aisle. A four-hour rail journey was approaching, just long enough to immerse herself properly into someone else's life and hopefully forget about her own.

Her own story was a whole other matter. Needless to say, she was fed up and frustrated at having just discovered that her newly launched podcast series, which she had poured her heart, time and effort into, had spectacularly flopped. If she hadn't been so keen on searching for her listener count, none of this would have happened. Three was a number that only included herself, her mother and her best friend. Three was failure, no matter how positive one tried to spin it. It struck her that perhaps changing the series to be more about how one could overcome failure might be a future topic series.

She scanned the aisle for something to read. Her eyes landed on a brilliant sapphire book, right at eye level in front of her. She picked it up just for the colour alone, noting the beautiful gold threading woven into the spine. She flicked to a random page rather than reading the cover - one of her many bad habits. She could barely recall the title or author of any book that she read, which made her sound absent when recalling great reads to others. She glanced at her watch. Her train was due to depart in 15 minutes, so there was no mad rush. She would read for one minute and then decide if it were a keeper. If not, then the book would be placed back onto the shelf. She scanned the first page.

'*Our days are full of insignificant events that take us from birth to death in what amounts to a journey of nothing. From nothing to nothing. Days filled with the monotony of small and quite stupid activities, which are grossly insignificant in the grand scheme of things.*'

Catherine's eyes widened. Her mind filled with the notion of insignificant events, and she wondered how much of her life filled that criteria? Her pulse quickened as she realised she was bordering on what might become a full-blown existential crisis, right in the middle of Paddington Station. Wasn't she too young to be forced into such a significant crisis? She reflected on her job, which wasn't significant at all. She doubted whether anyone knew how much thought went into keeping the company's cloud ordered and tidy. She continued reading, hoping to find a better bit.

'There probably isn't a heaven or a hell to look forward to after the small and stupid has ceased.'

She felt her stomach forming a tight knot at the depressing tone of the words, wondering if her podcast series had indeed been small and stupid? Maybe that's why it had only accumulated three listeners? Accumulated seemed the wrong choice of words when discussing only three, however. She became aware of a man standing in the aisle next to her suitcase, his path obviously blocked by it. If she completely ignored him, he might go away. Couldn't he just walk into the next aisle and go around? The man stood square though, defiantly staring at her. It was obvious he wasn't going anywhere.

'You got yourself some light reading there?' A well educated voice seemingly belonging to the man emerged from behind the suitcase. It seemed at odds with his heavy stance. He was apparently nosey too, and remained standing in the same spot, now waiting for her to answer.

Out of habit, she immediately dropped her gaze to the man's left hand to check to see if he was married. A bad habit, but necessary, given she was still hoping to find a soul mate. At 33, she was tired of being alone and any opportunity to find a partner to share her life with was still on the books. She noted the unintended thought-pun, given they were both standing in a bookstore and congratulated herself.

She did a quick inventory of appearance, not seeing a wedding ring nor a mark where one had been taken off. Mid-forties, dark hair, curls at the nape, deep-set laugh lines and a recent trip abroad given his tanned skin. Either that or a pretty good fake tan? She ruled him out immediately as she followed his mismanaged attempt at fashion. He was dressed in brown from his feet to his head as if he'd been transported from the seventies. He was a mission-brown rectangle if she were accurate. Her gaze stopped on his brown striped tie, and she must have looked a bit disappointed because he apologised.

'So sorry to interrupt. I'm just looking for a book myself.' He looked at the book in her hand. 'Metaphysics and philosophy I see. That's Fallow's book on The Futility of Being Human. Not the happiest of reads if you don't mind me saying so.' Then he waited for some sort of response, brown eyes wide and eyebrows perched high on his face. They stayed there, insisting that she respond.

She inwardly sighed. He wanted conversation which was going to be awkward given she had no interest in brown rectangles.

'Oh goodness, is it?' She feigned alarming surprise and quickly turned the book over. He was most certainly waiting for something profound to erupt from her lips, given she had picked up such a well-titled book. 'Oh,' she said, sounding a bit disappointed that the brilliant blue of the cover didn't seem to match the cracker-dryness of the title. Her mind was blank with intelligence and full of disappointment over the blue that had promised so much more. If she were honest, she had been lured and cheated by colour alone, but perhaps that wasn't the conversation he was after. The silence lasted too long, and so the man spoke again.

'It's not a bad read in all. I read it whilst flying over China a few years ago.' The man seemed to be filling in the missing words of conversation for her. He then gave up and squeezed his way past her suitcase.

'I've not yet been to China,' she finally said, hoping that he would keep moving.

He frowned and stopped in his tracks.

She frowned back, knowing that she needed to say something else because he still wanted more. Maybe he was a pilot and had actually flown the plane himself? The words hung in the air, not knowing where to fall.

He stopped frowning and smiled. 'Well, you must put it on your bucket list. It's quite marvellous in places. Makes Paddington Station look empty given the density of the crowds over there. Are you interested in metaphysics and philosophy then?'

No, she thought to herself, not wanting to express the words.

He reached for a book on the top shelf titled 'Quantum Entanglement.' It looked like it had too many pages for Catherine's liking in the context of train travel. She wondered how to respond to his question. Could she be interested in metaphysics and philosophy? She wondered what metaphysics even was. A cross between philosophy and science, perhaps? At that moment, given she had picked up that particular book, maybe she could be? She also didn't want to disappoint the man, who had sounded quite hopeful - for a brown rectangle, that was.

'Yes,' she said confidently, flicking her hair dramatically. 'I love questioning everything, although I'm not sure I'm in the mood right now for something so heavy.' That was brilliant. She smiled at her clever response hoping that it was enough to have him move on, as well as make her sound super-clever.

'It's definitely heavy,' he agreed. 'Certainly that, and it gets you thinking... which isn't always a good thing in certain situations, especially on trains. I prefer to mostly look out of the window and ponder simple pleasures. I'm a bit of a happy ponderer if the truth be told.' His phone buzzed, and he checked the message. 'Must go. My train is due to depart. I'm off to a conference in Glasgow to speak about artificial intelligence scaffolding. Enjoy the book if you decide to buy it, won't you.' Then he was gone.

Catherine was again standing alone in the bookstore. She found herself stuck on his final words. She had no idea what AI scaffolding looked like and wondered if he had thrown that in to impress her. However, there was a possibility that she might enjoy the book. Out of respect for him, especially given he had finally walked away, she opened up another page to give the book one last opportunity to invite itself into her train journey.

'Most life events aren't monumental enough for historical noteworthiness or powerful enough to cause more than a small and hardly noticeable glitch in the fabric of everything. Thus, the reality of small lives, played out by billions of small, insignificant human beings...'

No. Catherine had read enough. This book was about despair and bleakness. By the time she got to her destination, she would be depressed. She didn't want to feel futile at that moment. She wanted to feel excited that she was going on a journey that had been a long time in the planning. She glanced at her watch. Nine minutes until her train left. She put the book back onto the shelf, the brilliant blue cover inviting other people to pick it up and investigate. Even if people only read a few words from it, she surmised that it had done its job in getting people to reflect on life and, indeed, feel futile.

She wheeled her suitcase to the fiction section, bumping into several shelves and knocking down the books that had their corners sticking out on the lower shelves. The woman at the check-out glared at her before calling over.

'Be a bit more careful, Luv.'

'Sorry,' she called back, wondering why the woman didn't keep the narrow aisles better managed. She berated herself for being so judgmental as she picked them up.

She needed a different book. One that might encourage escapism and allow her to vicariously inhabit someone else's world. Maybe she could lead a more exciting life, one with less futility, by doing this? She smiled at her conclusion. Four hours of escapism, that's what she needed.

A book caught her eye. She smiled when she saw the title. 'Consequences.' That was a metaphysical moment, given the fact that the dryness and futility of the doomsday book had made her reach for a second one. She almost wished the brown rectangle was still there to have noted this profound coincidence. She handed over the eleven pounds to the sales assistant and made her way to Paddington's Platform Three, where her train was waiting to depart. Settling into her comfortable first-class seat, a treat for such a journey, she got her ticket out, ready for inspection. She already felt spoiled with a small bottle of sparkling water and a packet of crisps on her seat tray. She opened the book, took a deep breath and invited the characters in.

TWO

WHITE KNUCKLE FLYER

With ruffled ginger hair and newly 26, Andrew smothered Rupert with morning kisses, then languidly sat back to watch him dress. He couldn't resist playfully grabbing as Rupert hurried past him, trying desperately to find his shoes. Both had been thrown off the night before and were now hiding under the bed, probably in shock from having been a silent witness to the night before. He aimed his phone at Rupert, once suited, and took yet another Instagram perfect shot. He was fully aware of the envy that others would feel at his apparent good fortune. Then, a few moments later, he leaned out from between his blue pinstriped linen curtains and waved to Rupert, who was heading back towards his car.

He grinned. The first week of pure, unrelenting lust in any new relationship was always the best, especially when one had found a diamond amongst the coal. A pearl amongst oyster-filled shells. He had wanted to spoil Rupert from the moment they had met. Life now seemed more exciting, despite the exhaustion from the constant sexual ache between his legs. Colours were more vivid, and there was a definite optimism that enveloped everything as a result. Every moment seemed to be electrified - probably due to all the hormones being released, he surmised, but nevertheless, still an excellent free high to be had. Jonathan smiled to himself as he pulled the doona back onto his bed.

He also concluded that a wild juicy ride of Rupert, cocktails and a few forbidden white lines had also resulted in a hammer-pounding headache, a small price to pay for such outrageous fun. It had been a sexual Michelin three-course adventure in which three stars could have been given to the dessert alone. Andrew never shared secrets about his romantic adventures but knew he had found a partner in crime. A perfect parallel. It was a mind of likened complexity, corruption and a body that caused ripples in space itself when it quivered.

Rupert, whom he had met the week before at a friend's party, was an incredible find. Well, it wasn't so much of a chance find, per se, as Andrew had quickened his pace to catch up with Rupert the moment he had spotted him. It had been a perfunctory meet, greet and lay the 'I want you,' right at Rupert's feet. At least he thought it was in that order. A deliberate overt proposition rather than a chance meeting where two minds and bodies could foster compatibility over time. They were entwined together in a spare bedroom four minutes later, after which Rupert disclosed that he hadn't quite caught Andrew's name. Andrew needed a Rupert in his life. A man to indulge, spoil and worship. He had got Rupert, and rest assured, he would look after him. That much he knew. His cock agreed, nodding with the thought.

Rupert, in fact, was nothing short of a god-like statuesque beauty. Blonde, buffed and blissfully sculptured. He was now

Andrew's muse, his lover, and now his new addiction. Andrew needed addictions in his life like others needed oxygen. He needed to operate in a haze of swirling extras. Otherwise, life was too dry for him to savour, like eating dry crackers without a topping. Rupert was the caviar, the creamy cheese, the delicate smoked salmon that made Andrew want to devour everything whole. Flavours merging together, they created one greedy bang of an experience. Just like Rupert, when he had been in his mouth. That had been a bit of a bang too, and Andrew reflected that he had probably been a bit greedy too, in retrospect.

He surmised that there was just nothing better in this world than losing oneself in a haze of body parts, sweat, juices, and the unexplored. He stepped back to admire his bed, now eagerly and patiently anticipating the next chapter of this wonderful romance. Drunk as the proverbial skunk and as high as an Elon Musk rocket he had been last night.

'Fuck!' he yelled out to his apartment, his only witness to this fugitive word. He was a corner-hugging Ferrari on the other side of straight, and he loved it. All of it. He most certainly loved all of Rupert.

ON THE OTHER side of the city, Matt Harmon, noir-black curls at the nape, strands of grey at the temples, and 36, placed a succulent kiss onto the peachy white arse that belonged to Miss Cindy. He slapped it, playfully leaving his signature mark, and she giggled. He, too, had woken to a flood of excruciatingly good memories after his night of raw passion, in which he had shown the strength and flexibility equal to an Olympic gymnast. His black and white silk sheets were drenched in both of them, giving off that 'morning after' fragrance. The sort of smell that, if bottled at a perfumery, would make people sniff, grimace, turn away, and then sniff again, trying to work out what the contradiction of like and dislike was all about.

He stopped to admire his reflection in his full-length mirror. His family of six-pack, biceps and quads were a reflection of hard work and discipline. He refused to compromise on the time he spent with them, and his gym time was never negotiable. Shortly, Miss Cindy would return to her life as a fitness instructor at his gym, and he would most likely only ever utter 'hi' to her again. He smiled, acknowledging that the left side of his face was probably his best angle because it showcased his rather cute and sexy dimple, which always got him to first base. He snapped his image with his phone and then waited for the likes. Then he remembered he needed to send a text.

'Don't forget you are having dinner at my place tonight x.'

His girlfriend Felicity, texted straight back, as she always did. 'xxx.'

MEANWHILE, in a most affluent suburb of London, a 56 year-old man was tied up. He was positioned in a neat, Georgian white-washed three-storey terrace, fringed with black gutters and a lacy black balcony. Not with pressing appointments for work, which would have been far more socially acceptable, but rather, swinging from a homemade bondage apparatus. Husband Greg was spanking him lightly in all sorts of dark and mysterious places, and the man was shrieking a song of lustful pleasure. Greg alternated spanking with tickling, which extended the song into a chorus and verse of pleasure and pain. A hood protected the man's face. Well, it was more of a badly homemade mask in the form of part of a silk pillowcase and some elastic nicked from a pair of pyjamas. It was finished off with a piece of felt from an old hat found in the back of his wardrobe. His Zorro-like identity remained a secret as the small camera, set up at one end of the room, silently witnessed this amateur debauchery, only showing its moderate interest by blinking red on occasion. Blink. Blink. Pause. Blink.

LOUISE HAMILTON, 53, and two suburbs away, was drinking a cup of Earl Grey tea after watching several episodes of 'The Lost Abbey.' It had been a 'series binge' in which she now felt sated from having gorged in such a manner. She often parked herself into an altered reality that provided solace and escape from the routine of her day job. Her nightlife mainly consisted of home, pop her nightie on, watch tv and then sleep. It sounded boring, except that technology allowed her to transform into a chameleon. In her world of technology, she could transform into literally anyone. A displaced Victorian, or perhaps Edwardian depending on the moment. Sometimes, in a wild moment of bravery, she even imagined herself as a flapper, but that was rare, and mainly after too many pink gin and elderflower tonics. She was currently in a stupor of heritage heaven, complete with a new hair-do. A softly swirled pompadour style which she wore with a deep sense of dignity. She felt fabulous. Decadent, even, if she lingered in the moment long enough to savour its effect.

AT SEVENTEEN THOUSAND feet above the English Channel, Kate Hemsworth, 33, was belted as tightly as would allow her to breathe into her plane seat. She could tolerate the occasional cup of Earl Grey, but on most days, she preferred a double shot coffee. She hadn't had a relationship in too many years, and nor did she watch historical dramas. She peered out from the window contemplating the strange half-reflection looking back at her. She could just make out the outline of the landscape below her. The sun was brilliant at this altitude, reflecting off the white cliffs of Dover, and the sheen made the English coastline look like it was edged in silver foil. Leaning further, almost resting her nose on the plane window, which smelt like hundreds of other noses that had gone before, she could see the deep green of the patchwork fields below, which struck her as resembling an alien landscape compared to the parched ochre dunes from her hometown in outback Queensland.

The plane started to descend further, and her ears blocked painfully. She yawned, trying to unblock them, and then the plane took a sudden steep and sharp turn to the left. She felt her pulse quicken and checked it on her watch. It was racing past a hundred and twenty. She took a few deep breaths and remembered her calming mantra. 'Anchor, calm and breathe,' she repeated to herself, trying to slow her breathing. It did nothing. What was the point in having a relaxation mantra if it did nothing when needed? Why was she on this plane at all? Flying had never been a comfortable experience, and the fact that she had boarded the plane at all was a bit of a miracle for someone with such a profound fear of flying. However, the alternative was six weeks on a cargo ship rolling around in random waters, so flying had seemed the easier choice.

However, here she was. This move she was making… this hugeness, would change her life because it had to. She hoped that all the shit, currently stuck to her person, would fall off, allowing her to emerge as a certified normal human being. She needed to feel good about herself at the end of the day, and right now, things had crumbled around her. Her job had been stifling, her relationships were failing, and she felt an overwhelming sense of despair on most days. She was becoming someone that even she didn't recognise anymore.

She yawned again as the pain intensified in her ears and her pulse galloped away. The plane hit some turbulence and was descending in great awkward leaps with the engines roaring and whining. She felt as if she were on a small boat in a vast, turbulent ocean. She clenched the armrests tightly, noting how her knuckles turned pearly white. Breathing in and out, she felt herself getting dizzy. She knew not to swear out loud in her panic. She had once done that on a previous flight causing a great deal of alarm to everyone around her.

'Why don't you eat some of these?' a flight attendant had asked, plonking no less than ten packets of salt and vinegar crisps onto her lap at once.

Her ears were painfully throbbing as the plane descended some more. She looked out again as a form of distraction. She could see a highway of planes in front and behind the plane, which gave her a sense of comfort that others were most likely also suffering in their descent to the promised land. She wondered how many of them were in her state of mind, escaping from hell and yet still with a small glimmer of hope for the future? London historically was a city of new beginnings and promises of better things to come. It was a place where dreams could reboot and previous identities could be lost to the wind.

Her recent depression, which had plagued her, hadn't been so much a black dog per se, as a dog at her side would have been a comfort. Instead, her depression had taken the form of a drenching, suffocating fog. A wall of thicket and deep unhappiness that had its roots firmly planted in her childhood. She had felt cut off from her world, behind a veil of blackness. She was lost in a world that she could barely touch, see and hear. It was closing in, judging by her insomnia and bouts of crying. She hid it from the world ever so cleverly, not through pride but a fear of what would happen if the illness was acknowledged by others. She would be labelled as something she wasn't prepared to be. She had become an excellent actor in hiding her reality.

Kate had felt emotionally exhausted all of her life. There had seemed to be no control over the recurrent depression that paradoxically hit just as things were going well. She was functioning with limited productivity, with third-degree emotional burns. A rawness that made her vulnerable to running, hiding and escaping the realities of life for respite. Sometimes she was so tired that she just wanted out. To be dead, she thought to herself. The bluntness of that thought required a bit of space around it. Then it required further analysis. It was a drastic thought at the best of times. The nothingness would settle matters once and for all. Rather than kill herself at that moment, which she had figured would be no different to just 'being asleep', she had reasoned that she would give herself a London shot first. A dose of much needed better.

This was the start. The first hint of what was to come. If it all failed, then the end would be arranged. An end already carefully researched and waiting in the form of pills and alcohol as she couldn't imagine blowing her brains out with a gun. That was way too confronting, and if the truth be told, too messy. Allowing others to bear witness to the dark insides of her brain seemed somehow quite unfair to them. She also wasn't sure if her blackness was contagious if released. Her details planning for the end hadn't quite been finalised just yet however, and were on ice until London had shown its hand.

Her ears painfully popped as the landing gear engaged with a dull thud. She looked out to see the city unwinding before her as the plane started its final descent into Heathrow. The Thames weaved around familiar landmarks such as The

Shard and Tower Bridge. It looked hopeful even from this height. The flight attendants instructed everyone to buckle up and then returned to their own seats. Kate shut her eyes instinctively as the runway accelerated towards them. She wondered if death would be a good thing if the plane did hit? One minute she would be here, and then there would be nothing. She might feel the impact and then go upside down as her seat rolled, or perhaps feel herself being flung around. Then there would be radio silence. It might be easier than working out how many pills she would need. She gripped the armrests so tightly that she was sure she would leave permanent indentations in them.

There was a dull thud as the wheels landed, the nose came down and then an enormous roar as the engines competed against the plane's brakes and the reverse thrusters were engaged. She felt herself forced forwards from the inertia, and then the rush was over. The plane slowly cruised to the terminal gates, and condensed passengers sprung up from everywhere, stretching and clambering to get off before the seat belt sign had even been turned off. She was alive though and had survived. She felt like jumping for joy. Most people don't see a landing as a cause for celebration, but it was a sheer miracle that should be dutifully noted in the grand scheme of things for someone like Kate.

As she waited in customs, she reflected on the journey thus far. It had been relatively easy to start this new life. She had bought a plane ticket, packed a suitcase, got on a plane and then sat there. Then she had got off. New ground, new turns, new air and new faces. Kate took a deep breath. There was no turning back now. No one would ever be able to tell if she were running towards a new life, running away from a past life or perhaps a bit of both? Only she knew all of that, and she would keep it a secret just as she always had.

She was now officially a risk-taker, a woman on a mission.

What was that thing her life coach had once told her? He had sternly said that weakness was for losers when she had confided her feelings about things. Kate wanted to be a winner for that moment, and every subsequent moment, so her cloak of artificial optimism would suffice for now as her favourite attire.

THREE

THE UNIVERSE SPOKE

S ix months later.

KATE TIGHTLY HUGGED her coat around her. The London wind felt icy and unforgiving, forcing her to walk pitted against it. The rain that was lashing her face was so cold that she couldn't tell if it were droplets of water or ice crystals that were stinging her cheeks. She carefully negotiated her way across the hectic London street, dodging the multicoloured taxis and the red and blue double-decker buses. She noted how her heels audibly clicked on the pavement, providing her with a sense of proof and connection with her route. How many other people had walked this very trail on their way through their own life story, she wondered? How many layers of human story were etched into the ground beneath her? Dirt road would have preceded pavement, and field would have stretched to the horizons before that.

She concluded that every person's thoughts, dreams,

ambitions, and histories have been absorbed into that space. They all must go somewhere, she reasoned, noting the regular rhythm of her heels. Otherwise, what was the purpose of a thought? It had to mean something rather than have such a short impact in people's minds. Surely a thought made a difference to the tapestry of everything? She loved that aspect of London. The sense of history and the feeling that you were part of some linear human continuum. A place that encouraged mindful wanderings, in between everything else. London had generously given her a little bit of itself to own, for the time being. It had resulted in a feeling of belonging that she hadn't experienced before. By comparison, back home in the Australian outback, she had instead belonged to a vast isolation. A space that had, at times, seemed to go on forever. Even the silence out there had felt deafening and defeating.

When a much younger Kate had stood in the outback, amongst the silence, the universe had once introduced itself to her. A private moment just between the two of them when perhaps she had been too young to be introduced at all. She had stood, small in the ochre paddock that had stretched for a hundred miles, and the universe had enveloped her on first meeting. It was everywhere and everything. It had demanded to know her worth. Not polite, not kind, but relentless with this needy connection. Did she feel small and irrelevant standing before it, or did she feel connected and mighty too? Did she remember that she was a higher-order animal on a tiny blue planet that revolved around one of its countless suns, connected to everything that was? Or had she forgotten? Was she destined to be a small human who would breathe, live, and then die without further understanding her place in the vastness? There was no escaping the enormity of the meeting.

Kate had felt insignificant, however, when pressed. She

had stopped for a moment to attempt contemplation and had looked up, trying to calculate the size of space and everything that was above her. She couldn't. The more she thought about it all, the smaller she became. Eventually, she became so small that she lost herself entirely, just for a moment. The universe had punished her for her lack of courage, her lack of succinct answer by enveloping her in dark matter. Punishment for not having the courage to stand in her rightful place and own it. To understand that she, as a human was a reflection of the greatness itself. Not just skin and bones and a conscious, temporary mind, but more than that. So much more if she could just see it.

The meeting had left her with an overwhelming uneasiness that made her wonder why she was trying so hard to get life right in the first instance? What was the point to it all when it appeared that she was just a tiny, random animal on a planet, suspended in a nothingness that was too big to even comprehend, where life shouldn't even exist? She was so small that compared to the size of everything, she was virtually nothing. She was nothing before she was born and would be nothing again at the end of her life. What was the point to the middle? At that moment, it had seemed futile to even try. At that moment, Kate and her sense of despair had been woven together as one.

A taxi splashed rain onto her legs, snapping her out of her ponderings. She could now see the name of the legal firm that had offered her a position. 'Plaid and Potter'. It stood out as being out of place in a street better known for boutique clothing retailers and tourist shops, but the fabric irony in its name wasn't lost on her. The urge to smile was definitely there as an option for such a literary connection. Disappointed that it wasn't going to be realized, the smile retreated. Kate didn't mind. It was better to feel something than the numbness that had gone before when the depression, out of spite, had frozen her feelings with its darkness. Smiles could come later.

She shook the rain out of her hair once back in her office as if she were a dog. Fragments of memories flooded in from childhood. Her Golden Retriever Bella, running in from the seasonal rains through the house. Her mother's shrieks at the trail of paddock-red paw prints and the fragrance of wet dog hair. Kate would turn towards the commotion only to be sprayed with saliva droplets, wet dog and ochre, as Bella shared with her. The memory wasn't whole anymore. Instead, it was a series of snippets of moments that seemed disorganized and silent. It was as if she were watching a silent film in which she was observing herself. She was sure there should have been more, such as all the in-between bits but couldn't access the memory further. Her reminiscence was interrupted by her assistant buzzing her and informing her that her two o'clock clients had arrived.

She should have remembered her umbrella, an accessory she had never owned in the dryness of home. Her lack of diligence meant that she had returned from lunch looking like someone who had swum laps during lunch, rather than a professional woman due to meet new clients in a matter of minutes. She buzzed her assistant for a towel, knowing that her request would be dutifully carried out, such was the power attached to her position. Her assistant would undoubtedly appear in a short time with the towel. The action, logically defying time itself. A wormhole known only to her assistant, perhaps?

By the end of her ponder, a fresh, dazzling white towel from the firm's bathroom linen cupboard was handed to her, complete with an equally dazzling, whitened grin, mainly due to the sensational memories from the night before. Jonathan then waited for his verbal reward, a bit like Bella had done after sharing her wet hair with Kate. An acknowledgement of his exceptional speed, efficiency and showmanship was necessary to dopamine-ready him for the next work challenge. Andrew also secretly wanted praise for his lovemaking to Rupert, as he felt he had exceeded all human expectations. It was so good that it needed to be acknowledged, even if only tangentially through his speed in obtaining the towel. Once he had received his verbal pat from Kate, his subsequent, oozing happiness would be infectious-ready. He would then spread it throughout the office, free of charge, no cough necessary and to those not immune to the effect.

Kate wouldn't have been described like that. Her only infectious trait was to spread darkness. The ambient room light would dim when she entered a room. A simple observation with no exaggeration. It was the way she was. Kate wasn't intentionally melancholy, but an unfortunate cloak of bleakness seemed to be stuck to her all the time. Humiliating too. At social gatherings, those around her would escape from her rather bleak accounts of life, mid-sentence, as if urgent business was calling them away. When people asked her how she was, only needing to hear a meaningless 'good thanks', Kate would instead tell them. A bit literal and far too truthful for most people's tolerances.

She would recount every nuance and detail of all of the challenges facing her in life. Receiving eyes would slowly glaze over and admit to lateral looks, this way and that, escape being the only comfortable response. She was the lactose, the gluten, the antichrist of vegan, the disguised grain of wheat that had no place in today's sensitivities. This explains why the ambient light in the room would dim. Kate literally sucked out energy by drinking from her own truth, leaving a reality that most couldn't even pretend to want to share with her.

Kate had been born with a happy demeanour, so she had

been informed by her late Aunt Natalie. She had once been a fat, bouncing buddha of an infant. Her chuckle had been constant, so joyful in fact, it had offended life itself, which in turn had decided to drain the chuckle out of her. A juvenile offence of too much positive spirit. As a result, she had been turned into a charcoaled etching of herself. Blackened and trapped in a reduced dimension in which to exist. If she remembered how to link the emotion to muscle memory, smiling was saved for monumental occasions only.

A random drunk dude at a bar had once explained over too many vodka shots that her nonchalant expression was a tremendous asset to her. She had been vaguely interested through her drunken haze at the thought that she had been blessed with any asset. She had verbally probed the random, slurring man at the bar for more details. Happy to oblige but struggling to link the words together coherently, he had explained that if she ever faced a chimpanzee, which he had added, happened 'jack squat' that, if she smiled at the chimp, it would most likely eat her face off. He added that monkeys didn't like being smiled at, so she would be fine. He had then grinned at her waiting for some reaction at this clever revelation, adding that he would be happy to eat her face off too if she wanted.

So, had thought Kate, her face would remain intact because she didn't smile. Definitely a small victory amongst life's more complex challenges. She shook her head at how bizarre thinking could be when pissed, wondering why the random man had started thinking about monkeys and her face in the first instance. She turned down the invitation for the random man to eat her face off and sank three more shots, glad to still have a face at all. Being shit-faced was better than being no faced.

Kate glanced at herself in the office mirror. 'Seriously?' She scolded her reflection. Her mascara had run down her cheeks, making her look like a sad clown, and her hair had frizzed into a dome on her head.

Her foundation, strategically applied to cover a few red patches from harsh summers in Australia, had escaped down the London drains in sympathy with the rain. The look was not a pretty sight, nor did it emulate professionalism. In the third drawer of her desk was a small bag, full of makeup for a just-in-case moment such as this one. Underneath that was a bottle of gin, for occasions just like this one. Her stress could be relieved with one large swig, which of course, she did right then, followed by a sneaky second. Too easy. She waited for the warm to start, which, right on cue, spreading throughout her, filling her with confidence and ease.

She popped a mint into her mouth for breath freshness and started to comb through her frizzy mane. Having an unlimited supply of booze tucked away for any occasion had proved to be a lifesaver. Kate rarely had the inclination to calm her anxieties the hard way, which required too much effort on her part. Her calming mantra had proven ineffective on the plane trip, so she had chucked it at Customs. She reclined in her chair, new confidence oozing through her veins, and read the brief for her new clients.

FOUR

SATAN SPEWED OUT

Another couple was divorcing and systematically being piped through the sausage process of couple's counselling. Kate was there to help sort out the remains of what had once been a promising relationship, once full of hope. She was a legal referee in a heated fight between two animals. Not an inappropriate label given how people behaved when they wanted the same shit. Animals that at times, attacked to a legal death.

So far, nothing had softened the dislike they now held for each other. Love had turned into hate and a desire to destroy the other. This meeting was a mandatory mediation appointment. They were to try to sort things out before their case progressed to a courtroom battle. Roger Leslie, wanted this, and Prudence Leslie, wanted that. In essence, that wouldn't have been an issue, only they wanted the same things, and neither would budge. Kate shook her head at the list of 'non-negotiable items'. A cast-iron cooking pot, a mobile phone, one queen bed and a faux Persian rug.

'Seriously?' she muttered to herself. How much was that

stuff worth, she wondered? Quickly doing the calculations in her head, it was a couple of grand. Their legal fees would run into the tens of thousands. However, it was the fight they wanted, not the stuff. According to the paperwork, their kids were becoming depressed, as neither would negotiate appropriate access either. Roger was fighting over a third of a per cent discrepancy in a fifty-fifty split. Was it pride, she wondered, or belligerence?

Both of them had more money than sense too. This wasn't a financially struggling couple. Both were professionals earning more than enough. She thought back to her own divorce and felt her chest tighten. She wondered if it were easier if both people wanted out? Did that lessen the pain, she wondered? She hadn't wanted out, and she hadn't seen any hints of her husband's affair either. The news had been thrown at her after dinner one evening. Then Ethan had literally walked out of the freshly painted doors to their newly built home twenty-three minutes later. She was given the divorce papers to sign, and her life as she had known was over. It was nothing short of brutal. No couple's counselling, no discussions. Just a moment in time where one door slammed, and a vast nothingness had presented itself.

Her life, ten years married to Ethan, had been sucked into a void, along with hope itself. Her subsequent depression grew into a black hole devouring the previous ten years with relish. It was as if that ten years had never been. Those years had now been replaced with nothingness and pointlessness that had made their relationship seem redundant from the start. All the good bits were eaten away by his ruthless affair and a deafening silence.

That had been six years ago, and Kate had locked herself away from the world, caring for her injured self as she might have cared for a fragile, wounded animal. She was familiar with fragility, having already cared for herself with the same degree of introspection all of her life. 'Take control and don't let go because there is no one there to catch you', her little voice had repeatedly told her growing up. She'd had plenty of time to repeat the mantra because her mother's charade of actually liking her own children couldn't be sustained past six o'clock in the evening. They were sent to their rooms so that her mother could pretend they didn't exist. Kate would lie there in the blackness, holding it together for fear that the monsters would come and get her if she showed any hint of weakness. Later in her life, upon reflection, she figured that she must have let her guard down because the depression monsters got in and opened up housing estates inside of her. They were property tycoons by the time she was twelve.

After Ethan, she had wrapped her smashed sense of self in the sensible words of encouragement spouted by her friends and colleagues. Two weeks of pity they had given her, and then they had forgotten about her pain, assuming her to have bounced back. So, she hid everything from them and herself. She built a nest of what her subsequent therapists called 'self-love' and then had gently placed her smashed form into the nest as if one were replacing a baby bird back after it had fallen out. Her therapists had been proud of this metaphorical action until she had disclosed that she kept it subdued by dousing it with alcohol. Then she had wrapped it, as one might have wrapped an Egyptian body, with infinite layers of protection, swapping cloth for attitude. No-one would ever hurt her little self-bird again. Then she had cultivated enough anger to keep anything and anyone away from it.

She had thrown herself into her work after losing Ethan, which had provided a form of solace. A legal and theoretical context in which displays of true self weren't necessary for promotion nor accuracy in her workplace. She had defined her new self as a workaholic and had turned her anger and hurt into a raging desire to be the best. Her lingering anger towards Ethan was outed at anyone male. A legitimate punishment for such betrayal, and she became known as ruthless and tenacious. Any man that resembled Ethan, whether in looks, mannerisms or words, was crucified. A wrath of fury was unleashed from her petite frame that impressed and perplexed every judge who witnessed her outrageous performances in the courtroom.

She knew not to give a death stare to the man sitting opposite her. He would ultimately pay her well for sorting out what was stupid and infantile behaviour. She took a deep breath as he launched into a tirade about his wife, Prudence. Kate looked over at Prudence, sitting diagonally opposite to him. A thin, wiry woman who was doing her best to remain calm. Kate admired her at that moment, as she would have already ripped his head off had he been saying the same things about her, figuratively, of course.

Kate noted Prudence's jaw clenching as her husband listed her flaws, inadequacies, and inability to please him. Her hands ever so slightly tightened around each other, having been neatly placed on top of the table in front of her. The woman was throttling him in her mind at that point. Kate was sure of it. Roger had never guessed at the violent fantasies that had regularly been played out right under his nose in his wife's mind. Kate wondered if this display of blatant control had been the norm and wondered how Prudence had been conditioned to remain so silent. A quick hit here and there, behind closed doors, might have done the job she surmised? Either that, or she had been reduced into silence through regular verbal assaults.

Kate vicariously enjoyed participating in what was really going on behind the charade of pretence that her clients arrived with. It didn't take much to press a few buttons and watch them transform into their honest normal. Kate wanted deterioration from the moment they arrived. The heated exchanges and the costumes falling, allowed her to feel. Akin to cutting, bleeding and being in the moment rather than as a passive observer. Kate did whatever was necessary to induce this state, something which her colleagues often quietly shook their heads to. If she couldn't feel the nuances of her own life, then why not immerse herself in the emotional expressions of her clients? Was it so wrong to drink a little of their blood every now and again? She wiped her lips with her fingers at the thought.

Her job was to note slight changes in behaviour and posture, which was part of her expertise. When she was cross-examining someone in court, noting when they became uncomfortable helped with her line of questioning. Sometimes it was a change, ever so insignificant. The person might blink more rapidly, breathe more deeply, or look around when answering a question that raised accuracy issues. She was like a hawk, peering into their space and watching for the slightest movement that might indicate an uncomfortable reaction and an opportunity for her to swoop. Individuals were often advised to sit as still as possible and have their hands in their lap when up against her. 'Don't move, don't breathe and keep your eyes straight,' they would be directed by hopeful defence lawyers. They would drill into their clients, 'don't ever let her see your weaknesses.'

In this case, Kate would wait until Prudence reached the point that Kate had coined 'the big bang', albeit in a legal context. If she had to stop and describe it, she would have noted it as a climax. A legal orgasm of sorts for Kate. A moment where the pain that had welled up inside of her could be released as her clients reached their own breaking points. A vicarious way for her to tag along with their pain. She would sit watching, as her clients slighted each other and wouldn't help. She wanted the explosion. She wanted their hate vented out so that she could feel it, just like Ethan had goaded her anger but hadn't allowed her to express it. She could remember how much he had hurt her and how much she had wanted revenge by witnessing hate again. Revenge offered power. The antithesis to helplessness.

Kate never wanted to feel as insignificant as she had in front of the universe that day either. Silence and a lack of feeling were akin to being nothing. She could at least exist by feeling and hating. She allowed the idiot man Roger to continue his tirade. A litany of complaints fell from his mouth, and Kate knew that the climax was coming. With every nasty insinuation uttered out of his mouth, the tension began to build. He recounted why he had felt the need for his affair with his work colleague. Kate had heard it all before. His wife had stopped giving it out in the bedroom. He was sexually frustrated and misunderstood, and along came 'Miss Blow Job' herself, and wifey became redundant. Kate allowed him to run himself out and watched as Prudence blinked back tears. The man was a parasite in her mind. However, taking sides wasn't what this was about, and Kate needed to remain impartial so that the full force of Prudence's own fury could unleash in one go.

The climactic big bang exploded precisely nineteen minutes into the meeting. It was nothing short of spectacular. Roger almost lost the rest of his receding hairline as Prudence finally reached that point where she could listen to no more. Her voice filled the room as she finally opened her mouth and uttered five words. Precisely placed for maximum impact.

'Shut the *fuck* up, Roger.'

The word fuck was always so powerful when uttered with an affected accent, Kate thought, and even more entertaining when the owner wore an expensive triple strand of pearls.

Kate was having fun. The explosion resulted in a loudly animated and aggressive argument between them, with wrath never seen before in her firm. It was all let out with Kate scribbling notes along the way, her own adrenalin fuelling the script. He had been impotent in the bedroom, she had lost interest, he started to work more, she lost herself in online shopping, working longer hours and white wine. He had then started an affair, and so she spent more money to punish him and had worked even later. She hated his father, and he had hated her mother. Her dog had pissed too many times on the carpet, and his stinking feet had apparently offended people in social situations. He hadn't wanted the roses in the front garden, and she fucking well HATED the colour of the leather recliners he had chosen. Lastly, her name was PRUE. She had always been PRUE because she had hated PRUDENCE since she was ten and had told him this for the past FIFTEEN FUCKING years. Now they hated each other and wanted to see the other suffer in PAIN! Both of them released their internal Satans, and the pent-up anger filled the room, turning it into a raging and burning inferno. Kate's heart warmed.

Other lawyers thought that Kate was inappropriate and unprofessional at times, some suggesting hints of psychopathy in her methodology. Kate liked it that way, and she wasn't breaking any rules by doing it. Her criticizers could go jump if she were being blatantly honest. What was wrong with creating a bit of tension and then sitting back and watching what happened? The truth came out far more easily when people's emotions became more extensive than the protective shield that they carried. There was nothing wrong with getting to the truth, no matter how you got there. It was the truth that mattered, nothing else.

They finished the Satanic part of their feud after eight minutes and sat back in their seats. Both of them were sweating and red-faced, having forgotten that Kate had been their silent witness. Kate paged Andrew and asked him to bring in coffee and biscuits. Now that the raw emotions were out of the way, Kate could negotiate terms and conditions.

Forty-five minutes later, they walked out of her office with a signed document to take this and that and leave each other alone except for when they had to hand their poor, suffering children over for access visits. Another two innocent lives ruined amongst adults who should have known better. She got the cooking pot and he, the faux Persian rug, which her dog had patched yellow. He took the queen bed mattress where he had played out his affair whilst she had been out doing overtime, and she the bed base. Neither wanted the mobile phone and the rest of the contract to pay out, so Kate tossed a coin and handed it to Roger. Real estate was to be shared. Shares to be divided equally, and spousal maintenance and child support agreed upon. The marriage was over, and so was any pretence that they liked each other. Prue gave Roger the bird finger as a parting gesture, still wearing the three-carat diamond bought for their tenth anniversary. It sparkled.

FIVE

AN EXORCISM... REALLY?

That evening, as she was soaking in warm lavender bubbles, the room bathed in a soft light from sandalwood candles, she reflected on her life. She swirled the spa water with her fingertips and dared to touch on the life that she had just run from. Run she had. There was no doubt in her mind that this had been one massive sprint. Her life had felt so painful and so wrong that running had offered her the hope that perhaps there was something better far away. It was that or end everything. A work opportunity had presented itself and so here she was. Was that even possible, she wondered? She inhaled the lavender scent deeply, waiting for a release of tension that didn't present itself. Could she really get it 'right' given she was in her thirties? Wasn't she supposed to have her shit together by now?

She had run from the not-so-subtle advances of Matt Harmon, a man who refused to acknowledge her complete lack of interest in him. Matt had worked for a rival firm and their paths regularly crossed. That situation had been more than appropriate to run from. It could never have worked despite his feigned protestations. Kate didn't want that man or any man for that matter. That message had been delivered to him bluntly with news of a move to London. She smiled, remembering his attempts at trying to attract her attention.

He had once told her that her intelligence was a rare commodity amongst his colleagues and that at times, he craved intellectual banter - hers, in fact. Maybe that was it. Maybe he had just wanted to have her mind? A mind fuck, perhaps? She wondered how that would feel if she felt nothing in the first place? Would he, too, feel nothing as he ground himself into her, finding that once there, that the enticing space was, in fact, empty? She would have laid there, feeling nothing, being nothing, saying nothing. A void in amongst the bedsheets. She would spare both of them the humiliation and move to the other side of the planet instead.

She had also run from her family. Too many siblings made from parents who didn't understand the concept of birth control. Her parents had shown little leadership concerning the moulding of any sense of a family unit. They had been more concerned with running their cafe than raising well-adjusted children who numbered nine by the time Kate was born. As a result of allowing a brood that size to raise themselves, they had morphed into a bit of a dysfunctional mess.

Most of them had turned to religion for solace and comfort, except for Kate and her oldest brother. This difference had been interpreted as a sign of non-conformity by the rest of her clan, so the two had been ostracised. Every time the family met, they would attempt to convert her into beliefs she simply had no time for. They saw her defiance as odd, given they were all made from the same flesh and blood, and punished her for daring to step outside what was expected. Kate felt like a solitary leaf on her family tree, having been pruned off and planted into a space all by herself.

Her mind wandered back to Matt Harmon. She shook her head. He didn't have the right to invade her mind, and he shouldn't. She recalled how he had sent weekly bouquets of flowers in a relentless pursuit that had amounted to nothing. She sat up in the bath, wanting to change the narrative in her head. She had better things to do with her time than wonder about what-ifs from a past that had no relevance anymore. She unplugged the bath instead and dried herself off. The last thing she needed was another complication. What she wanted was to find peace. Men were not part of that plan and would never be in the future, either.

Right now, she was warm, a little drunk and almost content. She poured herself another gin, mixing it with a rose tonic- water and sank into her comfy chair. Pinpointing the exact moment that she had decided to move countries was easy. It had been during a moment of insanity when things had become absurd at the outback cafe. An innocent visit back home, where she had hoped to gain some space and peace from the relentless office politics at the law firm.

Instead, she had become embroiled in an argument between two of her sisters and her mother. All of them had decided that the visit could also serve as a long-overdue religious conversion. It was a hounding of scriptures and reasons as to why Kate's life would be more manageable if only she invited God into her life. She had tolerated the indoctrination of ideas for the first few days until her mother had suggested, with a serious expression, that perhaps what Kate needed was an exorcism.

'A fucking… what did you say?' she had asked her mother in disbelief.

'An exorcism. Belinda from the post office said that her daughter Emily had more track marks on her arm than any railway station. They found actual demons inside of her. That's what was making her do all the drugs.' Her mother had whispered the word drugs as if it were a secret.

'Are you actually being serious?' Kate had asked, her eyebrows higher than the huntsmen spiders squatting in the timbers of the cafe's exposed beams.

'Don't accuse Mum of lying Kate,' Stella had fired back, her eyes already squinting in fight-mode.

'I'm not,' Kate had said to her older sister, who had yet to leave home and still wore her hair in pigtails.

'It's true,' snapped back her sister, Cath. 'I was there when the demons left Emily's body. It was awesome. She was talking in like a whole other voice. Kind of deep and manly.'

'Really?' Kate sounded cynical at best.

'Yeah, Kate, really.' Stella puffed herself up, just as she had when they had been growing up.

Her mother, at this point, had sat herself down in the cafe massage chair. It was entirely out of place and something you most likely would find at an international airport or a shopping centre - certainly not in the middle of nowhere in the Australian outback. Her father had bought it on a whim, and now it sat in the cafe, offering shiatsu massages to tourists who left red dust in it and too much sweat. Each time anyone finished a massage, they would leave a complete outline of their body in the chair.

Kate wasn't sure how everything played out exactly. As her mother was justifying the need for an exorcism, God himself had intervened on Kate's behalf. He had suddenly activated the massage chair and lowered her mother into a lying-flat position. From this moment on, it was chaos. Kate's mother was a little on the round side and couldn't get herself back up. The airbags then inflated and secured her mother in place. Stella and Cath then panicked, accusing Kate's demons of harming their mother. At this moment, Kate had turned and walked through the doors to the cafe and back to her car. Enough was enough.

Her last image of them was bordering on the ridiculous. Her mother, legs flailing and spewing nasty crap at her, and her sisters, waving their hands in the air and shouting about demons. The huntsmen spiders had started to crawl down the walls wanting a taste of the action, and a couple who had just arrived at the cafe after a long drive, stood motionless at the scene that greeted them.

Kate switched on the ignition and had driven with frenetic haste for the next thirteen hours. When she returned home, she had immediately applied for a job in London which was about as far away as she could get. There was going to be no return. Her heart was now closed shut and could not be opened again.

The irony in her act was that her family had no need and no intention of contacting her again anyway. She had left them before the end of what they had deemed a necessary redemption. That was mutiny as far as they were concerned and punishable by the sentence of eternal silence. They would have laughed at her sense of self-importance, thinking that they cared whether she existed or not.

SIX

TIME TO EXPOSE YOU

Andrew greeted Kate with a smile that was a bit too much for such an early start on a cold morning. She shot him back a fake one, given that her own smile muscles were still in early retirement. Andrew always aimed to be there before Kate, often arriving at the office before the sun rose. He wanted to have everything just right for his boss as she arrived and avoid her filthy temper when things weren't organized. It was more a survival skill if he were honest. He opened the daily diary on his computer.

'Alright. Give it to me,' sighed Kate. 'What's on for today?'

'Okay. You have a new client coming in at nine. I'm not sure what it's all about, as he wouldn't say over the phone. A bit mysterious. However, I did manage to get a bit out of him.' He leaned over and handed her a yellow client folder with a solitary piece of paper in it. 'Oh, and don't forget you have a video conference at three to discuss the Smith case and you're meeting with the local paper at four-thirty to do a story on 'Progressive Women in Law'. Other than that, you have heaps of free time to prepare for tomorrow.'

'Tomorrow?' Kate looked at him blankly.

'Court? Big day. The Howard second interim. The third Wayne hearing and also, the second hearing for Banks.'

Kate groaned. 'Bugger. I'd forgotten I'd agreed to do that journalist thingy. Damned reporter got me cornered in the loos at court last week. Can't one of the others do it? Isn't Louise free at that time? What about Anna? She's only just got back from hols. Surely she has some time to do that?'

'Nope, afraid not,' frowned Andrew. 'I already asked. Everyone else is busy. Looks like it's just you.' He gave her an encouraging smile. 'You're progressive enough. Just give them a few dynamic quotes, and remember to smile for the photo. I think you are there to inspire other women to study law, not put them off it.'

'Very funny. Can you send me the details for the reps for tomorrow's cases? I want to make sure there aren't any nasty surprises. Last time I did Wayne, they sent in a surprise QC at the last minute.'

'Actually, I've got them here if you want a printed out copy?' Andrew quickly shuffled through the pile of paperwork on his desk, finding whatever he had been searching for. 'Right. You are up against Hartwright for the Howard as per last time. Mr Foldeur again, for Wayne and…' he frowned. 'Can't see a name for Banks… I'll need to follow through with that inquiry.'

'Foldeur was such a prick at the last hearing.' Kate thought back to her previous interaction with him, remembering the haughty and arrogance of the French QC. 'Do you have any idea as to who might be representing Banks?'

Matt typed into his computer. 'I'll see if it's been updated yet. Hang on a sec…' He searched the screen. 'Yup. They've updated the lists overnight. 'It's an M. Harmon who will be representing Banks.'

Kate stared at Andrew. Had she heard him correctly?

'Sorry, Andrew. Who is the sub again?'

'Harmon.'

'Harmon? What's the initial?'

'M. Let me see if I can get his first name,' he said, typing something into the court information lists.

She stared at him in disbelief. Surely not Matt. He was not going to say, Matt. Please don't let him say Matt. Maybe M is Michael or Mitchell. There must be lots of Harmons out there in the world. The world was massive. Lots and lots of people. Billions of people. Dear God, please let him not say Matt.

'It's… hang on a min…' He searched the screen. 'Got it. It's a Matthew Harmon.'

'Are you sure?' Kate was staring at him in disbelief.

Andrew ran his eyes over the list again. 'Yup. Definitely.'

'Right.' She felt feelings arising. That was unacceptable as Matt didn't deserve them. She momentarily believed in the Law of Attraction. After all, she had thought about him the night before in the bath. This was the universe responding to her thoughts. How do you un-think someone she wondered, and reject the universe's offerings?

Kate turned to walk to her office and then stopped. She turned back to Andrew. 'Can you do some digging for me in terms of who this Matthew Harmon is, Andrew? He's not a legal I've come up against before in the UK. Find out everything you can.' That was only partially a lie, she thought to herself. It was true that she hadn't come up against him in the UK before. Why she hadn't just owned up to knowing Matt, she wasn't sure. However, she didn't want her past to chase her here into this near-perfect reality. She could not and would not combine her past with her now. It would tarnish it and ruin the possibility of hope.

'Already onto it, Kate,' replied Andrew, already tapping on the keyboard.

What the hell? Kate thought to herself, once settled into her office. Matthew Harmon was here in London? You had to be kidding. She lost herself into the past, remembering his relentless pursuit. His inability to accept defeat. Every week, the same dozen roses, always white. She was still staring into space, wondering what the hell Matt Harmon was doing in London when Andrew buzzed her.

'Your nine o'clock has arrived, Kate. I've found out some info about Matthew Harmon, so I can give you that after your meeting, perhaps? I'll have him sit in the blue room.'

Shit. She hadn't even opened the new client folder. 'Yes, Andrew. Thanks, blue room is good. Email me through what you have on Harmon.'

She quickly opened the new client file. It didn't offer much in terms of her new client. Mr Daniel Parkes, age 56. Lives in West London. Wants advice re partner. She sat back in her chair. He was probably yet another man wanting to leave his wife. She immediately berated herself for her assumptions.

DANIEL PARKES WAS SITTING at the top end of the boardroom table in the blue room. He was a mess. Well, inside he was. On the outside, he had achieved a look of respectable. He had made an enormous effort that morning to look like he had his shit together. With the help of a tailored, grey woollen suit and shiny black, patent leather shoes, he had hoped to at least give some sort of impression as a professional businessman. He had run into the budget barber for a quick tidy up of his hair and had shaved for the occasion. Reaching into his pocket, he pulled out a mint and chewed it quickly, hoping to hide the fumes from his drinking the night before. He usually wasn't a big drinker, but life had become complicated lately. Drinking was the only way to soften and cushion these new complications.

Kate Hemsworth had come highly recommended by two of his associates. She had a reputation for knowing when to break balls, and she did it quickly and effectively. Money wasn't an issue. He would throw every cent behind this woman to sort this horrible mess out. Mess wasn't the right word, though, he surmised. Disaster, awful, monumental cock-up of a nasty scenario. Only he wouldn't be able to describe it that way to the lawyer. Best to remain polite and professional and keep what was going through his head contained. He didn't want his own balls damaged in the process if she thought him weak. He had prepared what was needed to be said, and he would leave it at that. The rest would be for this Kate woman to sort out.

Kate opened the door and greeted her client with a warm good morning and a firm handshake. She quickly noted the new hair-cut, expensive suit, patent shoes and the smell of the mint. Within seconds she had assumed him to be an emotional wreck trying to keep it together. Sitting down, she clasped her hands together on top of the table and then she smiled as best as she could.

'How can I help you today, Mr Parkes?'

Daniel quickly crunched the rest of his mint and then took a deep breath. 'I need some legal advice in terms of my partner… I mean my ex-partner.' His voice wavered. 'I'm in a spot of bother, I think?'

Kate's pulse quickened. This sounded interesting. 'Well, you have come to the right place. Take a deep breath, and let's start from the beginning,' she said, picking up her pen.

The words tumbled out of Daniel's mouth as if relieved to be escaping. 'My partner… I mean, my ex-partner is apparently not who he claimed to be. I met him at a bar…

and he introduced himself as Greg, and well, we clicked, as sometimes you do with people. I took him home that night and it was nice. We cultivated a friendship that I'd not really experienced with other men. It was quite real. Lovely, in fact.' Daniel momentarily lost himself in his memories.

He shifted in his seat, trying to get comfortable and took another deep breath. 'He stayed with me for eighteen months, to be precise. Inseparable we were. I loved him, and in fact, married him.' He instinctively reached for his ring finger and twirled the patterned, silver wedding band he wore.

'Go on,' said Kate, interested in where this was leading.

'Well, it was all going fine until his wife phoned him.'

'His wife?' Kate was confused. She put her pen down.

'Yes. His wife. He'd had a wife before he met me. Never let on. Never mentioned her. Not once. No hint. Didn't mention his three kids either. She had even reported him missing. His name wasn't Greg. It was Barry, and he had been married for thirteen years to Linda Evans. They had three kids together. Three! Then he just left and went back to them.' He looked up at Kate with a grief-stricken look on his face. 'His name wasn't even Greg. It was Barry and I suppose we're not even properly married now?'

Kate knew she had lost him temporarily. She buzzed Andrew. 'Can we have some tea in here, Andrew? Asap.' She turned to Daniel. 'You do drink tea, Mr Parkes?'

'Yes,' was all Daniel Parkes could manage before crumpling into a sack of pent up tears.

Daniel excused himself and went to the bathroom, where he took several deep breaths. This was far harder than he had imagined. The feelings that he had cultivated for Greg over the past eighteen months were real. Real to him anyway. Talking about him left him feeling raw. The bond had felt genuine. Now the genuine feelings had been turned inwards, slicing through his heart like razor-sharp barbs. They were physically hurting him. He shook himself and zipped up his trousers. There was such a fine line between love and hate. Right now, he needed to hate Greg because loving Greg was killing him. This entire situation that he was facing was too much.

Kate was trying to get her head around the complicated story that Daniel was telling her.

'Let me know if I have understood this correctly,' she said, referring back to her notes.

He nodded.

'You met a man named Greg approximately eighteen months ago. You entered into a de facto relationship with him before marrying him. You believed him to be single and supported him financially. In total I understand, because Greg was not in stable employment at that time?'

He nodded again. 'Yes, that's correct.'

'Then, after approximately eighteen months, a woman by the name of Linda Evans phoned your house and explained that she was the lawful wife of a Barry Evans whom she had married thirteen years earlier. During the marriage, they had three children, Aaron aged twelve, Drew aged ten, and Mary aged six.'

'That's correct.'

'You then confronted Greg, and he admitted he was actually Barry Evans. You added that Greg – or Barry as he was lawfully known, left your home after a couple of weeks of enthusiastic encouragement from Linda Evans. He returned to his marital home, with Linda stating to you that 'Barry had never liked men before.'

'Yes.'

'Hardly the actions of someone who had been in a happy relationship, don't you think?' Kate looked over at her client. 'Does a happy person simply get up and walk out?'

'It's confusing. When he was with me, he *was* happy. At least I thought he was happy. He seemed happy. He acted happy… I don't know… those words were spoken by Linda, though. Greg never said them… I mean Barry.'

Kate went on, looking through her notes.

'Now, starting three weeks ago, you say that you received several texts that said, *'Time to expose you,'* and *'This is going to get complicated.'*

'Yes.' Daniel put his head in his hands.

'Okay,' said Kate clasping her hands together again. 'What are we talking about here? What sort of trouble are we dealing with, Daniel, and have you taken this to the police yet? This sounds more like a police matter?'

Daniel looked up at her, his face now white. 'Well, we did a bit of stuff together that was… I don't know… stuff that pushed the boundaries a bit. You know… it's not really something that I want to involve the police with. You know how it is in the bedroom?'

Kate looked directly at him. Her blue eyes meeting squarely with his brown eyes.

'Well no, actually, I don't know,' she said. How the hell would she know? She hadn't allowed anyone into her bedroom for years, let alone start experimenting in dodgy sexual practices.

'It's a thing', he said, after a long pause, in which he avoided eye contact.

'A thing?'

'Yeah, kind of a fifty shade thing. Lots of people do it.'

'Do what?' She needed him to be specific.

'Stuff with ropes… you know… like…' He stopped, shaking his head.

'… and you decided to film it just for what… posterity?' Kate hadn't wanted to sound incredulous, but that's exactly how her words came out. Filming in the bedroom was always risky. She was forever dealing with the consequences of films being made public by someone seeking revenge.

'Something like that. It was just a bit of fun. I wore a mask thing anyway. To protect my identity,' he added, having reassured himself.

Kate immediately thought of Zorro and tried to suppress the smile begging to be released from her lips. A genuine smile at that. 'Not so much fun now, though, I imagine?' she asked.

'No, not really,' replied a dejected sounding Daniel Parkes.

'Are you sure that this is about the films? Could it be something else? Can you think of anything else that someone might want to expose? Why is it going to get complicated too? How many people knew about all of this?'

'Only Greg… I mean Barry. I kept that side of my life private. Very. I certainly don't publicize my sexuality activities, if that's what you mean.'

'So, you believe that it has to be Linda and Barry behind this?'

'I can't think of anyone else, and I'm sure it was it was Linda's number on the text messages.' Daniel looked her square in the eyes. He looked certain.

'Do you have the actual texts so that we can check the number?'

'No. I deleted them as they came in. I also didn't bring my phone today either, sorry.'

'What?' Kate looked incredulous. 'You deleted them?'

'Yeah, sorry.'

'All of them?'

'Yes. I thought if I did that, the problem might go away?'

'Did you at least take some screen shots?'

'No. I panicked.'

'Did you at least call the number back?' Kate asked.

'Yes, once. Only I got a generic voice message. I'm pretty sure Linda is the one who sent me the silent calls as well.'

'The silent calls?' asked Kate.

'Yeah, for about a week, I received calls where there was silence on the end, and then the person would put the phone down. At one point, I was getting five… maybe six a day?'

'Did you not think of blocking the number?' asked Kate.

'Well, yes and no. It may have stopped it, I guess… but then they might have changed the way they got at me. Better the devil, you know, I suppose.'

'And you are sure this can only be Linda Evans?'

'Well yeah - this all started the minute that Greg went back to her. He must have told her about the films. No one else would do this, I'm sure.' Daniel shifted in his seat. He was beginning to feel uncomfortable.

'Okay, so we assume this is either Linda flying solo or Linda and Barry working together. Tell me about your work Mr Parkes.'

Daniel seemed to brighten up for a moment. Work was something that he was inherently proud of. It was something that he could share with this highly competent woman that might make him feel less of a complete loser at that moment. A way to regain some shred of dignity, perhaps. God knows he needed some.

'I own a consultancy business. It's global, actually. We offer foreign investors specialized real estate and share market advice. I have offices in New York, San Francisco, here in London and three in Asia. About to start one in Sydney too.'

'Average turnover?' Kate was blunt sometimes.

'Well, last year, we took in a profit of just over seventeen million pounds.'

'So, you do this well.' Kate was impressed.

'Well yeah – I guess I do.' Daniel smiled for the first time that morning.

'So, if I have this correct, then Barry Evans was well aware of the financial aspects of your company, and now he and his wife think they can financially blackmail you, I'm presuming? I'm just taking a wild punt on where this is heading, Mr Parkes.' Kate raised her eyebrows, allowing them to emphasize the seriousness for her.

Daniel shook his head… 'I don't know… really? Do you think they are going to ask for money? Is this what this is all about? He never seemed the greedy type. His wife though, is something else. She wants to humiliate me. She's irate. Seems that she blames me for everything. I suppose that he told her about our lifestyle and it's not hard to search online for my company details. I suppose if she has the films, then she knows she could make some money?'

'Daniel. Usually in these cases, there is a demand for money. I imagine that will come later. I doubt whether they would just put the films out there for a laugh. If they know that they can make a financial gain, they probably will. You said though, that Barry hasn't actually said anything to you. Most of the animosity is coming from Linda?'

'Yeah, she seems really angry about it all. I'm not surprised, really. He left her believing he was dead. I would be angry too… but it's not as if I encouraged him to disappear. I honestly didn't know. However, she seems to be venting all of her anger in my direction. It's rather unpleasant if I'm honest.'

'Well, from a legal perspective, blackmail is similar to extortion, both being serious criminal offences. In this case, it's the threat of public humiliation that we would look at. Right now, given they aren't asking for anything in return, it isn't what we would deem 'with menace' either. They also haven't posted them. Currently, this is an idle, general threat to expose you. I think we can start with a stern desist letter. If the films were to be released online, we could get them under the privacy act, and they would be facing jail time if you were able to be identified in the films. If they make threats as well, it can carry hefty prison time.'

'Right.' Daniel felt shards of emotions shredding his chest open. He instinctively placed his hand on his heart, trying to take in some deep breaths. He couldn't imagine his Greg sitting in a jail cell for years on end. It was unbearable.

Kate didn't seem to notice as she stood up.

'Pardon me if this sounds a bit awkward, Daniel. I'm trying to work out possible intentions. If Barry Evans was, in fact, married and had three children, then he was, in fact, bi-sexual, I'm thinking? Or was he straight and playing along, knowing that he could do something like this in the future?'

Daniel stared at her. He hadn't thought about that. Greg had seemed perfectly happy in their relationship. Really genuine. 'I don't know. I don't think anyone could feign that sort of thing if they weren't genuine?'

Kate tried to get the images of a naked Daniel 'Zorro' Parkes whipping a faceless Barry Evans out of her head. 'Our time is done for today.' She reached forward and shook his hand, again with a tight and powerful grip. She noted the dampness on Daniel's hand. His shake was limp, a trait she abhorred. Kate had always believed that one's character should extend out of a handshake, giving the other person an indication as to whom they are dealing with. Limp meant a defect, a weakness of strength.

'Daniel. I want you to keep a diary of every message and phone call you get. Take photos of all messages. Send them to the cloud, email them to yourself. Don't delete anything. I suggest you also write up a comprehensive account of the entire relationship. Include every detail that you can. We will need all of it in case this goes further, and we have to act quickly. Don't go near Barry Evans or his wife. Don't meet them and most certainly don't hand over any money if they ask for it. Do you understand that?'

'Yes.' Daniel could feel his heart thudding in his chest. Anxiety was welling in him, and tears were forming in his eyes. 'What about the police, though. Do you think I should speak with the police?'

'At this stage? No. I think this can be dealt with by a stern letter. The police really couldn't do anything right now anyway. If they start to threaten you, however, then it's a game-changer.'

Kate stopped in her tracks. She could hear the words coming from her mouth and had surprised herself. The police. Of course, in theory, he *should* go to the police. However, this was the first fascinating case she'd had fall onto her lap in ages. If he notified the police at this stage, then she would lose control of it. However, if she handled it herself, she could probably sort it out within a week. Once Barry and Linda Evans knew who they were up against, she was sure they would simply back off, and it would be a case of menace or blackmail if they did anything further. It was just a matter of a stern letter for now. Then she could take the credit for having sorted it. It was something a bit different to her usual caseload. Deep down, she doubted whether they had the balls to do much more anyway. No. Calling the police was irrelevant and unnecessary. She was certain.

She articulated her summation. 'Everything right now is still under control, Daniel. Calling the police at this stage is unnecessary. I have enough to start with. I'll engage a private investigator to see what we can find out about Barry and Linda Evans. We'll do a bit of searching from the office as well, just to be sure. In the meantime, I'll be able to draft a letter in the next couple of days that should deal with this. Once you have proofed it, we'll send it straight to them.

Should stop this nonsense in its tracks. My assistant will be in shortly for you to sign our contractual terms and conditions for legal representation. Are you good with all of that?'

Daniel nodded. The woman didn't have the reputation as the outback bulldozer for nothing, he thought. She was like a machine. He loosened his tie, took a deep breath, and slumped into his chair. He was exhausted but relieved that he had this woman finding a way forward.

SEVEN
WILLOW-GREEN AND BLONDE

Kate belted her kickboxing instructor just below his knee pads, letting out a guttural scream in the process.

'That's my girl! Kick it hard. Harder! Let it out!' Tod sounded energised as if excited to be attacked by Kate, who was clearly unleashing her inner beast.

The release felt good. Raw anger spewed out from deep inside of her. Her screams were unedited and honest. Harder and harder, she kicked. Sweat was flying from her face, her teeth were gritted, and a guttural roar was escaping from between her lips. The more she kicked and screamed, the more she felt the anger escaping from her body.

Tod yelled loudly over the class of warrior women. Ten professional businesswomen by day and pure crazy during kickboxing classes. If he hadn't had a neon sign above the door to his gym, Tod was sure the police would have paid him several visits. The women honestly sounded like they were being tortured rather than enjoying themselves.

'Ten more seconds! Go for it! High kick! Low! Inside!

Okay, last one... put your energy into it, ladies! Time up! Okay. Good work everyone. Take a breather.'

The class stopped kicking. Kate sank down to the floor in a squat position, hunched over, trying to get her breath back. It felt like both of her lungs were on fire. She could feel the reverberation of the kicks as they had met her feet. 'God, that felt so damned good,' she gasped.

Kate attended kickboxing twice a week, rarely missing a class. The room was full of women just like her. All of whom needed to kick the shit out of something other than those closest to them during the day. It was the only time they could express their feelings without being accused of being neurotic or highly strung by their colleagues. Or, in some cases, being arrested for assault, according to Chloe, who had finally snapped and kicked a particularly obnoxious co-worker in the shins.

'That was amazing,' panted Anne, lying on her mat next to Kate, her hair matted with sweat. 'Better than any fuck if I'm being honest.'

Kate smiled. Anne was also straight to the point with what she said.

'I call my kicking bag after my boss James, you know. Every foul line he directs my way during the day, I kick the shit out of him, here. Lucky for him really, otherwise I'd be kicking the shit out of him in front of his shitty mother, who won't stop dropping in and ruining my shitty workday. Next round, I'm kicking the shit out of her. Way cheaper than therapy.'

Kate nodded in agreement. 'Yeah, I've named my boxing bag after several lawyers I've dealt with recently. Seems better than punching them on the spot - hey?'

Tod interrupted them. 'Right!' he shouted. 'Get up and grab a partner. I want a 1-6-3-2 jab-right uppercut-left hook-right hand and then a 2-3-2 right cross-left hook-right cross...

Go! Go! Go! You should have already started. On your feet, ladies! Let's go!'

They all moaned but jumped to their feet anyway, ready to hit anything that stood in front of them. Kate walloped Anne, who yelled at her.

'Your fucking turn next, Hemsworth!'

ON HER WAY HOME, her car hugging the wet, winding road, she felt considerably better. The tension from the day had eased, and she had managed to release more of the ancient anger that she carried around with her. A therapist had once labelled it ancient anger, and the name had stuck. Mainly directed at her family, especially Cath and Stella, who had taken great delight in antagonising Kate at every opportunity. Kate had rarely fought back, and the layers of indignation that she had suffered over the years had morphed into a quiet, bubbling rage. Every bit that she managed to get out though, was good. It stopped it from spewing out uncontrollably at inappropriate moments. For example, if someone cut her off on the road, in court when a client said the wrong thing, or when someone pushed in front of her at the supermarket.

The afternoon interview with the reporter had been disappointing at best. A young journalist who hadn't planned her questions adequately to make the most out of the interview. The meeting was over in ten with a quick photo of Kate at her desk with her law books blurred in the background. Kate hadn't helped the struggling journalist either, which she knew was a tad passive-aggressive. However, she wanted to teach the young woman a powerful lesson about doing due diligence.

Kate wondered in fact, if she had found the questions online because they seemed to have little relevance to anything legal. Asking Kate what she liked to eat for breakfast seemed irrelevant at best. Perhaps she could have asked Kate about sexism in the courtroom or how female law partners often were paid less than their male colleagues. Toast and marmalade seemed trite by comparison.

She pulled up outside her terrace and sat for a bit. Tomorrow she would see Matthew Harmon again. A person whom she had assumed had exited her life because she had made it impossible for him to see her. What the hell was he doing in London anyway, and why was he now representing Angela Bank's ex? Next to flash into her mind was an image of Daniel Parkes wearing his Zorro mask, with a faceless man in bondage. Kate shook her head. Stupid idiots, she thought to herself. Why would you film that and not control where the images went? That was just asking for trouble.

COURT DAY WAS ALWAYS an early start. She arrived early to re-read the briefs that Andrew had printed off and placed on her desk. Hot coffee was brewing, and soon Andrew would bring her a croissant and some fruit. She had to eat before her first appearance. Otherwise, she would feel faint and irritable before mid-morning recess. With low blood sugar, she could potentially rip someone's head off if not careful. Her court attire was ready on the back of the door, freshly dry-cleaned and spotless. Her leather briefcase was wiped clean, and a small handbag with makeup, a toothbrush and hairbrush were ready for the lunchtime freshen up.

There was no mucking around for Kate. This was a time where she needed to excel. A poor performance would not only cost her clients dearly but also would damage her reputation. She needed to ensure that she had all the case facts in her head and a strategy already rehearsed for cross-examinations. She reached for the Banks case and felt a wave of anxiety. Matt Harmon would be facing off with her in the room. Bank's ex-husband had a history of booze, drugs and domestic violence, which they had already proven to the court. Harmon was hardly going to fight for his access demands which were ridiculous to start with, based on such a flawed character. Harmon wasn't one for throwing away victories, so why was he there, fighting a lost battle? None of it made sense, but she was sure that the truth would reveal itself reasonably quickly.

The morning went as planned. The Howard case was pretty straightforward. Mr Howard had broken down under cross-examination when the judge had allowed evidence collected by a private investigator, proving his numerous affairs. Fifty per cent access with the children was granted, and Mrs Howard received the family home, a generous spousal maintenance allowance and half of Mr Howard's personal wealth. She had, after all, sacrificed her own career to raise their four children, which was dutifully noted by the judge.

The Wayne case ran overtime as Mr Wayne had hired Foldeur for a second time. The case meandered and was bogged down in legal frivolities, all designed to throw the scent off Wayne's nasty narcissistic personality. It was a shame that the scent of Foldeur's wig couldn't be thrown off too. It honestly smelt as if a cat had taken a pee on it. If Kate were frank, it needed burning, preferably with Foldeur catching alight as well.

In the end, the judge himself got swamped by the masses of verbose legal arguments that Foldeur had randomly thrown into what should have been a quick hearing and decided to set a whole-day hearing two months later. He directed Kate to ensure that her client was ready to answer the complaints raised by her ex-husband, adding that both parties needed to come back with some manners.

'Prick,' mouthed Kate towards the silk when the judge's back was turned.

'Want some?' mouthed the silk, leering at her.

Kate held up her little finger and laughed at him.

There was an opportunity to freshen up during the lunch recess. Kate re-applied her makeup and brushed her teeth. She tidied her hair in preparation for the afternoon session. Harmon would be arriving at any moment to face off against her in the courtroom. This was a critical hearing for Angela Banks. It was the second hearing as the first had been hijacked, again by frivolous and unnecessary legal arguments, a regular tactic used to slow things down and take the heat off one person's own wrongdoings. It mostly backfired though, because the judges weren't stupid. Usually, when one person slowed things down, it meant they were hiding something and stalling the reveal of the truth. It gave Kate an excuse to go in even harder. Mr Banks had been an arsehole in real terms. An abusive drunk who took too much shit and had made his wife's life a nightmare. Kate's job was to put that into a more user-friendly context and then present it to the judge in a linguistically pleasant manner. Drunk, drug-fuelled arseholes didn't make great parents, and Angela's children needed Kate to protect them.

She entered the courtroom, settled her nerves and had a last look through the case. Matt Harmon walked into the courtroom ten minutes later. He was hard to miss. Tall with black curly hair that was streaking early-grey at the temples. Vivid, blue eyes leapt out from his face, framed by long boyish lashes. A cheeky smile with a dimple on his left cheek and a fit body that was neatly presented in a grey silk suit. Only the best for Matt Harmon. Kate glanced at him, but he was speaking with his client earnestly. Fine then, she thought. Cool, it is. I'll pretend I don't even know you too.

They fought hard. Kate presented her evidence, and Matt

would counter-argue just for the fun of it. He resembled a vulture when cross-examining Angela Banks, picking away at the remnants of her marriage and suggesting that Angela had been instrumental in stuffing up her relationship. At one point, the court was forced into recess due to a frail Angela bursting into tears after Matt accused her of not meeting her husband's sexual needs. The judge was appalled, and Kate shot Matt a dark look which was met with a raised right eyebrow as if Matt was asking her what he had done. Formally reprimanded by the judge, Matt walked back to his seat and then shot her a grin. She shook her head at him.

Kate fought back after the recess painting his client as a self-obsessed alcoholic drug user, which was easy to prove given the numerous police reports tendered to the court. Kate was becoming more frustrated in how Matt portrayed Mr Banks as some sort of victim, which he clearly wasn't. Why this man's childhood was brought into the equation was a no brainer. In Kate's mind, what happened in your childhood stayed in your childhood. Adults needed to act like adults. She stopped her thoughts in their tracks, the irony not lost on her. It was context, she reasoned. This man surely could not be blaming his parents for *all* of his dysfunction?

The dialogue exchange went for three hours, backwards and forwards, with the evidence stacked against Mr Banks. The court recessed as the judge went away to make orders, and Kate and Matt were left in the courtroom, their clients having left to get coffees through separate doors.

Kate had expected Matt to walk over and explain himself. Why was he in London? Why hadn't he contacted her before the case to let her know he was acting for Banks? Instead, he sat, zealously typing notes into his laptop, refusing to look her way. This infuriated Kate even more. There was no way she was going to walk over to him. He was the one who had turned up on her doorstep, so that job was his.

The judge returned, and orders were made in favour of Angela Banks. Her husband was ordered to undertake mandatory drug and alcohol rehabilitation before applying for further access to their children. He would be granted weekly supervised access in the meantime, and that was that. Property settlement would be dealt with through mediation, as per the agreement already tendered to the court, unless communication broke down and they needed to settle issues in court again. Kate knew the judge would rule in favour of Angela, so there was no real sense of victory.

Angela Banks left the courtroom in tears. Hardly a win when her marriage was now over, and there was no hope in getting away properly from a bastard like the one she had married. Until the kids had grown up, which was another fourteen years into the future, she would need to accommodate that awful man into her life at least once a week. If Kate had been capable of crying, she probably would have cried too, if she were Angela Banks, that is.

Surely Matt would now come up to her after the case and explain himself? He didn't. He walked out with his client, patting him on the back and explaining that they could go again as soon as he had completed his drug and alcohol rehabilitation. This cheered Mr Banks up enormously and gave him hope that he could return to have a third go at shredding his ex-wife's reputation and emotional composure. Kate walked up behind Matt and was just about to say something when a young woman approached him. Kate had seen her in the courtroom but hadn't known who she was. Kate disliked her immediately. Blonde, tall, fit and looked pretty swanky in her willow-green blouse and tailored grey skirt, she was the sort of woman that made Kate look plain and stumpy.

'Well done, Matty,' the woman said, placing her hand gently on his arm. 'You shook that woman up beautifully.'

Her voice was pretty, and it was apparent that she had been privately educated by the rounded vowels that she dribbled all over him.

Matt smiled at her, not wanting to wipe anything away.

'… and you gave that other legal a run for her money,' the blonde continued. 'She thought that was going to be easy, you could tell in her opening. Loved it.'

Kate felt fire rising in her soul. Her inner rage was ignited in a flash.

Matt turned around to leave and was suddenly facing Kate. The blonde woman's hand was still resting on his arm. He stared at Kate, and an awkward dome of silence surrounded them. Neither said anything. They simply stared at each other. Kate was trying not to unleash her inner beast. Not in front of that woman anyway.

The blonde woman sensing the tension pulled Matt away. 'Come on, let's get a wine or something.' He turned away quickly, without acknowledging Kate at all.

Kate went to say something, but for once, her mind was blank. She was left standing there, open-mouthed. Was she angry because he obviously no longer wanted her? That had been a pretty public way to let her know. Punishment for having rejected him, she surmised. Or worse still, was she angry because she wanted him and was in denial? That was a stupid thought. She didn't want anyone. That was one fact she knew for sure. She was angry because he hadn't shown any interest in her, and he should have done, even if only out of professional courtesy. That was screwed up too.

She shouldn't even feel angry. She revved her car noisily instead. Stuck in a long traffic jam at the end of a long day, she had found herself trapped with her own thoughts. She revved her car again. She was behaving in an infantile manner, that much she knew. It didn't help to intellectualise her anger, to rationalise it or even understand it. If anything, the process made her feel angrier. Where was her control? 'Stuff this bloody traffic!' She banged her hands onto her steering wheel. Her anger was welling. She had transformed from slightly irritated to full-blown rage in less than five minutes. There would need to be a release. There would *have* to be a release if she were to find normal again.

An accident on the road ahead had blocked both lanes of peak-hour traffic, and no one was going anywhere. She knew it was time to do some deep breathing before she exploded. She thought back to the relaxation techniques taught to her by her meditation teacher. A patient older woman who had told Kate that if she slowed down and spent more time relaxing, that she might just open up her chakras and allow the rage within her to slowly ease itself out. Maybe it's the blonde woman's chakras opening that Matt likes, she wondered. Bang! Ten out of ten anger. She hit her horn, keeping her hand on it for way too long, venting her frustration. The person in front gave her the bird finger out of his window. She gave one back, hitting the horn again and sent another bird finger along thirty seconds later, just because she could.

Two hours later, feeling like a coiled spring from the horrendous drive home, she sank into a hot, soothing bath. She lit some vanilla-musk candles and invited Vivaldi to caress the silence. Then she had poured a glass of champagne and had laid back to take her first deep breath of the day. Her lower abdominal muscles barely allowed the breath in, such was her tension.

People were so predictable, she thought, especially when relationships broke down. What made people turn on each other? All that love. All those promises and then they morphed into people wanting to hurt and destroy each other. They don't care what they throw at their other half in the courtroom. No boundaries, just the need for revenge. She thought back to when she had laid in Ethan's arms sharing her secrets with him. The moments of absolute trust where she had felt like she had fully belonged in the moment. Only it had been a lie, all of it. Whilst she had been lying there feeling so safe and so complete, he had felt incomplete, apparently. So incomplete that he had chosen to shag and trust another woman. Kate wondered if that woman had laid in his arms as well, sharing her own secrets? Ethan would have been full of secrets from both of them. Kate wondered where hers had sat. In the corner of his mind, somewhere unimportant perhaps? Why hadn't he told her that he had felt incomplete?

Kate thought about the way her own marriage had ended. It was safe to do this now that the champagne had numbed her. The one thing she had never been able to do was un-love Ethan. Different to many of her clients who spoke about their ex-partners as if they would gladly run them over if they had the chance. Ethan had walked out so fast that there wasn't time to undo all the love she had felt towards him. He was there, and then two hours later, he wasn't. A clean-cut as if he had been killed suddenly in a road accident. No more arms to lie within and no-one to tell her secrets to. Half of her was missing as if suddenly amputated. Three weeks after he had walked out, she had discovered she was pregnant. She had phoned him.

'I'm pregnant, Ethan,' she had told him, knowing that he had always wanted a baby.

'Don't expect me to love you just because you are pregnant,' he had replied icily.

There was no love left. It was as if it had run out. 'I'm not coming back,' he had then stated coldly. 'You should also know that Fiona is pregnant, and it's mine.'

Her mind, her soul and her heart had then shattered into

several thousand tiny pieces. She felt them disintegrate around her. Shards of memories and love. The two of them together, being released from her physical being.

Kate lost her baby at nineteen weeks. She thought she had sailed through the danger period. No reason had been given for the sudden cramping and early labour. It was 'just one of those things,' the nurse had told her gently, placing the tiny little girl into her arms. She had grieved alone, lost in a darkness that blinded her, crying for her baby girl and crying for the one man she had trusted to love.

She made it her mission to at least clear up the mess he had left behind. She would find those fragments of herself, and she would put them away somewhere safe. She didn't know how to rebuild the old version of herself anyway, but it seemed negligent to not find them and put them somewhere. Everything that had been, was gone. There was no Kate left from the Kate and Ethan era. She would need to find a new way to live and rebuild a version of herself that could not be as easily hurt.

The new Kate had no sense of who she was. In silence, only her footsteps now walking the floorboards, she existed rather than lived. Sometimes she would imagine the sound of Ethan laughing and the sound of a baby giggling. That was the other life. It was the life that she should have lived. The life that another woman had stolen from her and lived as her own life instead. Each day that passed separated the two lives. Fiona, glowing and happily pregnant, and Kate, fading into somewhere else. A place where she was someone that simply walked, talked and breathed.

They were still together. The Ethan and Fiona show. Their first baby had been born healthy and then their second. The universe had no sense of dignity, Kate surmised. Allowing such a horrible duo to procreate and then raise smaller versions of themselves seemed like it should have been illegal. Her baby, whom she had named Sally, was no more. Sally had never stood a chance, even though Kate had been prepared to love her more than anything else in her life. The universe had killed Sally for a reason she would never understand. She was a failure as a wife and a mother, and Fiona had taken everything from her, including hope.

Kate had always wanted to feel loved. The sort of love that you feel when you aren't making any effort. When you are 'being' in your own skin, and someone loves you for it. When you aren't thinking about clever or witty things to say or worried about your clothes or unbrushed hair. It wasn't until she had met Ethan that she had felt anything close to unconditional love. Then she had lost it and had felt as incomplete and as wretched as a heroin addict without heroin. It seemed that love had been offered to her in a temporary arrangement. She had tasted it, become addicted to it and then was cut off from it.

HER PARENTS HAD DECIDED to move to a remote outback town just as Kate was entering high school. It had been hell that place. All of it. Their sudden desire to open a cafe was bewildering to everyone who knew them. It was supposed to have been a tree-change to become 'more at one' with Mother Earth. It was most likely a mid-life crisis in which the two of them had decided to chuck the towel in and make a run from everything. They knew nothing about running a cafe and spent every day relying on the locals to buy coffees to survive. The locals put up with them because no one new ever came their way and they got discounted meals in return. It was a symbiotic relationship paired with sheer desperation. The suffocating ochre dust settled on everything, including the drunk tourists who invaded the town at night after eight.

In the end, Kate's only option for education was a

boarding school, hours away by red road. She arrived understanding her place as the new girl, put her head down, and worked as a strategy to survive. She worked hard enough to earn a place in law school, and once there, she understood her place as a 'country girl from god knows where.' Shunned by the old money, the school tie club, the boys' club and the city chic, she again immersed herself in her studies and understood that no one was ever going to give her a break. She had fallen between the cracks, somewhere between dysfunctional parents, nasty siblings and an inability to network.

She finished off the third glass of champagne, her mind flicking back to Ethan. 'How ironic,' she directed towards the champagne bottle. 'Ethan was the only human to love me, and then he didn't.' She clicked her fingers. 'Just like that.'

She poured another glass of champagne, finishing the bottle. The alcohol hit the sweet spot, and she felt a warmness gliding through her. There would be no more ruminating for the time being. It numbed the pain and allowed her to float for a while listening to Vivaldi. For a while, her mind was still, and she was no longer tormented by the realisation that no one loved Kate Hemsworth. Not a single person in a world, teeming with billions of other human beings.

EIGHT

WE'LL SEND THEM A LETTER

'And a good morning to you, Kate,' beamed Andrew as she walked into the office. 'Spring is here. I can feel it in the air.'

The air had a warm feel, and some of the spring flowers were releasing sweet scents into the air. Kate had celebrated what had looked like the end of a long and cold winter with a new spring outfit. She'd matched an emerald knee-length pleated skirt with a diamond pink blouse, adding nude pumps, which gave her a bit more height to her petite frame. Pearls and a splash of fresh fragrance added class, and the effort wasn't lost on Andrew.

'Looking very fresh, Kate. Love the pink with the green. You look like a pink crocus, emerging from the thawing ground.'

'I'll take that as a compliment?' asked Kate, smiling.

'Of course. Now, before I forget, Daniel Parkes has been in touch.'

Andrew flipped into work mode. 'He's sent through some texts that he says he received last night. I've forwarded them to your email, and here are your client folders for today.' He handed her six green and yellow folders.

Kate sighed. 'That reminds me, Andrew. Has the private investigator got back in touch yet with the info about Barry and Linda Evans?'

'No. They said something would arrive by the end of today, so I'll keep my eye out for that coming in. I'll let you know as soon as that happens.'

'Okay, I'll draft the desist letter to them first thing, and if you can email that onto Parkes for his approval, that would be great. I will also need you in my room in twenty. I need another set of observations done on a client. It's a complicated case, and I want to do less writing and more observing.' Kate felt that something wasn't right with the client's story and wanted to concentrate on her body language and what wasn't being said.

She opened up the attachment once in her office. She could see that Daniel had received several texts from an anonymous source the night before. This time, he had taken screen shots.

10.03pm. 'I told u that I would expose you. You have a lot to lose.'

Daniel Parkes: 10.23pm. 'Who is this? Linda? What do you even want me to do?'

10.31pm. 'We need to make a deal.'

11.18pm. 'What do u mean? Make a deal? Who is this?'

12.03am. 'Meet and discuss. Café Red, Wharf 3, River Front. 4pm.'

End of text exchange.

Okay, thought Kate. They had made a move. However, they hadn't threatened anything new. They appeared to want to negotiate. Her guess was that they would ask for money if Daniel was present. Therefore, she would need to get the cease and desist letter over to them before lunch as a priority, hoping to deter them from going ahead with the meeting. If they ignored the letter and insisted on a meeting, she could go to the police. There would be time then for the police to determine what needed to happen before any meeting. No harm done, and Daniel wouldn't need to meet whoever this was.

She called Andrew and told him to email Daniel as soon as she sent the draft letter through. Also, he was to let him know that the letter would be delivered via courier later that morning, so he was to return it as quickly as he could. She added that he was not to go to the four o'clock meeting for any reason.

The ten o'clock teleconference was short and sweet. Andrew arrived promptly to take notes. Kate watched her client closely, wanting to better understand what Harriet Bowles was trying to articulate, as none of her recent accounts of events had made much sense. Kate resented representing someone whom she thought might reflect poorly on her in court. It could result in a potential legal loss that Kate could not, and would not, tolerate.

It wasn't long before Kate had found several holes in what Harriet had been telling her. It turned out when under closer observation that Harriet looked to the right when telling a lie and a gradual blush rose from her neck, venturing into her cheeks. Harriet had been adamant that her husband was the one having the affairs. Kate managed to dig a bit deeper, at which point Harriet confessed her own string of infidelities which, in the end, amounted to no less than five.

She gave Harriet a shove in the right direction. This would be a divorce without a court hearing. Otherwise, her entire tennis club was going to know who she had been shagging each week after Thursday night tennis had finished. Given she had done the rounds of her friends' husbands, it wasn't going to be in her best interests. Harriet had thought it was an excellent idea and said she would send in a list of what she wanted to take with her from the marriage and that she would be reasonable. Kate had told her that this was an excellent idea, and they had parted on respectful terms. 'Play fair,' were her parting words to an embarrassed Harriet Bowles.

Andrew buzzed Kate at eleven-thirty, informing her that he had made contact with Daniel. he had returned the draft email saying he was happy with it, and wanted to come in just before four, given that was the time that whoever it was, had wanted to meet him. His anxiety was through the roof, and he would feel safer sitting in her office. If he was a no-show for the meeting, they might phone him, and he wanted Kate to be there, in case they did. Kate thought this sounded a bit like progress was being made.

JUST AFTER LUNCH, the law firm held their weekly colleague get-together. It was a time to catch up and mingle with each other. It wasn't uncommon for this to be the only time the busy lawyers saw each other all week, as most of them were continually popping in and out of offices for meetings and appearing in court. Often, they only knew each other by a wave or a quick hello. Kate wondered if she should mention anything about the Daniel Parkes case to Tracey, one of the senior partners, just in case things went wrong. However, Tracey didn't show for the meeting, instead being held up in court. Kate didn't want to approach any of the others in the firm because she didn't feel that she knew them well enough.

After the housekeeping, it was time for the weekly presentation. All the lawyers were on a roster and required to give a ten-minute presentation on an interesting legal topic. Louise, who had worked at the firm for the last twenty-two years, was 'it' for this week. She had chosen an interesting topic on 'Why we need to stick to the truth.' This was a notorious issue for lawyers, especially those who found themselves defending people who weren't innocent but were declaring themselves as such. It didn't take a brain surgeon to work out how fundamentally difficult this could be when trying to defend and stick to a shred of truth at the same time. Kate found herself thinking about Ethan and the damage his lies had done.

Then her mind wandered to the awful behaviour that Matt Harmon had displayed in court, parading his client's lies before the judge as if they were solid truths. It hadn't done either of them any good. Lying in court was a no-brainer. So why had Matt stooped to that level? Her mind moved on to his desire to have sex with her. Was she attractive enough for someone like Matt Harmon to want to have sex with her? Then she remembered. He had only wanted her mind and not her body. Really, she should have taken it as a compliment, shagged his arse off and then given him the flick when he wanted more or when she was done.

She was snapped out of her thoughts by applause. Louise had finished her talk, and everyone was starting to mill around having coffee and tea and some of Jill's chocolate mud cake as she had rostered for cake duty. Cake duty was always a bit of a joke as everyone knew that none of them ever had time to actually make a cake. They were all store-bought and usually from high-end bakeries and, as a result, inherently delicious to eat.

'What do you think about this whole honesty thing then, Kate?' asked Louise. A woman who was practical, on time and straight to the point.

Kate immediately thought of Ethan and Matt and wondered herself. She went to reply, but Louise had already moved on, being congratulated by someone else for her succinct presentation.

Kate arranged to have the letter couriered to the home of Barry and Linda Evans by two. Instructions were left for the courier, that if no one answered the door, it should be delivered instead to Barry's place of work.

Four o'clock approached, and Kate buzzed Andrew.

'Has Daniel arrived for his appointment, Andrew?'

'No, not yet. He's probably stuck on the tube as King's Cross had a fire alarm go off, so the authorities have closed several lines down.'

'Do we know if they received the letter?'

'Well, I left it at reception waiting for it to be picked up, and nothing has been relayed by the courier company or reception about a delay, so yes. Should have got to Linda by two-thirty at the latest.

Kate sat at her desk and reflected on calling the police. Should she involve the police, or was this something that she could sort out quickly herself? It technically was skirting around menace and could even lead to blackmail if she weren't careful in managing it. So far, she had done things sensibly. She doubted whether anything else would happen. If she went to the police, they would take over the matter, ask too many questions and leave her with little involvement. She liked to see things through to the end anyway.

At four-fifteen she phoned Daniel herself and got his voice message. She left him a message to call her back urgently. Then she asked Andrew into her office.

'Where the heck is Daniel? He should have been here at four.'

Andrew shrugged his shoulders. 'No idea, I'm afraid. I'll go and call him again. The trains are back up and running, though.'

Oh God, thought Kate to herself. What if that idiot has

gone to the café anyway and something has happened? She felt herself panicking and was wondering if she should pour herself a gin when Andrew buzzed through.

'Daniel has just got back to me. He should be here in a few minutes.'

Daniel Parkes soon charged into her office, puffing and panting as if he had just run a marathon.

'Sorry, I'm late. I got held up on the tube. There was a fire.'

'Have a seat, Daniel. I'm relieved it was only a fire.'

'So, what now?' asked Daniel. I'm presuming they will only be highly annoyed that I didn't show up at the café and got the letter instead? They aren't likely to go and put the films up anyway, are they?'

'Doubt it, as that will get them into enormous trouble, which has been clearly explained to them in the letter. That is, of course, if they are thinking this through properly. The problem with this sort of thing is that once the films are released online, you tend to lose control of them as people download them. You can't take them down as easily as they take on a life of their own. However, these guys aren't hardened criminals, so my guess is that they will now back off.'

'Really?' Daniel Parkes looked relieved. 'Well, that's good news. Excellent news.'

Andrew brought in some tea and left-over cake, and nothing happened. There were no texts or phone calls from Linda and Barry. At five, Kate called it a day. The letter had obviously done its job.

'Daniel, my best advice is to go home and sit tight. Again, do not text back. Do not meet with them and certainly don't hand over any money. My guess is that they thought you were going to show up and now don't know what to do because they have been officially warned by us. It's a good sign, actually. It means that they don't have a sincere plan.'

'I agree,' sighed Daniel. 'Greg… I mean, Barry never had any mean intent inside of him. I did all the planning and arranging when we did anything. He just followed. It's Linda who is behind all of this, I'm sure.'

'Well, we are still waiting for the investigator to get back to us. I was expecting something at the end of today. So, go home, relax if you can and just keep things calm. I'm sure we have this sorted out.'

Daniel got up and straightened his coat. 'You don't think that I should go to the police… just in case?'

Kate shot him a look that said 'no' without actually saying anything.

'No. I didn't think so. I'm sure you can handle this yourself,' added Daniel. He handed her a piece of paper.

'What's this?' she asked.

'The security pin number to my office. 418729. Just incase anything happens to me.'

'Thanks?' she said, a little surprised. 'You're going to be fine Mr Parkes.'

He was already hurrying out of her office.

NINE

A BUNCH OF FLOWERS

Spring had all but disappeared the next day, and Kate arrived at work having battled freezing wind and horizontal, lashing rain. Despite her best intentions with having remembered an umbrella, she was still soaked through as the parking station was several blocks from her work. She still hadn't got used to the notion of the London spring, which was colder than the winters back home. It seemed that cold and rain were the main breakfast choices that England served up each morning. Indeed, the warm spring air had blown itself over to Germany since yesterday.

Andrew was diligently working at his desk as Kate arrived.

'Oh, wet poodle alert,' he said, noting the state of her.

'Yeah, what's with this weather?' Kate ran her hand through her hair which was now forming tight curls which were springing up in all directions. 'This was after remembering an umbrella too.' She laughed instead of feeling offended, as she knew her hair misbehaved when wet.

'There's a hairdryer in the toilet cupboard if you need one,' Andrew added.

'You're a lifesaver. Who thought of putting one in there?'

'I did. It seemed sensible,' he said, looking pleased with himself and taking his gaze towards Kate's hair.

Andrew had never been late to work, not once since he had started at the law firm. Andrew had graduated in commerce but hadn't been able to find a job as a new graduate. Not an unusual scenario across the board, as graduate jobs were becoming harder and harder to secure, especially given the way things had gone after so many lockdowns due to Covid. The lack of interviews in his chosen field had come as a shock. In the end, he applied for the Legal Assistant Position out of desperation. Surprisingly, it had suited him with the necessity for excellent people skills, attention to detail, organizational aspects, and the hours suited his social life. It was like he had been made for the role.

'So, what's on for today?' Kate asked.

'The private investigator re the Parkes business has finally got back to you. There's an email waiting for you with those details. Your nine o'clock has been cancelled as she has had to go away and says she doesn't want to do a zoom. You're seeing a Mrs Wards at ten, Mr Simmonds at eleven and an adorable elderly couple at twelve to go through some end of life matters. You have two new clients after lunch and your kickboxing class at seven. You're on cake duty for next week too. Louise has asked if you could meet with her three o'clock client as she may get held up in court. It's just to go through and sign an Affidavit, by the way, so not complicated. Oh, and these arrived for you.'

He picked up an enormous bouquet of white roses from behind the desk and beamed at her. His face asked a million questions. 'Not going to ask, of course, who they are from. It could be that Mr Parkes thinks you have done a tremendous job… or they could be from a secret admirer? Would you like me to put them in some water?'

'Is there a card?' asked Kate, smiling as genuinely as she could. She already knew who they were from.

'Yes. In fact, there is,' said Andrew reaching around the side of the bouquet and pulling out a small white envelope that had *Kate Hemsworth* written on it in neat cursive handwriting.

'Thank you,' said Kate reaching over to take the card.

'They smell gorgeous,' beamed Andrew, inhaling the perfume deeply. 'There's nothing like the smell of a rose, is there?' He was dying to know who had sent his boss such a beautiful bouquet.

'Can you put them into a vase? We do have vases, don't we?' asked Kate, looking around for one.

'Yes, of course. I'll go and get one from the lunchroom.' Andrew was already off towards the lunchroom before finishing his sentence.

Kate wandered into her office with the small white envelope in her hand. She knew who had sent the flowers. The same person who had sent her the same bouquet every month in Brisbane. The same flowers, the same long stems. She sat the small white envelope down in front of her and stared at it. *'Kate Hemsworth,'* it said quietly in what she guessed was the florist's handwriting.

Andrew knocked on her door. 'Flower delivery,' he smiled, and sat the huge display down onto her desk, now displayed quite perfectly in a tall, crystal vase. 'So, do we know who they are from yet?' he inquired cheekily.

'Yes. They are, in fact, a thank you from Angela Banks,' she lied. There was no way she was going to mention Matt Harmon's name. The gossip would be excitedly spread around the office before lunch, she was sure. There was no way she was ever going to let on that she had known Matt

Harmon in a previous life. To do so might infect her new one.

'I'll make you a flat white?' he asked, happy that Angela Banks had been so thoughtful towards his boss.

'Thanks, Andrew. Can you make it a double shot though?'

Kate looked at the white envelope, willing herself to open it. That one action would bring their entangled past into the now. There would be a point of no return once she opened it. Matt Harmon and his desire for her would again be in her life, despite how far she had already run from it. She picked up the white envelope and quickly tore it open. Inside was a small yellow card.

'Good to see you again. M.'

What did that mean? That was it? She felt disappointed and then reprimanded herself for feeling anything at all. The message hadn't been the same as the ones she had received for the ten months in Brisbane at all. Those messages had been full of possibilities and sexual innuendo. This was just blunt. What did he even mean, 'good to see you?' What did 'good' even mean?

Andrew came in with the coffee.

'Andrew, I think it would be nice to share these around the office instead. Can you put them on the front desk at reception so that everyone can enjoy this gift from Angela? They are a bit big for my desk. I'm going to find it difficult to see my clients.'

'You sure?'

'Yes.'

'Okay. Will do so,' said Andrew picking up the vase and taking it straight to his own desk instead. Roses were his favourite flowers, and these had the same perfume as the ones that Rupert bought for him. So what if he had no room to work properly. He would sit inhaling the perfume all day, which he found to be a natural aphrodisiac.

The day was full after that. Clients were coming and going, and legal matters were sorted. The private investigator had uncovered trivial information about Linda and Barry Evans but nothing to suggest they were in any way dangerous. They looked like they had been your average Mr and Mrs from the suburbs, that was until Barry had walked out and Linda Evans had reported him as a missing person. Kate thought that the police hadn't done due diligence in finding him. Perhaps it really was that easy for someone to disappear? It appeared that he had managed it for well over eighteen months, right under everyone's noses.

It didn't explain, though, how Linda Evans had finally located Barry and had managed to get hold of Daniel's private mobile phone number. Kate surmised therefore, that they were bluffing with their threats. With no existing criminal records, it was hard to imagine them escalating things further. She was confident that Linda was behind it all. Revenge for Daniel having borrowed her husband and anger at having to imagine Barry in bed with Daniel. Kate was also confident that she had made the right decision in not going to the police. This was a simple domestic matter and well within her jurisdiction. Given that nothing else had now transpired, it seemed like it was case closed. An odd situation for a city lawyer, but one which she thought she had handled well.

KATE WAS in fight mode during kickboxing. She kicked the living daylights out of every single rose that she had been sent. Twelve perfectly good reasons to kick hard. Matt was playing with her. Sending her the same flowers as when he had been pursuing her and now rubbing her face in the fact that he now wasn't interested. She was sure it had been 'good' to see her – so good, in fact, that he had left with the blonde woman. She could only imagine what they had done after the wine they were going to drink. She gave one final kick that she imagined was going to connect with the blonde woman.

'Hey, Kate! Easy on!' shouted Todd, who had been kicked off balance.

'Sorry,' she snapped back, kicking him again and sending him flying.

THE WEEKEND ARRIVED and given she had tied up all the loose ends at work, it was hers for the duration. No clients, no courtroom and no Matt Harmon. The weather had again warmed, and a weekend road trip seemed like a perfect choice. She packed a small overnight bag and jumped into her car. She was on the motorway by seven and heading north. Just for a moment, she was free of everything. She searched her phone for something to listen to, deciding on a random podcast about overcoming a sense of failure by Catherine Watters.

She made it to Edinburgh by the end of the day and booked into a small boutique hotel not far from the castle. After showering, she wandered around the old part of the town, singing with bagpipes of varying pitches. She caught snippets of conversations as she walked, sometimes being able to decipher the broad, thick Scottish accent and at other times wondering if it were even the English language that she had heard. She stood under Scott's Monument, craning her neck to the top of the darkened stone, and then walked up the Royal Mile, noting the cashmere, tartans and Haggis in leadlight shop windows.

This part of the city was old - ancient by Australian standards. The buildings were arranged all higgledy-piggledy too. Some tall and narrow, standing shoulder to shoulder, following the shape of the winding roads and others like Giles's Cathedral, stood stately and towering over everything else. Kate loved their lilac, cream and powder blue colours and neat square windows edged in lace.

She found a small restaurant tucked away in a quiet back street.

'A table for two, Madam?' asked the front of house waiter, despite only seeing one of her standing in front of him. He looked over her shoulder as if trying to find the other part of her couple. They were fully booked aside from a cancellation, and one person didn't generate as much income as two.

'No, just one, thank you,' she replied.

'Certainly, Madam.' He whisked her towards the back of the restaurant.

She tried to guess the age of the restaurant as she hurried after him. She was sure that it was much older than any building in Australia. The ceiling was relatively low with exposed darkened beams, and the surfaces of the walls were bumpy and thick in places. A fire roared in the front part, despite it being spring. It was the sort of place that oozed comfort and cosy.

She started her feast by sculling a dark glass of red wine. The earthy and mellow taste slid down her throat, coating it in a sense of peace. She added fresh oysters and lemon for entrée, pairing them with champagne. She chose salmon linguine for her main, and finished with a thick and rich chocolate mousse. She deliberately avoided thinking of anything that might stress her during dinner, instead, practising the mindfulness techniques that her meditation guru had taught her. Stay with the flavours, the textures and the aromas she reminded herself. It was an exercise in enjoying the moment rather than spoiling it with issues from the past, the now and the future. The candlelight flickered on the table, and she observed it as it weaved, danced and created shapes in the air. Something so simple and yet so beautiful, she thought to herself and only noticed if someone took the time to watch its performance. The stress eased out of her, and for a moment, she felt deeply content.

Walking the streets of Edinburgh afterwards was different. She allowed her mind to wander freely without constraint. She was happily numb from the bottle of vintage red she had indulged in during her dinner, so thinking about the hard stuff seemed a bit easier. She admired the view below her as she climbed the ancient cobbled roads, glimpsing the blue of the sea through the gaps in the buildings. She loved the sense of the ancient here, imagining the old sailing ships that must have anchored just offshore. She sometimes wished that she could hear the echoes of the past and hear the city's rumination and stories. Instead, all of those voices had been lost to the wind, and all that was left were the buildings they had inhabited.

She gazed downwards from the top of the castle walls, the alcohol encouraging her thoughts to ramble. Was she finally happy? This latest version of her, at least? Was this the place where she could safely state, 'I am happy?' Happiness had eluded her for much of her life. It had ducked and weaved around her only to flee from her grasp. She acknowledged that she theoretically should be happy now and that perhaps happiness didn't show its hand unless asked to? Maybe grateful was the word, at the very least?

It was better than it had been in the past. Uncomplicated. Did she need anyone in her life, though? Would that make her 'happier?' She thought not. Every person in her life had hurt her, so why complicate a stable situation by introducing complications? She would strive to be the best in her career. That would be enough. She wondered if she should also include the notion of being liked by people too? Maybe that should be something that she might concentrate on more as well.

'AM I happy?' she called out to Edinburgh. A few people looked over at the drunk woman and smiled themselves.

A red-haired guy in his twenties shouted over the road to her, 'On ya Luv. You go be as happy as you like.'

She continued her walk down the winding streets. Her mind, too, winding its way around the twists and turns in her own life. It seemed to Kate that everyone was pursuing the idea of happiness, almost as if it were the elixir of life itself. Happiness to Kate was elusive, and every time she thought it sat in her hand, it would slip away. She thought back to Ethan, who had been a source of happiness for her. She had always believed that he had been her soul mate, and she, his. They had done everything together, as a finely tuned team. Two people who saw the world through four eyes and two connected minds. She cynically wondered if that was the definition of codependence? Then it had all crashed down around her, and happiness had been replaced with nothingness. Losing Sally had replaced the nothingness with an eternal numbness that sat quietly in the back of her mind, painting her soul with eternal despair.

Kate now saw the world through this despair. Her mind was devoid of colour and vibrancy. Walls built to protect herself were now so thick that she doubted if she could let anyone in, even if she wanted to. That's how it would stay. She too, had built a fortress around her, similar to the one around Edinburgh Castle, perched so confidently on the clifftop. This castle was still standing after hundreds of years… over a thousand if she remembered correctly. Even having been built on a volcanic part of the earth and after defending itself countless times throughout history, it still stood with conspicuous dignity. So why was building a fortress around her own heart any different? She was now built to last too.

The next day she spent a few hours in Edinburgh before

setting off back down the motorway. Most of her colleagues would think her mad to have done a weekend visit to the other end of the UK. Kate always laughed at how they thought the distances between cities were enormous. It had been ten hours each way, from her home to her boarding school. A few hours on the motorway, by comparison, was easy.

The following week flew by, and there was no further news from Daniel concerning any films being uploaded, no bouquets turned up, and the only thing that went wrong was when Kate forgot that she had been on cake duty and had forgotten to buy a cake for everyone. Andrew had been sent out in a state of panic to find something that would feed approximately twelve people in less than an hour. He had, of course, risen to the occasion and had brought back a freshly made, triple-layered vanilla and chocolate cake from a specialist cake store.

'I *know* people,' he winked at Kate as he opened the box to show her his spoils.

'I honestly don't know what I would do without you, Andrew.'

'You would cope, I'm sure,' said Andrew as he made his way out of her office with the cake, ready to place it centre stage in the meeting room.

Kate winced slightly. He hadn't meant to touch a raw nerve, but she knew what he meant. She would cope if she were the only human being left on the planet. She honestly didn't need anyone, and that probably wasn't a good thing.

TEN

IT'S JUST SO SATISFYING.

The court lists were officially up, and Kate was in for a busy week with six clients requiring her representation. Andrew arrived with the list and placed it down on the desk in front of her. She ran her eye down it and then stopped when she saw the name Harmon leap out at her.

'Fuck!' left her mouth before she could prevent it.

'Kate!' Andrew had never heard her drop the f-bomb before. 'Can I help?' he added as an after-thought, wondering what might have caused her to react like that.

Kate knew she should stop swearing. It was a problem in her own head as well. Kate found the word *fuck* so damned satisfying, though. It summed up really shitty moments in such a precise manner. No other word had the same effect, so she wasn't sure if she even should give it up.

Kate deflected his question. 'I know I should stop swearing, Andrew. Set up a swear jar this morning. I'll put a pound in each time, I swear. The money can go to a charity of your choice.'

'Done,' smiled Andrew.

He left to choose a charity that might benefit from regular small donations, and Kate was left staring at the court list. Why was Harmon still around? Had he moved to London as well? Why?

THE NEXT DAY, it was the same scenario in the court as before. Matthew Harmon played verbal games with Kate's client and tried to slow her down using every cross-examination tactic he knew. He would stall on small irrelevant details, which irritated the judge to the point where he asked Matt no less than five times,

'What is your point, Mr Harmon? You seem to be more interested in distressing the woman.'

Kate was ready to kick his arse by the time the judge left the room. She threw her files into her bag and stormed out to find Matt. That case should have been quick and easy. Why was Matt doing this? He was nowhere to be seen. Kate was furious. She texted Andrew to get her a number or an email to contact Matthew Harmon. He sent it back in less than a minute.

Kate immediately fired an email his way. Usually, she would allow herself to calm down before writing anything impulsive, but she was steaming with fury. Her stress levels were hovering around ten. He was playing with her. Playing with her clients. It wasn't fair, and it wasn't professional.

'Dear Matthew, your conduct in court has been inexplicable. It is unfair on my clients and utterly unprofessional. Please stop immediately. Have you moved to London or what? I received the flowers. Sincerely, Kate Hemsworth.'

She hit send before editing or proofreading it. After ten minutes of deep breathing, she went into her sent folder to see what exactly it was that she had written. It wasn't exactly her best email, but it said what needed to be said, albeit in a relatively terse and disjointed manner. She was relieved that she hadn't sworn at him, which could easily have been done. A response arrived in her inbox almost immediately.

'Dear Kate, what a delightful coincidence to see you again. Glad you liked the flowers. Yes. Have moved to London. Perhaps we should catch up for dinner soon? Cheers, Matt.'

Kate was bewildered. She re-read her email again. She hadn't said she had liked the flowers, and why was Matthew Harmon now living in the same city as her?

Andrew knocked on the door and interrupted her thoughts.

'Houston, we have a significant problem.' His face was unusually serious.

'What's up, mate?' asked Kate, realising that Andrew had never looked like that for the time she had known him.

'It's Daniel Parkes. I think he seems to have gotten himself into trouble.' Andrew handed her a note.

'We have him, and the matter needs to be resolved. Don't go to the police. You know what this is about.'

Kate shot Andrew a panicked look. 'Who delivered this? This is a joke, right, Andrew? Tell me this isn't Daniel Parkes that they have?'

'I don't know. It was handed in at reception, just before five, and the girl down there has no recollection of who handed it to her as she was on the phone at the time. She was apparently taking notes and literally just stuck her hand up to grab it. I walked in a few seconds later apparently, and she just handed it to me.'

'Seriously?' said Kate. 'Don't we have security cameras down there?'

'No, we haven't really required cameras before. Police?' suggested Andrew. 'I could call them now if you like.'

'No. Don't. Not yet, anyway. Let me just get my head around this.' She thought for a moment. 'What does this even mean - We need to resolve this? Where is Daniel?' She looked at the note again. 'The language seems a tad amateur, wouldn't you agree?'

'Yeah. It's not very well written. Although, are notes like that usually better writen?'

'No idea. This is my first.'

'I'm not sure where Daniel is. Do you think we should let the police know?' said Andrew slowly, looking at his boss. 'It may be badly written but the note definitely suggests that Daniel has been kidnapped.'

'Well, we can't be sure of that yet, can we?'

'What would you like me to do?' Andrew sounded as if he were ready for action. 'Try to find him?'

'Yes, I think that should be our priority. Tell the temp at the reception desk that she needs to get some form of ID from everyone who hands things in next time. Don't alert her to the fact that anything is wrong, and maybe you could look into some cameras for reception?'

'Sure.' Andrew swept out of her office, hoping to catch the temp before she left for the day.

Kate bit the end of her pencil, thinking about her next move. Nothing sprang to mind. Andrew swept in again a few minutes later.

'Kate. There's another problem.' This time he looked as white as a sheet.

'What?' asked Kate, almost scared to hear his reply, imaging that a body had been dumped in reception.

'Can I sit down?' he asked, looking physically sick. He sat and then took a deep breath.

Kate held hers.

'This.' Andrew held up a note from reception.

Kate looked blank. 'What's that?'

'It's a note from the couriers.'

Kate was confused. 'Why? What's the issue?'

'The couriers we booked to deliver the letter to Barry and Linda Evans?'

'Yeah?'

'They didn't pick up the letter. They turned up, but it wasn't at the desk. The temp forgot to give us this note, which they wrote.'

'I'm confused. Why did they write a note?'

'They were covering themselves. Wrote a note to say that there was no letter to be delivered and left. The temp doesn't seem to know why either. The letter disappeared, so she says - although she seems to think 'someone' may have picked it up too. Vague. Just vague and empty, I'm afraid.'

'Like she lost it?' Kate shook her head. 'How does a letter go missing? Are you telling me that she actually lost the letter to Barry and Linda Evans?'

'I believe so? Although depending on which version you believe, it either went missing or some random dude picked it up.'

'So, it never left most likely?' Kate's heart was thudding in her chest. 'No-one else knew about it, so some dude wasn't likely to have picked it up. She must have forgotten and lost the damned thing. How do you lose a letter? What's her name again?'

'Alex.'

'Has anyone told Alex that she is incompetent?'

'Would you like me to?'

'No.'

'She said she couldn't find it when the courier came in but then she says that she remembers someone else picking it up. This note from the courier has been sitting in her 'to-do' pile for the past week.'

'A week? A whole bloody week? Are you saying that a

whole week has gone by and that Linda and Barry never got the letter from us? At all? This is a disaster.' Kate put her head in her hands.

'Sorry.' Andrew apologised on behalf of the temp. It was hard to know what to say next.

Kate held her breath and counted to ten in her mind, hoping to clear her mind. 'Go to your desk Andrew and advise the temping agency that we are returning Alex. Don't go into too many details. Organise a new temp through a different agency for tomorrow. Why have we still got a temp anyway?'

'It'll be another two weeks before Georgina is back. Her mother died, remember.'

'Oh yeah. It's a perfect little storm down there, isn't it?' Kate sounded pissed off.

'I'm so sorry, Kate.' Andrew looked devastated. He felt as if he had let his boss down.

'It's not your fault Andrew. Let's sort Alex out first. Have you tried to make contact with Daniel to make sure he isn't just sitting at home? This could just be a bluff? Although why someone would write a note like that as a bluff is beyond me.'

'I called his office. His work said he's off sick for the next couple of weeks. He has the flu apparently.'

'Okay, that's slightly more positive than him just disappearing. In fact, that works quite well for us.'

'How?'

'He's not technically missing, is he? He's just sick.'

'If he's been kidnapped, how did he phone his work to let them know he was going to be away?'

'Good point Andrew. Maybe Barry and Linda got him to do that? It buys them some time too, if no-one is officially looking for him? No-one else knows about this note, do they? It buys us some time too.'

'I suppose so?' Andrew didn't sound convinced.

'Did the temp even read the note?'

'Apparently not. I was walking past and she was on the phone. Handed it to me without even looking up.'

'So we literally have no idea where Daniel Parkes is?' Kate looked out of the window, as if hoping to catch a glance of him.

'Nope.'

'Great.'

'I'll go sort out the temp. They shut at five.' Andrew hurried out of the room.

She looked at the time. It was almost five. She never drank before six. It was her rule. An hour and three minutes to wait. If she only had one now, then she could still drive home, later. She stood staring at the bottle of gin that she kept in her drawer, wondering if breaking her own drinking rule was of any consequence. Nothing popped into her mind that was of any use concerning Daniel Parkes and where he could be. He may just have the flu? The note though. Someone was claiming to have him. Where? She poured herself a double. Her emotions were running too hot for her to concentrate. She skulled it in one.

Why was she not calling the police? She should do, especially if this were now a kidnapping. The note had told her not to though. His work thought he had the flu, so the police might think the same. However, her own reputation would be shot to pieces if didn't say anything now that she knew about the threat. She could get done for professional stupidity and possibly hinder... no... definitely hinder a criminal case. That would be enough to destroy everything. She couldn't risk it though. She had already sat on all of this for too long. 'Shit,' she said out aloud angrily. She should have sent Daniel off to the police from the start. Why had she thought that she could handle something like this?

The alcohol calmed her down, allowing her to retake

control somewhat. There was a change in her. A small thought at first that grew larger. Why couldn't she handle this herself, she pondered, pouring herself a second drink. She looked at her watch. She could take a taxi home and leave her car in the overnight parking.

Andrew knocked on her door, discretely ignoring the gin bottle and glass on her desk. 'Okay, I've updated the temping company. I think they were disappointed that I called them a minute before they closed for the day. I've organised for a new temp to start in the morning and I've also ordered in some cameras for reception. It's not too hard to install them. What can I do now – call you a taxi?'

'No thanks, I'm fine,' Kate said. 'I just had a small one,' indicating to the bottle. 'I'm okay to drive.' She didn't want Andrew to think that she was a rampant alcoholic. It was bad enough with the swearing and the current situation she had embroiled him in without adding further dysfunction into the equation.

'Let's just sit this out for tonight, at least. Not do anything rash. Linda and Barry Evans are not big-time criminals. This has to be a scare tactic. We don't even know for sure if they even have Daniel? I'll drop past his place on my way home and check he isn't there with the flu. You never know.'

'Okay. Are you sure, though? What if…' he paused, raising his eyebrows, not wanting to ask the obvious question that was hanging in the air.

'They won't do anything to him. Well, I hope they won't do anything stupid. I'm going to assume not.' Kate was obviously flustered. 'It's already been over a week since they were supposed to meet with him.'

Barry and Linda hadn't got her letter to back off. They would have gone to the cafe, and Daniel wouldn't have shown up because he'd been sitting in her office at that time. That must have angered them, she presumed. They supposedly now had Daniel in order to blackmail him over the films? This whole exercise had to be based on financial gain. Now they were getting more demanding, but no body had been delivered to her yet and no demands for money either. She assumed that would come next.

'Well, call me if you need me,' offered Andrew, meaning every word. His boss sounded like she had things sort of under control… at least he hoped she had. She had reassured him at the very least. This was well away from his area of expertise, though. Maybe she was used to people doing this sort of thing all the time anyway? After all, this was the legal world, where perhaps the rules were broken to sort things out? He was glad he had chosen to join the firm. Commerce, by comparison, would have been very dull.

He walked out of the office to see Rupert waiting out the front.

'Hiya,' Rupert said, putting a protective arm around Andrew's waist and drawing him closer.

Andrew kissed him. 'And a good evening to the most gorgeous man on the planet.'

Rupert grinned.

'I've had quite a day actually…' Andrew shot Rupert a conspiratorial look. 'You won't believe what just happened.'

'A bit of office drama? Excellent,' smiled Rupert, who was quite fond of getting involved in things he shouldn't.

Where the heck was Daniel Parkes? Kate wondered.

KATE ASKED the taxi driver to stop at Daniel's address. She waved the taxi on as she didn't think it a great idea if he waited and then saw her peering through the windows of a random house. There was clearly no one at home. None of the internal lights were on. She shivered as the freezing wind picked up strength. Treading carefully and quietly, she made

out of the courtroom, as he had on countless occasions, the sight of her had turned him on. She had pissed him off in the end though, by refusing his advances.

He hadn't meant to move to London when he had. It wasn't like he had chased her halfway around the world deliberately. The career opportunity had presented itself coincidentally, and it had been a good move for him. It had made sense at the time. When he had seen her name on the court list, he had also done a double-take. Then he had felt anger at her rejection which he had channelled into the courtroom. The flowers were a bit of an after-thought to remind her of his past efforts, and the email was a cynically saturated and moronic attempt to have a dig. Anyways, he was shagging Felicity now, so in reality, nothing serious could actually happen between them anyway.

However, if there was any chance of finally bedding the one and only Kate Hemsworth, then he should. He would. He would charm her, want her, and she would want him in return. It was as if it were supposed to be. Now that there was an opening, however slight, he could work his way in, like he always did. A quick dalliance or two which he would keep from Felicity. Neither woman would know, and that was best all around. Then he could add another notch to his sexual prowess belt, something that he was inherently proud of.

He carefully worded his return email. If she were interested, then he should not frighten her off by being too keen. Being complacent, however, might drive her away too. They should meet quickly. He smiled to himself. Life could be so damned good sometimes. He projected forward a couple of weeks. A Saturday afternoon shag with Felicity, and then he could move on to Kate in the evening. Now life was talking to him. He caught sight of his reflection in the window. 'You still have it, Harmon.' Then he smiled at himself, patting his cock with assurance in his pants.

'Hi, Kate, great to hear from you. How about we do dinner to properly catch up? I'm free this evening as it happens. Matt.'

'Hi, Matt. Sounds good. Where and what time? Kate.'

'Weatherspoons on Regent 7.30pm? Matt.'

'See you then. Kate.'

MATT SMILED. That had been easier than he had anticipated. The thought of having two women in one day turned him on. He had done it before. Three, regularly, when he was at law school. Women had been easy to find and willing to open up for him. Sex made him feel powerful. Wanted. He liked taking charge and then have a woman be vulnerable in his arms. The thought of finally… possibly… having Kate made him feel excited. He walked back into his bedroom, where Felicity was just finishing doing her hair and was about to leave for work. He would take Felicity now to alleviate the desire now coursing through him.

'I love staying over. You know that, don't you?' She smiled as she tied her blonde, waist-length hair into a ponytail.

Matt smiled. He walked up to her, and standing behind her, he gently kissed the back of her neck, knowing that this would have the desired effect. She moaned, turning her head towards him. He gently nuzzled into her neck, blowing onto her ear and then gently kissed her cheek. He traced his finger gently down the side of her neck and over her shoulder. Her hips responded, moving ever so slightly from side to side and then pushing back into him.

'Not now, Matt, I'm late as it is.' She pulled away from him, needing to finish getting ready for work.

Matt gently turned her around. He needed her and would get his way. He always did. He knew the moves. Felicity would do anything he asked her to. He knew what to do in order, the exact moves that would have her moaning, passionate and begging. He placed his hand on the back of her head and took a handful of hair. Then he gently pulled her towards him.

'Matt… ' Felicity's breathing became short. 'We don't have time. I'm serious.'

He brushed his lips against hers, found the zip on the back of her skirt and lowered it down. It fell to the floor. Women just wanted a bit of attention, he thought to himself. Act romantic and sexy and watch the magic, he thought to himself. Placing one hand onto the inside of her thigh, he felt her give into him.

'I'm going to be late.'

'Probably,' Matt said, guiding her to the bed. He laid her down and started to kiss her.

ELEVEN

BLACK LIKE QUEEN VICTORIA

That was easily done, thought Kate to herself, as she zipped up her black skirt, which she had teamed with a black blouse. Kate wore black just as Queen Victoria had done when mourning Albert. Given her morals were about to become a thing of the past, black had seemed an appropriate choice of attire for mourning a loss of future ethics. It was her way to acknowledge that she had stooped to a new low without having to say anything at all.

Andrew noted Kate's all-black number and took a deep breath. She had done this once or twice since arriving at the firm, and it hadn't taken long for her colleagues to understand her intended message. He would need to be delicate with her and tread carefully.

'Coffee Kate?' That always worked. Start with a safe daily routine first. He knew she needed her morning coffee before doing anything else.

'Yes. Double please,' she shot at him, striding past and into her office. He heard her door shut with a hint of frustration.

Andrew sighed. She had walked too fast past him to make him feel like the day was going to get any better. He would pop a blueberry muffin in with her coffee. That might sweeten her up? He rushed out towards the bakery deciding to buy a dozen in case any of the other lawyers were also in need of a bit of kindness.

Kate sat down in her chair and stared out of the window. The view from her office gave no hint as to the mess that was currently plaguing the inside of it. The river sparkled in the spring sunlight, and boats were trailing each other in meandering lines. Tourists were congregating on the bridges taking selfies and enjoying the warmth of a spring day out in London. It looked nice outside, she thought, having a sudden urge to run from the building and take a boat ride somewhere. She couldn't, though, and this mess would be worn as a cloak of stupidity until she could sort it out.

She had back to back clients that made further strategizing concerning her later date challenging. Clients moaned at her for the entire day about their problems, and by the end of it, she had felt more like a psychologist than a legal advisor. It was after five before she was able to stop and take a breather. There had been no news from Daniel or news about Daniel. No more notes had been handed in at reception. Kate had sent Andrew around to his house posing as a salesman if any neighbours had asked questions. Andrew had reported back that everything was quite aside from the dog next door, who had snarled at him through the side fence and sounded like he would have happily torn him to shreds had he ventured into its territory.

There was no sign of Daniel. Nothing. His work confirmed that he was taking the whole week off from the flu virus. Kate decided that no sign of him was better than bits of Daniel being sent to her through the mail or perhaps seeing him in some sort of amateur hostage film. More silence meant that nothing had happened. Or did it? What if they had just killed him and dumped his body somewhere? The police would find the body and track his last movements to her office. She took a deep gulp of her gin. It was only a few minutes after five, but the six o'clock rule was now irrelevant anyway under the circumstances.

She was planning on walking to meet Matt at Wetherspoons so she could technically drink as much as she wanted to anyway. She had a second drink, and then she changed into her dress that had been hanging on the back of her office door for the day. Then she sat and stared into space. What was she about to do? Use her body to gain an ally?

Andrew was heading out the door as she left.

'Wow, you look great,' he smiled spontaneously. She did. For a woman who had worn black all day, she now looked refreshed and approachable. He had given her a wide berth all day, only contacting her when her clients had arrived to show them in. She gave nothing away, despite it evident that she was on her way somewhere special.

'Have a good one,' she smiled at him.

'I'm going to have a good one,' thought Andrew as he remembered that Rupert was taking him out to the theatre and then dinner. The conversation would be charged with attraction, and dessert was bound to be spectacular. He hoped, though, that the next day there was some resolution to the Parkes case. He was in up to his neck as well. He wondered if he should say something about the smell of alcohol on Kate's breath. It was becoming evident that she was regularly drinking at the office and that it might become obvious to clients. Reflecting on her earlier mood, he decided to put the issue on ice for the time being.

• • •

MATT WAS WAITING for Kate at the restaurant. He had sat fidgeting, having got there way too early. He ordered a vodka on the rocks and then a pint of lager. He wasn't sure that they mixed very well with his nerves. He'd stared at the entrance door, wondering what she would be wearing and whether she would smile when she saw him. He would smile a little, he thought. Not to be too keen. Keep it cool.

The door them opened, and there she was. Kate Hemsworth, wearing an understated but classy dress in ruby-red. He liked the pearls and the heels she had chosen, one being class and the other being pure provocation. He followed his gaze from her heels up her legs and then to the hand that she had extended towards him. He imagined leaving her pearls on as he shagged her later.

She approached him with a warm but controlled smile and shook his hand with a firm grip. He lingered a moment, looking into her eyes for any signal as to what she might be feeling. There was nothing except a confident blue stare that met his, her pupils remaining a constant size, indicating that she hadn't felt excited to see him.

'Good to see you again, Kate,' he said enthusiastically, hoping to ignite a spark.

Kate took a deep breath. The aim of this was to create an ally. If she had to work him, then so be it. Work him she would, no matter what it took. She ignited her inner strength and smiled back.

'You too, Matt.' She reached forward and kissed him on both cheeks.

Having chosen the simple ruby-red dress with a single strand of pearls, she had wanted to look elegant and sophisticated, which might help to give the illusion that she was there for more than a meeting destined to end up between sheets. Although the heels were another matter. They screamed urgency no matter which angle you looked at them from. She had an urge to lie on the table and get the deed over and done with so that she could concentrate on moulding her alley to help with the important matters. However, that was too hasty. She would be charming, witty and interested in everything Matt said. It wasn't like he would be an ugly encounter if there was a silver lining to all of this. He had at least made an effort with his appearance.

'So,' she said, smiling back at him. 'How have you been?'

'I'm good. You?'

'Good.'

The exchange stalled.

'So,' Kate said, trying again. 'In London for long?'

'I think so. Got a job here for the next few years if I want to stay.'

The conversation was jilted and awkward. A few more drinks would help. The gin had worn off already, and she felt too raw to relax. She didn't want to bring up how he had treated her in court as that would be a killjoy. Kate ordered a bottle of wine and quickly downed the first glass. She felt the familiar feeling of warm courage begin to fill her. She had a second. Matt did the same, and the awkward exchange began to thaw as they remembered their shared past. They ordered a second bottle, the wine loosening up any second thoughts about the meeting.

They laughed when they both ordered the same meal for their main. By the time they were digging into some chocolate desserts, they were sharing quirky cases and stories of eccentric judges back in Australia.

Matt's phone lit up several times during the night, which clearly irritated him.

'So stupid to have given clients my mobile number,' he complained to Kate, eventually switching it off. Felicity could be so damned clingy, he thought to himself.

Kate felt out the mood between them. So far, so good. She

thought it would be stupid to suddenly launch into the whole Daniel Parkes matter as there hadn't really been a good moment to have discussed something so heavy. Right now, it was groundwork time. She needed time to feel her way into Matt's trousers, so to speak. She shook her head. Her thoughts were playing in the gutter, helped by too much alcohol.

Matt wasn't sure what was going on. Kate had refused to even look at him the whole time he had been pursuing her in Australia, so he couldn't fathom why she was giving him so much attention now over dinner. However, it looked like she was keen and up for it, so he was too. All he had to do was be patient, and she would be a sure conquest by the looks of things. He wondered if he were being too presumptuous and then figured that he had already put in an enormous amount of groundwork for this moment. He deserved some success with it.

They split the bill, and Kate followed Matt towards the exit, wondering what happened next. She was hardly a pro at this sort of thing, smirking at her own internal pun. Matt however, asked her outright if it was going to be her place or his? They decided on hers, which relieved Matt because he couldn't be sure that Felicity wouldn't suddenly turn up, given she had been incessantly texting him all evening. Kate's place would be better. Safer.

It wasn't a romantic shag. It was a tear their clothes off, go hard, and put their clothes back on. It was over in under ten. No kissing either. Just a fast and furious pounding and Matt had loved the simplicity. This was a woman who knew what she had wanted. No emotions either. None of that messed up love stuff that was inappropriate for a first encounter. Just a friendly, hard exchange. The best. Easy to walk away from too. No emotional entanglement. No obligation to whisper sweet one-liners afterwards.

Kate wasn't sure what she had expected. She was relieved at first when he hadn't wanted to kiss her and then had spent time worrying about her breath. Was that the reason he hadn't wanted his face near hers? He was out of her door a few moments later.

'That was great, Kate. Really good. We should do this again. Soon. Text me,' he had called as he was leaving.

That was it? Kate reflected in the bath, soaking off his sweat. God, she hoped it had been enough to hook him. She hadn't felt anything. Not even partly aroused. She hadn't done much either. He had taken her clothes off and then had taken his off. After putting protection on, he had put her into a boring missionary position and then had banged her for a bit. Then he had flipped her over, doggie and had thrust until he finished. She had been a moaning rock, making sure she made all the right sounds until he finished. It really hadn't been anything to remember. It seemed a tad ironic that she had been worried at times during the past six years about missing out on sex.

They repeated the exercise the following afternoon. They were at Matt's place this time, as Felicity was out of London visiting her parents for the day. This time, he lingered, and she responded. He kissed her slowly enough for something in her to re-awaken. Suddenly and out of the blue, there was a connection between her mind and her body. She returned the gesture by tracing her fingers around his muscular torso and he had sighed from her touch.

This time, the play was slower. Lingering kisses and tongues that danced with each other. They had slowly caressed each other, noting how the other responded. When Matt had turned Kate over, she was genuinely moaning from her body being alight with desire.

This time, he had made her ready for him, and the pleasure she felt as he had thrust deeply into her was as absolute as the first time she had merged with Ethan. She had been encompassed by an awakening of every cell in her body. She had wanted and needed Matt to the point where she too, had exploded with an ecstatic release.

'I want more,' she texted him perfunctorily as soon as she got back into her car.

'God, yes,' he had texted back.

He was already shagging Felicity before Kate had finished kicking the shit out of Todd at kickboxing that evening. Her kicks weren't nearly as hard as they had been in previous weeks, and Todd wondered what had changed. Kate only knew one thing. Now that Matt was hopefully hooked, she needed to break the news about Daniel Parkes.

TWELVE

STRATEGY AND ADVANTAGE

The weekend was quiet, and no news was good news as far as Kate was concerned. She didn't know if her lack of action was a sign of apathy or paralysis from fear. She feared searching online for anything that might leave an incriminating digital footprint as there was no need to implicate herself further. Deep down, part of her hoped that nothing would happen and if she ignored it all, it might just go away. Daniel might just turn up, having gone away somewhere on a holiday perhaps? Maybe he had gone to a relative's house to be cared for until he felt better? She called Andrew into her office as soon as she arrived on Monday, hoping that Daniel had been in touch with the office.

'Morning, Andrew.'

'Morning, Kate,' he replied cheerfully, hoping she was in a better mood. He placed a double shot coffee and a chocolate croissant in front of her for good measure.

'Yeah, look… sorry about last week. Goodness, this looks delicious. Where did you find this?' She picked up the croissant and as she did so, flakes of delicate pastry fell to the plate.

'No probs. It's a new week. The local bakery is having a French theme for the week. They make their own croissants which I think are better than the ones the French make. Although, I have only been to France once, so I'm no expert. They are super-flaky as you can see. Any news?' Andrew was hoping that Kate could alleviate his rising stress over the Parkes matter.

'Unfortunately not. He may just have the flu as his work said? He could be in a hospital for all we know? Someone knows where he is, because they informed his work. I wish we knew who.'

'Really? Do you think he may have flu?' Andrew shook his head. 'Doesn't really explain the note though.'

'No. I was just being hopeful. It is Monday morning after all. Plenty of time for the rest of the week to go pear-shaped. I'm just hoping that no news is good news. There's something else I want to clear up with you by the way. It's about Matthew Harmon.'

'The new legal rep who was in with the Banks Case?'

'Yeah, that one. Matt is actually an old colleague of mine. I was quite shocked when I heard his name the other day.' She looked up at Andrew trying to determine how the comment had gone down. He didn't seem horrified, so she added a bit more to her confession. 'I thought I'd left him in the past.'

'Okay.' Andrew didn't know what to say next. Kate had appeared to feign knowing him last week, and now she was owning up that they had been colleagues? Weird. He wondered if the flowers had been from Matt as well and not Angela Banks.

'I think I owe you a bit of an explanation for that? We don't need more intrigue and conpiracies flying around right now.'

'It's okay. You don't have to…' Andrew hoped she would explain anyway.

Kate quickly outlined the situation, leaving out the strategy part. Andrew didn't need to know about that bit.

'Well, I think it's a good idea to get his opinion, to be honest. I mean, it's not like we have a heap of people helping us with this situation.'

'I haven't actually asked him yet, although I'm sure it will be fine.'

She hadn't sounded as confident as she had wanted to. She hoped that Andrew hadn't picked up on her change of tone.

'Yeah, especially if you two knew each other? Coincidence that you both ended up in the same courtroom, don't you think? Definitely though, another opinion would be good.'

'Yeah - weird.'

'Maybe it was meant to be?' Andrew loved the idea that fate sometimes intervened. In this case, reuniting two people back together again.

'Well, right now, we are up shit stream without a paddle, and I have a missing client, perhaps taken by a couple from suburbia who appear to have lost the plot. I feel like a headless chook.'

Andrew's eyes grew wide as he imagined Kate as a headless chook.

'It's okay Andrew. We say that stuff in Australia. It's figurative. Not real.'

MATT WAS SITTING in her office during their lunch break, lured in by the promise of a quick lunch dalliance. He liked the word dalliance. It reminded him of a time before he was born, where sex was undertaken behind a veil of mystery and a more polite guise. A dalliance now was often perfunctory. A banal exchange of give and take.

Kate made sure that Andrew was out at lunch and then locked the door to her office. There was nothing to gain from sharing this strategy with her colleagues. Then she cleared her desk. It was Matt's fantasy to have Kate in her office. He had asked her not to wear anything under her skirt so that he could face her away from him and lean her over her desk. The perfect, non-emotionless exchange between two consenting adults. Sex for sex's sake and nothing more. He had pulled her head back to pull her into him, and she had been surprised by the gesture. It was rough and hard, but not so much that it was unpleasant. She liked the rawness of it, the honesty with his desire. This man wanted her for sex, and she wanted him for so much more.

Afterwards, and trying to sound as nonchalant as possible, she popped in some info about Daniel Parkes. It was not too much to start with, but rather the exchange from their first meeting when Parkes had received the alarming threat. Matt was on a high after sex with four women in less than seventy-two hours. Felicity, Kate and the twins from the gym. Life was excellent at that moment for him, although Kate didn't need all the details. He smiled broadly at her, that was, until Kate got to the bit about Parkes being missing.

'Seriously, Kate? What did the police advise?'

'Nothing.'

'Nothing?' Matt was surprised. 'They aren't usually that useless.'

'I haven't actually been to the police yet.'

'What? Why not?' Matt was obviously confused.

Kate said nothing.

'Kate? Why haven't you gone to the police? You have a kidnapping note.'

'He may have the flu.'

Matt stared at her. 'I'm speechless.'

'I thought I could handle the matter myself.'

'You what?' Matt sounded incredulous. 'He may have the flu? Are you serious? Has anyone seen him for the past week? He could be dead, Kate.'

There was an uncomfortable silence.

'You haven't involved the police? Holy shit. I can't believe you haven't contacted the police. This is bad.' He sat and stared at her with a look of utter disbelief. He was clearly bewildered.

Kate held her breath.

Matt shook his head and got up as if about to leave. 'Kate. What were you thinking? Seriously? You haven't been to the police after a client came to you after having been threatened and is now missing? Presumably, kidnapped? How does any of that make sense? How can he have the flu when you have that note in your posession?'

'You've said the same three times, Matt. I hear you. No. I didn't go to the police as I have also reiterated three times.'

This was the moment when the strategy was either going to get to the next level or come crashing down. Matt had to like the sex enough to want to help her. Otherwise, he would walk. She studied his body language closely. He considered walking. Having Kate was about merging power. Not that she realised how much power she actually carried. That was what made her so damned alluring. The fact that she had such a low opinion of herself whilst everyone else stood back and looked at her with sheer awe. He wanted some of that. He wanted people to look at him with the same awe. The two of them were dynamite together. He liked that and deep down, he wanted and needed more. He would help her, even if just to rescue her and play the hero to secure their merge. That came with risk, though. Was she worth the risk?

He did a quick risk assessment in his mind. Legally, it

would be his word against hers that he knew about any of this. He could say that she hadn't told him anything. As far as anyone knew, they were just having a professional fling, and that would be the extent of it. He could advise her, have her and then go back to Felicity any time he needed to. Plus, he shouldn't forget the girls at the gym. Yeah, that worked for him, although he needed to appear softer. He was probably scaring her off at that point.

'Right', he finally said. 'I could walk through that door right now, Kate Hemsworth, you know that.'

Kate followed the arc of his arm and stared at the door handle.

'You are in the shit. Deep shit right now over this. You do realise you could be charged with God knows what? What if Parkes is dead, Kate? What then? Are you going to be hiding his body if it turns up? Throwing it into The Thames?'

'I'm fully aware of the enormity of this, Matt, but thanks for going over it again. And no, I don't have any plans for body disposal just yet.' She was dripping with sacrasm.

There was another lengthy, awkward silence.

'Why, though?' Matt asked, sounding a tad exasperated with her. 'It's not like you to be so legally… stupid.'

Kate shook her head again. 'The issue wasn't that serious when Parkes walked in. That's why I thought I could handle it.' She shrugged her shoulders. Matt was beginning to annoy her. She could eat so much humble pie before the act wore thin. She just wanted some help, not a therapy session. The berating and demanding line of inquisition wasn't what she needed at that moment.

His tone changed to utterly exasperated. 'Linda and Barry already have enough on you to KNOW that you won't go to the police. You can't now, even if you wanted to! What have you done, Kate? How did you ever think that this was a matter for a cease and desist letter? That's rookie thinking, and you aren't a rookie! Not that your letter even got to where it needed to go.'

Matt studied Kate, who now seemed genuinely overwhelmed. This wasn't a woman feigning anything. Kate needed his help. Would she have done the same for him, he wondered? He sat back down.

'We need to fix this,' he continued. 'How?' He could walk, or he could stay. It was his decision. He stared at her. Was she worth it? Maybe? Yes. 'Let's write down everything we know about this Daniel Parkes, and Linda and Barry Evans. The fact that nothing, well, we presume that nothing has happened yet, suggests they don't know what to do. I agree that money is the underlying motive behind this. I might do a bit of digging myself. See if there is anything that your investigator has missed. That will be my priority after work today. It's a starting point.'

Kate let out an audible sigh. The tension had been building in her to an uncomfortable level. She hadn't known which way Matt would go. He was going to help her. Now he was talking.

'Well, I didn't ask the investigator to do much in the way of Parkes' business,' she offered. 'I wanted to know what I was dealing with in terms of this psycho couple from the suburbs. It would be useful to see what is going on within his business as well, I agree. He gave me the pin to his office if that helps, only I haven't wanted to stride in there, in case I get noticed.'

'Okay then, let's sort out this side of things first. Kate, write down everything you know and see where the gaps are. I'll be in touch soon. I have to go. I'm fully booked for the arvo. Oh, and that?' He pointed to the desk. 'That was sensational, Kate. The rest of it was just complicated.' There was no hug goodbye. No kiss on the lips and no smile as he left. It seemed wrong, thought Kate, and then she berated herself for having expected more.

After Matt had left, she walked over to her bookcase, reached between two volumes of Torts and removed her phone, which had silently recorded the entire exchange. The action was below the belt and illegal. However, she may in the future need to prove that Matt Harmon knew precisely what had been unfolding, both in terms of their relationship as well as the details of the Parkes matter. Dividing the seriousness and potential consequences between the two of them might just take the heat off her a bit if things went wrong. She encrypted a copy of the recording and then sent it to her personal email. Then she deleted it from her phone. Just in case she ever lost her phone, or Matt gained access to it.

She worked until late. Partly out of guilt for having resorted to illegally recording Matt and partly for having had sex with someone to gain an advantage. It was mainly however, to atone for having made such a monumentally unprofessional decision to handle the Parkes case herself. Driving home, she mulled over the facts. There was nothing more to decipher from any of it, though. Had Barry and Linda Evans already uploaded the films, and if so, was Daniel Parkes already floating down The Thames? How would she even know if the films had been uploaded? Trying to find something like that online would be like trying to find a needle in a haystack.

KATE SAT on her lounge room floor later that evening, her laptop overheating on her lap. She yawned, feeling exhausted. She hadn't made any progress either. After watching poorly made films on the internet, she needed a break. None of the actors looked remotely like Daniel Parkes dressed like Zorro. Thank Goodness. The average couple having sex was also highly off-putting. Too many hairy arses and lousy acting. How desperate would you have to be to find that a turn-on? She sat, wondering what her next move should be. Then a text from Matt alerted her.

'You awake? Urgent.'

'Wait, I'll call you.'

He answered his phone before it had finished its first ring.

'What's up?' she asked.

'I'm in his office now,' Matt whispered.

'Office? What office? Whose office?'

'Parkes' office.'

'Parkes? What? Why? How did you get into his office? Did you use the pin?'

'No. I didn't need to. I'm dressed as a cleaning dude.'

'What? A cleaning dude. Seriously? Why? How did you get in without the pin?'

'Door was open. Other cleaners are here. Look, I'm going to have a scout around. I'll call you back in a few minutes, okay? I just need you to know where I am in case something goes wrong.'

'Hang on a min. Why are you *in* his office? Couldn't you have searched for info online?'

'No. I tried finding info through a couple of sources, and no one called me back. Given the urgency in sorting this, I had to think creatively. This way I can see if he's been in this week. Rubbish.'

'Rubbish?'

'Yeah, I'm checking his bin to see if he's been here.'

'A cleaner, though?'

'Yeah. I saw it in a movie once. Turns out it is easy to walk in somewhere if people think you're a cleaner. You kind of just walk in, as I did. I just wore cleaning clothes. If I'd used the pin, it would have logged me into the system alerting people to the fact that I was here. Especially given they think he is away with the flu. This is much safer.'

'Well, don't get caught. This isn't a movie, Matt.'

'I won't get caught, I promise. Now I'll go have a look around and then call you back. Okay?'

Kate sat holding her breath for what felt like the full ten minutes it took for Matt to phone back. She practically leapt onto her phone.

'Holy shit,' he whispered into the phone, so faint she could hardly decipher what he was saying.

'What?' Kate asked.

'I think I just found his phone in his office. Top drawer. It's not even password locked. At least I'm presuming it's his phone. Weird hey. There are messages which have come through, with no response from him too.' He scrolled through the phone. 'Weird though, there's talk of a Harry in all of them. Wait… give me a sec to figure out what I'm looking at. He hasn't deleted any of these messages by the way. They are all still here.'

'Strange as he said that he had deleted them?'

Matt quickly read the most recent messages. 'Okay… yup, I've got the thread of the threats. Looking at this, the first message is from a mobile number, which you said was Barry or Linda's number?'

'Yeah… Daniel said he thought Linda most likely. Then the messages went to a private number, most likely through an online service. I'm presuming Linda realised it was stupid to threaten someone without hiding her caller ID?' Kate paused mid-sentence. Something was niggling at her.

'What's up?' asked Matt.

'I'm just trying to remember…' she thought back to precisely the words that Daniel had used. What had he said? She had asked him if it was definitely Linda's number… 'He said he had got a generic voice message when he had called her back, that's all.' There was something else niggling at her. What had he added? 'He said that he was certain no-one else would do this, and yeah - he also said that he had deleted all the messages. That's why he didn't bring his phone into the meeting.'

Matt took a deep breath. 'Okay, well firstly, he didn't delete all the messages. Second, he gave you the pin to his office and third, he's left his phone in an unlocked drawer without password protecting it. Fourth... that's not conclusive about the number belonging to Linda, Kate. Did you check that the number actually belonged to Linda?'

Kate's heart immediately sank. 'He said he'd deleted everything, so there wasn't a way to check.'

'Well he obviously hasn't deleted anything. It's all here.'

'Why would he lie?'

'No idea. I've got a couple of contacts on the phone, but there's no Barry or Linda listed here either.' Matt rechecked. 'Nope. No Linda here.'

'Try the name Greg. Remember, Daniel knew Barry as Greg initially. Remember, they were the most likely candidates to try to blackmail him because of the films. No-one else knew about them.'

'And that's certain?' Matt asked.

Kate held her breath. The silence was enough for Matt.

'OMG, Kate. Have you checked that it was Linda or not? How do you even know if the threats are coming from Barry and Linda?' He paused, looking for a Greg on Daniel's contact list, which was incredibly small for someone who ran a business the size of the one he was in. 'Look, I'll have to call you back as I can hear a vacuum cleaner on this floor.'

Kate sat very still. What had Daniel *actually* said? He had looked at her confidently enough, but then she remembered. He had shifted in his seat. She had missed the connection and hadn't done her job.

'SHIT.'

Kate phoned Andrew, waking him in the process.

'So sorry, I know it's late, Andrew. I need to know something urgently. Did anyone ever check to make sure that it was Linda Evans who had called Daniel? Do you remember exactly what I said at the time?'

Andrew's mind was groggy. 'Hang on a sec.' He sat up in bed, trying to think. 'You said that Daniel had told you it was Linda's number. Didn't we then organise for that temp to get onto someone who could reinstate deleted files on the phone or something, only then he went missing before he had brought his phone in?'

Kate remembered. 'Bugger. I'd forgotten we had organised that. Did we ever follow up on any of that?'

'Don't think so. We asked Daniel to bring his phone in and then he disappeared. We never got to do it.'

'Shit. Just shit,' repeated Kate.

'Agreed,' said Andrew.

'Well, it seems that no one has checked, Andrew. Matt is in his office now. Cleaning.'

'Cleaning? Why is he cleaning at this time? In whose office?' Andrew was confused. 'So, we don't even know that this is Linda Evans sending these threats?'

'No, we don't. Not yet. Matt is trying to check it now. I can't believe we didn't check to make sure.'

'Well, to be fair, Daniel seemed sure and he didn't ever bring the phone in. I didn't follow up on it all.'

'Not your fault,' she quickly replied. The buck stopped with her. She had forgotten to check the details. A stupid mistake.

KATE PACED AROUND her lounge room. How had they all made such a fundamental mistake? It was so stupid. Why hadn't they checked to make sure that the number actually had belonged to Linda? If it wasn't, then they had all been sent on a wild goose chase, chasing what amounted to be a semi-dysfunctional couple from the suburbs who had nothing to do with Daniel's disappearance. Daniel Parkes had been so adamant that it was Linda and Barry behind it all, that they had all just gone along with it.

Why hadn't Matt called her back? She called his number. It doesn't take that long to check one number against another.

Matt answered in a hushed voice. 'The real cleaner has turned up. I can't speak. I'll come over, okay? I'll be over soon.'

He arrived precisely thirty minutes later, still wearing his cleaning attire, with a folder in his hand.

'This has just got a lot messier, Kate.'

She looked at him quizzically.

'You probably need to sit down. You're not going to like this.'

Kate sat, saying nothing and wondering how any of this could get any worse.

'Omg - there isn't a body is there?' She looked at Matt as white as a sheet.

'No, of cousre not. Can I have a drink though?' asked Matt. 'It's been a bit of an evening so far.'

She poured them both double scotches and then waited.

'Okay. Daniel Parkes isn't actually Daniel Parkes.'

Kate looked at Matt blankly. 'Sorry?'

'He's been using a fake name.'

'What?' Kate was bewildered.

'Turns out, his real name is Harry Rainer. He's 56 and CEO of 'Rainer Consulting Services.'

'Hang on.' Kate was trying to mentally catch up. 'What?' She couldn't think clearly.

Silence.

'Wait…' said Kate, trying to make sense of it all. 'Are you saying there is no Daniel Parkes at all?'

'Not that I know of.'

'Okay. So how did you find his office then?'

'What was the name of the business he told you he ran?'

'HRC?'

'Think about it. Harry Rainer Consulting. All I had to do was search online for HRC. I ended up at the right address… in the end. So, our Harry Rainer, formally know as Daniel Parkes, is actually an extremely wealthy businessman.'

'Yeah… I knew that much,' confirmed Kate.

'No, I mean really wealthy… he's listed in the top one hundred.'

'Really?'

'Yeah. So, this changes things a bit, wouldn't you say?' Matt looked at her. 'What have you got yourself into Kate Hemsworth?'

'I don't think I know,' was all Kate could say.

'There's more.'

'More?' Kate held her breath. 'How can there be more?'

'Yeah. That number? The one you assumed was Linda Evans?'

'I didn't assume. That's what I was told,' she said defiantly. Kate's heart began to race.

'Not Barry and most certainly not Linda Evans,' Matt said.

Kate looked at Matt, terrified of what he was going to say next.

'Whose number is it then?' she asked, her voice going quiet.

'It's a number belonging to a David Mason, who lives in San Francisco and is the Manager of Harry's Company out there. He's the one sending the threats.'

'What?' Kate was lost. 'Why?'

'The threats, Kate. Never came from Barry and Linda. They are coming from within his own business.'

Kate shook her head. She needed time to digest all of this and re-set her internal compass. She had been lied to. Majorly. She hadn't spotted the lies, though. A substantial professional mistake. She felt her face burning from the humiliation.

'Why didn't Daniel tell us who he really was?' She sounded defeated. 'Did he know that Linda wasn't behind all of this?'

'My guess? Probably didn't want us to know because of the films. He probably thought he could get away with the name change in amongst his panic that the films would be publicly released. I think he actually thought it was Barry and Linda Evans threatening him, though. He assumed it was going to be an easy fix, I believe. The threats are real, though, and it does look like he's disappeared.'

'Doesn't make complete sense.' Kate was up and pacing. 'He approved the letter I drafted to Barry and Linda Evans. They wouldn't have known who the hell I was talking about if they had even received it. We referred to him as Daniel Parkes, remember? So why would he have allowed us to send a letter to them using that name?'

'Unless he is known as Daniel to them as well?' Matt suggested. 'I'm sure he thought it was Barry and Linda.'

'Maybe?'

'Well, think about it. He meets Barry, who is also hiding under an assumed name. Probably wants to protect what he has, so he decides to hide behind a false name too. Coincidence most likely that they both changed their names at that time.'

'Omg,' said Kate sounding frustrated. 'Is there anyone actually telling the truth in any of this?'

She looked at Matt, realising that she certainly couldn't be included in that. Matt, looking back at her, tried to keep his expression the same. He wasn't included in the truth set either.

'What a total arse of a mess,' said Kate. 'Are we sure he thought it was Linda Evans behind all of this?'

Matt thought hard. 'I think so. I think he knows that the films could cause a professional scandal, so he came to you hoping to stop Barry and Linda from releasing them. Otherwise, he wouldn't have come for help.'

'But it isn't Barry and Linda.' Kate shook her head. 'Fuck, Matt. This is serious.'

'I don't think Harry knows it's David Mason making the threats. In fact, I'm certain of it,' added Matt.

'Hang on,' said Kate. 'If Mason's number is in Harry's contact list, then why didn't the phone number show up as his when he called?'

'Well, I wondered about that too. It looks like several calls were made to Harry that day, most likely business-related, by David Mason. However, Harry didn't have his number listed under a name for some reason. I'm going to guarantee that Harry wears reading glasses and doesn't bother to wear them most of the time. I would say this is just human error on Harry's part. He's assumed it was Linda's number, heard a generic voice message and so has gone along with it.'

'Dumb,' said Kate. 'This is getting worse by the minute.'

'Yeah, but it happens. If you cross-examine ten witnesses to any situation that has unfolded in front of them, you will get ten different versions. People believe what they want to believe. Not necessarily the truth. They also make mistakes. There's no way he would have gone along with the cease and desist letter either.'

She stared at Matt, frowning. 'Well, how did you find out that the number belonged to David Mason then? If it wasn't on his contacts and didn't come up under his name?'

'I googled the number.' Matt waited for the simplicity of his answer to sink in.

Kate shook her head. 'All we had to do from the start was google the number? Are you kidding me? Although I'll give us some credit that Parkes didn't bring his phone with him. Couldn't he have googled the number? Omg. I'm stuffed. Totally stuffed.' She slumped down into her chair.

'No. Not yet, you aren't. We haven't tried to sort this out yet. We just need to calmly think this through. Stick to the facts. Be meticulous. We're not stupid, Kate. Let's combine our intelligence together here.'

'Really? You have hope?' Kate didn't. This had turned into one enormous shitty mess.

'I do have hope Kate,' he said, acknowledging that his reply could also apply to their partnership. 'I always have hope.'

An hour later, after discussing the case again from start to finish, Kate suggested they just go ahead and speak with Linda and Barry Evans to see if they had any idea where Harry might be.

'Not keen on that. It also means that we are then linked to Barry and Linda.'

'Hear me out. It makes sense. We might get a better idea as to why Harry was so worried about the content in the films. He might have mentioned this David Mason to Barry at some stage? Also, we'll meet them somewhere public. Keep them away from the office.'

'Harry, Harry, Harry.' I need to do a permanent mental switch from Daniel,' said Matt. 'I hope no one else decides to change their name. I'm having trouble keeping up. Yeah, I suppose it's worth a try. You want to call Barry?'

'Yes. Harry, not Daniel,' added Kate. 'Must remember too. I'll call one of them. Whoever picks up first.'

'Okay. You have sold me on the idea. I agree. We can

gauge how much scandal is contained within the films and see how much trouble Harry is in. Speaking to the two of them might help. Organise it for tomorrow. We need to find out some more about this San Francisco dude as well and we may just get some info from Barry. I'll do the work myself. Use an internet cafe and cover my tracks. I suggest then that we meet up after lunch?'

'Sure,' agreed Kate. It sounded like a start in the right direction.

THIRTEEN

HAIRS GROWING EVERYWHERE

Kate worked until lunch, which proved to be a welcome respite given everything that was going on. The next bit of her day was more tricky. She needed to arrange a time to meet with Barry and Linda, but she couldn't be sure they knew him as Daniel. She wrote down what she wanted to say and then tried calling Barry Evans at work, ensuring that she blocked her number first. He was in a meeting until later.

She then phoned Linda Evans at work. She panicked when it went straight to voice mail.

'Hi, this is Linda. You've called BJ Services. Leave me a message, and I'll call you right back.'

Kate quickly thought. She would need to leave a number. She took a deep breath to keep her voice calm and steady. She could leave a message but not say where she was calling from.

'Hi Linda, this is Kate. I was just wondering if you might give me a call back to discuss a sensitive issue? Hoping for a meeting late afternoon or early evening to discuss with you and Barry. Thanks.' She added the number and then quickly changed her voicemail. That way, Linda wouldn't know where she worked or what her last name was. She waited.

Linda phoned back within a few minutes. Kate allowed it to go through to her new voicemail.

'Hi, this is Linda. Not sure what this is about. Can you call back and give me a bit more info?'

Kate hadn't given her enough. She called back, again getting the voicemail.

'In regards to an old friend of your husband Linda. Nothing to worry about. Thanks.'

Linda was intrigued. She called Kate back. 'Yeah, sure. Barry is free too. Can you get back to me with a time and a place? I've got to go out for a bit to run some errands, so if I don't get back to you immediately, that's why.'

Linda hadn't asked any questions though. Did this mean she didn't want to incriminate herself whilst at work? It could mean that. Most people would have asked. Kate called back.

'Hi Linda, this is Kate returning your call. I was hoping to meet in the city at around six? Maybe we could meet on Westminister Bridge near the Eye? I'll be with my colleague Matt, so we should be obvious. If necessary, I'll call your mobile at six and give you both a wave. Thanks, see you then.' Kate stared at her phone. That had sounded really suss. Two strangers asking to meet on a bridge? She hoped that Linda and Barry were curious enough to follow through with the request.

Matt popped in a few minutes later with some sushi.

'Here, eat. You look like shit.'

'Thanks, Matt.'

'My pleasure.' He stuffed a large piece of salmon roll into his mouth.

'They have agreed to meet us at six. On the bridge near the Eye.' She filled him in.

'Good outcome Kate. Now think of the questions that we

need to ask. We need to know the extent of these films. At least Barry can give us his side of the story anyway. Then we can figure out how much damage they can do. That's a start with this mess anyway. I suppose then we can see how much of Harry's work he shared with Barry. Whether or not he ever mentioned this David Mason?' He leaned back on the client chair, resting her feet on her desk. 'You do know Kate, that this is dire shit here. You should have gone to the police.'

'I still know that, Matt,' she replied, sounding fed-up. 'As you have now pointed out several times, thank you. I'm not dumb and nor am I deaf.'

'I'm not saying you are.' He squeezed some wasabi onto his salmon. 'Love this stuff. Clears out my sinuses. Okay, important question. Why didn't you go to the police? Give me your thought processes. I said it the other day. It's not like you to make such fundamental mistakes.' He stuffed the entire piece of green salmon into his mouth and then quickly unscrewed the lid of his water bottle. 'Shit hot,' he spluttered, his face going bright red and his eyes watering.

'I know this looks bad.' Kate sounded defensive. 'It's not every day that a man walks in with a threat like that. I suppose given how he explained everything, I assumed it was a simple cease and desist matter. Be fair though, Matt, if I had taken it the police at that point, there wasn't much of an actual threat going on.'

'True, but it got worse,' he croaked, his throat on fire.

'I still thought it was under control. I stuffed up. I agree. Can we move on?'

'Yeah, yeah, keep your hat on. You were unlucky that he chose you. See? That's one of the drawbacks of having a high profile online. Means that people click on the first name they find, which is yours. Kate Hemsworth… super lawyer.' He covered another piece of salmon with wasabi, wanting his throat to catch on fire again.

'Remember he lied to me too, Matt. Not exactly an average client walking in off the street in the end now, was he?'

'True, I'll give you that. By the way. This David Mason, the guy who is sending the threats, has some serious background. I had some info come in this morning about him. Thus my reason for being here, aside from feeding you. You haven't eaten anything yet, Kate. Eat.'

She opened the plastic lid and squirted the soy sauce onto her salmon. She wasn't in the least bit hungry.

'You do know that I'm going to charge you for all of this work?' he added.

Kate looked up. He was smiling at her.

'Plenty more places to have some fun.' Matt beamed at her.

Kate frowned. Was he insinuating that she could repay him with sex? Matt was a complete douche at times. She smiled back as part of the strategy. All Matt ever thought about was sex, so nothing had changed there.

'Well, we could start tonight with repayment? Actually, no. Not tonight,' he added quickly, laughing nervously. Shit! He had forgotten that Felicity was coming over later that evening. 'Tomorrow. We can start tomorrow.'

Kate didn't say anything, as her mouth was full of salmon and rice.

KATE CANCELLED the last two of her clients as she was running late by four. She couldn't afford to be late for the meeting, and she needed time to prepare. She asked Andrew to send out feelers asking if anyone would like two additional consults, using the excuse that she was feeling sick, and Louise kindly agreed to take both.

'Happy to do that, Andrew. Just send me their details,' Louise cheerily messaged back.

Andrew smiled. Louise was a sweetheart. The rock of the firm. She was always the first to offer assistance to everyone else.

KATE MET up with Matt at the tube station opposite Big Ben. People were milling everywhere, admiring the Houses of Parliament and taking photos of the boats trailing down the river.

'How do we even know what they look like?' she half-shouted to Matt as a large double-decker bus went past them. They walked over the bridge which was teeming with tourists and commuters.

'Got that sorted. They have their photos plastered all over Facebook. Look for a woman with bright red hair walking with a tall, dark-haired dude of about fifty-five. He's got to be well over six foot. Hard to miss even with these crowds.'

They walked down the stairs past a hawker selling everything from small plastic red buses to blue bobby salt and pepper shakers.

'Come get your souvenirs here,' he called out to the eager tourists, revealing a few rotten teeth inside his mouth.

Kate huddled close to Matt. It was freezing. Hail had been forecast, and the dark thunderous clouds had begun to show themselves on the horizon. She stamped her feet, trying to warm them up.

'What's with the weather in this city? One day it feels like spring, and then the next mid-winter. They should be here soon, I hope. It's bloody freezing.' She looked up at Big Ben as it chimed six.

'Not everyone is as punctual as you are, Kate, and it's peak time. We need to give them a few extra minutes. Hey, I can't believe they didn't even ask why we wanted to meet them.'

'Maybe that's a sign of their guilt? Not wanting to give anything away?'

'Maybe?'

They looked out over London.

'I love it here, you know,' said Kate, the comment coming out of left field.

'Me too. I didn't at first, though,' said Matt sighing, as he leaned out, looking towards Big Ben.

'Why not?' asked Kate.

'I think it's just so profoundly different to home. It took me a while to settle in. It's a much faster pace which is good, but I kind of miss how laid back things were in Brisbane. Here? There are a million different stories all being told at once.' He smiled at her. 'Just a bit noisy sometimes.'

'Very poetic there, Harmon,' she said, smiling back. 'I loved it, the first time I saw it,' she said, allowing the wind to blow her hair off her face. Never alone, or bored and always in the thick of life itself.'

'Well, you came from somewhere where only the sheep talked to you, didn't you? I imagine anywhere with some people added would be better.'

'True.'

The two of them stood for a while, leaning on the stone bridge next to the river. Kate pulled out a hair from her head and dropped it into the water. She watched as the river took it away.

'What did you do that for?' Matt asked, looking perplexed.

'Just to be a part of it all. My DNA is now a part of the Thames. A part of London. Part of something much older than I will ever be.'

'Getting deep there, Hemsworth.' He smiled. Kate was an

enigma compared to most women. Hard on the outside, yet sometimes, she just dared to show a more vulnerable side of herself. He didn't believe that she ever stopped musing about everything. Her mind was always on the go.

'I think that's them headed our way now,' Matt said a few minutes later, peering over to the other side of the bridge.

A couple was walking towards them. The woman looked about fifty with a bright red pixie cut. The man was tall with darker hair.

Matt looked at Kate. 'Remember, don't mention anything about Harry and the kidnapping. We are just getting info about the tapes and maybe a bit about David Mason. The last thing we need is these two seeing an opportunity to make some money with the media and go selling some half-cocked story about kidnapped businessmen and crooked lawyers. Also…' he added, 'don't use Harry's name either way because we don't know what name he gave them. We'll have to get into the topic without using his name.'

'I gave her Daniel's name remember.' Kate raised both her eyebrows at him.

'Oh yeah, so you said. That was lucky. Just checking 99.' The nickname made her smile. He had called her that back in Australia when they had worked on cases together.

'Hang on a min,' Kate quickly added. 'Do we know that Linda knows about the films?'

'Did Harry mention it to you when he was telling you about the phone calls?'

'When she first found out where Barry had been?'

'Yeah.'

'No, I don't think he said anything. She may not know.'

'Right then, she may be about to find out.'

'Isn't that going to drop a bombshell on her lap?' Kate looked concerned.

'Probably?' Matt said. 'Okay, you ready? It's showtime.'

They greeted the couple in a professional and friendly manner, and Linda and Barry seemed happy to meet, despite not knowing exactly why. The truth was that their lives were dull, and being asked to meet in the city had added spice and excitement to their suburban, domestic routine. Linda was also curious. This could be the news that they had been left with an excessive amount of money from a friend of Barry's. It was worth the trek into the city, and anyway, the girls at her Thursday morning pilates class would drool over their lattes at her good fortune. It was definitely worth following through.

They had only just finished exchanging pleasantries when hail started stinging their skin. There was no way they could continue the chat out in the open.

'I know a café not far from here. Happy to go there?' Matt shouted, over the sound of the hail.

They ran, like everyone else, trying to escape the sharp pings of the icy balls into the café. They were soaked. They sat down at a window table, and then there was an awkward silence. Kate wondered how they were going to get from discussing hail to bondage films. Matt, however, just jumped right in.

'Kate and I really appreciate you guys meeting us today. It's a very sensitive issue that we are dealing with. We can't tell you all the details, but we would appreciate your help concerning some films that a previous partner of yours says were made?'

Whoa, thought Kate to herself. We don't know if Barry knows him as Harry or Daniel, and he has just opened up the topic by chucking it out onto the table. Clever move, Matt. Although Linda may have just found out something she knew nothing about.

'Yes. I wondered if this might get brought up,' said Barry looking uncomfortable. 'I presume you are speaking about Daniel?'

Linda shook her head. It would have been too good to be true that they were about to become wealthy from someone else's demise. It was about those bloody films.

'Yes,' said Matt. 'Daniel Parkes?' So, Harry had kept his true identity hidden from Barry? Both had done the same thing by not revealing their real names to each other.

Kate wondered how on earth that had lasted for eighteen months. 'Your help would be very much appreciated,' she smiled.

Barry nodded, gulping down some water.

'Yes, so we believe that there were some films made?' Kate glanced at Linda to gauge whether she knew about them or not. She didn't look overly surprised. 'Is this right?'

Linda interjected before Barry could reply. 'I told you, Barry. I told you this would come back and bite you on the bum. I have no idea what you were thinking, being with that bloke in the first place when you were married to me. You hadn't said anything about separating, and you traumatised the kids. We thought you were dead, for God's sake. Don't you roll your eyes at me, Barry Evans. Why were you making commercial porn anyway? It's disgusting.' She shook her head and turned the other way in a grand gesture of disgust.

Meanwhile, a young waitress had snuck up on them and was standing at the table with her jaw now planted on the floor.

Matt raised his eyebrows at her.

'Ready to order?' she asked in a higher than usual pitch.

'Yes, thank you,' said Matt, trying to appear nonchalant.

She leapt into action, took their orders and scurried away.

'I don't think Barry was making commercial porn, Linda,' Kate said gently, trying to break the stand-off at the table. The words porn and disgusting had been hovering over them, and no one wanted to pick up the thread of the conversation.

'Well, what would you call it?' she asked Kate.

Matt jumped in. 'Creative expression Linda. It was creative expression. We can express ourselves in many ways. Daniel and Barry just chose that particular medium to do it.' Matt sounded so in control and so full of shit. Kate was impressed and tried not to smile.

'My arse, it was creative expression,' retorted Linda. 'It was two old men who should have known better, spanking each other and showing it all off for the world to see. Hidden behind ridiculous masks as well. It's embarrassing. There's no other word for it. Embarrassing Matthew. I'm sorry, but I'm not buying creative expression.'

Barry piped up. 'It wasn't for the whole world to see Linda. It was just between Daniel and me. No-one else was ever supposed to see it.'

They must have both had the same thought at the same time because Linda and Barry suddenly looked at Matt and Kate, their eyes very wide.

'You haven't watched any of it, have you?' asked Barry looking terrified.

'Of course not,' said Kate quickly. 'No, not at all.'

'Well, that's a relief then,' snorted Linda. 'I don't want his hairy arse making it onto the news and then blocking up my newsfeed, now do I? Let alone giving the two of you nightmares.'

'I don't have a hairy arse, actually, Linda.' Barry sounded indignant. 'I got it waxed.' He looked proud of himself.

'So you waxed it for that, Daniel, but not for me? Like that, is it?'

Barry sighed and another silence descended over the table.

'You do actually have a hairy arse by the way, just for the

record.' Linda piped up again. 'It's much hairier than it was ten years ago too. It happens to men as they age. Your ears are hairier and your nose.'

'Well, you have more hair on your...' Barry was fighting back.

'Shut up, Barry. The police are trying to hear intelligent information from us. If you have something to say, make sure it is grown up... and intelligent. That is, if you can manage it,' she added, folding her arms.

Barry had been told. He shut up, sighing loudly again.

Matt and Kate looked at each other. Linda thought they were the police? That wasn't a bad assumption, thought Kate.

The drinks appeared just at the right time as Matt regained control of the table.

'Barry. When you made these films, the intention was that they would be between just you and Daniel. Yes?'

'Absolutely.' Barry sounded adamant. 'Neither of us had any intention of releasing them. It wasn't commercial porn, as you so kindly called it Linda. It was just a bit of fun.'

'What did Daniel do with the films after you had made them?' Matt softened his tone to dispel the obvious tension.

'Well,' said Barry thinking hard. 'We would watch them and see what we could improve on for the next film and then Daniel would store them.'

'Store them? Where?' Matt asked.

'Let me think.' Barry paused, trying to recollect. 'Oh yes, I'm no tech-head, but I think he did this really clever thing and sent them up there.' He indicated up into the sky with his hands.

'What do you mean up there?' Linda interrupted. 'Like up to heaven for the angels to watch? Not likely. Maybe they went into space for the aliens to watch? Makes no sense Barry. No wonder we've never had any visits from aliens. Imagine. Oooh that looks like a nice planet. Look at what they do on that. Most likely, the films went down there.' She indicated to the floor. 'To hell, where all the other people who made bad porn went, after they died.'

The waitress had just arrived at the table to ask if they needed anything else. She quickly diverted her stare and hurried off to the adjoining table.

Kate jumped in. 'Did he send them to the cloud, Barry?'

Barry nodded animatedly. 'Yeah. The cloud. His work one, I think. I always used to joke with him about what would happen if the cloud burst and all that stuff came pouring out while he was at work.' He smiled with a hint of nostalgic love.

Matt smiled. He wasn't far off the truth. When someone did hack into the cloud, the info literally did come falling out, and, in this case, that is precisely what sounded like had happened.

'So, was Daniel concerned about anyone at his work ever finding the films?' Matt asked.

Barry shook his head. 'Not really. He said that the safest place to store them was at his work. He said it was way safer than keeping them on his laptop.'

Matt sighed at the dead-end reply.

Kate tried. 'Barry, did Daniel ever say anything about work and if anyone was causing problems?'

'Yeah, he did. He said there was a takeover attempt, but that happened way before I met him. He mentioned it a couple of times. Not in any great detail though.'

'Do you remember any names he might have mentioned at the time?' Matt pressed him, hoping he might remember.

'Gees, it was ages ago. Let me think. A David someone? Honestly, I can't remember. Maybe David? He didn't talk much about his work and it wasn't something that I asked him much about.'

'So, are you going to tell us why you need this

information or is it like hush-hush?' asked an inquisitive Linda.

'Hush-hush, I'm afraid, Linda.' Matt sent her the biggest smile that he could muster.

Kate could see that he had Linda wrapped around his little finger.

'I see,' said Linda eyeing him squarely. 'Like that is it?' she asked, nodding slowly at him.

'Absolutely like that,' Matt answered, nodding back.

'And your information has been invaluable. We can't thank you enough,' chimed in Kate, not wanting to feel left out.

'So, if you two know about the films, how many other people do too?' Barry sounded stressed.

'Oh, it's fine,' answered Matt sounding reassuring. 'I can assure you categorically that the films are safe. Our inquiry simply relates to Daniel and where you stored the films. Nothing to worry you.'

'So why not just ask that Daniel fellow yourselves?' Linda was thinking clearly.

'We have. There are two parties involved, though, and we wanted to see if Barry knew where they had been stored. The matter we have is all about testing intention and subsequent storage, that's all. There's some new legislation coming in.'

Kate winced. That sounded suss at best and hardly a legitimate reason why they had needed to meet Linda and Barry in a public space without giving them their last names. What new legislation? Intention and subsequent storage? It sounded a bit wishy-washy.

'What? Am I in trouble?' Barry looked as white as a sheet.

'No, not at all, Barry.' Matt tried to sound as reassuring as he could.

'My understanding is that you can't be recognised in the films anyway, Barry.' Kate smiled at him.

He seemed to instantly relax. 'Yes, of course, we were careful about that.'

'Unfortunately, as much as we would like to tell you more, we can't at this stage.' Matt stood up to leave.

'So, you just needed to ask about where it was all stored?' asked Linda looking puzzled. 'That could have been done over the phone from the police station?'

'We needed to check that Barry understood about intent of storage, that's all. Anyway, we prefer to put faces to people that we deal with,' smiled Matt. 'It's always nicer to chat rather than speak into a phone, don't you think?'

'Well, you have our number if you need us again. Anyway, we have to go as well,' said Linda, sensing that the meeting was over and that she wasn't going to get any further information. 'We thought we might do a fish and chips at the river. Have a bit of a splurge, given we're here.'

'Thank you,' added Barry, not really knowing what he was thanking them for. Perhaps keeping his dignity intact, he wondered to himself. Deep down, he missed Daniel, but Linda had been there since he was nineteen. They went back such a long way. Linda couldn't give him what Daniel had given him, and she would never understand what it was that they had shared. He had tasted a different life with Daniel but was now happily back into the fold of his family again.

'SO, we can now confirm that it was sent to Harry's business cloud,' said Matt hurriedly, leading the way back over the bridge to Kate's office. 'Probably hacked from there by this David Mason in San Fran. I haven't even had time to fill you in yet about the digging I've done on him. However, meeting Barry and Linda has certainly ruled them out of the equation, which we had already surmised.'

'This is complicated,' sighed Kate. 'Haven't we just impersonated police officers?'

'We didn't say we were the police. They assumed that. So, technically, no.'

'I suppose so.'

'Look, there is a lot of background to understand concerning Harry's business structure and this David Mason chap, Kate. I'm busy tonight, but let's meet up again tomorrow afternoon. I've got some important stuff in the morning to do but could meet you after lunch. Can you take another afternoon off?'

Kate felt uneasy. She hadn't taken a day off since she had started at the firm. One afternoon had already been an issue for her. However, this mess needed sorting, so she hoped that taking another one-off and backing it up with a weekend would be okay.

Matt handed her a thumb drive out of his pocket. 'Go through everything on this and have it etched into your memory by tomorrow afternoon.'

'Sure.' Kate looked at the thumb drive. 'Where did you get this stuff?'

'Just take a look. It's enlightening, to say the least. I called in a few favours,' he added.

'Should I ask?' asked Kate. 'How did you do all of this so quickly?'

'Best not to ask,' replied Matt.

Matt said his goodbyes as he had Felicity coming over for dinner that evening. He wanted to feel cleared of Kate and all this stuff before she got there.

KATE KICKED TODD, but her mind wasn't on the job.

'Come on, Kate, you're like a limp bean tonight. Gets those legs up higher.'

Todd had them do a circuit to finish off, but Kate felt exhausted. Usually, the class invigorated her, but tonight, the effect had been to simply drain her. She ran her bath as she always did after kickboxing. Her stomach and abdominal muscles were in a tight knot. She did some deep breathing and felt them start to give. It was the first deep breath she had been able to take all day. She sipped the white Riesling she had chosen for her bath time soak. She downed a second glass waiting for the warm moment. It didn't appear.

'Stuff that,' she said out aloud. She needed help tonight. Her stress had been rising for days. She stepped out of the bath, covered in a cloak of bubbles and threw a towel around her. Carefully placing her feet on the tiles so that she didn't slide, she gently tiptoed into her kitchen. At the far end was a red cupboard that she called her 'special place.' She opened it and smiled. Inside there were several heavy-duty drinks to choose from, ranging from an aged brandy, some Baileys, Rum and Tia Maria. There was also a very nice black label malt whisky that she had picked up when in Scotland.

She poured herself the scotch. Grabbing some ice cubes from her freezer, she started to make her way back to the bath. Having second thoughts, she went back and picked up the bottle. At the same time, she sculled the scotch. That way, the warm feeling would be activated before she got back into the bath. Sensible and why delay it further? This whole sorry situation was definitely dire enough to allow more drinks into her system. She would drink until the calm feelings started, and then she would tackle the information on the thumb drive.

The bath felt different after the warm feeling had been ignited. She felt herself sink into a relaxed apathy. Nothing seemed as dire anymore, the alcohol having melted away the seriousness of the situation. Not even the fact that she was sleeping with Matt Harmon seemed to worry her.

'All for a good cause,' she said to the empty glass, pouring herself another. After the water had started to go cool, she topped it up again, not wanting to leave. After doing that several times, she poured a third and then dried herself off and made her way to her couch. She put the thumb drive into her laptop and settled down. The computer lit up, and she opened up the file called David Mason.

'So far, so good,' she told the glass.

Several pictures of a Chinese man dressed in a business suit appeared, standing outside an office block with HRC signage. She presumed it must be in San Fransisco? He looked confident, too, as if he knew his worth. There was another file called Background. She clicked on that. David Mason, as she had guessed, had anglicised his Chinese born name. Huang Fa Lee had been born in a remote village in Northern China. He had studied in Beijing and had acquired an undergraduate degree in Finance. He had then gone on and had done an MBA. He had worked in Hong Kong for a while and then had moved to Shanghai. After three years there, he had moved to San Francisco and had worked in Senior Management with Harry's firm for nine years. This was a good bit of background information.

Okay. She took another look at the information, not seeing anything that looked out of place and clicked on the last folder that had been named 'Concerns.' Matt had jotted down some notes concerning possible motives. Included were several detailed financial reports and a history of an unsuccessful takeover from a rival company in Shanghai. The information looked complicated. Kate stared at the information, which looked liked a series of shapes on a screen rather than anything of interest. She suddenly felt overwhelmingly sleepy. If she could just take a power nap, she would cope much better at digesting all of this.

Her head sank into her couch. All she needed was ten minutes, and then she could go back to the information and process it all. Her mind eased into her safe place. Over seven billion people on the planet, and yet, in this place, it was always just her. Her mind didn't seem to feel different imagining itself in the vastness of the universe, nor in the secret place in her mind, which at times seemed just as endless. Perhaps, they were both just as real as each other? Just for a moment, she felt a sincere sense of completeness, a oneness with everything around her. She allowed the blackness to lead her away. Deeper and deeper she sank until she became nothing.

SHE AWOKE the following day with the sun streaming in a little too bright for her normal waking time. At first, she lay, enjoying the warming light and then realised she had clearly overslept and wasn't in her bed. She had a throbbing headache pounding from behind both eyes and a pain in her neck from lying on the couch. She put both feet onto the floor, immediately feeling sick. She had less than ten minutes to get out of the door.

She gathered her clothes hurriedly and stood under the shower. She could smell alcohol oozing from the pores on her arms. She scrubbed herself with shampoo and conditioner, hoping to wash away the night before with something more heavy duty than soap. She then sucked on a mint and sprayed a strong perfume onto her blouse. Then, giving her hair a quick brush, she was out the door. Eight minutes and fifteen seconds, not bad, given the pounding from inside of her head.

She assumed that she might still be over the limit, so driving wasn't going to be an option. She hurried to the train station and jumped on the first train headed into the city. It was horribly crowded. She had been lucky to find a seat and felt like a sardine might, layered into a tin, only she was in a metal carriage, and people were swaying all over the place as they hung onto the straps for dear life. The carriage smelled of last night's dinner, deodorant, perfumes, sex and booze.

She was interrupted from her thoughts by the sound of a woman's voice.

'Kate. Hi. I didn't know you took the train into work.' It was Louise from the firm.

'Hi, Louise. What a surprise. No, I don't normally… my car… broke down.'

Louise hadn't been so lucky to get a seat and was swaying precariously in front of Kate, holding on to the arm strap tightly above her. She was dressed in a red and pink floral dress, black tights, a rose-coloured cardigan, topped off with a flowing black woollen coat. She looked like someone's idea of femininity. Kate had no way of moving away. She was trapped. A certain audience for the excited Louise who had never seen any of her colleagues ever venture onto the tube with her.

'Now, Kate.' Louise was beaming. 'You don't need to worry as I had your clients in yesterday afternoon. You are feeling a bit better, I hope?'

Kate looked at her blankly. How could Louise know she was hungover? Then she remembered.

'Yes, thank you, Louise. I still have a bit of a sore throat, though.' She quickly changed her speaking voice to sound like she might be in a bit of pain.

'You poor dear. It's going around, you know. First, it was Covid and then back to influenza. Not nice, I hear this year. I'm all sorted, though. Had my shot.' She grinned at Kate as if she had shared a secret with her and was waiting for a response. 'You do know that Influenza Type A has actually mutated this year?' She paused for effect. 'Just like that Covid virus did. It's knocking off the young mostly. Dropping like flies, they are. Terribly concerning. Some are even dying at home before they can seek help. Terribly alarming.'

Louise always sounded so precise when she spoke. Every word was carefully and crisply articulated. She spoke in such a compelling and intellectual way. What she said she meant, and it seemed to flow from her so neatly. Kate felt that most of the time, when she spoke in social situations, it was like her words had been placed into a clothes dryer, and they came tumbling out and not necessarily in the correct order. It was hard not to feel intimidated by Louise just for that. For sounding so 'together.'

'Yeah, I probably should get a shot too.' She smiled at Louise, trying to match her early morning optimism and say a whole sentence using the minimum amount of words necessary.

'I saw that Matt Harmon was in the office yesterday. Did you two know each other in Australia?' asked Louise, leaning into Kate's knees as they went around a tight corner.

'Yeah. We did, actually.' Kate tried not to look surprised. She had assumed that no-one had seen him enter from the side entrance.

There was an awkward pause. Louise had wanted more information than that but wasn't rude enough to probe. She smiled instead at Kate and then looked out of the train window, thinking of something else to discuss.

'Well, I'll need to catch up with you this morning Kate. It shouldn't take long. I've got to update you on a few things your clients did from yesterday. Charles Bryne, in particular, had me a bit worried. His affidavit, as it turned out, was full of small mistakes, let me call them.'

Kate shook her head. 'Really? Did you explain the concept of perjury to him? I have, a million times.'

'Yes. I think he was trying to push things as far as he could, quite deliberately, actually.' Her eyes went very wide. The thought of anyone trying to bend the truth in an affidavit was bordering on the abhorrent to her. 'You'll need to watch that one carefully.'

'Thanks for seeing to that, Louise. Hugely appreciated.'

Louise beamed at Kate. 'I do my best. I really do.' Her smile lit up the entire train carriage.

Kate was sure that she did. Louise was the backbone of the firm. Single and utterly devoted to her career, she would do anything to help any other lawyer in the firm. She also expected nothing in return.

The train pulled up at Westminster, and most of the train got off. It was one of the busiest train stations, and the effect was a wave of people all moving in the one direction as if the tide of nine o'clock had come in. Kate followed the herd, having lost Louise in the process but secretly relieved because she didn't want any more questions about Matt, nor her supposed illness.

Andrew was in her office with her coffee. He noted the overuse of the perfume and wondered if she had been drinking again? He hoped not. His father had been an alcoholic. What do they call them again? A functioning alcoholic, that was it. Although he hadn't ended up homeless and destitute from it, Andrew knew the problems that secret drinkers could face and hoped that Kate wasn't falling into the same pattern. Smelling alcohol on her breath well before midday was becoming the norm. Anyway, there was a idea sitting in his head that he needed to relay.

'Kate. I was thinking. Have you considered going and looking for Harry yourself?' Then he handed her the double shot latte.

Kate stared at him. 'Sorry?' She was surprised at such a bold statement coming from Andrew.

'I think it might be a good idea.'

'Where would I even start? Harry could be anywhere at this point, Andrew.'

'Matt gave me a thumb drive to look at, that's all.' He held up a similar red drive to the one Matt had given Kate. 'He asked me to look through it all, and I did last night. Actually, Rupert helped me. He's a bit of a whiz at collating info. I think Matt said you would look through the info too? So, what do you think? It looks like David Mason is up to his neck in it all, doesn't it?'

Kate looked blank. She delved into the hazy recollection of the night before. A bath. She remembered the bath because it had been warm and relaxing. Then there was the bottle of black malt. She remembered getting that. More bath and then the couch, or was it the couch then the bath? An image of a well-dressed Chinese man popped into her head. Nothing more.

'I'm not sure, Andrew. How about I wake up first? Get this coffee into me. I'll discuss this at lunch? Come see me during lunch and we'll go through it all.' She was stalling for time. What did he and Rupert know that she didn't?

Andrew left, giving her a nod. Whether it was an acknowledgement that she needed to wake up, meet again or that he knew that she couldn't remember, she wasn't sure.

'Fuck.' Kate searched in her handbag for the drive. It wasn't there. It was still plugged into her laptop at home. Now she couldn't read anything. Great. She would need to rely on Andrew's interpretation of it all at lunchtime. She imagined telling Matt that she had explicitly chosen to get herself so pissed that she had blacked out, just at the time that she was supposed to be doing some reasonably heavy-duty assimilating of essential info. No. She would never admit to being so useless.

Andrew arrived back into her office on the dot at 12.30. Just as he had started to comment on how polished David Mason had looked in the pictures, a text came through on her phone.

'Hope u have a passport. The flight leaves at 5.20pm. MA529 to Hong Kong. Meet u airport at 2.30pm dep. Heathrow Terminal 4. Confirm asap.'

Kate stared at the message. 'Why is Matt asking me to meet him at the airport?' She looked up at Andrew.

'Oh, God. Yes. Should have mentioned,' said an apologetic Andrew, 'Matt phoned whilst you were dealing with your eleven o'clock client and asked me to book a couple of flights for you.'

'What?' asked a bewildered Kate. 'To where?'

'Hong Kong.' He waited.

'Hong Kong?'

'Well, Matt agrees with Rupert. Harry left the country and is in Hong Kong, by the looks of things. Matt said this morning that he wasn't kidnapped in the UK. Left of his own free will. However, when he got to Hong Kong, he then got himself kidnapped. We think. That's when the note was sent.'

Kate stared at him. 'What?' Kate stared at him.

'Did you read the info on the thumb drive Kate?'

She shook her head.

'I didn't think so. It's complicated, as in there's a lot to read.'

'Yeah, I'm gathering that. I can't just fly out of the country, though, Andrew. Hang on, the kidnapping info isn't on the thumb drive, is it?' That made no sense. Matt would have told her when he handed it to her.

'No. He has contacts.'

'Contacts?'

'Yeah. I think you might have to fly over. You're like really implicated.' He paused. 'Matt explained it all when he phoned.'

'I'm confused.' Kate stood up as if going somewhere and then sat down again.

'Why not let Matt explain it all this afternoon?'

'What, on a plane to Hong Kong? Do you know how ridiculous that sounds?'

'I don't think you have a choice. Matt knows people over there who have offered to help. You should probably go at this point. You kind of need the help.'

Kate wished she had read the information. Obviously, there was more to it. 'Right,' she said, '… and Matt couldn't have told me all of this himself?'

Andrew raised his eyebrows at her and shrugged his shoulders. 'I think he did try to contact you late last night or early this morning? Several times?' He lowered his gaze.

'What? Did he?' She glanced at her phone. Andrew was right. Matt had tried calling her five times that morning. It was probably his last call that had woken her up. 'What about my clients, though? I can't just fly out and leave them.'

'I've already sorted that, Kate. You have a good friend in Louise, it seems. She said that she bumped into you on the train this morning. Just adores you. Wants to help with your potential influenza in any way she can. She also said that she had convinced you to get an influenza shot next year.'

Kate couldn't keep up. She texted Matt. 'WTF?' It was as if her life had just been taken over by Matt, Andrew and now Louise.

'See you at 2.30 to check in,' came the response, followed by a smiley face.

'How long am I supposed to be in Hong Kong?' she asked Andrew, who was halfway out the door. He stopped and turned around.

'Oh yes. Matt said you might ask that. He told me to ask you, how long is a piece of string?'

'Not helpful!' called out Kate as Andrew disappeared.

S0 Harry hadn't been kidnapped in the UK? Then he had flown out of the UK and then had got himself kidnapped? Was that even her responsibility? How was Matt even finding all of this out?

Kate stared at her desk. Maybe she should just call the police and tell them she had made a stupid mistake in not telling them and go from there. She could face the consequences. She was a grown woman. She paused for a moment. Theoretical consequences were one thing, but the actual consequences could be professionally dire. Daniel hadn't been kidnapped at first so maybe there was a way out? Although, now he had? It could mean the end of her career. She shook her head. There was no way on this planet that she was going to jeopardise her career. None. She had worked too hard and for too long to get to where she was at. She had put all of her eggs into her career basket. All of them.

She had sacrificed kids along the way as well. She paused, listening to her own narrative. She hadn't had kids because her only baby had died. Then she hadn't met anyone. No, she didn't want to meet anyone. Kids were a complicated issue too. If Sally had survived, she would have loved her with all her heart, but being a single mother may have been difficult. Maybe it would have been better to think of her warped narrative instead, as it was less painful. Either way, semantics aside, if she lost her career, she would lose her new self. No. Whatever it took to clear up the mess she had got herself and everyone else into, she would sort it out.

She called a cab and went home to pack a suitcase and grab her passport. She had never even been to Hong Kong before. The only fact that she knew was that the airport landing there was one of the most spectacular in the world.

She felt the sweat start to bead on her hands. It meant flying. Out of the blue, with no weeks of meditative preparation possible. Above everything else though, she needed to remember the strategy. It was all she had, and her life had just gone from bad to worse.

FOURTEEN

MILE HIGH CLUB

Kate arrived right on time and lugged her hurriedly packed suitcase through the automatic doors. Matt was standing in a line at a cafe. He beckoned her over.

'We've got time for a coffee before checking in. Want one?'

'Not really. I've had enough excitement for one day. Want to explain to me why we are even here?'

Matt could see her anger bubbling to the surface.

'I'm sorry. Okay? It was our only option with the info on the drive and the info my sources sent me.'

'Your sources? At some point, I need to be filled in, Matt. Soon?'

'Yeah, let's go find a seat, and I'll update you with everything.'

They walked across the terminal to a quieter corner and sat down.

'Look,' said Matt. 'I have good info that Harry is in Asia. Somewhere. He checked in to a hotel in Hong Kong before the kidnapping notice arrived. We know that much. At some point, he has presumably been kidnapped, or whatever you want to call it, by someone in Hong Kong, and we're assuming that David Mason is behind it. Then we got the note.'

'How do you know all of this?'

'I've got good sources, Kate.'

'Good sources? You sound like a bloody detective.'

'Every good lawyer needs their sources, Kate. Even you know that.'

'So why would Harry travel to Hong Kong without telling us?'

'Well, that's what we don't know. Maybe he thought the crisis was over? Maybe he thought he could handle things himself? Something has drawn him here, and we need to know what.'

'So, how do you know that David Mason is defintely our suspect?'

'We don't. It's just an educated guess based on the fact that his number started all of this. I'm just following all leads concerning his actions. Kate - you can't just stick your head under the sand with all of this and pretend it didn't happen. You have a missing client who came to you for help.'

'I don't get why we have to actually go to Hong Kong, though? This seems a bit extreme. I don't understand what we can do over there that we couldn't have hired an investigator to do for us.'

'I've got good contacts over here, that's why. People on the ground are willing to go the extra mile for us. If we start too much investigating in the UK, then we may get noticed and implicated if anything goes wrong.'

Kate sighed. 'Are we safe doing this?'

'Yes, Kate. Of course. I would never lead you blindly into danger.' He frowned slightly. He had already involved her with danger. Felicity was still on the scene and would put up a fight if she ever found out about Kate.

. . .

KATE STRAPPED herself into the plane seat, doing a good impression of calm. She looked around her as they settled in for takeoff. None of the other passengers seemed in the least bit worried about imminent death as the plane leapt into the sky after takeoff, maybe to then crash back towards earth. She gladly took the champagne from the flight attendant and sculled it. As the attendant walked back up the aisle, Kate asked for a second.

'Certainly, Madam,' the attendant smiled at her.

'Steady on Kate. I need your mind clear for some strategy work during the flight.' Matt looked at her glass which was already half empty.

Kate stared back at him. He had used the term 'strategy' right in front of her. Was he inferring anything? She downed the last of the champagne.

'Both of us have a lot to lose, Kate. Just keep that in mind.'

'Are you mansplaining?'

'What?'

'Mansplaining. Pointing out to a woman what is logical and obvious about a situation, assuming they are too stupid to think logically for themselves?'

'No.'

'Yes, you are.'

'No, I'm not Kate.'

'You just did. I know we have a lot to lose. That's why I contacted you for help. That's why I'm sitting on this plane with you. That's why I'm going to Hong Kong with only a few hours notice.'

Matt sighed. 'Sorry if I mansplained.' Matt needed Kate to be on-side during the flight. He couldn't imagine anything worse than being trapped next to her if she was in a bad mood.

'Genuine?'

'Yes, Kate.'

The engines began the whine that would soon turn into a roar. Kate was pushed back into her seat as the plane accelerated down the runway. Faster the plane went. Kate looked out of the window, knowing that everything was out of her control at that moment. Fate would decide what happened next in more ways than one, she thought. Reaching takeoff speed, the nose pushed into the air, and they were up.

'Don't you just love flying,' beamed Matt a few minutes later as he peered out of his window seat. 'It's so nice to be up here. No complications, just looking out over the world.'

'Absolutely,' said Kate, gripping her armrest tightly as the plane banked sharply to the right. In her mind, it was going to continue its lean and tip over. It was hard to even describe how much she hated flying, but she wasn't going to show her fear to Matt at that moment. The strategy she had devised did require a degree of fake. She needed to keep Matt working with her, so figuring out what kept him happy was imperative. She needed to curb her anger at some of the stupid things he said to her, that much she knew. She also guessed that he liked his women to be fearless which she could be at that moment.

Soon after the early flight snack, Matt plugged in his laptop. 'Time to do some serious stuff for a bit, and we can then play later.' He winked at her.

'Did you just wink at me?'

'Yeah. Do you have a problem with that?'

'Why would I have a problem?'

Matt sighed again. 'I'm sorry if I winked.'

Kate popped into the toilet and downed another valium. She was biting too much at Matt and if she continued, was going to get him off-side. She waited a few minutes for the drug to mix with the alcohol. A woozy feeling coursed through her veins, instantly transforming her from stressed to relaxed. She smiled at her reflection. That was more like it. Now she needed to go back to Matt and stop biting his head off.

She sat back down in her seat, now wholly fearless and ambivalent about whether she or anyone else on the plane survived the flight. She studied the flight screen and could see that they were travelling at six hundred miles an hour and that it was minus fifty-two degrees outside. She laughed. The sort of laugh that starts as a chuckle and ends as a snort.

'You okay there?' Matt asked, seeing a demonstrable change in her mood.

'Yeah, perfect,' she replied, smiling.

Matt opened up the files that had been on the thumb drive and went back over them. He had already worked out that she hadn't looked at them properly, given she didn't seem to have any idea as to what was going on. Kate was finding it hard to take in the financial details of Harry's company. In his haste to expand internationally, he appeared that he weakened his defence structures concerning possible takeovers. Something to do with shareholder percentages?

David Mason was believed to have set up his own company in Los Angeles in direct competition using a dummy director, whilst heading Harry's company in San Francisco. Then he made a move to buy out Harry's weakened business, and the two became professional enemies. Kate sighed. She felt so sleepy with the full effects of combining alcohol and valium now strengthening. She rested her head against Matt's shoulder and could feel the deep resonance of his voice on her cheek as he talked her through the details. His suit jacket was spiced with the aroma of his cologne, and as she nestled down, his voice became fainter and fainter.

The sound of the seat belt warning woke her a few hours

later. Her stomach lurched. Calm and soothing, the captain's voice had announced that they would soon be hitting a bit of turbulence, and it was best if they kept their seat belts on. Turbulence was Kate's worst nightmare. Once turbulence was severe enough for the flight attendants to sit down and buckle up, she started to panic. Her fingers gripped the armrests tightly.

Matt noted her panic. 'These beasts cannot fall out of the sky Kate. You can switch the engines off and do a nose dive for thousands of feet. They start up again. They can fly upside down if they have to.'

She gave him a faint smile as the plane dropped suddenly.

'Yup. All good,' she said, gripping even tighter.

The plane lurched and dropped for twenty minutes. Some passengers loved it, shrieking in delight as they fell. Others gripped their seats like Kate, silently praying for it to stop. One unfortunate passenger heaved into a white flight bag.

Then it stopped. The seatbelt light went out, and the flight attendants appeared beaming and smiling, offering coffee and tea as a consolation for the unexpected ride. Kate could not fathom how anyone would want to do this for a job, yet they did. Day after day. Endless takeoffs, landings and turbulence. It sounded more like hell to her.

Matt leaned towards Kate sometime after and whispered to her. 'In exactly one minute, I want you to follow me into the bathroom over there. Don't ask,' he added, putting his fingers onto her lips.

Kate watched him go into the bathroom a few rows in front. The red light went on, indicating that the bathroom was occupied. Was Matt asking her to have sex with him on the plane? Could she do that? The valium and alcohol said yes.

She waited a minute and then had a quick look for the flight attendants. They were busy unfolding blankets and laying them across passengers for the sleep part of the flight.

Quietly, she unclasped her belt and then made her way slowly towards the bathroom so as not to draw attention to herself. She pulled the dividing curtain across behind her so that other passengers wouldn't see which toilet she had gone to. She then tapped on the door discreetly.

Matt opened the door and ushered her in. Then he quickly locked the door again.

'Right,' he said, turning her around to face him. 'We have about five minutes in here before we need to leave. Don't speak. Just do what I say.'

He turned her around, which was difficult given the lack of available space.

'Kneel on the toilet,' he told her.

'Protection,' she whispered quickly.

'Of course. I came prepared. No pun intended.'

The thought excited her. This was crazy. At any moment, the flight attendant might notice that both of their seats were empty and that only one toilet was occupied. They could be caught. She steadied herself using one hand on the wall and reached behind to pull him towards her.

She felt him push into her. 'God, yes.'

He moved quickly and with urgency. Kate gasped.

For a moment, they became one as a feeling grew and built inside of Kate. She let out a moan and felt Matt's hand cover her mouth.

He let out a gasp and then stopped, his weight heavier on her back as he caught his breath. Kate dropped her head down, recovering and coming back into the moment.

'Babe,' he whispered. 'You are amazing.' He glanced sideways and caught his reflection in the mirror and grinned.

At forty-one thousand, five hundred and seventy-two feet above Russia, in well below freezing conditions and going at speed hard to imagine, Kate Hemsworth had just had sex with Matt Harmon.

Kate smiled. That had felt genuinely good, which had surprised her. The drugs and alcohol had stopped her internal chatter long enough for her to feel. Not used to feeling a full range of emotions, the sense of danger had excited her. She liked the way that Matt knew what he wanted and when.

'Clean yourself up and then leave a few minutes after me, okay?' He zipped up his pants. 'Welcome to the mile-high club, I'm presuming?' He didn't add the fact that this had been his ninth conquest in the air. Then he left the bathroom quickly before anyone noticed the two of them in there.

Kate locked the door again. She looked at herself in the mirror, looking deeply into the pupils of her eyes. She wasn't sure what she was looking for. She had connected with something deep inside of her during their encounter. What was that? Matt was reawakening a part of her that she had buried a long time ago. She stared at herself, her pupils dilating from the attention. How close could she really get to Matt Harmon, given this was a strategy?

Matt went back to his seat, feeling amazed that his suggestion had been played out. In a million years, he had never expected her to agree to that. Kate had played so hard to get in Brisbane, and this new version of her was excellent. He was one lucky man, that much he knew. Women though. Who the bugger understands them.. he thought to himself, shaking his head.

Whether it had been strategic or not from Kate's perspective, Matt was a new man for the duration of the flight. Perked up by the thought that Kate was now willing to have an adventurous relationship with him, he told her about his own life, growing up in rural NSW, something she hadn't know about him.

'I thought you were a city boy?'

'Not always. For the first ten years of my life, we lived on a pig farm.'

'That's different. How big?'

'Not massive by your standards out west, for sure. About six hundred acres. Just out of Armidale.'

'Cold country.'

'Yeah. Winters were freezing. We moved to Brisbane after that. My Mum got sick and needed to be around a major hospital.'

'Is she okay?'

'Yeah, luckily, her treatment worked. We still have her around.'

Kate smiled. It was nice hearing about Matt's previous life. She hadn't known he had been briefly married either, to a woman named Carla.

'Yeah, look. If I'm entirely honest, we got married because the sex was great.'

'Why doesn't that surprise me?'

'The only problem was that we had nothing in common. Once the novelty of the sex stopped, so did our relationship.'

'Has she remarried?'

'Yeah, lives in France now with a new husband. Has three kids as well. Weird. She said she would never have kids when we were married. Absolutely adamant. Then got pregnant with her new bloke two months after they were married.'

'Ouch?'

'Yeah. I was a bit surprised when she told me.' He sank back down into his chair. 'Might have a bit of nap before we arrive?'

THE DESCENT into Hong Kong was spectacular, with the dazzling afternoon sun shining off the high risers, which looked as if they were rising from the ground as stalagmites might. The sun shone on the water as they descended towards the small Hong Kong airport island of Chek Lap Kok. Matt instinctively reached down and placed Kate's hand into his as the plane descended.

'You got this, Hemsworth.'

'Yup,' she managed to squeak, her fingers tightening around his.

'Did you know that the landing into Hong Kong is one of the most turbulent in the world?' he volunteered.

'Did that fact come out of your mouth intending to be helpful?' she asked.

'Yeah?'

As if on cue, the plane started to bump as if being driven on cobblestones. Then it swayed, side to side. It descended in leaps rather than gradually. The engine whined and then roared. They approached the runway, the plane a see-saw, and just as they were about to land, the plane pulled up momentarily before hitting hard on the left wheel. Kate had yelled out along with a few people as the plane then careered sharply to the right and then was pulled back onto the runway. They were still going too fast, though. Kate shut her eyes. This was it. They were going to die.

'We're going to die,' she told Matt with her eyes tightly shut.

'Don't think so. Not this time, anyway,' he told her, trying to redeem himself for his last comment about the landing.

The plane was brought back under control, and they slowed down to a halt.

Kate opened her eyes.

'All over. We have indeed survived,' Matt smiled at her.

'Good.' She took a deep breath. 'That was awful.'

Soon they were standing in the warmth of a Hong Kong afternoon sun outside of the airport terminal, waiting for a taxi.

'That sun feels good', said Matt, facing towards the sun and closing his eyes, soaking in as much as he could.

'Doesn't it?' said Kate, agreeing with him as she did the same. 'There is nothing like a bit of sun. That's the one thing I miss the most about Australia. The sunshine. I think it makes you feel better overall.'

'Yeah. Totally agree.'

They took the taxi to the hotel. Matt had booked them into a prestigious five-star hotel in the heart of the city. It was so high that Kate had to strain her head back to see the top.

'How many floors is this thing?' she asked, craning backwards.

'Over a hundred, I think from memory,' said Matt allowing the porters to take their bags. 'Wait until you see the view from the room.'

'Have you been here before then?' Kate asked.

'No. I saw the pictures on the internet when I booked. It looks kind of amazing up there. Believe me.'

They took the lift to the 98th floor, and the view was indeed spectacular. The room had floor-to-ceiling windows that gave them a three-hundred-and-sixty-degree view of Hong Kong. They were like birds in a nest that had been perched high above everyone else. Kate could see mountains in the distance and Victoria Harbor with tiny boats on it. There were so many other high risers. The room itself was enormous with a marble spa bath and a king bed with a huge plasma tv. There was an extensive mini bar and lounge area for relaxing.

'You did good with the room, Matt. This is amazing.'

'It's sensational, isn't it,' agreed Matt, looking out of the window. 'It's good to be here with you, Kate. We may as well do this in style. My shout for all the glorious moments we are going to share within these walls.'

Kate had been enjoying the moment until he had so blatantly monetised their relationship.

Matt finished unpacking his bags and then turned to Kate. 'Let's go for a bit of an explore, have an early dinner and then we can catch up with my man on the ground here.'

'Your man on the ground?' asked Kate, having no idea that there even was a real man on the ground.

'Yeah. I've got someone here getting some info for me, and we're going to meet him later this evening. It should help orientate us in the right direction for finding Harry.'

Harry. That man had caused her an immeasurable amount of trouble. Had it really been the case that he had innocently searched for a lawyer and her name had been the one his eyes focussed on? She literally had to keep this mess under wraps. Otherwise, it would also be the first thing that people saw when they googled her.

THEY STROLLED AROUND THE CITY, which overpowered every sense with its lights, traffic noise, smells and speed. It *was* a city on speed, Kate deduced. The neon signs became more apparent as dusk fell, lighting up the city like a Christmas tree. The traffic sounded like the roar of the winds when they had come tearing over the paddocks back in Queensland. They dodged the army of commuters making their way home as they walked to a stylish waterfront restaurant.

'Now this one I am familiar with,' he told her as they admired the spectacular view across the Bay from their window table. 'Came here for a business conference a few years ago. It does the best duck in the world. Seriously. You have to order it.'

'Well, I love duck, so I might just do that,' said Kate,

nodding. She picked up the menu and put it back down. 'I can't read the menu, though. It's all in Chinese.'

'To be exact, it's actually in Cantonese. Most people here speak Cantonese rather than Mandarin. They do this cool thing here. It's called code-switching. You'll hear it when I order. They substitute English words for Cantonese words, and you get this cool hybrid language,' he said. 'Let me order for you. What would you like to drink for a start?'

'What do you think I might want? A stylish waterfront restaurant, a beautiful woman at your side and a balmy evening with a hint of warm breeze?' Kate asked, sounding more flirtatious than she had for a while. There was something about the warmth in the air and the view.

'Well, if you put it like that, then it has to be a dry martini, doesn't it?'

'Yes, please.'

He ordered martinis for them both in fluent Cantonese, and the waiter replied in a mixture of English and Cantonese. It was a mixed language that Kate had never heard spoken before and was precisely as Matt had described it. Matt then ordered them duck, followed by a lavender crème Brule. He added a flaming chocolate brandy as an afterthought.

Kate studied him at the table over the flicker of candlelight, now that the sun had set. She acknowledged that she had mixed feelings towards Matt, that was for sure. Sometimes she spoke harshly towards him and wondered if his own ambition threatened her. However, that made no sense, given they were both competent in their areas of law. Maybe he forced her to confront what she had lost in Ethan, namely being able to trust another human being? Matt was offering her healing, it seemed, and she wasn't sure whether she was ready, or not.

After all. They weren't actually in a relationship. Not from her perspective, anyway. She felt a pang of guilt as he smiled at her. Would he have ever guessed that she was using him to save herself? Lots of people used each other, she reasoned. For a multitude of reasons. How did people even climb the corporate ladder without using each other? That was life.

Matt was looking at Kate across from the table. The situation was undoubtedly complicated with Felicity being back home. Kate was a more complicated woman than his standard pick and didn't give things away easily. She was hard to read. In court, she was impenetrable, hard and gave off an illusion of strength. Behind closed doors, she was the opposite. He couldn't see how the two sides of her merged together at all. He smiled at her, seeing that she was deep in thought. If they stayed together, who knew where they could end up? The thought of merging as one law firm crossed his mind. Then again, Felicity was prettier, for sure. Unlike Kate, she was also easier to be around. Kate jumped on him for the slightest reason. He figured that Kate should be kept for his professional use and Felicity for everything else. He was glad that Kate couldn't read his mind at that moment, as she appeared content, sitting opposite him in the candlelight.

After dinner, they walked to the harbour foreshore and met with Matt's contact. He was a young man in his late twenties, Hong Kong-born. He had worked with Matt as a legal assistant a few years earlier on a case and had kept in contact. They shook hands, and the moment became serious.

'Tim, let me introduce Kate Hemsworth.'

'Very good to meet you, Kate. Matt has told me many things about you.'

'Hi, nice to meet you. He has?' She smiled at Tim, shaking his hand firmly.

'I suggest we go to a bar close by where we can talk more comfortably? Yes?' Tim indicated in the direction of a restaurant not far from where they were standing.

'Absolutely. Lead the way.' Matt was clearly keen to hear what Tim had discovered for him.

'Right, so this is what we know so far,' said Tim, opening up his briefcase. He placed his laptop and a wad of papers on the table between them.

'There are particular moments of interest, particularly in the financial history of the company. Not discrepancies as such, but tensions are apparent. You would have read some of this on the files I have already sent you.'

Kate nodded, feigning familiarity with the information. How she would justify missing two opportunities to understand what was going on was bordering on embarrassment. Now might be an excellent time to activate her mind and get things straight.

'So, Harry set up the first business in London, right?' She thought if she asked some generic questions, she might be given enough in the answers to follow what was being said.

'Yes,' nodded Tim. 'Essentially, he created a consultancy business in real estate investment. It offered large time investors advice on what to buy and when. Like you would call a 'high-flyers' consultancy. Those with cash to spend could create a lot more. But the risks were high. Thus the potential to make enemies along the way. No consultant has a crystal ball, and mistakes are made, but Harry's people were rich enough to absorb most mistakes.'

'So, some of his clients made money and some lost money, but on the whole, they were rich enough to absorb losses?' Kate mulled over the idea of being super-rich and not caring if you lost a millon dollars here and there.

'Yes. Most of the time. If they lost, they could easily recover. They had money to burn, the majority of the time, anyway.'

'Well, that sounds fair enough,' said Kate. 'Although, if I was trusting someone with my money, I'd be pretty annoyed if they gave me the wrong advice and I lost most of it.'

Tim explained further 'Harry decided to expand. He had huge amounts of money behind him, made firstly after several wise decisions during the dot com boom. He opened up an office in Hong Kong first and then floated it. From there, he expanded into Beijing and Shanghai. After that, he took aim at the States. He opened up two smaller offices, one in Los Angeles and the other in San Francisco.'

'With exactly the same business model?'

'Yes. He found a formula that worked fairly well globally. That's what made him so popular. He only floated the Hong Kong and San Fran sides of things, though. Set them up as separate entities before going on to sell the Beijing and Shanghai businesses. He kept a minority share in them.'

'And now he wants to set up in Sydney?' she asked, impressed by Harry's vision.

'Yes', added Matt, joining the conversation. 'But, the problem seems to lie in the opening of the American offices. Something has gone wrong with these. As soon as he opened the American ones, someone did some clever accounting and tried to manipulate the finances, giving the impression that the expansion into the States hadn't worked so well.'

'This is where David Mason comes into play,' Tim interjected. 'He was the CEO of the San Francisco office, and then we believe he set up another business in Los Angeles in direct competition to Harry. Trying to steal his clients and so forth. But...' he emphasised. 'Harry didn't know any of this.'

'Why not? How could Harry not know if competitors were circling?' Kate looked confused.

Matt explained. 'Dummy manager for a start. David Mason also manipulated the loss and profit of the company to get investors to sell their stocks. The price went down, and he then tried to buy all the stock and knock Harry out of the local American market. He tried, we believe to then inject cash into his own business, which subsequently failed. He also failed to buy enough shares to knock Harry out.'

Kate got the gist, nodding. 'So, we're talking insider trading? How did David Mason manipulate the finances so blatantly, though? Didn't anyone notice him?' Kate asked. 'Who got done for the insider trading? Mason?'

'No-one saw anything,' replied Tim. 'He had an extensive network of people in his team, as we have now uncovered, and he planted someone new into the company to do most of his dirty work for him. He looked squeaky clean in his role, and Harry never knew that the takeover had been instigated by him. Meanwhile, Harry was confiding in Mason and building up trust, and I imagine spilling his heart out to him. The guy who did Mason's dirty work got six years for it. Mason allowed him to go down for it, too.'

Matt joined in. 'Harry was giving Mason personal information without knowing he was giving it directly to an enemy.'

Kate was getting the picture.

'So, if Mason didn't manage to take the company over, what's the problem? I mean, all is fair in business. It was a failed takeover. I don't understand why he would then want revenge on Harry. Do you guys see my point?'

'Well, that should be the case, only it isn't. There is honour in business, and for someone like Mason, feeling humiliated in a failed takeover would have caused him great internal shame. He has had to watch Harry continue to thrive, getting richer by the day. Mason still wants what he cannot have.'

'… and this was all initially triggered by what?' Kate understood all too well how money could turn people. It was the one thing that feuding couples would fight to the death for.

'We think it was when Harry sold off his Beijing and

Shanghai offices, although we don't know why. He kept a minority of shares in both but sold them off for a substantial profit.' Tim sat back, shaking his head. 'Business can really bring out the worst in people.'

Kate looked at him. Little did he know just how much Harry had brought out the worst in herself.

'You know,' said Matt. 'There was something odd about the timing.'

'The timing of what?' asked Kate, jumping on his statement. Was he talking about her?

'The selling off. It seemed off because Harry had kept everything up until this point. Did he need the money himself, maybe?' Matt shrugged his shoulders.

'I'm still working on it, Matt,' said Tim. 'Okay, some other information has arisen. For a company that only deals with the exchange of information concerning real estate and shares, I managed to find that Harry has cargo shipments going from China to the US. All of the Asian offices seem to have been involved, with several shipments initially coming from Shanghai and Beijing. Then they were sold off. Now the shipments travel only from Hong Kong.'

'As in goods that he was shipping?' asked Kate, sounding confused. 'What would he be shipping?'

'That's the million-dollar question,' smiled Tim. 'That's what I'm trying to figure out because neither real estate nor shares require large container ships to leave international ports.'

'Wow. That's new. Shipping what?' Matt was clearly interested in the news. 'In the meantime, do we know where Harry is?'

'We have confirmed that he bought an airline ticket from London to Hong Kong last week. Not long after having been in your office, Kate. He arrived and made his way to the Green Lotus Hotel. We know he checked in and had dinner in the restaurant that night. The next morning, he checked out and hasn't been seen since. Then apparently, you guys got the note.'

'So why haven't the police been involved from this end?' asked Kate. 'Why wouldn't he have told us that he was leaving the UK? This makes no sense.'

'The police are not aware that he is missing,' replied Tim. 'His work believes that he is off sick.'

'... and because we don't want them to know,' added Matt, looking at Kate with his eyebrows raised.

'Yes,' agreed Tim. 'You don't want to be going to the police now. That time has long flown away. Matt explained it all to me in terms of you wanting to solve this yourself. Look, be assured. I think we can find Harry. I don't believe that Mason would kill Harry anyway or send the films out. This is a bluff. Mason has found Harry's weakness by hacking into the company cloud and taking the films. I doubt if he knew what he would find in the cloud and then a stroke of luck! Films that he can use against Harry. He thinks he can throw his weight around. Lucky for us, he doesn't have much weight.'

Kate and Matt smiled at the same time.

'So, you think this is a storm in a teacup, Tim?' Kate asked. 'I'm confused that if you are so easily able to find all of this out, then why has Mason got off without being charged?'

'Corruption. Lots of it in Hong Kong, unfortunately in the circles surrounding business. It's hard to say categorically, Kate, but I think it can be sorted out.' said Tim, 'It's a bluff and scare tactic, I believe,' he added. 'He's probably assuming that you guys would keep it all in-house as well, hoping to sort it out quietly, especially when you got threatened yourself. Finding those films must have seemed like gold for him. Anything he could use as leverage against Harry would be an asset for him. Mason would know how much it would frighten Harry to have to go and see you in the first instance. He would know Harry well enough to know that he wouldn't want details of his private life out there. We don't know what is exactly in these films either. Enough for Harry to jump on a plane and travel to Hong Kong in a hurry. It's a perfect blackmail situation.'

'Right,' said Matt. 'That's helped enormously, Tim. Let's meet again in the morning? We'll work on finding out where Mason is, and hopefully, he will lead us to Harry. Then we need to investigate this cargo that is being shipped around.'

Kate looked at Matt. Thank God he was helping her with this, if only so the responsibility for this monumental cock-up could be dispersed amongst more people, taking the heat off her a little.

FIFTEEN

THE GREEN BEAN MOMENT

Andrew woke mid-morning with Rupert's long limbs wrapped around him, and smiled at the prospect of a lazy morning ahead. Saturdays allowed him to unwind as a coiled spring might and shake off the stresses from his working week. Rupert had given him a sense of belonging again, after the undignified way his parents had reacted when he'd announced he was gay. Any sense that he belonged anywhere had been shattered by his mother's histrionic silence. Neither of his parents had spoken to him since his announcement. He had been turfed from the family nest unceremoniously and without an opportunity to explain anything with them.

Andrew had been educated at none other than the Richard III College for Boys. This exceedingly expensive and fine institution promised to turn young boys into strapping young men ready to lead the country into a positive future. He had indeed turned into a strapping young man, but in the eyes of his parents, that fact had now become obsolete.

Andrew had been nick-named 'Daffodil' by his peers

due to his bright and sunny disposition. He was always the first to say hello in a room and was notorious for nursing sick students with tea and biscuits. If anyone had a problem, they would turn to Andrew first for his calm and nurturing advice. He had graduated with academic excellence and had been accepted into one of the most prestigious universities in the country. His first plan had been to study Commerce-Law, something that both of his parents had encouraged.

Jean and Brian were proud of their son's academic prowess, and he was the talk of many late-night dinner parties. Jean even spoke of his potential in leading the country if he kept going as he was, although that was usually after too many drinks. His father expected nothing less, having been a scholar himself. Andrew's path was glued into place without room for deviation. A typical overachieving set of parents and a son who wanted to please them.

Jean, not understanding that Andrew had clearly been interested in men since his early teens, had expected him to date young ladies that she'd hand-picked from the 'crème de la crème' of available social circles. 'Influential families,' she had called them, full of people who would help him climb the ladder towards his inevitable success. The young ladies would go on to breed perfect stock, iron his shirts crisply and entertain his colleagues with lavishly organized parties, done with a finesse that only the well-bred knew how to do. They would know *whom* to invite and *when*. This obsession was endless, and his mother made it her mission to find him a wife.

More often than not, when he was home from school and college, he would be forced to endure dinner parties where he would be placed next to some girl from splendid heritage. He would be polite, but he never felt anything stir in his pants. He went on dates to appease his mother a few times, but they were more 'good times' out rather than nights of passion. His groins had stirred first for another boy many years earlier.

He tried to unsuccessfully date a few girls at university. Being the first year out of home, they were eager to be picked. He felt nothing, and they never noticed. It was towards the end of his first year when he finally met his first man. It was the night of the annual college party, notoriously a wild night on the social calendar. Andrew got dutifully smashed, and so did Max, a fellow first-year student on exchange from Texas, also good looking and popular with the girls. Max had approached Andrew towards the end of the first set.

'Hey, what's up?' he had drawled at him with his Southern accent.

'Not much, actually. The band is okay, don't you think?'

Andrew was struck by the young man's good looks. Prominent chiselled features and two rows of impressive white teeth that had grinned at him. The sort he'd only seen in the movies.

'They're okay.' Max smiled at him, holding his gaze.

Andrew noted the brilliant green eyes that had looked right into his. 'I'm Andrew, by the way.' He had held out his hand to shake his.

'Max.' They gripped hands, and both knew at that precise moment that they had sealed the deal. Max led Andrew to a quiet place outside in the garden, dark enough to be discreet. He had pulled Andrew's jeans down and had taken him hard against a wall covered in climbing jasmine. Andrew had discovered the meaning of life, and couldn't get enough of Max from that moment on. It really had been that simple.

What wasn't so simple was how he was going to break the news to his parents. He decided not to complicate his relationship with them during university as this would lead to an inevitable demise of all supporting monies that they sent to him. He quite liked not having to work and study, and he usually had enough leftover at the end of each week for extras. If they cut him off, he'd become instantly poor. That seemed like too much effort and change in living standards.

He had dropped hints to his mother as a sort of softening for when the real news was broken. Whenever news about progressive gender issues could be raised, he did so. None of that went down well. They were more akin to little verbal landmines that blew up in his face. His mother would portray disgust on her face. His father would boom out that 'all gays will die from aids,' which made Andrew wince. He explained time and time again, that wasn't the case anymore. He also explained that nowadays, this was also highly offensive to say and he would be cancelled and trolled if he dared utter them in public. His father would look at him as if he was the one being disrespectful. There really wasn't any hope with any of it.

He completed university with honours, but without Max at his side. He had returned to Texas in his third year, which was the last that Andrew had heard from him. The fire in his belly had gone too, after years of striving for excellence. He didn't feel that success was the end-game anymore and had his heart set on being authentic, instead. Andrew wanted happiness, not a huge bank balance. Looking at his own father, who was exhausted by fifty, he didn't want his own life to deteriorate as his father's had. He wanted to meander through life with balance, enjoying the journey along the way. He dropped the law component of his degree and concentrated on the commerce part instead.

He'd sent out his resume to firms willing to employ new graduates and had received a handful of first interviews. He never managed to get a second, though. He just wasn't competitive enough, the feedback had relayed. For every job he'd applied for, there were fifty different versions of him also applying, and some of the applicants knew precisely what to say, when to say it and how to present. He just couldn't be bothered to play the game like that, and if the truth was told, he didn't really want to go into commerce anyway.

He had religiously attended his parents' weekly dinners, and it was during one of these that the truth had exploded from his mouth. His parents believed that his position at Plaid and Potter was a suggestion of better things to come. However, Andrew had gilded it somewhat from personal assistant to para-legal. He'd not told them that he had dropped law whilst at univesity. He didn't feel bad about lying as he had become used to bending the truth to protect his own platform of being. Therefore, given his career was established and humming along nicely, his parents had perceived that marriage should follow shortly afterwards. The truth about his sexuality had been blurted out between the mouthful of green beans he had been chewing and the corn kernels that were waiting patiently on his fork for ingestion.

At that moment, he had been sitting next to Dr Molly Clarington-Ridge. She had arrived as an unexpected gift from his mother and was her idea of a good match. Molly had arrived with lights in her eyes and a hope that Andrew would find her attractive. She was a newly graduated doctor and had just joined her family's GP practice in the next village. She was clever, witty and potentially a great catch. Andrew was sick of pretending though, and trying to appease his parents. Molly had just finished recounting her heritage to some long-lost Scottish Earl from the 12th Century when Andrew blurted it out. He hadn't meant to. Speaking when one's mouth was full of green beans was hideous at best.

'I'm gay.'

There was silence. Molly had almost finished a sentence

about her family tartan, then the two words had been spoken. Silence can be deafening depending on the context. Such was the ferocity of those two words leaving his mouth that one green bean, partially mashed, escaped his mouth and landed in the middle of the table. Everyone stared at it.

It looked somewhat lost. Alone and wedged between the red wine carafe and the gravy jug. So did Andrew. Not having planned on announcing his sexuality, he didn't have a second sentence and no words to buffer the bluntness of his revelation.

'Right,' said his father, slowly putting down his knife and fork.

His mother was staring at the green bean, her fork now motionless next to her mouth.

'Are you?' asked Molly, trying to break the awkwardness of the moment. 'That's nice.' Then her voice had trailed off.

After that, it had been a wall of parental silence. An exercise in meditative control. His father had looked like he had wanted to rip his head off, and his mother was blinking back tears. Molly had tried to compensate for their silence by chattering on about anything that she could think of. She covered elderly incontinence and the need for regular bowel check-ups after the age of forty. She ended with a horrible story about what she experienced in ER during her internship when a patient's aorta had blown out in front of her.

The green bean sat there as a token of Andrew's sexuality. It was a reminder of the words he had uttered. No one wanted to acknowledge that it was there. If it were ignored, then perhaps the whole topic of sexuality could be ignored too. Molly gave up just before finishing her brandy-soaked pears, which had been served with a delicate French mascarpone and cherry sauce. Thanking Jean and Brian for the delightful evening, she smiled at Andrew and said cheerily,

'Well, it was nice to meet you, and good luck with it all.'

Then she was seen out by Brian, who had then returned to the table.

'Please remove that disgusting green bean,' his mother instructed his father. As it turned out, the bean had been a euphemism for Andrew himself, and he was removed from the house and never invited back again.

AS HE NOW LAY, watching Rupert, though, he felt complete. There was no pretence in this house, just an honest journey that was allowed to be explored at one's own pace. It was a better way to live. An easier way to live. He was sad that his parents hadn't accepted him for who he had been born to be. Still, he could never trade his sexuality to re-establish the relationship between them. Not ever.

LOUISE HAD SPENT the previous evening curled up in her recliner chair watching a BBC series set in a historically notable house. The idea was that a modern-day family would be transported back to Victorian times and live as an aristocratic family would have done so from that era. She loved it. Now that she had finished the Abbey series, she felt she had found a passion to indulge in. She dipped her spoon back into her container of rum and raisin ice cream that sat on her lap. She searched for a raisin. Finding one, she dug it out of the ice cream and popped it into her mouth. This solo action provided her with enormous satisfaction.

After a busy day at the firm, she liked nothing more than to shut the world out in the evenings and watch her new flat-screen television. It was state of the art, with four speakers that were positioned around her chair. Sometimes the effect of the surround sound was so good that she felt that she was in the actual television scenes. She dug for another raisin.

Her cat Mildred purred on her lap. Sometimes, knowing that no one was ever watching, Louise would allow Mildred to lick the ice cream off the end of the spoon. Then she would pop it back into the ice cream and have some herself. Her clients would never have guessed that the same woman who would stand up in court with such courageous wit would curl up with a cat on her each evening, with such self-imposed solitary simplicity. Louise was an anomaly. A challenging and professional lawyer by day and a meek and mild home-body by night.

She had decided early on not to have children. She didn't feel that she had the energy to raise a brood herself. Anyway, she had only ever popped in and out of relationships, with none of them going anywhere. Now it was too late to have kids, and she had lost her need for sex altogether. It was just her and Mildred, and she had found contentment. Any frustration about how her life had turned out was transposed into her courtroom character. It was here that she could relay to the world if she were feeling disappointed with how things had turned out. No one would know. She could channel any unresolved anger into the cross-examination stand, and everyone would just think that she was doing her job. It worked well for her. There had been times however, where she had looked at her small life and wondered if she should have made it a bit bigger.

That night was to be a small, simple night. Find the raisins, watch the television and give Mildred some ice cream when she asked. Her mind wandered to Kate. She had been a bit surprised when she had gone into Kate's office to update the files that afternoon and had found such an extensive number of bottles of alcohol hidden around her room. She wondered if Kate had a drinking problem? It was an exciting thought, and she dug a bit more eagerly into her ice cream in search of another raisin. Kate, sitting in her office drinking. She chewed the raisin with vigour.

MEANWHILE, on the other side of the planet, Kate and Matt hadn't had sex. They were exhausted after the flight and had literally crashed and burned the minute they had sunk into the king-sized bed after dinner.

Matt was woken early morning by a phone call from Tim, who wanted them to meet for breakfast downstairs.

'Wake up, sleepyhead,' Matt turned towards Kate and gently brushed the side of her face with his hand.

Kate had woken quickly. She was a light sleeper at the best of times. She brushed his hand off instinctively, as she would have done a fly.

'What time is it?' she asked.

'Tim-time. He wants us downstairs in thirty. Breakfast and another meeting.'

Kate sighed. She was so relaxed in the bed. The mattress was soft and had moulded perfectly to her shape. She felt as if she had sunk into a sublime position.

'Just five more minutes,' she said as she fought the urge to go back to sleep.

'I'll jump in the shower first and then you, okay?'

Matt leapt out of bed, naked. Kate watched as he walked towards the shower. His body was well defined. His backside was small and muscular. She liked that. She also admired the bulky biceps that held her so well. His arms made her feel safe from the world. She rolled out of the bed and looked out of the window. They were soaring in the Hong Kong sky. Ninety-eight floors above the rest of the world. It really was breathtaking. The boats on the harbour looked like insects, leaving tiny trails behind them on the blue canvass they skimmed across. The rising sun illuminated the water with diamond-like sparkles. There were hundreds of sky-scrapers in the landscape, each vying for attention. The one she was in was one of the tallest. It made her feel important, knowing that she was one of the few people at that moment, so high in the sky.

That thought triggered off something else. The notion that she could also have Matt Harmon any time she wanted as well. Money or strategy, both had got her the same results. Whether it was opportunistic to take him in the shower of the eight hundred dollars a night room simply because she was there, or whether it was part of the strategy, who cared? She would go and make his morning for him. She tapped on the shower door, and he opened it. Then she surprised him by kneeling down.

FELICITY WAS ALSO KNEELING DOWN. She was missing Matt and had gone for a girls' night out. A bunch of happy women who were juggling careers, kids and partners. They had met at a local wine bar and had enjoyed a few wines, comparing notes about their week. Most of them had met through the twenty-four-hour gym except for Nat, whom they all knew from the local health food shop where they bought their protein supplements, kale powder and smoothie blends.

Felicity hadn't had a great day at work. She was exhausted. She had been asked to suddenly take on some of Matt's workload as he had gone to Australia. His mother had been taken ill. That was what the firm had told her anyway. This had confused her though, as Matt had texted that he was in Hong Kong on a business trip. She had consoled her muddled and tired mind by having one too many drinks after recounting the minutiae of the situation to her friends. Now she was throwing up her drinks and chicken curry into the toilet. Nat was holding her pony tailback as she heaved.

'You'll be okay, Luv,' cooed Scottish Nat, who was a fair bit older than the rest of the girls. She had been a smoker all her life, and now as the owner of a health food store, the irony had made the girls laugh when they had found out. Over the past twenty years, the box a day habit had resulted in a deep and resonating timbre to her voice.

'Yup,' repeated Felicity, retching again.

'Matt will be back soon, don't you worry. He's a good catch that one. Handsome as anything.'

'I know.' Felicity gulped in as much air as she could.

'You know Luv, I'd be hanging onto him. You two planning on staying together then... long term, are you thinking?'

'I hope so. I'm going to ask him to move in with me when he gets back. We've seen each other long enough for me to know that he's the one. It feels right.'

'Oh, Luv, that sounds lovely. Well, I hope the two of you make it. Now come and rinse, and we'll go back to the others.'

Felicity missed Matt more than ever at that moment. She texted him.

'Missing you, babe. Wish you were here xxx.'

She didn't get a response and then remembered that there would be a time difference. She assumed he was probably in a meeting, or perhaps still asleep.

'Yr busy or asleep, I suppose. Talk later x.'

KATE HEARD Matt's phone vibrate with a message as she was dressing.

'You're popular,' she smiled at him. He was already

bounding around the place full of optimism, about the day ahead.

He glanced at his phone. 'Tim's waiting and getting impatient by the looks of things.' He quickly deleted Felicity's text and then smiled at Kate.

They met Tim, already halfway through a massive plate, stacked up with items from the breakfast buffet.

'Great, you guys are up,' he smiled at them. 'Join me. I have some news about Huang Fa Lee, aka David Mason.'

Over breakfast, Tim explained that Mason had suddenly taken leave from the San Fransisco office for personal reasons and was in rural China, somewhere just northwest of Longnan. His mother had apparently been taken sick.

'Must be the season for sick mothers,' chuckled Matt, explaining his own excuse for being absent from work.

'Exactly,' said Tim. 'You two need to go and check why he is really at his mother's house. I can guarantee his mother is not sick. You may find Harry there.'

'Really? Are you sure?' asked Kate.

'Yes. It would be the perfect place to lure someone. Out of the way too. I've mapped out a travel route for you. His village is quite a long way from here. It's about fifty miles out of Longnan. My guess is if you want to find Harry, then that's the place to start. I can't guarantee that he will be there, but I don't think we will be finding Harry without Mason. My guess is that wherever one is, the other will be close by.'

Kate remembered something that she had meant to say at last night's meeting but hadn't remembered to at the time.

'This is a bit lateral, but has anyone actually seen the films?'

'The films Harry made with Barry?' Tim asked.

'Yeah.'

Tim nodded. 'I've seen them. We managed to hack into

the cloud account pretty easily as well. Harry used his birthday as his password. It really wasn't that hard.'

'And?' Kate was curious.

Tim shook his head. 'Well, pretty amateur stuff. Fifty shades and all that. Not terribly pleasant to watch. However, Harry had his identity pretty well covered up for most of the time, so I'm not sure that Mason has much to blackmail him with in the first place. He wore this kind of hood thingy.' Tim tried to demonstrate the hood thingy with his hands, showing how it sat on Harry's head. 'It's a pretty ridiculous look.' He gave up.

'I thought Zorro?' offered Kate, trying to keep a straight face.

Tim and Matt both laughed at the mental image of it all.

'How many films are we dealing with?' Kate asked.

'Eleven, I think from memory. They were doing this calendar theme, so it was one film for each month of the year. Quite inventive when you think about it. Number twelve was thwarted when Barry made the leap back to his family. Can you imagine the Christmas special they had planned?'

'I'd rather not,' smiled Kate. 'It sounds positively ghastly.'

'You sounded English just then,' grinned Matt, looking at her.

'I suppose it's going to happen given I now live there. Duffer,' she accentuated.

'Duffer? That's like a century-old.'

'Yeah, like you,' she laughed.

Matt became serious and turned back to Tim. 'So, getting to Longnan. How long is that going to take us?'

'About nine hours by my calculations. I've tried to get you guys there as quickly as I can.' He pulled out a map.

'Old school. I like that,' said Matt.

Kate looked at him inquisitively.

'The map. Old school. Cooler than google maps.'

Tim showed them the city of Longnan. 'The village you want is farther to the northwest. However, you need to get here first.' He had circled in red the city of Longnan. 'So, you'll take a train from Kowloon to Taimaiz. Then I've booked you on a bus that will take you to Shenzhen.' He reached into his bag and pulled out two tickets, 'I've booked you on a flight and the car will be waiting for you at the airport, in Longnan. That's about four hours or so.'

'Christ,' muttered Matt under his breath.

'It is a long way. China is a vast country, you know.' Tim folded the map and handed it to him.

'Couldn't we just phone him?' Matt asked, being facetious.

'Um… let me think about that…. no?' laughed Tim. 'You have to go there. Hopefully, Harry will be there, and you can sort this out… nicely.' He accentuated the word nicely.

'Aren't we assuming a lot? That Mason will firstly be where he says he will be and secondly, that Harry will miraculously be there too?' Kate raised her eyebrows at Matt and Tim. 'It would be a bit of a miracle don't you think? Do we even know what we are suposed to say to him?'

'We are assuming a lot,' agreed Tim. 'But, we have to start somewhere.'

'We can discuss it on the way there,' nodded Matt. 'Think of a strategy.'

'True. Right then,' said Kate, standing up and ready to go, 'where and when does this bus leave?'

'You have thirty-five minutes. I'll meet you out the front in say ten and drive you there.' Tim packed everything back into his bag. 'Whilst you guys are doing that, I'm going to go and do a bit of poking around the docks. I'm going to find out what was in the containers that Harry has shipped out. As soon as I know, I'll call you. If I can't call because you are out of mobile range, I will leave messages with the 'Red Pride

Duck'. It's a small restaurant in Schuzalan, Mason's home town. I'll be cryptic, so expect a lot of messages from your sister if that's the case.'

Matt was impressed. Tim was amazing. He had thought of everything.

Kate made a quick call to Andrew forgetting the time difference. It was the middle of the night in the UK, and the answering machine kicked in.

'Hey Andrew, it's Kate…'

'Hope you're not phoning anyone at home?' Matt called out.

She quickly cut the call short.

'Did you block your number or say anything?' he asked, looking worried.

'I'm not dumb, Matt. I'm supposed to be in bed with the flu. Of course, I'm not going to leave a message from Hong Kong at the office.'

'Well, thank god for that.' He went back to packing his bag.

Kate looked down at her phone. She hadn't blocked her number, so it would have shown on the office machine. She had spoken a few words but had spoken, nonetheless. No one would find out, she hoped. Andrew was always on the phone during the day, so that number would disappear down a list. Andrew was usually the only one who used that phone anyway. She went into her phone's settings and changed it to private.

Tim was waiting for them after they had checked out.

'Look, guys,' he said, sounding serious. 'Mason has no existing history of being violent. Ruthless, yes, especially in business. However, don't underestimate him. If you find him with Harry, then play it cool and contact me before going in like some dynamic cop duo would. You are lawyers, not cops. Remember that. All we need to do is see that Harry is alive and well, and this matter is shut. The contents of the containers are for personal interest only.'

'Well, I'm not going to mess with some idiot.' Kate looked inquiringly at Matt.

'I agree,' said Matt quickly, shooting her a similar look.

'Good. Glad you guys have understood that.' He gained Kate's eye contact with the mirror as he was driving. 'Be aware and be careful. I hope you have all your devices fully charged too. Don't use the power-up frivolously. It may be hard to find the power out there. Here.' He passed something to Matt from the front. 'Portable chargers and some plug adapters. You have enough there to keep going for a couple of days, but...' he paused. 'Just use everything and then switch it off again. Save your power for when you need it.'

They were soon waiting for their flight to Hanzhong. Kate felt sick. Another flight to deal with. It didn't get any easier no matter how many times she did it. She and flying were just never going to have a better relationship no matter how hard she tried. She downed her trusty valium and waited for it to kick in. Matt had gone off to find something to read on the flight, having heard Tim's warning about not using up the power on his devices.

So, what now? She thought to herself. She had got Matt truly on side. She was getting worried, though. Was he taking the relationship more seriously than she was? He had slotted in next to her so quickly and effortlessly. She had to admit that they made a pretty functional couple. Together, they would make a formidable team. Except this wasn't about forming a team. This was about strategy. Her strategy. Get Matt to help sort the problem out and then resume her career where she had left it. Iron out a stupid mistake. God, she hated making mistakes.

Marrying Ethan had been a mistake too, in hindsight. She had trusted him. Told him her secrets. Then he had shat on her. No one, not even Matt Harmon, was going to find a way in and do that to her. Never again. He would remain a part of something bigger. A way out of the mistake she had made when she had thought she could sort something out that had been bigger than her to start with.

Did she feel bad? She checked herself. Was sleeping with a man to gain something so wrong. Really? In this world where everyone was fucking everyone else, was it really that bad to offer herself to a man in return for the future of her career? She smiled. She had this under control, just as she'd had control of all the other men in her life, except for Ethan. He hadn't allowed her control. He had walked too fast for her to get her bearings.

How many men was a bad thing she wondered? How many men had she bedded so far in her life? She counted them in her mind. Twenty-three. Twenty-two for strategy and one for love. She had offered herself twenty-two times out of gain. How bad was that? Was it so wrong to have seen ways to further herself in life by being on the right side of someone? She had bedded her human rights lecturer when she had been having personal problems with her parents. He had listened, and then he had asked her to drop her jeans. She had complied with the promise of fatherly guidance and better grades. It had worked well, the arrangement between them. Kate was only too pleased to know that she would graduate in human rights with excellent marks. All part of the plan.

She had slept with her best friend's boyfriend at one point in her fourth year. They had been drunk, and he had promised to get her tickets to the Law Ball, which had sold out on the first day. Kate had missed out. They got drunk, and the next minute she was saying thank you to him for the tickets. Was that really so bad? The ball was the last opportunity for some significant networking, and Kate needed it. He hadn't remembered the next day anyway. He'd been as smashed as hell.

There were others. There was a random guy in her third year Torts class. He had been popular and had been in charge of the debating teams for the inter-university competition teams. Kate saw no harm in having him in the library, near the rare books section, just as the library was about to close. She made the team, and it was something else that she could put onto her resume. The system worked. Men were primed for such offers. They were easy. Kate could get what she wanted by offering sex.

The pattern had continued until Ethan came along. He was different. She had wanted him because she had loved him. True love. It had felt different to anything else she had ever felt. She had wanted to touch him, trace him and taste him. She had loved the scent of him. She had laid in his arms after passionate lovemaking, just enjoying being there because it was Ethan who had been holding her. She had kissed him with feeling, enjoying the warmth of his breath on hers.

When they had made love, it was the act of making love. Not just sex. Not simply a journey to climax. Different. It was two bodies intertwined. It was sweat and touch and feeling. Kate had made love to Ethan like a bee took nectar from a flower. Delicately, patiently and lovingly. Then he had suddenly walked out. There was no acknowledgement that she had meant anything to him. Later, when she lost their baby, and she held the tiny little girl next to her, it was one half that grieved, not two. Hate had replaced love, filling every crevice in her being. Deep-seated hate that would serve as a protective wall for anyone in the future who dared to come too close. Kate was angry with Ethan, and she had locked that anger away, deep down, in case it spilt out and became dangerous.

There had been more than one occasion when she had imagined revenge. Revenge against the woman whom she saw had taken her husband from her. Revenge against the husband that had torn her soul to shreds. How dare she, Kate had ranted to herself on many occasions, drunk and pacing in her terrace. That woman had deliberately taken Ethan from her. She imagined breaking into their house and setting it on fire or shooting them both. She would watch them die and enjoy their suffering. The fantasies would become complicated, though, as Kate's practical side often interfered with the joy of her fantasy acts of revenge.

Halfway through a fantasy, she would stop. What if someone saw her number plate? Or a security camera caught her? She would need a gun with a silencer – where the hell would she get that? If she burned the house down, then she would make sure their pets were out. Then there was the fact that she couldn't really see herself from hurting anyone in real life. That thought would be shunted out as it interfered with her ability to continue the virtual punishment. She could never get mindful revenge and enjoy any of it. That frustrated her as well. She then hated herself for being so weak.

The fantasies became an escape at night. Just before she would fall asleep. Instead of going to a safe place as her meditation teacher had instructed her, Kate would go to a dark place. The imagined house where Ethan and his woman now lived. She would imagine breaking in as they were away at work and waiting. Waiting in the wardrobe for one of them to return. She would take aim, laughing at their terror. The same terror she had felt when the door had clicked shut the night when he had walked out on her. The same fear as when her baby had slid from her, too soon to survive. Then she would shoot them one by one in cold blood and then leave. If she couldn't have her Ethan, then why the hell did this woman have him?

The following day, she would be full of shame from the content of the fantasies. As a lawyer, it was her job to encourage people to follow the law, not create ways to kill each other. The fantasies worsened over time, with the execution methods becoming more and more horrific. Even for Kate, she was becoming worried about their violent nature and how much she enjoyed watching Fiona die every night in front of her. Kate needed to vent the anger out. She knew that. It was bottled up inside of her, dangerously brewing somewhere in her subconscious. She drank more, numbing it, hiding it and keeping it at bay. Taming it to do as she asked and to leave her alone when she needed it to. She wondered how many other women had these fantasies? To kill the woman that had taken their husband, best friend and lover? She drank to subdue the rage burning within her. She dared not think of what might happen if she allowed her beast to unleash itself.

SIXTEEN

BELLIGERENCE

'Did you wonder if using Matt as part of a strategy was a bad idea?' The woman then leaned forward, waiting for her to respond.

Kate was thinking hard. Taking herself back to the six months before, in China.

She shook her head. 'No. The strategy was all that mattered.'

The woman frowned slightly and looked down at her notes.

There was a heavy silence hanging in the room.

'Let me ask you another question, Kate. If you had your time again, would you have used Matthew Harmon in such a …' she paused, trying to find the right words. 'Practical sense?'

Kate looked at her in the eye.

'I knew what I was doing. Matt was a way for me to fix everything. What's so wrong with that?'

'Why don't you explain that to me?' asked the woman gently.

'Why don't you go and fuck yourself instead?' asked her patient, turning and staring out of the window.

SEVENTEEN

TOO MUCH PAPER

Matt returned, looking rather chuffed at the number of magazines he had collected for the flight.

'These should do it. It's only a couple of hours anyway. Betting their in-flight entertainment is all in Chinese anyway. I've got women's stuff, health, holidays and real estate. Take your pick.'

Matt had also texted Felicity whilst he had been magazine hunting.

'Babe – you missing me? Busy here. Won't be long, and then I'll be back.'

Felicity had jumped on his text. Still feeling sick from her overindulgence the night before, she had been mindlessly scrolling through her phone when the text came in.

'Hey, sweetie. Good 2 hear from u. So want u back. How's yr mother?'

Matt was taken aback. What was wrong with his mother? Had something happened to her? How would Felicity know? He stopped to think for a second. Then he remembered. He had told Geoff at the firm that he was going to Australia because his mother was ill. He had told Felicity that he was in Hong Kong on a business trip. Shit. She would be confused.

'Hey, babe. In Hong Kong, remember. Told the office I was in Oz to keep things simple. Let's keep it that way.'

There was silence. Felicity now held quite a bit of power. He needed her to keep mute as to where he really was. A bit of softening wouldn't go astray, he thought.

'Love you, babe x.' That should do it. She loved being reassured as to how he felt about her.

She sent kisses back almost immediately. 'xxx.'

A moment passed before another text came in from Felicity.

'So… what's the secret in Hong Kong?'

'Not really a secret, babe. Have a great job opp! Just want 2 keep it private. You and me only, babe.'

Felicity smiled. It was a job! Of course. That made sense now. Matt was confiding in her. 'Of course. You and me x.'

'Only you and me, babe xxx.'

The flight was uneventful except for their descent which became bumpy through the clouds. Matt and Kate had flicked through the magazines and then had napped mostly, their jet lag catching up with them. Kate was too exhausted to care about dying from a bad landing. She was awoken as her ears started to react to the descent.

She yawned, and her ears popped.

'All better?' asked Matt, smiling at her.

'Yes, thank God. I hate it when the pressure builds up like that. I end up walking around with most of my hearing gone if they don't pop.'

The plane landed safely, and they made their way through customs.

'So, they drive on the right?' she asked as they walked towards the hire car.

'Yeah,' said Matt. 'I've heard though that driving in China isn't for the meek, even in the smaller towns.'

'So, you've driven on the right before?' asked Kate loudly as a military plane flew overhead. The airport was used for military and commercial planes, resulting in twice as much air traffic. It was loud and busy.

'Not really. Have you?'

'Not really? What does that mean?' Kate stopped and stared at him.

'I've done online gaming. That counts, doesn't it?' He smiled cheekily.

'No?' Kate didn't sound convinced.

'I think I'll do all the driving Kate, no offence. It's just that you still look half asleep.'

'Fine by me. So, you think you can figure out driving on the right?'

'Yeah, seriously. Been driving on the right for years, online. Shouldn't be that different.'

'Unless you crash into something.'

'I'm not going to crash into anything Kate.'

'Well, just concentrate harder than you do for gaming. Okay? It's not like we can get another few lives from anywhere.'

'Gotcha. I've driven on the right before, so don't panic.'

'For real?'

'Yes.'

They got into the small, no-frills hire car.

'Okay, shouldn't be too hard,' Matt reassured her as he started the engine, smiling. 'Everything is just on the opposite side.' He looked at his watch. 'I figure that it's going to take us a good three and a half hours to get there. I think it gets dark around six-thirty, and I don't want to be on these roads in the dark, so we need to get going.'

They drove into the mountains. The road wound and

wound around the steep cliffs. It was nothing like the landscapes back home in Australia nor England. It was raw, sleek and stunningly beautiful. Matt took it slowly. The roads weren't that great in places as debris from small landslides scattered on the edges, and there were massive drops that could send them plummeting to their deaths if Matt didn't corner accurately. The traffic was insane, though, given the driving conditions. Other drivers didn't stick to the supposed speed limits and would overtake on blind corners or come around a corner on the wrong side of the road. Sometimes Matt would go around a corner to find a local on a bike with a carrying pole. He was constantly swerving.

'These people! Don't they know that cars can kill them if they get hit?'

He swerved again as a cyclist came around the corner too fast and not wearing a helmet. A cow wandered into the road, and then a random group of people appeared as he turned a sharp corner.

'I'm going to end up killing someone if this continues. Why don't they understand the concept of keeping to the inside?' He was getting increasingly frustrated.

'They seem oblivious to the fact that this is a road that cars use. Just slow down a bit Matt. We aren't trying to meet a deadline.'

They eventually arrived in Longnan after five hours of hard driving, feeling utterly shattered.

TIM WALKED along the pier to the docks. There were boats, cranes and shipping containers scattered along the bay. He was interested in port thirty-seven, which Harry Rainer had reportedly used to export cargo containers. Tim had gone through his company carefully and systematically, looking for anomalies. There was no apparent reason for him to have needed to ship cargo from Asia to America. What cargo? It made little sense. He had agreed to meet with a contact at the docks. An old friend of his family who managed the paperwork for exports. He might be able to give him some info about what was in them without getting either of them into trouble.

He found the door to the office and knocked on it.

'Tim, it's nice to see you,' greeted an elderly Chinese man in broken English. He smiled a toothless grin at him and patted him on the back.

'Hi Eric, long time, no see.' Tim raised his voice to just less than shouting, as Eric was three-quarters deaf. Eric was a mandarin speaker, and Tim wasn't. The exchange would need to be in simple English.

They shook hands.

'It very nice, Tim. Been way too long. I last see you when you were…' he stopped and thought for a moment. 'Yes, twenty-one. Your family good? Yes?'

'Yes, Thank you, Eric. How's your wife? Is she any better?'

Eric's face dropped. 'She worse Tim. the cancer, you know. Not long now.' He pointed to his right side.

'I'm sorry to hear that, Eric. That's dreadful news. Pass on my best wishes, won't you.'

'You good soul Tim. Now, why you here, Tim? Why you need to know from me. I do you a favour, yes?'

Eric was a good friend of his father, and their friendship had spanned forty years, including a session of Thai Chi once a week, which they had never missed.

'Yes, Eric. I need to know about some containers that left the dock?'

He handed Eric a piece of paper with the cargo numbers and dates for when the shipments had gone out. There were three recently, with several containers being moved on each trip.

'I go and see on computer. You come and make coffee. Yes?'

'Sure, yeah, thanks.'

Tim followed Eric into the cluttered office of port thirty-seven. Eric put oversized glasses on and started to type into an old computer.

'You help yourself to coffee, please, Tim.'

Tim made himself a cup of instant coffee in a mug that had seen better days. Luckily, the coffee hid the yellow rings on the inside of the cup. Tim wondered what superbug he was also ingesting.

'I see,' murmured Eric after perusing the computer. 'So, the containers are sent under name of Harry Rainer. The contents received by Mr David Mason at other end, in San Fransisco. Let me see. Here. Rainer signs for them, then they go to LA by rail. That odd, Tim. Why then take them from this port and then by rail? It odd. They would normally go direct. We have many ships that go from Hong Kong to LA.'

Tim was interested in what Eric was saying.

'So, initially, the containers get sent out for shipping from here under the name of Harry Rainer and then you are saying that they then get sent to LA by rail from San Fran?'

'Maybe?' Eric looked confused as he studied the computer more. 'It say the name changes to David Mason at the other end. It strange.'

'Does it say what is in the containers?'

'I should be able to find that out for you.' Eric leaned forward carefully, following the prompts on the screen. 'Right. I have that information. In June of last year, it was paper. Then in September, it was more paper. January paper. The extra cargo looks like white goods for other companies.'

Tim frowned. Why would Harry Rainer export paper from Hong Kong and then send it to San Fransisco and then on to LA? Tim wondered if Harry Rainer knew about any of this. He should do, given his name was on the paperwork? It made little sense, though.

Tim pulled his phone out. He searched in his photos for a picture of Harry Rainer. He showed it to Eric.

'Eric. Have you seen this man?'

Eric took the phone and studied the photo.

He nodded. 'Yes. That is the man I was just speaking about. That is Mr Harry Rainer. Very nice man.'

Tim was surprised. 'When did you see Harry?'

Eric thought for a bit. 'A few days ago. Yes, Tim.'

'Here?'

'Yes, Tim. He flew from London, he said. He is the owner of whole company. Very important man.'

'Did he say why?'

'Yes. He said he need to find out about his business. I said I would help, and we arranged a proper appointment the next day, but he never came back.'

Tim's face fell. Harry Rainer must have figured something out about the containers and was coming to sort it out. That's why he had made the sudden trip to Hong Kong. What was being shipped out? He doubted it was just paper. How was David Mason implicated, aside from being the signatory at the other end?

Eric handed Tim some paper. 'Don't look at this now. You not supposed to have it. Yes?' He waited for Tim to agree.

'Sure, Eric.'

'Wait until you not on these grounds. Otherwise, I can get into trouble if anyone sees I give you paper.'

As soon as Tim was off the docks, he looked at the paperwork. Two more containers had been shipped recently, originating in Hong Kong. They were in transit, due to arrive shortly in San Fransisco. Tim wondered if Harry had found this out too? Maybe he had flown over to San Fransisco to explore the lead?

. . .

MATT'S PHONE BUZZED. 'It's Tim,' he said, putting him on speaker so that Kate could hear what was being said.

'How's Longnan guys?' asked Tim.

'Pretty nice. About to have dinner. Exhausted though. What's with all the bicycles on the roads out here?' complained Matt.

'Oh yeah – I should have warned you about those. I've picked up some interesting info.'

'What?' Kate's ears pricked up.

'Turns out that either Harry or David Mason have been shipping paper cargo on behalf of the company.'

'Paper?' Matt sounded surprised.

'Yeah, and I can't be sure, but Mason is doing an interesting manoeuvre with the cargo by transporting it from San Francisco to LA by rail.'

'Paper. Why paper?' asked Kate. 'Harry doesn't make paper, does he? Would he need that much paper?'

'I don't think it's paper,' Tim said. 'I think there is more to this. I'm thinking along the lines that Mason may be using Harry's business to do some importing? What do you guys think?'

'Hard to prove. We'd need a bit more info, I reckon, to prove something is amiss.' Matt shook his head.

'Yeah, but what doesn't make sense,' added Kate, 'are those films. What's with the films? If Mason is busy moving cargo around, then why bother to blackmail Harry with the films? I just don't think the films are that important, especially if Harry can't be identified. This isn't adding up.'

There was a silence in the room.

Kate was the first to piece it together.

'Shit. I can't believe we have all been that stupid.' She was up and pacing.

'What?' asked Matt and Tim at the same time.

'Guys. There were no films!'

Tim sounded confused. 'I saw them, though.'

Kate stared at Matt and then at the phone as if Tim were supposed to see her too.

She held her hands up in the air expecting the penny to drop with them.

There was silence. She continued.

'Well, there were, but this hasn't been what any of this has been about. It was Harry who told us that the first note was about the films he had made.'

Silence.

'Think, guys! Harry assumed the note was about the films. We never questioned him over that. Like we never assumed that he had got the mobile number wrong in the first instance. We just went along with what he was telling us. What if all along this has nothing to do with the films? The evidence may well have been anything! Harry had a guilty conscience for doing the films and jumped, thinking that's what this was about.'

Silence.

'OMG. Am I the only one who can see this?' Kate was getting frustrated. 'The original message didn't mention films per se. Remember? It just said it was going to expose the truth. It was Harry that said the truth was all about those films. We didn't check the phone number in the first instance either. Remember we thought it was all about Linda, Barry and the films. Then we shifted to David Mason and the films. Now it's obvious this probably has nothing to do with the films at all!'

'Oh shit,' Matt said. There was another lengthy silence.

Tim spoke first. 'Harry must have figured this out too. The evidence could be about what is in those shipping containers.'

'Right. So, he's found something out about the shipping containers. That makes more sense.' added Matt. 'Explains why he jumped on a plane and raced over here. We're still guessing, though.'

'But what doesn't make sense is that it was Mason saying to Rainer that he would expose the truth – as if Rainer was the one at fault.' Kate shook her head in frustration. 'I agree. We're jumping to conclusions a bit.'

Matt stared at Kate, realizing their fundamental mistake. 'We went and met with Barry and Linda as well.' He shook his head. 'You couldn't make this up if you tried.'

The three of them sat there in amongst their stupidity, with the mobile phone witnessing all of it.

Tim sighed. 'So, yeah, this makes the situation a bit different. However, we still have Harry missing, and now it probably isn't about the films. This is more serious. We don't even know which one of them started all of this. Look, I got info that there are two more containers in transit as well, right now. So, we need to keep an eye out on those.'

'Absolutely. That's a good lead, Tim,' agreed Matt. 'I suppose the original text, going back to it, was more that Mason was threatening to expose Harry as a smuggler of some sort? Maybe blame him for whatever he could come up with? If Harry does know what's in the cargo containers, then Mason is trying to blackmail him? We don't know for sure and the change of signatory at LA doesn't add up.'

Kate did a quick summation. 'So, Harry supposedly comes to me thinking that his ex-lover is blackmailing him over porn films because he feels guilty for having done them. We get sent on a wild goose chase trying to find the films and stop some random dysfunctional couple from the suburbs from releasing them. Meanwhile, Harry smells a rat, maybe about the threats? He goes to check into what has been happening? Maybe even trying to cover his own tracks? Who knows? He panics and flies over here to sort it out. Mason gets wind of his arrival, and they meet. Mason does what, kidnaps Harry and takes him to his mother? Why take him all the way here? How? That bit doesn't make sense. Not with another shipment on the way to San Fran.'

Matt jumped up. 'No, you're right. He's probably not in rural China with his sick mother at all.'

Kate stared at Matt. 'How do you know that?'

'Maybe that was Mason's cover to get from San Fransisco to Hong Kong without alerting anyone? I mean, it's the same excuse I gave for being over here. Think about it.'

Tim groaned in agreement.

'Why would Mason come to Hong Kong, though? If he's based in San Fransisco, then surely all he has to do is go and meet the cargo over there?' Kate looked perplexed.

'Because he found out that Harry was here, that's why.' Tim sounded frustrated. 'You guys need to get back to Hong Kong. It's more likely that David Mason is here. Although does he have Harry here as well? That's our million-dollar question right now.'

'This is why we are lawyers and not detectives,' said Matt. 'We would make shit detectives, hey.'

'You mean we have to make that journey, again, in reverse tomorrow?' asked Kate, suddenly feeling overwhelmed.

Matt nodded. 'However, we'll check in on Mason's mother on the way out. No point in having come all this way if we don't do due diligence.'

'Yeah, seems a bit pointless, and then we can at least rule out Mason being here.' Kate agreed.

'I'll book your flights and send them through. I'm going to be trying to find out what Mason or Rainer would be doing shipping paper from Hong Kong, across to San Fransico and then hijacking it and taking it to LA. One of them must know what is going on. Maybe we can track down where the heck Harry is as well?'

KATE SAT on the bed with Matt. 'Get me a drink. I need to be wiped out for a few hours. This is crazy shit. This is not what I thought we were dealing with.'

Matt agreed. 'I'll go get something for dinner and some booze. Then I'm coming back to eat, drink and get very merry with you. Then we shall see where the evening takes us.'

Kate inwardly sighed. She just wanted to drink, not do anything else. Matt's mind seemed to always lead to sex. However somehow, she knew that he would get his way, as there was still the strategy to consider.

After they had eaten, Matt pushed up against her in the bed. It was obvious that he wanted her. Matt needed sex like an alcoholic needed wine and a drug addict needed a fix. When he was younger, it hadn't been like it was now. When he was younger, he wanted sex because it made him feel good. It was a physical release that pushed the re-set button within him. Now the act simply made him feel normal and less depressed about himself. After a few days without sex, he started to slump. He would start to think about sex. Obsess about it. He tried to remember the most prolonged period it had been since he had gone without sex recently. Five days? Six? That's why having many women on the go at once worked for him. He could go from one to another, ensuring that his supply was always there. So far, Kate had been there consistently for him. That may well slow down in the future, so if he kept Felicity on board as well as the gym ladies, he would have an assured near unlimited supply. It gave him hope for the future.

Kate was tired though, and a bit pissed after her drinks over dinner. Matt had bought enough alcohol to comatose them both for a week. Kate drank enough to find her warm spot and then a bit more to stop the self-recrimination playing out in her head. She had well and truly mucked the entire situation up from start to finish. Her only hope now was if Tim and Matt helped her sort it all out. Perhaps their combined intellect would prove to be bigger than the plans that David Mason and Harry Rainer were currently executing?

She sighed. Would she allow him to take her, even though she was so tired? She had to admit though, that the last couple of times had felt genuinely good.

Afterwards, he felt re-set, like the world was good again. A nice meal and a good shag after a long day. He lay behind Kate, kissing her gently on the back of her head. He could get closer to Kate if he wanted to. It was an easy relationship, with a genuine understanding of his needs. He hoped that it would stay that way. He fell into a deep, contented sleep.

Kate didn't sleep. Her safe place was alluding her, and something was niggling at her. She had been projected out of her safe place when her mind had started to wander concerning possible adverse outcomes for the situation. She could see herself unemployed, struck off her professional register for getting herself caught up in this mess. Her mind went around and around all night, tormenting her. Her strategy was so far working with Matt though, looking at the bright side. She hadn't felt overly aroused by him, hadn't fallen in love and nor did she feel some yearning to stay with him after the mess was sorted. Had Matt remembered protection just then? She hoped so.

She could go back to her old life, well it was her new life, once all of this was over. The move to the UK had been the best thing she had ever done for herself. A line in the sand. It had turned out so much better than she had anticipated. All she had to do was deal with the rumination and this temporary setback. Temporary? It had better be, she thought. She turned in the bed and looked over at Matt. His body was illuminated by the full moon, streaming through the curtains. The moonlight traced the contours of his body down to where the sheet was draped over his groin. He looked peaceful, serene and as if he had found the true meaning of contentment. She felt a stab of resentment. When would she, Kate Hemsworth, ever find the same feeling?

EIGHTEEN
CIGARETTE SMOKE IN HER FACE

The woman smiled pleasantly towards the middle-aged woman sitting across from her. Kate had at least brushed her hair today and looked a bit more together than she had the last time she had seen her. Less frazzled with the world, the counsellor noted.

'How are you today, Kate?' she asked her, hopefully.

'I'm good, I guess. Same as I was last week. Surprise, surprise, hey?'

The woman noted the slightly defensive tone in her voice and knew not to push things. Otherwise, Kate would shut down again. The idea was to get her to open up, find her feelings again, and articulate them.

'Have you had a positive week?' asked the woman.

'I suppose so. Nothing bad has happened. I didn't die, and the sky didn't come crashing down. The earth wasn't hit by a meteorite, and humanity wasn't wiped out. I've also been well behaved all week, if that's what you are really asking. I don't think I've offended anyone. Yet.'

Kate lit up a cigarette, her hands shaking slightly. The

counsellor discreetly made a note. She paused with her questions, not wanting to take the bait. Kate often threw out comments designed to inflame. If she were to acknowledge them, Kate would wind up, something she didn't want. Her job was to unwind her.

'So today, I thought we would work on some feelings work. How we feel, why we feel and how we explain our feelings to others,' she said, crossing her fingers that Kate would agree. After months of weekly sessions, Kate had made little progress in terms of being able to tell her how she had felt, other than to throw insults towards her. The only way for Kate to move forward was to do the work.

'Sure. Let's talk about my *marvellous* feelings,' Kate responded with a slight sarcastic emphasis. She took a long draw on the cigarette and blew it in the direction of the woman.

'Ok,' smiled the woman. Kate had given her a figurative bird finger, A polite fuck-off. Kate was like a stubborn mule. You had to drag her to get her to participate. She knew this was out of self-defence. Kate didn't want to open up because she was scared of what was going to be unleashed. The only reason she allowed her to smoke during sessions was to keep her calmer than she might be otherwise. There was a fire raging deep inside the belly of Kate Hemsworth, and her counsellor didn't want to be in the firing line when it erupted, as it might possibly do.

NINETEEN

MAYBE PARIS?

Tim made another visit to Eric, to explore some of the issues a bit more deeply.

'Eric. How are you?' he asked, patting him gently on the shoulder.

'Tim. I am lucky man. I see you two days in a row.' Eric grinned at Tim.

'I'm the lucky one,' replied Tim. 'You are helping me enormously.'

'How I help you today, Tim?'

Tim showed Eric a picture of David Mason.

'Have you seen this man recently, Eric?'

Eric looked and nodded.

'He was in same day that Mr Harry Rainer visited.'

'What did you say to him. Can you remember?'

Eric stopped to think and then nodded.

'Yes. I remember now. He ask me if his boss had been in yet. I say yes. Then he asked where he was staying as he forgot where? I say I didn't know. He asked if I was seeing Mr Rainer again, and I said yes, the next day. He said he would come back the next day. He said he was supposed to meet with him but had lost the meeting place. Was on a piece of paper, and then he lose all the details.'

'Thanks, Eric. That's what I needed to hear.'

'All good, Tim?'

'Yeah, the information makes a lot of sense.'

He phoned Matt the minute he left the docks.

'Hang on, let me put you on speaker so that Kate can join in.'

'Hi, Tim. How did you go?' Kate joined the conversation.

'I think we can categorically say that Mason has Harry. I've just finished speaking with my contact at the docks. Both Mason and Harry were here on the same day, asking questions. Then Harry disappeared. Where are you guys, by the way?'

'We're back. Just checked in at the hotel. That was one long couple of travel days. I wouldn't want to repeat that any time soon,' Kate said adamantly.

'I'm presuming there was no sign of Mason anywhere?'

'No. Just his mother, as we thought. We pretended to be lost. No sign of anyone else at the house.' Matt smiled, remembering how they had feigned a wrong turn and how surprised Mason's mother had been when they had knocked on her door asking for directions. They had talked with her for ages, showing overt interest in her garden.

'I like the idea of a trip to San Fransisco actually, suggested Matt. We need to wrap this up.'

'Me too,' said Tim. 'Only we can't all go at once. I suggest that you and Kate look for Harry and Mason here in Hong Kong. I'll travel over to San Fransisco and see what I can find out about the containers. Once we have some evidence about what Mason has been up to, we will have more of a bargaining position to work with.'

Matt thought for a moment.

'That sounds like a plan. I'm not sure how we are going to find Mason, though? I suppose Kate and I should start by digging around at Harry's Hong Kong office?'

Tim agreed. 'Look, we know that Mason said he's off visiting his mother, according to my source. I doubt if that is widely known. The Hong Kong office might just know where he really is. I'm hoping we can find some places he might be if we ask around locally.'

That reminded Matt that he needed to speak to Felicity. She was the one holding his location as a secret for him. He needed to touch base to reassure her before she started wondering what he might really be doing in Hong Kong.

Kate turned to Matt after the phone call. 'Something is bothering me with all of this,' she said.

'What?' Matt panicked, thinking that she had read his mind about Felicity.

'Well, if Mason wants to shut Harry up, then why the notes to me? Why involve me in the first place? Why didn't he just take Harry out quietly?'

Matt thought for a bit.

'I don't know. You've got a point. Mason really didn't need to do the whole cloak and daggers stuff, did he? He could have just taken Harry out quietly, and no one would have been any wiser. What are you thinking, Kate? Any ideas?'

'I'm not sure. I'm trying to piece it all together. I mean, he also threatened me not to go to the police. For some reason, he has me involved and yet I don't know why? It's not like we knew who he was at that point? I mean, I can understand Harry coming to us thinking it was the films, but not the rest of it. Especially the second note.'

Matt excused himself. 'I need to make a phone call Kate. Restless client, I'm afraid. I'll go down to reception to do it, so I don't bother you.'

Kate nodded. She could do with a few minutes alone. She was used to being alone, and since leaving the UK, she hadn't had any proper alone time to think. The space would be good for her. She poured herself a bath in the decadent 98th-floor hotel room, lay back and relaxed.

Matt found a quiet spot in the corner of the reception area. Seeing an adjoining bar, he ordered himself a vodka and then phoned Felicity's number.

'Hiya babe.'

'Matt! How's it going over there? Are you missing me?'

'Of course. Missing you heaps.'

Matt wanted to hear what she was thinking, hopeful that she still believed that he was in Hong Kong only for work and second, that she still wanted him.

'When are you coming back?' she asked. 'Have you had the interview yet?'

'Yeah, through to the second round. The interview process is pretty intense.'

Felicity took in a deep breath. He was sharing personal stuff with her again. This meant he cared.

'What's the job?' she asked, hoping he would open up further.

'Can't say too much, babe, but it's a good one. Based in London too, by the way, so no need to move. Head office wanted to do the interviews in person, so that's why I'm here.'

'I should have gone too. I have a heap of leave up my sleeve.'

Matt inwardly panicked. The last thing he needed was a surprise visit from Felicity.

'When I get back, I was thinking we should go away for a holiday together?'

'Yes, please. Where?'

'Anywhere you want.'

'Paris? I'll start looking around, shall I?'

'Yeah, sure.' Now he needed to steer the conversation into the real reason he had called. 'Hey, whilst I'm thinking about all of this, has anyone said anything at work about me?'

'Not really. A few people have mentioned that it must be hard having parents in Australia when you live halfway across the world, through.'

'Good. So, everyone thinks I'm in Australia?'

'Yeah, as far as I know.'

'Good. Babe. I have to go. You know what I want to be doing right now, don't you?'

Felicity smiled. 'Tell me, and please don't go so soon.'

Matt paused, thinking hard. Spending a few more minutes wouldn't hurt. He moved into the garden courtyard where he wouldn't be overheard.

'Well, firstly, I'm going to be wanting to kiss that neck of yours. Blow some gentle warm breath over your ears, your neck, your back. Then I'm going to ease in behind you and let you see how much I want you.'

Felicity closed her eyes.

'More,' she murmured.

Matt lowered his voice and took Felicity to a good place, one where she would love him even more than she already did. It was a perfect symbiotic relationship.

ANDREW WAS PANICKED. The temp had just handed him a note that had been hand-delivered earlier in the day.

'So, what now? You do nothing? I have Harry Rainer. Take this seriously, Kate Hemsworth. You contact the police? You're dead.'

Andrew was beside himself. He had just about interrogated the poor temp who had made a genuine effort to describe the man who had handed in the note. He was young, maybe twenty-three? Medium height, medium build… she didn't know… maybe he had a tattoo on his hand? She had only looked up briefly, as Louise had been asking her to type up some preparation notes for court at the time and then he had walked away before signing the drop off-book, which he was supposed to have done.

He berated himself for not having installed the CCTV system.

Andrew phoned Rupert.

'Rupert. Problem.'

'What is it? What's up?' Rupert knew that Andrew wouldn't have contacted him at work unless it was urgent.

'This is getting serious.' He read the note out quietly. 'What am I supposed to tell Kate?'

'Shit, Daff. That's serious territory. You think it's a genuine death threat?'

'I don't know?' whispered Andrew down the phone.

'Sorry. This sounds way out of my league,' added Rupert, also lowering his voice. 'I'm at work Daffy, I can't discuss this too much. People can hear. Open plan office, remember.'

'I know. I'm just out of my mind right now.'

'I would help if I could. You know that. I just have fifty pairs of ears hanging onto every word I'm saying at this moment. Let me call you back as soon as I can?'

'Please. I'm going out of my mind right now.'

Andrew paced around his desk and then went and sat in Kate's office. He was tempted to start drinking her gin which he had found one day when snooping around her office. He knew that was wrong, but it was always good to see what Kate was hiding, if only to protect her in the future. That was if she needed protection from her hidden treasures.

He supposed it was good that whoever had sent the note did not know that Kate and Matt were in Hong Kong. Whoever had written the note believed them to be in London. That was definitely a positive.

Andrew worked out the time difference. It would be just before midnight in Hong Kong. He hoped he wasn't going to wake Kate up by phoning so late. However, she needed to be updated.

'Hi Kate, it's Andrew.'

Kate hadn't been asleep. She had been lying on the bed, looking out at the sky risers around her. Hong Kong wasn't a city that slept, and she had found some comfort in watching the trails of traffic and the flashing lights of the city.

'Andrew. What's up?' She knew immediately that something had happened. He wouldn't have been phoning her at that time, otherwise.

'We had another note handed in.'

Kate sat up.

'What? Another note? Like the last one?'

She elbowed Matt, who was sleeping peacefully next to her.

'Huh?' he groaned, turning over.

'Wake up. Andrew's on the phone. There's another note.'

Matt sat up quickly, rubbing his eyes.

Kate put Andrew onto speaker.

'Okay, I've got Matt here too.'

Andrew fleetingly thought about why Matt would be up so late with Kate. Were they sleeping together? That thought could wait until later when he was with Rupert. They could discuss it further.

'Right', said Andrew, not quite knowing where to start. 'I received a note from the new temp. Apparently, she was handed a note this morning but was sidetracked by Louise, who was asking her to type up some court notes.' He paused for a breath. 'The note looks like the last one, but she's gone and left it sitting on her desk for hours before giving it to me.'

'So, what does it say?' asked Kate impatiently, feeling frustrated with the temps they were being sent.

'Oh yes, sorry. It says, *So what now? You do nothing? I have Harry Rainer. Take this seriously, Kate Hemsworth. You contact police? You're dead.*'

There was a silence.

Kate was the first to speak.

'Wtf. Dead? What the hell is that supposed to mean? Is that an actual death threat? So, whoever wrote that, and we are thinking Mason? Thinks that we are in London, right?' She turned to Matt, '… and wants to what - kill me if I go to the police? What's the taking this seriously bit mean? Am I supposed to have done something?'

'Looks like it. Shit.' Matt stared at her. 'Andrew, is it typed, handwritten… any clues on where it might have come from?' Matt was now wide awake. 'Did you put the CCTV in? Just send us a pic of it.' His words were tumbling out.

Kate interjected.

'Isn't this a problem for us, though? Does that mean that Harry and Mason are back in London?'

Matt thought for a minute.

'No. It simply means that they don't know that we are over here. Andrew, did the temp give anything in the description that might help identify the man?'

'Lots of questions.' Andrew sounded flustered. 'I'm trying to keep up.'

'Sorry mate. Just one at a time.'

'No cameras, unfortunately. The firm decided to do a proper job and get an electrician in to install it all. The temp said he had a tattoo on his hand. Other than that, he was of average height, brown hair and in his mid-twenties. Not much to go on, and the note is on similar notepaper, black ink, fairly neat handwriting… hang on, I'll send you a pic.'

'Can you ask her about the tattoo?' Kate asked. 'Like, don't get her too interested in your curiosity. Just ask in a vague sense?'

'That's not a bad idea,' chimed in Matt.

'Sure,' said Andrew, taking a deep breath. He was still clearly shocked. 'You should get the pic any second.'

'One problem in all of this,' added Kate. 'Why would he want to meet us over there if he is over here? Doesn't it mean there is a third party in all of this? Someone on the ground in London who is a part of all of this?'

Matt nodded his head as he was thinking. 'I think so? To be honest, though, we really don't know where anyone is. Let's run this past Tim and see what he thinks.'

'Andrew?' said Kate.

'Yes, Kate?'

'Stay calm. We're fine over here for now. Install a basic camera into reception and hide it. Ask the temp about the tattoo and then get back to us?'

'Sure. I can do that.'

TIM WAS NEARLY asleep when his phone rang.

'Well, it could be a bluff? We have to consider that. Mason might know that you are over here and has sent the letter as a decoy to make you think that he doesn't know. The second option is a third party somewhere in London who is trying to put pressure on you, although that makes no sense. I suppose the third option is… actually I can't think right now… I don't know if I have a third option?'

Kate sighed. 'Once someone starts talking death threats, I'm going to start to worry Tim. Again. I have no idea why this person thinks I know anything. It's stupid. Unless they think that Harry told me a lot more than he did when he met with me?'

Tim reassured her. 'Look, I'm out of here in the morning on an early flight to San Fransisco. The shipment is due the day after tomorrow if it stays on schedule. I can either intercept at San Fransisco or head on down to LA. Given that Mason meets every shipment personally, he should meet this one as well. Whether he has Harry with him, nearby or what, is up to me to find out. I doubt it. That's why you guys have to start looking first thing in the morning. The note means that Mason's plan is progressing. We just have to catch up. Let's not panic, though. Agreed?'

Kate and Matt agreed.

TWENTY

MILDRED WAS KNEADING

Louise sank into her lounge chair. Mildred was kneading and sucking on her woollen cardigan, purring contentedly. Louise was enjoying watching a new television series that was in sharp contrast to her usual heritage diet. Something had stirred in her. She wasn't exactly sure at what moment in the universal lineage of time that the shift had even occurred. She thought that recent events had pushed her ever so slightly off course and into a new place, previously invisible to her. A darker layer in which things may not always be as they seem.

She had cut her hair, too, into a jaw-length bob, something she had secretly wanted to do for a long time. She was now a daring flapper, a woman who might take risks if offered to her. So naturally, she had chosen something far more daring to watch on television.

Her spoon dug blindly into the ice cream, searching for the squishy texture of a raisin, but her eyes were glued to the television screen. The story had gripped her imagination. The male lead was sleeping with a journalist. A young woman, undoubtedly legal but barely so. It would have been abhorrent if his wife hadn't been sleeping with the family's photographer. It was scandalous. They proceeded to lie to each other, their colleagues, and strategy seemed to be the platform they were operating from. The spoon made its way to her mouth, and she felt excitement when her tongue felt the squishy sensation of raisin within the cold of the ice cream.

'It's time, Mildred. The world has been hiding so much from me.' Mildred said nothing, her eyes had glazed over, and a small amount of drool now oozed from her lips. She was oblivious to the progressive movement unfolding around her.

'Maybe I should start living my life a bit more strategically too?' She wasn't sure exactly what that might entail, but it sounded daring and fitting for such a moment.

She gave Mildred a little kiss on her vibrating head and smiled. Strategy. She felt it suited her.

TWENTY-ONE

MOTHER AND DAUGHTER

The woman coughed from the cigarette smoke being blown into her face, which indicated disrespect. Her patient was oozing passive aggression from every pore. She would ignore the behaviour in the hope she would see no use to it.

'Kate. When you think of actions and consequences, what do you think of?'

'Nothing. I think nothing. How many times do we have to go through this? I think nothing.' She tapped her head. 'There's nothing in here. Got it? I honestly don't know why you think that the secrets of life are hiding here. They aren't.'

The woman took a deep breath. She was not going to let Kate win. Kate would need to start co-operating. Otherwise, things were never going to progress.

'When you say nothing, do you mean that you feel nothing, or perhaps that you have no words to describe what you are feeling? There's a difference.'

'You know what?' muttered Kate. 'You have no fucking idea, do you? You sit there in your suit with this grand sense of autonomy. Great. We all know that you have your shit together. Maybe it was given to you on a plate. So, what? Are you going to tell me how to run my life? What I should think? How I should feel? That I'm supposed to have these words, or those words or the right words and somehow be able to even tell you how I'm feeling? Really?'

The woman sat back. The hostile reaction had been better than the long silences that had been occurring over the past few months. Kate had said something, at least. She leaned away as another puff was sent towards her.

'I'm trying to help Kate,' she said calmly.

'Go fuck yourself,' said Kate. 'What's the point anyway? I've ruined everything.'

Kate was speaking in platitudes, almost as if she were an angry teenager. It was as if they were replaying a mother and daughter dynamic rather than one between two adult women. Baby steps, thought the woman. One small step at a time. This case was one of the most complicated she had been given. So far, they had made little progress. It felt like she was being let in and just as quickly, shut out again.

There were so many defensive layers to get through until she could reach her client. Down and down she went, hoping that somewhere, deep inside of her, was Kate. Then she would try to release her and guide her to a better place, out of her own misery. Kate had to understand that there were consequences to actions. No matter how painful it was to deal with them, she would need to turn around and face them if she had any hope in recovery.

TWENTY-TWO

RED TALONS AND HIGH HEELS

Tim landed in San Francisco with a clear mission in his mind. With Matt and Kate in Hong Kong following up on the Mason lead, he needed to get his homework right in San Fransisco. Eric had given him the name of a contact at the docks. Someone on the ground might be able to provide him with some information. Tim wondered if it would be better to let the whole shipping transaction run itself out so that he could stand back and watch how it unfolded. However, getting some info before the containers arrived at the port could be extremely useful. In the back of his mind, he knew that there was a slight possibility that the containers would indeed contain paper and nothing else. However, that was highly improbable with the way things had been going and the fact that paper was so random a commodity in Harry's business. No company had a use for that much paper, that much he knew for sure.

He was trying to guess what it would be if it weren't paper. Drugs perhaps? Smuggling drugs was a high-risk venture. This was also plausible given the clientele of Harry's business, though. However, smuggling drugs wasn't easy. You had to be clever, and you had to outsmart Customs in China as well as in the US. Whomever they were dealing with was perhaps very clever. That was something to note, he thought, and be wary of. He had a moment of worry about Kate and Matt. He hoped they would be sensible if they found anything, especially Mason.

He made his way to the port area. The day was sunny and warm, with a brisk breeze skimming in from off the water. The Golden Gate bridge was majestic, its vibrant colour making it stand out boldly against the sapphire blue of the water and the cerulean of the sky. Tim liked America more than he loved China. He liked the freedom of action in America over the tightly controlled Chinese way of doing things. One day, he would love to move here. He could see himself happy in America, establishing a consultancy business where the sky was the limit. He imagined uncensored access to the internet and freedom with his political thoughts. Hong Kong wasn't a bad place to live, but the cost of living was also becoming harder to manage. He kicked a stone on the pavement and watched it fly forward. He, too, might move forward if he placed himself within the right setting. The optimistic plan gave him something to think about as he strolled towards his meeting point with Eric's contact.

The contact turned out to be a woman, which surprised Tim. It wasn't that he was sexist in his thinking, but that the name of his contact was Jayme which he had assumed was a variant spelling of Jamie or James. The majority of men who worked at the port were solidly built and rough around the edges. On the other hand, Jayme was not what he had expected. Petite, and no more than five feet two. She wore red hair extensions down to her waist and had the longest acrylic nails he had ever seen. To compensate for her height, she wore stilettos that NASA would have seen from space. Red, glossy and painfully high. Tim was captivated by her creative appearance from the moment he laid eyes on her. She seemed to hold her own as she barked orders for the guys loading and unloading. It was easy to see the amount of respect the men had for her. She spotted Tim standing waiting for her and approached him, smiling.

'Let me guess? Tim, right?' she asked. 'I'm Jayme. Nice to meet you.' She held out her hand for him to shake.

'Hi. Thanks for meeting with me. I appreciate it.' Tim smiled back at the cheerful face beaming at him and shook her hand, avoiding her talons in the process.

'All good,' she beamed. 'So, you know Eric then? He's my man over in Hong Kong. Sweetest man on the planet. Said you would be coming in and that I was to be extra nice to you.'

'Well, that's a good start,' smiled Tim. 'I hope you're nice to me too.'

Jayme laughed. 'So, Eric tells me you are interested in a shipment coming in from HK, due to arrive tomorrow?'

'Yeah. I have the paperwork here with the cargo info on it.' Tim took out a folded piece of paper that Eric had given him from his pocket.

'Look, why don't you come up with me to my office. We can talk better from there. Also, I'm dying for a coffee. You want one?'

'Yeah, thanks, that would be great.' Tim followed, wondering how anyone with heels that high, could walk that fast.

She ushered him into a chaotic office that looked as if someone had thrown stacks of papers around, with every available surface covered in documents.

'Excuse the mess. It looks worse than it is. Surprisingly, I actually know what's in all of these piles.' She sorted through a pile and then pulled out a piece of paper.

Tim interjected.

'Are we good for confidentiality here, by the way? I just want to check before I go on any further.'

'Shit, yeah. All good here, Tim. Eric and I are like this.' She crossed her fingers together. 'You wouldn't believe how much we have helped each other over the years. I owe him big time. Anything you say stays in here. Lips sealed, I promise.' She drew a figurative zip across her mouth and then dropped the imaginary key into the wastebasket next to her.

She sat down at her computer. 'Right, so as far as I'm aware, every couple of months, we have a shipment that comes in from Hong Kong under the name of a Harry Rainer. The containers look to have been shipped from Hong Kong. The next one contains paper. All headed to San Fransisco and then on to LA. Weird.' She paused. 'Going by rail to LA? Maybe a partial drop off in San Fransisco? I might have a look into that. That's not usually how we do things.'

'Yeah. The cargo sent to LA by rail doesn't make sense as Harry Rainer has his business based here in San Francisco. It's perplexing as to why the cargo is then being sent on to LA. Did you say there might be a partial drop off?'

'Maybe?' Jayme studied the screen. 'Not this time by the looks of it. Although, it's hard to tell because of how the paperwork is being done.' She frowned.'That's interesting. Yeah, look, these are huge containers for paper. He's bringing in two forty footers each time. That's a shit load of paper. How many people does he have working for him?'

'Not enough to use up that much paper. That I know for sure,' replied Tim.

'By rail too.' Jayme was searching through the paperwork looking for the forwarding information. 'It's got me intrigued, that's for sure.'

'Yes. Also, the name changes, at that point on the paperwork to a David Mason.' He looked at Jayme inquisitively.

'David Mason? Really? That's unusual. Normally we like the cargo to go door to door under the same name. For obvious reasons.'

'Thus me being here. There is a small chance that Harry Rainer doesn't even know that these shipping containers have been brought into the country under his name. Well, I think he does now… but he didn't until recently.'

'Okay.' Jayme shook her head. 'I can see why you are concerned. I'm glad you've raised this with me, Tim. It certainly has me alarmed. What do you want to do next? Why hasn't this Rainer guy come in with you to sort this?'

Tim looked at her. Nothing sprang to mind. He said nothing.

'Right. Okay. I'll not ask,' Jayme nodded her head slowly. 'Okay, so I'm assuming there is something pretty serious lurking around in the background here?'

'Essentially, yes. I wanted to see how it all played out before doing anything, though. Watch the shipment being taken from San Fransisco down to LA and see what happens at the other end. I think it makes sense to watch how it unfolds than jumping in too soon?'

'Not usually how we do things, Tim. However, Eric wouldn't have sent you over if you weren't trustworthy. Legally I'm supposed to report anything unusual at the time of any notifications.' She paused, thinking. 'I trust Eric, and I owe him, big time. I'll tell you what. How about I haven't been officially notified, given this conversation hasn't taken place yet? I'd like to do a favour for Eric. As I said, he's covered me a few times in the past.'

Tim smiled. 'I'll take that.' That was a relief. Jayme appeared to be on side.

'What are we dealing with here, do you think?' She chewed the end of her pencil.

Tim had an urge to tell her everything. However, he held back. She would have to report a suspected kidnapping to the police. That was dumping her into some serious shit. 'Not sure. Drugs?'

'Drugs? Nah, we would have found drugs. Our guys have the best sniffer dogs in the world.'

'Well, I don't think it's only paper?'

'How do you know that they don't use a shit ton of paper at their offices?'

'I don't?' Tim was using a minimum amount of words in case he said too much.

'So… let me understand this better. Between you and me.' She leaned in towards him and lowered her voice. 'You need to sort this out a bit before I go formal because?'

She left the statement hanging.

Tim left it hanging too.

'You have to give me something here, Tim. I need something for my own curiosity.'

Tim thought hard about choosing the right words. 'I have friends. They have been put into a difficult situation.'

'That will do. If it has to do with friends and Eric thinks I need to help you, then done deal.'

'Thanks,' replied Tim. That was a moment and a half.

'Right. So, what's the plan? You got one yet?' Jayme looked at him quizzically.

'Sort of. I suppose my next question is why the name changes on the documentation and how that happens?'

'It shouldn't.' Jayme frowned. 'No way should cargo that's imported have a change name in transit, which is what this is doing. I also don't see a signature of recipient either. It's like it comes in, changes name and then disappears.

Almost as if it's overriding the system. The rules have been bent there, that's for sure.'

'Not surprising with what I'm thinking. Who checks the cargo at this end?'

'It's a stringent process. We take the dogs in and we x-ray if we need to. We check the weight of the containers against what we know is inside. If something is amiss, we do a pretty thorough visual, plus we do a manual search. So, you know Tim, it may just be paper. We would have found anything obviously wrong, by now, for sure.'

'Can you do an extra check for me?'

'What, like a visual?' asked Jayme.

'Yeah, can you just stick your head in and see if it's paper?'

'Yeah, sure. I was planning to, given how intrigued you've got me. I'll have to do that under a different pretence, though. Otherwise, it's going to raise alarm bells down here. My job is coordination, not inspection.'

'Thanks, Jayme, I appreciate it. Lots. Before I forget, and this is important. Do you happen to know if anyone meets this cargo before it gets sent to LA? Someone has to be changing the name on it.'

Jayme looked through the paperwork. 'I don't think anyone does. There's no actual signature on these. Looks like it gets done automatically somehow. That can't be right.' She frowned again, looking serious. 'This is just not an appropriate process. The name seems to just change, as you say. I can see that the name on the import is Harry Rainer, and then the transit and pick-up confirmation is David Mason. I can't tell you whether David Mason actually shows or not. Not my area. Looks like someone has set it up to do that from this end. Weird.' She shook her head. 'I can't tell if anything gets dropped off here either. The paperwork doesn't specify.'

'So, not something that would normally happen?' Tim asked.

'Shit, no. It's illegal for a start. Looks like we have a bad apple here. Right. That's something else I'll need to sort out. I'm glad you came in. This could be a lot bigger than just Rainer's shipments. It could be an indication of something bigger? We don't know, do we? Could be happening on multiple shipments.'

'I wasn't sure what to expect, coming in to see you.' Tim stood up and extended his hand to shake Jayme's.

'Anything for Eric, Tim,' she said, gripping his hand firmly. 'Seriously. I would do anything for that dude. He's one in a million, and as I said, he's saved my butt a thousand times.'

Tim left the shipyard feeling confident. He now had a plan and an ally. Well, a sort of a plan anyway. If Jayme could at least eyeball the contents of the cargo, he may well get a heads up as to what he was dealing with.

Jayme called down to him from her office.

'Hey! Be careful.'

He waved up at her. 'All good,' he called back. 'You too.'

He sent over an email to Matt and Kate rather than wake them. He had made them a facetious mailing address, for the time being, as it was too risky to send anything to their work emails. Email seemed more sensible than trying to coordinate the time differences with phone calls.

'Hi guys, going well here. Have made contact with a woman called Jayme at the port. She will be visualizing the containers when they come in. Says there is some level of discrepancy at her end, which she is going to investigate. She's going to hold off on official action until I've seen what happens in LA. Will have egg on our faces if the containers just have paper in them though.

IMPORTANT: Jayme says that David Mason is probably

not coming in person to meet and greet the containers in San Fran. So, he is probably still in Hong Kong before he heads to LA, or alternatively, he could already be there? We need to figure that out. Also, we don't know if he greets the cargo on the same day that it arrives? Taking a punt on that info. Assume he is still in HK for the time being and search hard.

Hope you are getting some leads on where Mason might be. I'm sure he is going to lead us to Rainer. I will pop into the San Fran office and ensure that he isn't here before heading up to LA tomorrow.

Cheers, Tim.'

KATE AND MATT were staring out of their hotel window as if they might just spot Mason down below in the multitude of people and night lights below.

'Let's try to work this problem through. Be logical. We need a starting point.' Matt then looked at Kate expectantly as if she knew what to say next.

'Don't look at me,' said Kate. 'I'm still thinking this through.'

There was another long silence between them. Tired from all the travel and the complexity of the situation, neither of them had any idea where to start. It was like finding a needle in a haystack they hadn't yet found.

Kate was the first to speak. 'We know where Mason works, right? We also know where Harry would visit if he were in Hong Kong. It makes sense to start with the most obvious possibility.'

'True.' Matt agreed.

'So. If Harry were in Hong Kong to do business, he would go to Head Office. Simple. So, we should start there.' Kate took out her phone and looked for directions.

'You reckon if we just walk in there and look like we're

meant to be there, that they will let us in?' Matt frowned. 'We're going to have to come up with a pretty good reason for being there.'

'Any ideas?' asked Kate,

'I don't know. Is there a reason as to why two lawyers from London might need to go to the Hong Kong office?'

'I can't even think straight, to be honest. I'm exhausted. I need sleep.' Kate yawned. She was spent, and the jet lag was catching up with her.

'Hey, look at it this way Kate. This is a bit of excitement before you have to go back and deal with all those feuding couples. It's got to be worth it just for the break with routine.'

Kate smiled. 'Yeah, you have a point there. I just don't want this to backfire in our faces. We've made good headway so far, but we have a lot to lose, Matt.'

'I know,' he said.

He felt a panic rising in him. He knew that the cost of stuffing this up could be their careers and more now if anything had happened to Harry. He felt his anxiety building and knew he needed a hit of something to calm himself down. Alcohol or sex?

'Want to fuck?' he blatantly asked her. It was a no-frills proposition.

The comment caught her off guard. They had been in the middle of planning the morning. Now, out of the blue, Matt suddenly wanted sex.

'Let's give the people of Hong Kong a bit of a show,' he suggested, moving towards her and wrapping his arms around her waist.

Kate looked at him blankly.

'I'm up for it if you are. Sex right here. In front of this expansive window.' He smiled at her hopefully.

Kate stared at him. He wanted sex in front of the window of the hotel, ninety-eight floors up?

'What if people see us?' She looked out half expecting to see people already sitting at windows with popcorn in their hands.

'They won't. Not properly. The windows are tinted. Anyway, they would have to be looking pretty hard if they did. Don't you want to risk it, though? What if someone was watching?'

'Well, what if they film us? What then?' she asked, sounding concerned. 'You know, crazy lawyer couple filmed having sex, straight onto YouTube or something.'

'What, someone out there sees us and then happens to have amazing filming equipment on the spot? Nah, it won't happen. Come on, be daring. Let's just do it. Not think about it too much.'

'Matt, this is nuts.' Kate looked out of the window. Given how high they were, there wouldn't be too many people who could see, she supposed. The risk element turned her on, though. The thought that someone might see them released adrenalin. What were the chances of being seen? Minimal. How would Matt regard her for joining in? This had to be worth a million brownie points in his eyes. Suitable for the strategy and keeping him motivated. Was that too callous an argument to make her want to do it? She did want to do it, though. Her body was already responding from the anticipation. Was wanting Matt part of all of this too?

'Okay,' she said, starting to strip off her clothes. 'Let's do this.'

Matt was shocked. He'd thought Kate was going to most likely slap him in the face for the suggestion. Instead, she was already half-undressed.

Kate and Matt gave the seven million inhabitants of Hong Kong a show they would never forget, ninety-eight floors into their sky. Matt was in heaven. Sex on tap and as dirty as hell.

TWENTY-THREE

LOUISE BECOMES SHERLOCK

Louise was feeling more adventurous than she ever had. She had dedicated a considerable amount of time to binge her way through the new TV series. She was now ripe for letting loose into the world. She saw the world through new eyes, which meant in a practical sense that she was looking at things more carefully and taking more notice in what people were doing. She had deduced that previously, she had worn blinkers, not even aware that they had hidden so much from her.

She loved the whole cloak and dagger aspect of this new underworld, where evidence was collected from careful observations and deduction. She felt like Sherlock, her mind alive and refreshed with new connections and desires. She curled up in bed with Mildred and entered the day's events into her new diary. She had read that a sleuth always takes meticulous notes from their observations and records them regularly.

I had been standing in reception asking the new temp to type up some notes when the most extraordinary thing happened. A young man strutted in and thrust a note at the temp. He did not utter a sound. Instead, he simply nodded at her and then turned on his boot heel and walked off. The temp read the note and then phoned Andrew immediately.

I asked the temp what was in the note as she seemed quite upset. She said it contained something about Kate and a client. I asked if I could see the note, and she said yes, before breaking down in tears saying that she wanted to leave this 'shit hole of a firm.' This is what it the note stated.

'So, what now? You do nothing? I have Harry Rainer. Take this seriously, Kate Hemsworth. You contact the police? You're dead.'

The content demonstrates that an eyewitness such as the temp, was unable to relay the intensity and seriousness of the situation. More involved in her own feelings and desire to leave the firm, she did not prepare me for the contents. I was not prepared for the deadly seriousness of the note, which also, upon reflection, seemed somewhat amateur at best. A real villain would not speak like that. It is perhaps a contradiction in the true sense.

As per the coaching I have undertaken for detective work, I quickly got out my iPhone, and took a picture of the note as evidence. This is one of the most important things you can do with fresh evidence, in case something happens to the original. Get your evidence, file it and then think carefully and methodically before doing anything rash.

The man in question was aged about twenty-five. He had short brown hair, was of medium build, and I believe was Chinese. He had a tattoo on his right hand. An interesting tattoo indeed. I noticed it because I recently saw the image in a documentary about Chinese Gangs. It's a four-animal depiction. A dragon, a turtle, a bird and a tiger. This was a marvellous coincidence to then see one up close.

This could be my first foray into my new life. Imagine if I hadn't been 'on my guard,' I would never have noticed these details! Of course, it raises all sorts of issues. Who is Harry Rainer? Why was *the note handed in like that? Why did the temp contact Andrew and not Kate, and is Kate going to be murdered?*

Louise sank back into her pillows. There was so much to understand about the situation. She couldn't wait to get started and put all the pieces together. She doubted if Kate was going to be actually murdered, though. Most people intending to murder didn't publicize their intention so blatantly and use such cliched language. It was some sort of definite threat, though. She thought that the best place to start would be with Andrew in the morning. She was sure he could enlighten her as to why a Chinese gang member had visited the Plaid and Potter legal firm to hand in what amounted to a clandestine note with a veiled threat of murder. Her whole body shook in excited anticipation.

ANDREW ARRIVED in the office early, but not in his usual cheerful attire. He and Rupert had gone out for a pub dinner the night before, choosing a venue in an area not wholly familiar to them. The intention had been to shake things up a bit with their routine. However, things had gone from bad to worse as they had been noticed by a group of men, standing at the bar.

One of them, tall, solidly built and heavily tattooed, followed Andrew into the toilet.

'What's yr problem lad?' He spat at him in a thick Scottish accent.

Andrew had said nothing.

'Did ya hear me lad?' The man raised his voice. 'I'll tell you that ya have a cheek. Look at ya. Do you look like us for instance? Are ya supposed to be in this pub, lad? Do ya think that this pub said, come on in, to someone like you?'

Andrew remained silent. He was holding his breath. He knew that if he said anything that it would inflame the situation. He was also in the middle of a long pee that required a few more moments of concentration.

The man approached him. He aggressively poked Andrew's arm with his finger.

'Soft baby skin. For the little baby boy.' He spat into the urinal. 'We don't do baby boy softness round here. We do men like me. Do ya understand, baby boy?' The man then stood tall and cracked his knuckles.

Andrew remained silent. He finished and zipped up his jeans and turned to wash his hands.

'Ya aren't going anywhere right now, lad. This is my fucking place. For my fucking people. Why would you think a baby boy would be welcome in here?'

The toilet door opened, and a man stepped inside. He quickly exited, seeing what was transpiring.

'So, the question is baby skin, babyface boy. Are ya going to fucking leave, or do you need some encouragement?'

The man pushed Andrew in the chest, forcing him back towards the wall. He stood over him, bulging biceps covered in tattoos of faded hearts, skulls and memories.

'See that there wall there, pretty boy? Ya face is about to leave a significant imprint on that beautiful brickwork. A little bit of baby art for the toilets so that I can remember you by.'

Andrew felt trickles of sweat running down the side of his right temple. He was thinking strategy when the toilet door flung open.

Rupert charged in with his right fist raised and clenched. He stopped in front of the surprised man, and then he swung backwards before anyone had said a word. His fist hit the man's jaw, sending him flying into the wall. There was a nasty sound as his head hit the brickwork, hard enough to knock him unconscious. He fell to the ground with blood pouring from his nose.

Rupert and Andrew just stood there. Frozen to the spot. Andrew was the first to speak.

'Fuck, Rupert.'

'Well, I suppose that did the job, didn't it.' Rupert stared at the man, now lying flat on the floor. 'He's not dead, is he?'

'No. I can see his chest moving.'

'Thank God for that.'

'Yeah,' replied Andrew in shock. 'He was a giant prick though. If he was dead…'

'He is alive isn't he?' interrupted Rupert looking alarmed. 'What if I killed him?'

'He's breathing Rupert. Look at his chest.'

Rupert studied the man's chest which was slowly rising up and down. 'He's alive. Thank God.'

'Yeah, of course. I was just saying though, where do you think people like that go when they die?'

'Prick heaven, I imagine. What an idiot.'

'Is there such a place?' Andrew sounded dubious.

'Definitely. Now, why don't we go somewhere else for dinner?' Rupert asked.

'Yeah, I think so,' Andrew replied, still staring at the bleeding, bulky man on the floor.

'We'll let the guy at the bar know a man has unfortunately collapsed in the toilets on the way out.' Rupert opened the door, keen to leave. 'Oh, and that he hit his head as he landed?'

'Yeah. That works.'

The man at the bar called an ambulance and thanked Andrew and Rupert for reporting the incident.

With that, they ran from the pub and onto the nearest bus.

'Seriously, Rupert. I didn't know you even knew how to punch someone.' Andrew was quietly impressed.

'Well, apparently, I do. Lucky for you, the other gentleman who went into the toilet tipped me off. Said you were in trouble. If he hadn't, I don't know what might have happened to you.' He kissed Andrew gently on the forehead. 'I've watched a bit of boxing. The key is in the surprise. Hit first and think later. It worked too.'

Andrew looked at Rupert's knuckles which were bleeding from the hit.

'You're hurt. We'll go find a chemist and get that sorted before we do anything else.' He loved Rupert more at that moment than he had ever loved another human being. 'I might take up boxing Rupert. What do you think?'

LOUISE WAS ALSO in the office early. She was on a fact-finding mission. Putting it all together, as it was known in the trade. The trade, of course, being the dark side of the light world. A world in which she was now dipping her toes into. Firstly, she thought that she should scout around Kate's office looking for stuff, although she wasn't sure what stuff exactly. After all, there was no point in announcing her curiosity to the world before she had something to say. Situations like this were best left undercover, so to speak. She said a quick good morning to Andrew and then realized that she couldn't be seen in Kate's office if he came in to do something himself. She needed to think fast.

'I'm going to work from Kate's office for a bit Andrew. I'm working on the Miller case this morning. I need to pick up a couple of files.'

Andrew smiled but didn't say much. He would stay low this morning.

'Are you okay, Andrew? You're looking a bit pale this morning.' She studied his face, which was as white as a sheet.

'I'm fine. Had a bit of an incident last night.'

'Oh gosh. That doesn't sound very nice. Why don't you make yourself a coffee and then come and tell me all about it?' She immedaitely berated herself. Now she would be interrupted before she had even started.

Andrew went to the kitchen to make himself a double shot espresso, and Louise raced into Kate's office. She wasn't sure where to start, but perhaps a file on Rainer would be a good acquisition? If she could find that, she could take the hard copy back to her own office and have a detailed read of it. She sat in Kate's chair and looked through the desk drawers as a start. She was slightly shocked to find an extensive collection of empty gin bottles in Kate's desk drawers. She'd known about the third drawer gin, but now the other drawers were full too.

She went to the filing cabinet. She had four minutes left by her calculations. Time to turn the coffee machine on. Get the mugs, froth the milk if he was having milk, that was. Then there was travel time from the kitchen to the office, slower than usual so as not to spill the coffee. She would need to work quickly before Andrew returned. She searched through the files and then came to a file with two stickers on it. That's a bit odd, she thought to herself, pulling it out. One sticker said, 'Daniel Parkes' and the other sticker said 'Harry Rainer'. She sat back in Kate's chair and started quickly skimming the information in the file.

It was mind-blowing. This wasn't what she had expected. All the hairs on the back of her neck were standing up. This was real. It was danger all merged into two files. There was a thumb drive too. She took it out of the plastic bag attached to the file and opened it on her laptop. Several files were in it, which she hurriedly opened. She was so engrossed in the material that she lost track of time. Espresso coffees don't require milk frothing time, and someone else had already warmed the coffee machine that morning. Andrew arrived fifty-three seconds earlier than expected.

Before she could put everything away, Andrew waltzed in with two coffees. He stopped in his tracks.

'I have a coffee for you too...' he started to say, staring at the files on the desk.

'... and I have the evidence, it seems,' said Louise, wanting to sound braver than she felt at being so obviously caught out.

'Sorry?' replied Andrew, doing his best to look surprised and confused.

'This,' indicated Louise, pointing to everything on the desk. 'I know everything.' This was, of course, totally untrue. She hadn't put any of it together properly. She was doing the 'bluff act,' just like the people had in her TV series. Bluff your way in, and then the other person tells you everything.

Andrew almost collapsed on the spot. He put the coffees down and just stared at Louise.

Louise looked at Andrew. The poor boy looked like he was going to die. She sighed. This was a moment of decision. What should she do? Then it hit her. She was going to help. She would help this poor young man and do something positive for the world.

'How can I help with this, Andrew?'

He took a deep breath. He may as well tell her. She seemed trustworthy, and to be honest, he was cracking under the pressure. He put the coffees down on the desk and sat on the chair.

Twenty minutes later, he had told her everything. She was gobsmacked. All of this had been unfolding around her, and she hadn't even noticed? A dark underbelly had been in operation right in front of her, and she had been too closed off, too narrow in her thinking and observations to suspect it. There was a Chinese gang member, a kidnapping, strange paper shipments, an alcoholic colleague, kidnapping notes and a gender-related attack. It was unbelievable in complexity and appeal. Far better and far more than she had ever anticipated.

She sat and processed the information before speaking. Then an idea hit her. Something proactive needed to be done.

'We could contact the man who left the note.'

'What, like just contact him and say what exactly? Do we even have any contact details?'

Louise thought hard. There had been something similar in episode three, or was it four? Three. It was three. Contact the individual and get them talking. That's what they would do.

'We just need a strategy,' she told Andrew. 'I saw him afterall, and I'm sure that we can find him.'

Andrew needed to contact Kate.

TWENTY-FOUR

PATRICIA WAS A MOVING STATUE

Matt felt restored, and his mind was now uncluttered. Kate was brilliant when it came to satisfying him. In fact, he was thinking about swapping Kate for Felicity when they got back to London. Turning Kate into his primary relationship and Felicity into his backup. That would work better for him, as Kate seemed more independent and less clingy. He could take Kate with him for networking events too, and their collective impact would benefit both of them, he was sure. He imagined that Felicity would buy the idea that he and Kate were simply old colleagues too. Felicity would never guess, especially if he reassured her that they were all good. Felicity was intelligent, but she wasn't street-smart for sure.

He shot a quick text to Felicity to start the groundwork.

'Hey, babe. Just thinking about you, as usual xxx.' He added kisses as he knew she loved it when he sent them.

'Me too,' she replied immediately. 'Can't wait for you to come home xxx.'

The word 'home' made Matt wince. He had already told

Felicity that he didn't do the whole domesticity bit. Once bitten, twice shy and all that. He had made it quite clear to her that he wanted to keep his bachelor status. This home thing was stupid and wholly conjured up by her own eagerness to be with someone. Only he couldn't be that blunt with her because she would then reject him altogether. He needed to keep her on board.

'Soon, babe. I promise xxx,' he texted back.

KATE AND MATT decided to go to Harry's Hong Kong office on the basis of being there to do some essential legal work for him. Given Harry was most likely not on the scene anyway, he wouldn't be able to deny that the arrangement had been made. They might just be let in if they looked confident and assured. Harry had given Kate a business card when they had met at the firm. She could use that as proof that she had met him in person. Kate wondered if they could go in based on analysing the legal business structure of the company and that Harry had asked them to do a check at each office independently. A legal health check for the business, so to speak.

Matt approached the reception desk. 'Keep your head up and maintain eye contact. Oh, and smile. Look friendly,' he whispered to Kate.

She did, beaming at the young receptionist.

'Good morning,' said Matt confidently. 'Matthew Harmer and Kate Hemsworth here to work in Harry Rainer's office.' He placed the business card on the counter.

Kate waited for the receptionist to ask for ID or paperwork. She didn't. Instead, she glanced at Harry Rainer's business card and then took her gaze quickly to Matt's face. She smiled.

Matt smiled back.

'You Australian?' she asked.

'Yeah. Have you ever been to Australia?'

Kate smiled. Matt had already changed the topic.

'Yes. I visited Sydney with my parents on holiday. It was wonderful.'

'Did you get to climb the bridge?'

'Yes!' Her eyes lit up, recollecting the memory. 'The view from up there was sensational too. Very cool.' She nodded, keeping her eyes on Matt.

'What floor do we need?' asked Matt, jumping in before the receptionist remembered to ask them for anything else.

'Well, I'll send you to the nineteenth for the time being. Out of the lift, turn right and go to the waiting room. Take the lift on the left, over there. I'll let Jasmine know that you are on your way.'

'Thank you. Sorry, I didn't catch your name?'

The receptionsist glowed. 'Tina.'

'Well, thank you Tina. Have a lovely day.'

'You too.'

'Do women always fall for you like that, Matt?' Kate asked as the lift was ascending.

'Seems so,' he said, with a straight face.

'Has anyone ever actually rejected you?'

'I don't think so? I've had a pretty good run.' He smiled at her. 'Oh, aside from you, of course... well, not now,' he added.

Kate held her breath. Now was not the time to be bringing up the past, nor her strategy. 'All you have to do is smile, and women just do as you ask.'

She noted the irony in her sentence. Matt hadn't guessed that she was less pliant than he believed her to be. He probably believed that she was one of those women as well. She wondered how he would feel if she were honest with him and told him about her strategy and whether his ego would be able to comprehend that he was part of something bigger.

They sat in the waiting room on the nineteenth floor, waiting for Jasmine to greet them.

'Now what?' Kate asked him in a lowered voice.

'Well, I suppose we wait for Jasmine? Although we don't even know who Jasmine is. Maybe we should search for her online? Find out who might be about to walk in? We also need somewhere to dig for info. We need access to the office that Harry uses when he visits, and we need access to whomever he trusts over here.'

'Well, that's a start,' she said hopefully. 'So easy. Just like in the movies.'

'Have you got a better idea?'

'Come on, Matt. This is like a bad movie script. Only we won't fare very well if anyone realises we're not supposed to be here.'

'Look, right now, in case there's CCTV, we need to get our laptops out and look like we're doing something productive.'

After fifteen minutes of tapping nonsense into their laptops, there was no sign of Jasmine.

'So, what now?' asked Kate. 'We can't just sit here doing this all day.'

'No, I agree. I suppose we could go for a walk? I've found the name of Harry's personal assistant. It's not Jasmine, either. We could go pay her a visit and see if she has heard anything?'

'Heard anything? Like how do you ask someone if they've heard anything suspicious without sounding incredibly suspicious?'

'It's fine, Kate. We'll figure it out.'

'Don't patronise me.'

'Patronise you? I wasn't.'

'Yes, you were. I'm asking reasonable questions. Stop being so literal.'

'Now I'm being literal as well?'

'Yes. If I ask something, I need an answer, not a platitude.'

'Wow. You're in a good mood.'

'See? There you go again.'

'Kate?'

'What?'

'Relax, seriously. Bickering doesn't look professional. We need to go and find Harry's PA. We need to remain professional and composed.'

'Fine.'

THEY LEFT the conference room and made their way to the top floor of the building, which was on the penthouse floor, complete with three hundred and sixty-degree views of Hong Kong. It was nothing short of spectacular.

'Not bad up here on the ninetieth floor, is it?' observed Kate peering out of the window, looking at the bustling city below her.

'Certainly, better than the view I have from my office. You're so lucky looking out onto the Thames in London. I get to look across to a bus depot. I wonder if I would be more productive if I had a better view. Worth a ponder.' Matt looked out. 'Soon, there will only be skyscrapers here. It's just chockers out there, isn't it.'

Kate looked out of the window. Their vista was dwarfed by so many buildings, all competing for attention. It reminded her of a rainforest where the trees grew taller so that they could bathe in the available sunlight. Hong Kong was a human forest where people displayed their wealth by climbing higher and higher. She wondered how high humanity could go before the foundations couldn't sustain the intentions any longer.

'Okay,' she finally said, coming out of her musings. 'I think we should sound like we're already in the middle of whatever it is that we are supposed to be doing. As if we're reaching out to clarify something that we have discovered. She may not know when we actually arrived? Jasmine never turned up, and if we are lucky, the receptionist only told Jasmine that we were here.'

'Agreed,' said Matt. 'So, we're looking for a Patricia Chang apparently. Her office should be up here somewhere,' he said, leading the way up a corridor.

The penthouse was white. All white. Stark and minimalistic, gallery styled. The ceilings merged into the walls, and the walls merged into the floor. Along the walls hung colourful artworks that leapt out from the brilliance of the white. It was stunning in effect.

They arrived at Patricia's door.

'Ready?' asked Matt

'Yes?' Kate nodded.

Matt knocked loudly.

'Come in,' called out a voice.

They walked in, oozing confidence and eagerness.

'Good Morning. Can I help you?' asked Patricia, a middle-aged woman who was impeccably dressed in black. She stood out from the white as if a living sculpture.

'Yes. Good morning. Matt Harman, and this is Kate Hemsworth. Mr Rainer said you would be expecting us this week. We're in from London to do the overview of the strategic legal plan for the company. We've been based on the nineteenth floor and thought it would be nice to properly introduce ourselves.'

Wow, thought Kate. Nicely done, Harmon.

Patricia looked surprised, but being highly professional,

remained calm. She immediately assumed the oversight in expecting them, had been her fault. It had been a busy week, and she must have somehow missed the memo.

'Could you excuse me for a moment?' She turned and phoned down to reception.

'Tina, I have a Matthew Harmon and Kate Hemsworth here to see me. Has Jasmine been informed?'

She waited as Tina replied.

'Oh, I see. Wonderful.' She turned to them. 'Unfortunately, Mr Rainer hadn't mentioned exactly when you would be arriving. He was in earlier this week but then, unfortunately, was taken ill. If I can be of any assistance, please let me know.'

Kate shot a look at Matt. So Harry had been in the office earlier in the week. A second definite sighting after he had checked out of his hotel. Again though, the message that he had been taken ill, just like in his London office. Matt shook his head slightly at Kate, alerting her to remain composed and not raise any suspicions.

Matt took the initiative. 'Do you happen to know when Mr Rainer will be back in the office by any chance? We were hoping to touch base with him whilst we were here.'

Patricia searched through some papers on her desk.

'He's due at a convention tomorrow. Giving a presentation, in fact. You might be able to contact him there? However, if he's not well enough, then it might have to wait until later in the week, I'm afraid.'

'Where is the conference being held?' Kate asked confidently.

'Let me see,' said Patricia taking a closer look at the documentation in front of her.

'He's presenting at the International Convention for Creative Investment. I'm sure you would be welcome. In fact, I recommend that you attend anyway. I know that a few of the Board will be discussing the strategic planning for aspects of the company, so it could be constructive for you.'

She gave them the venue details, and they thanked her profusely.

They smiled at each other as they walked from her office. Once out of earshot, Matt turned to Kate.

'That was far easier than I expected. I wonder if Mason is expected there as well?'

'Now, that would be too easy. There's no way both of them would be there, given Harry is supposed to be kidnapped, and anyway, wasn't the cargo due in San Fransisco soon? Personally, I doubt whether Mason is even in this part of the world.'

'Tim thinks there's a chance.' Matt pushed the lift button to get back to the nineteenth floor.

'Well, it can't do any harm to see if he's on the list of presenters. Hey - wouldn't it be amazing if they both showed up? At least this gives us a possible lead on at least one of them.' Kate felt a glimmer of hope for the first time since they had arrived in Hong Kong.

They searched for the conference online. Both Mason and Rainer were due to speak at it.

'Unbelievable. Do you reckon that there is any chance that Harry will actually attend?' asked Kate, thinking out aloud. 'The man is supposed to be kidnapped, afterall. What about Mason? What if he turns up? That would be something. The chances of Harry being there are probably between zero and zero, though. However, there may be a chance that Mason might turn up if only to look like everything is normal at his end. If he has got Harry, turning up at this convention would give him a tonne of alibis.'

'Well, Tim's latest update said that he hasn't sighted Mason in San Fransisco and that he usually doesn't meet the cargo anyway. So, he's either in Hong Kong to attend the conference and will then fly to meet the shipment in LA, or he is off somewhere with Harry. If we are fortunate, he will attend the conference and then fly over to meet the cargo. We need to let Tim know.'

Kate ran her fingers through her hair. 'The humidity here? Makes my hair go nuts.'

'Random,' replied Matt. 'Your hair looks fine. We need a break with all of this, Kate. Some good news. A positive sighting. Anything. I need to get back to work for a start. I've got some pretty hard-core cases coming up. I can't just be missing in action in Australia for too much longer.'

'Me too,' agreed Kate. 'I'm busy as hell next month. If I don't get back soon, then I'm going to go under with everything.'

'Well, tomorrow is the day,' said Matt. 'One of them, both of them or neither of them will be there.'

TWENTY-FIVE
MISSING EARTH

Andrew had arrived at work early, with his stress clearly showing on his face. Four of the lawyers who'd arrived for an early meeting had already asked him what was wrong, noticing his bleak expression. The attack in the pub had been enough to deal with, let alone everything else that was going on. If Rupert hadn't come in… he stopped the thought. Kate had managed to keep a lid on everything, but at what cost? Leaving him feeling overwhelmed and out of his depth, that's where. Maybe he should have gone to the police in the first place? That would have meant going against what Kate had wanted, though. Then Louise had popped in, out of nowhere. She wasn't someone he'd had a lot of interaction with since joining the firm, and she was the last person he'd imagined getting involved with. Now they were sitting together, either side of Kate's desk.

'So, Andrew. Where do we start?' Louise sounded eager.

'I don't know. Maybe we need to try to identify the guy who delivered the note?'

'And there's no film of him?'

'No. The firm wants wired CCTV, and the electrician can't make it in until next month. I could have set up a wireless system, but they wouldn't let me. Privacy act and all of that.'

'Well, lucky I got such a good view of him, especially the tattoo on his right hand.'

Louise opened her notebook.

'You kept notes?' Andrew smiled. Louise was full of surprises.

She flicked through the notebook finding the page where she had done a quick sketch of what she had seen. She showed Andrew.

'Sometimes, there are five components to an image like this. I only saw four, although that's not to say there wasn't a fifth that I just didn't catch. If there were just four, it might have represented the four seasons? However, five would represent the Five Principles.'

'The Five Principles? What's that?'

Louise was deep in thought. 'If that's the case, then I missed the earth. I suppose it could have been hiding on the other side of his hand? What do you think?' She stopped and closed her eyes, visualizing the hand that she had seen. She stopped for a moment holding her own hand up to the light and then turning it over. 'It could have been there, I suppose,' she surmised out aloud and indicating to the underside of her hand.

'I guess so?' Andrew held his own hand up to test her theory.

'He could have been creative and had the earth put on the under side. Just because I didn't see it, I shouldn't assume that it wasn't there.' She had learned never to assume any conclusion from episode four. 'Never assume that just because you didn't see it that it wasn't there, Andrew. It's an important thing to remember when sorting out a case like this one.'

'Where did you learn all this stuff?'

'TV would you believe. So,' she said, leaning forward with the sketch. 'You have an azure dragon representing wood, a bird symbolizing fire, a white tiger, which is metal, a black turtle, water, and earth is a yellow dragon. I didn't see the yellow dragon. I'm missing a dragon.'

'Wouldn't a dragon be hard to miss?' Andrew smiled for the first time that day.

'When you say it like that, I suppose not.' Louise grinned back at him.

'Do you think we can find this guy just based on a tattoo, though? Also, is it a great idea to find him? I mean, his note was a tad threatening.'

'Nah, this is all bluff, Andrew. The whole story is inconsistent and amateur. I don't believe for a minute that anyone is actually going to harm Harry Rainer and nor Kate. It's all a big bluff. If he was going to be hurt, then he would have been by now. There's a percentage.' She stopped for a moment and got lost in thought.

'A percentage of what?' Andrew asked.

'Ah yes,' she said, remembering. 'Eighty-five per cent of kidnapping victims are killed within twenty-four hours. The rest are completely open to negotiation.' Louise looked at her watch. 'No time to do too much right now, though. I'll put this on ice until the end of the day. Agreed?'

Andrew nodded. Louise had surprised him.

'And we are sure that going to the police is out of the question?' he asked.

'Do you want to go to jail?'

Andrew looked shocked.

Louise smiled. 'I'm sure you wouldn't, but Kate might. There's also the reputation of the firm to consider. Best that we keep this under wraps. Now, I've got an eight o'clock meeting to get to. All good for the time being?'

'Yeah, and thanks, Louise. You have no idea how much better I feel.'

'Always here to help Andrew,' She shot him a smile and then left.

He glanced at his watch, doing a mental calculation in regards to the time in Hong Kong. It was mid-afternoon, so a good time to call and catch Kate. He phoned, getting her voicemail instead.

'Hi Kate, it's Andrew. Can you call me asap? It's about Louise and the note.'

MATT AND KATE decided to take the afternoon off after having finished at Harry Rainer's office. Kate surmised that there wasn't much else to do until the convention the next day, so a bit of sightseeing seemed appropriate. She wondered if both Rainer and Mason would appear at the conference tomorrow, or maybe neither would? If they both did, then they had certainly hit the jackpot, although it made no sense if Harry was supposedly kidnapped. Either way, she needed to spend some time not doing anything that caused her further stress.

'I suggest that we try to de-stress for the rest of the day,' Kate suggested.

'Yeah, I might leave my phone at the hotel. Take my camera instead for the afternoon and have a moment for some silence. Sometimes I feel tied to the damned thing. Up for some sightseeing?'

'Sounds like a good plan. I wouldn't mind being unreachable for a bit. Just to take my mind off all of this. We've done as much as we can for today, anyway.'

'Yeah, I'll leave a message for Tim first, though.' He looked at the time. 'Actually, it's still quite early. I might leave it for a bit. He hasn't left any messages has he?'

'Don't think so. He would barely even be at the office, anyway.' Kate picked up one of the brochures from the hotel desk. 'Says here, that's there a cruise that leaves in an hour? Want to try that?'

'Well, it's sunny and warm, so yeah, why not?'

Kate couldn't agree more. She was tired, and she was stressed. A couple of hours out on the harbour would be lovely. She was sure that tomorrow would be an arse of a day no matter how she looked at it.

Her phone pinged just as she was placing it into the hotel safe. She listened to the message from Andrew. Something about Louise and a note? It was probably to do with the Banks case, and it could wait. He didn't sound panicked and he would have said if it were urgent.

They boarded the boat along with a few other passengers, having decided to exit the cruise halfway through and spend some time on the other side of the harbour.

'We can pick up the later cruise to get back. There are some amazing restaurants in that area.'

'How many times have you visited Hong Kong, Matt?'

'Five, maybe six. I love it here. It has an energy and pace that you don't find anywhere else.'

The boat, crafted in dark mellow timber with a vast red sail that billowed in the breeze above them, left the jetty. Along the deck were comfortable chairs for the passengers to relax and sink into. Drinks were offered immediately after departure.

'This is more like it,' Kate sighed. She was lying back watching the boat slice through the ocean blue waters of the harbour. There was a gentle breeze caressing her. She was in paradise just for that moment. The rest of the day would be one of simplicity. No more negatives, just drinks, food, sun and breeze. She shut out the voices of rumination and allowed herself to just be.

TWENTY-SIX

SLOVENIA AND PLASTICS

Tim made his way to the airport just as the sun was rising. A text came in from Jayme just as he was boarding his plane.

'Cargo arrived. Have gone and inspected cargo with sniffer dogs. All good. Have taken samples to test.'

Tim shook his head. There was no way that Harry Rainer's company was only shipping paper around. It made no sense.

He texted the exact words to Jayme.

'That makes no sense. Just paper?'

'Looks good so far. The samples may show something.'

'Ok. Heading up to LA now. Stay in touch.'

'No probs.'

HE RECEIVED a text from Jayme just as he was getting into a cab in LA after touchdown.

'Hey - remembered something. Case in Slovenia. Plastics.'

'?' He texted back. 'That's kind of random?'

'Need time to do some more digging.'

'I'm in LA and heading to the railway.'

'Cool. Talk soon.'

Tim had no idea how plastics and Slovenia had anything to do with a cargo of paper.

FELICITY WAS SITTING on her couch, flicking through TV shows. None of them interested her, and she felt unsettled. She texted Nat.

'Hey. What u doing?'

'Not much. U?'

'Want to go for a quick coffee?'

'Sure. Where?'

'Bo Boss in 30?'

'Sure. C u then.'

Nat arrived right on the dot.

'Hey, Felicity. What's up, my friend?'

It wasn't hard to see that something was on Felicity's mind. She looked stressed and as if she hadn't been sleeping properly.

She sighed. 'Not sure. You know when you just feel like crap but can't put your finger on why?'

'Yeah. All the time. What do you want?' Nat got up to order drinks.

'Flat white? Keep it simple. I suppose the caffeine will keep me up, but hey... I wasn't sleeping anyway.'

Nat placed the coffee on the table. 'Right. Start at the beginning, Luv, and we'll see if we can sort you out.'

'It's Matt. He's still away.'

'When was he supposed to be back?'

'I don't know. That's the thing. He told the office his

mother was sick in Australia. He's told me that's he gone for a job interview.'

'Maybe he doesn't want people interfering with the job application?'

'Maybe. Something doesn't feel right with it all, though. Can't you like zoom for a job interview? You don't need to fly halfway across the world.'

Nat frowned, thinking it over. 'I think the fact that he's telling you where he really is, means something.'

'Yeah, I suppose.' Felicity nodded, sipping on the hot coffee.

'What's your worry, Flick? Something's eating you up. I can tell.'

'I don't know Nat. I just have this awful feeling. Nothing specific. Just a stupid feeling. I'm probably just being hormonal or something.'

'Time of the month?'

'No. I just feel off.'

Nat looked at Flick intently. 'Is it something in your relationship that's bothering you, perhaps?'

'I don't think so. I feel comfortable in us, and I'm going to be asking Matt to move in with me when he gets back. I see no issues there. As for this interview in Hong Kong? He kept that pretty close to his chest. I didn't know anything about it until he suddenly announced that he was there. I don't know what the problem is. I just feel… I don't know… uneasy?'

'You might be going down with something, do you think?'

'Maybe?' agreed Felicity. 'I hope that's all it is. I've been flat out at work - especially having to take on some of his workload too. Maybe I just need a break?'

'That's probs all it is Luv. You'll be okay.'

. . .

TIM WAS STANDING in amongst hundreds of containers at the railway station. There were containers scattered everywhere and people milling around, unloading and shouting instructions to one another. It was chaotic. Tim could see why Mason had chosen to offload everything here. There wasn't as much scrutiny as in a seaport. If he were doing something illegal, then it would be harder to notice. He was just heading back to the hotel when Jayme texted him.

'Have news! Will need to speak to u soon.'

'Why?'

'Slovenia and plastics.'

Tim stopped in his tracks.

'???' he texted back.

'Search and then call me.'

Tim found a cafe, ordered a long black and then searched for Slovenia and plastics on his phone. Several sites came up for plastic mouldings. There was nothing that struck him as relevant. He texted Jayme back.

'Mouldings?'

'Add cocaine to your search.'

'Cocaine?'

'Yeah.'

He added this to the search term.

'Oh my god,' he said loudly. So loudly that several people turned to look at him.

He texted Jayme back.

'U positive???'

'Yup.'

HE READ some more from his search. According to the data, cocaine could be hidden into plastic and then extracted again. It produced a product that was up to ninety-six percent pure.

He could only surmise that Mason was importing cocaine from China into the US. He had found a way to hide it from the authorities. He did some more reading and then called Jayme.

'The plastic wrapping?'

'Yes. He's bringing in lots. Serious. I will set up a meeting with you, my Head of Customs and myself. I'll send you a time.'

Clever man, thought Tim. Each pack of paper had been wrapped in plastic for transport. The plastic wrapping had been laced with cocaine. Paper would never be a product that attracted attention at customs, especially given the small amounts coming through. He'd read that even sniffer dogs had issues smelling the drugs through the plastic as they added chemicals to the mix that put them off the scent.

He thought further into the problem. Harry must have found something out, and Mason had tried to stop him from alerting anyone? It sounded plausible, although not definite. Even if half correct, it meant that the game had changed. Mason was potentially more dangerous than ever. Tim stopped in his tracks. If he was right, then he needed to do two things. Firstly, he needed to warn Matt and Kate. He looked at his watch, trying to figure out the time difference. It was now six in the afternoon, his time, which made it three in the morning, their time. He phoned Kate's phone and left a message.

'Guys. I've got new info about Mason. Can you please put everything on hold? We will need to bring in the troops for this instead, figuratively speaking. Mason has been bringing cocaine into LA. Hiding the drugs in the plastic wrapping of the paper. It's too dangerous for you guys to meet him. I'm concerned as to how Mason might react if confronted. He has a lot to lose. Once I have talked with Jayme again, the police are going to have to be involved. Sorry guys. You should just hang tight till I get back if you can. I'm sure we can strike a deal re not involving the police until now - after all, he did blackmail you from the beginning.'

TWENTY-SEVEN

HUMIDIY MEANS FRAZZLED HAIR

Matt and Kate woke early, eager to make a start towards the conference centre. On their way out the door, Kate remembered that her phone was still in the hotel safe. She saw that she had missed a message and a phone call. The text was from Andrew, and the other was a message from Tim.

'Hang on, I'll just check these, Matt,' she called to him as he was walking out the door.

'Sure. Meet you at the lift.'

Kate checked her voicemail first and listened to Tim's message. It had come through five hours ago. Had Tim really just said that the police would be involved? Her heart started to beat so fast, she sat down on the edge of the bed. Now what? She had a decision to make. She could go with what Tim had said and wave goodbye to her career. Or, she and Matt could find Mason first. Then what? Even if they found Mason, there wasn't much they could do. Smuggling cocaine, though? She was thinking on her feet. Shit. Where was Harry? If this was about drugs, then was he still alive?

Should she let Matt hear the message or not? What would he do?

She banged her hand down hard on the desk in the hotel room.

'Fuck,' she yelled. 'Fuck! Fuck! Fuck!'

Matt rushed back into the room.

'Hey, what's the holdup? I had the lift waiting?' He looked over at Kate. 'What's happened?' he asked her, startled at the change in her demeanour.

'FUCK Matt. Just Fuck.'

'Calm down. Deep breath. What's happened?'

She switched her phone back on and played Matt the message.

'Shit!' he said angrily. 'Our careers are going to be over if this goes to the police. When did Tim leave that message?'

'Our time three.'

'They might have already acted on this, then.'

'I wish I had never well met Harry in the first instance. Not ever.' Kate was pacing backwards and forwards across the room, clearly agitated.

'Well, this is a problem, that's for sure. Mason is an actual drug dealer? I didn't see that coming. I thought maybe he was like smuggling fake watches in or something? I hadn't spotted him as a hardcore drug dealer.' Matt, too, was agitated.

'Me neither. Now what?' Kate held up her hands. 'What do we do next?'

'I don't know?' Matt was paralyzed on the spot. He had no idea what the next move should be.

Kate's anger boiled over.

'Well, I'm not going to just sit here and let Mason ruin my life. I'm going to the conference, and I'm going to find that idiot, and I'm going to force him into silence. Perhaps we could turn the tables on him? Tell him we know about the drugs, and we will turn him in unless he disappears or something. That at least solves half of our problem.'

'What? Does that even make any sense?' Matt thought for a moment. 'Actually, that's not a bad idea. If we gave him a heads up about the drugs and the police knowing, he might disappear.'

'Doesn't solve where the hell Harry is, though.'

Matt nodded. 'Yeah, but if we assume that Harry found out about the drugs, then Mason has to be involved. We might be able to get information from Mason about Harry in this process.'

Kate stood up. 'There's still a paper trail to Hong Kong, though. Harry flew here, and then we followed. Plus all the paperwork from the office.'

Matt stared at Kate. 'Get rid of it.'

'What?'

'The paperwork. Think about it, Kate. You have no CCTV at the office. There would be no proof that he ever came to see you.'

'Shit.' Kate shook her head. 'What about being in Hong Kong?'

'I could say that we were working with Tim. He'd cover for us. I've worked with him in the past.'

Kate walked around the room. 'Okay. I don't think we have a choice. I'll ask Tim to shred all the documents to do with Rainer. Let's get to the conference and find Mason and hopefully Harry - although we should steer away from being seen with him.'

'So why would we be attending the conference though? What if we can be seen? Also, don't forget we went into Rainer's offices.'

'True.' Matt shook his head. 'Let's just do this one bit at a time. Okay?'

'Well, unless you have another plan, then we need to find

him and fast.' Kate was already out the door as she said it. In her haste she forgot to text Andrew, asking him to shred the documents.

ANDREW POPPED in to see Louise at the end of the day.

'Heard anything? I got your message from earlier that you were trying to find me.'

'Oh yes, Andrew. I arranged to meet with the man who dropped off the note, only he didn't show.'

Andrew thought he had heard wrong. 'Sorry. Did you just say that you had arranged a meeting with the man?' His tone was incredulous.

'Yes. The one who dropped off the message. I arranged to meet at 4.30 this afternoon. I went and waited for fifteen minutes, and nobody bothered to show up. It shows me they aren't terribly serious or well planned.'

'What?' Johnathan was near speechless. 'How did you even get his contact details?' He looked confused. 'They weren't on the note.'

'Well, they were. On the back of it, actually.' Louise looked rather pleased with herself. 'The note was written on paper from a local hotel. The sort you would find provided in the desk.'

'Was it?' Andrew visualized the note. He couldn't remember seeing a number, but then again, he hadn't turned it over. 'How would you know who to call at the hotel, though?'

'Easy. People who write notes write other notes. I got lucky. Imprinted name on the paper. Just like out of a movie script to be honest.' She looked chuffed with herself.

'Wow.' Andrew was genuinely impressed.

'Yes. There aren't too many people named 'Lallan' in the

world, fortunately. He'd written a note to the housekeepers about wanting more towels left.'

'Louise, he could have kidnapped you too. I wouldn't have even known?' Andrew looked serious.

'Well, I wanted to jump whilst the iron was hot. Fortunately, though, he didn't.'

'Well, it was worth a shot at the very least. No harm done, I suppose?'

LOUISE SAW to her last client and then closed the door to her office. She was looking forward to getting home to settle down with Mildred for the evening. The temp at reception called to her on her way past.

'This was just handed in for you,' she said, looking bored.

'By whom?' Louise asked.

'Don't know. Just a man. He wouldn't sign the book either. I asked, and he refused. I could hardly call the police now, could I? Before you say anything, he was mid-forties, dark hair, probs from London and wore a grey suit. He was approximately six feet and smelled like he'd been drinking beer for a week.' The temp was sick of notes being handed in by random people and then getting into trouble for not giving the staff complete profiles. It wasn't in her job description, and she was going to put in a complaint if it kept happening. It was unprofessional at best to expect her to be more than her job title stated.

Louise read the note to herself.

'Thanks for the meeting. We now know what you look like. See you soon.'

She stopped in her tracks. This was the infantile way they were going to play this out? She stormed back into her office, feeling more cross than she ever had. Phoning the hotel, she asked to be put through to Lallan's room. She got an answering message.

'Don't you threaten me, Lallan. How dare you! So, what if you know what I look like? You could just have easily googled me. My face is all over the internet, and my full profile is on our firm's website. Why you wanted me to stand out in the middle of the street is anyone's guess. Ridiculous, all this cloak and daggers business. Now, either you want to meet me for a proper meeting to discuss this, or my offer to meet will expire. If so, then at some point, the police will be knocking on your hotel door. Goodbye.'

She put the phone down. That had felt good. This whole matter, though, had gone on long enough. She wanted to protect the firm's reputation at all costs, so all of this needed to be reined in. She stopped to look at herself in the mirror in the hallway before speaking to Andrew. Spectacular, she thought. Who would have guessed that Louise Hamilton could be so damned courageous? She liked this version of herself very much. Now all she had to do was think of her next move.

KATE AND MATT arrived at the convention centre feeling and looking frazzled. The humidity in Hong Kong had been overpowering that morning, and they were drenched in sweat by the time they arrived. The place itself was milling with hundreds of black suits, accompanied by black briefcases. It was going to be hard to identify Mason in amongst the crowd.

'Don't sign in, Kate,' Matt whispered as she started walking towards the entrance table. 'The last thing you want is a name tag right now. Let's just mingle.'

'We need the program, though. This place is enormous. We will also need to find a map.'

'Fine, we'll each get a program, but nothing else.'

Kate scanned the pages.

'Got him,' she said. 'Mason. Eleven. Black room on level three.'

'I've found Harry,' said Matt. 'Damn. Also at eleven but on the other side of the centre in the blue room. Look, if you feel like you can cope, how about I go after Mason, and you take on Harry? That is if Harry is there. If he isn't there, then run back to me and meet me there. It's about a three-minute fast walk from the black room to the blue room.'

'Okay. I doubt whether Harry will be there, though,' replied Kate. 'When I have confirmed he's not there, I'll run back to you, and we'll both go after Mason. We have a couple of hours before they are both due to speak, so perhaps we should take a good look at the black room to position ourselves properly. Ideally, we want to get hold of Mason after he has done his talk. No good if we get moved on by zealous staff before he is due to speak.'

Kate was thinking and planning. They would get one good chance to corner Mason, and they needed to. They had to warn him that the authorities were onto him. He would then run. Hopefully, avoiding the saga being told to the police. If they were lucky, they could just fly back to London, and no one would know about the depth of their involvement. Tim would need to conjure up a story that didn't implicate them too much about why they had been in Hong Kong. They might just get away with it. Harry would need to sort himself out, wherever he was, that is.

She wondered if that were mercenary. Leaving Harry. Not finding him. Not caring and just leaving him in her wake? However, he wasn't her responsibility, Not really. He was a man who had come into her office for legal advice. She had provided that advice, and then things had gone from bad to worse. It wasn't up to her to chase him halfway around the world, especially now that her career was at stake. Anyway, he had lied to her in the first instance. She suddenly remembered that she needed to ask Andrew to shred the documents. That had to be done over the phone she realised. There was no way she was going to write that in an email or text message. Lucky she hadn't texted anything in haste earlier. What time was it in London? Middle of the night. She would wait and then phone him.

TIME SLOWED as the moment approached. It was as if it started to stretch out in front of her, each second lengthening as if extending the mounting pressure. She knew what she needed to do, imprinted onto her by her past. She would drop Harry and all the concern she had for him. He would become someone else's responsibility. Run, leave and not care. It was and always had been there since she was little. When someone did you wrong, they run, and you run. You hide. A memory hit her, suddenly and violently. There was shouting. She was five... her birthday in fact. Yes, the memory was becoming more vivid. A day she shared with her older brother. She had waited all day for him to come home so that they could cut a cake that had been made for them.

She had waited until quite late, almost her bedtime from recollection. She knew that he had come home because the shouting had started. She positioned herself at the bottom of the internal stairs, alongside her parents who had appeared, possibly with the cake. Her brother had positioned himself halfway up the stairs, either having been stopped as he was going up or coming down. She couldn't tell. She looked for a cake but couldn't see one.

He was clutching something in his hand. A small white rectangle with red trim. He saw her, and despite the shouting in between them, he told her to catch. Then the rectangle was in the air, and falling near her feet. Kate reached over and picked it up. It was a small handbag. Her brother, still dodging the words being shouted towards him, had smiled at her. 'Happy Birthday, Podge,' he had said amidst the noise. She had felt a warmth pass through her. She smiled too. Fragmented yes, but still an intact memory coming back to life.

Now though, her parents had escalated the shouting, and it had turned into screaming. Rage was flowing, and things were being said that were just awful. She could tell because her brother's face was falling down, and hope was streaming from his eyes. Kate stood quietly as a silent witness. Everyone was so caught up in the indiscriminate dialogue that they had forgotten that it was being played out to a five-year-old audience. A fresh five-year-old that day too, having only been five for a matter of hours.

She had been standing there, on that spot, when she had first heard a chirping. She couldn't see where it was coming from but presumed that there was a little bird somewhere. Nobody heard its chirps aside from her, and she wondered if they might have been able to if they had just stopped their shouting. Kate had said 'hello' to the little bird although she couldn't see it and a warmth had passed through her. The song it sang was comforting compared to the rage surrounding her. She had wished that she was a little bird at that moment, singing sweetly against the tide of anger drowning the room. She would be able to fly away too, somewhere away from the destruction unfolding in front of her, now enveloping her. She could even fly inside herself, deep, deep down, and then the noise would stop. All she would hear would be the steady beating of her own heart. She would be protected.

Kate had watched as her parents accelerated towards the

cliff. They couldn't stop whatever it was they had started. There were no brakes and no stop sign, just a relentless screaming that was due to send them off the edge at any moment. They threw her brother out of the house just as they started to fall. It was save themselves or get rid of him.

'You are no longer our responsibility!' they had screamed after the ashen-faced sixteen-year-old.

Kate never saw her brother again. His crime had been a visit to the pub with his mates. She understood that this was naughty because of his age. She didn't understand though, how her parents could discard him, like the rubbish bin that went out on a Thursday night. Her parents had taught Kate that day that it is easier to wash your hands of someone rather than stop and work through a problem. It was an easy fix. She didn't know why they had done that at the time, though. It had been her birthday. Instead of giving her a gift, they had taken away her brother.

Harry Rainer was no different to her brother, or Ethan, who had left her without checking in again. It was her turn to leave someone now. To leave Harry and to be as selfish as her parents had been. As selfish as Ethan had been when he had shut the door behind him on their marriage. This was the time to put herself first. Not care about anyone other than herself. Her priority was to save herself.

Kate made her way to the room where Harry was due to give his presentation. It was full of black suits and white shirts. She sat down and waited. If he were going to show up, then it would be now. Just after eleven, a woman stood and made an announcement.

'Unfortunately, Mr Harry Rainer has been delayed, so, unfortunately, he won't be able to present his talk right now. We will try and reschedule him for another day, and we'll keep you all informed of this change. We will take a short break, and then we will hear from Tony Young at eleven-thirty. Apologies.'

Kate got up from her seat and ran. Fast. The black room was a good three minutes from where she was. If Mason had turned up, then he was due to leave the room at 11.20am. She and Matt had one chance to intercept him. She knew that she should be worried by the fact that Harry Rainer hadn't turned up. It meant he probably had been kidnapped and was in trouble. However, she would be ruthless. He was no longer her responsibility. He was on his own.

She spotted Matt near the side exit. He indicated for her to come closer. He put his fingers up to his lips and pointed to the stage. Mason was on the stage. Speaking animatedly about shares and sensible investing.

'It's him,' said Kate lowering her voice. She felt a surge of adrenaline flow through her body.

'Sure is. Look when he finishes, we have one chance, Kate. There's a small room to the left as you go out back here. It leads to the fire exit. We need to get him into that room.'

'Then what?' she asked.

'I don't know. Scare him about the drugs. Say that he needs to leave and shut up? It doesn't solve the Harry business though. However, it's half of the problem gone and he may tell us where Harry is.'

'Well, just remember that our careers are on the line if we don't do this.'

'I know,' said Matt.

TWENTY-EIGHT

SHE BOUGHT AN ENGAGEMENT RING

Felicity was out furniture shopping. Her double bed wasn't going to be big enough for Matt and herself once he moved in. Right now, she didn't mind the fact that he took up most of the bed when he stayed over. However, long term? She couldn't imagine being able to function at work properly if she was that uncomfortable each night. She had a king bed in mind, and just as she was about to walk into the shop, she had passed a jewellery shop.

Some ideas seem logical at their point of origin and others, afterwards, seem bizarre. Such was the decision that Felicity made at this moment. She spotted the ring in the window and then froze, mesmerised by it. A single diamond solitaire ring, shaped into an exquisite oval. She knew that she had to have it. Matt wouldn't mind, and it would save him having to buy one for her. Once they moved in together, it was a formality that they would get married anyway. Not that Matt had precisely said those words. In fact, he had sounded adamant that he didn't want to get married again, but there had been a gleam in his eyes. She knew she could win him over.

She had just stepped out of the shop when Nat caught up with her, having arranged to offer her opinions on mattresses.

'What are you doing coming out of a jewellery shop?' Nat hugged her warmly.

'I've bought something.' Felicity grinned.

'What have you done?'

Felicity held up her hand, showing the diamond on her finger.

'What? Did he ask you Flick? When?' Nat hugged her again.

'Not exactly. Not yet.'

Nat stared at her. 'Did he send you the ring?'

'Not really. I kind of bought it myself.'

'What? You bought a ring, just in case?' Nat sounded surprised.

'He's always busy, anyway.' Felicity was admiring her hand.

'Sometimes Flick, you do crazy stuff. This is one of them. You going to actually wear that?'

'Yup. Why not? It's just a bit of fun. It looks nice anyway.'

FELICITY, giddy from the sparkle of the ring on her finger, was lying on the bed, trying to bounce.

'Flick. Stop. No. Seriously. You're getting us funny looks.'

'You have to check the bounce factor. I'm being serious,' she added seeing the embarrassed look on Nat's face.

'I'm sorry,' apologised Nat to the salesman. 'She's just got engaged.'

'That makes sense,' he smiled.

'The softness is perfect on this one. Does it vibrate too?' asked Felicity.

'Yes. It's got the built-in massage feature.' The salesman reached down and turned it on.

'Bliss. Pure bliss!'

'Flick, you're a nightmare to be around some times. You do know that?' Nat smiled at her. 'At least you seem a bit happier than you were last night.'

'Yeah, I was just silly, I think. A bit of shopping has cheered me up. I still need to get a few other things if you've got time?'

Felicity had bought a new dinner set, towels, cushions, and a dining table for six by the end of the day.

'Anyone would think the two of you were getting married and setting up house together,' Nat had chuckled.

Felicity had looked at her with a knowing look. 'Well, we might be sooner than you think,' she said, twirling the ring around her finger.

Felicity arrived home with her bags of goodies and laid them out on her bed. The towels were the palest blue which would match Matt's eyes. The silly niggling fear that had overwhelmed her had quietened for the time being. This was going to be a new chapter for her and Matt. Her intuition was never wrong.

TIM SAT WAITING for the meeting to start. He felt nervous about discussing the matter with a stranger. However, he needed to trust Jayme. He hadn't heard back from Kate or Matt yet, which was frustrating. He would have liked to have included them in the meeting.

His laptop buzzed, and Jayme appeared, sitting with a man of about fifty.

'Tim.' Jamye smiled. 'This is Bart.'

'Nice to meet you, Bart. Jayme says you've given us something exciting.'

'Apparently so,' nodded Tim. 'So, you found drugs in the plastic you say?'

'Yeah,' said Jayme. 'I've not actually come across this before, and neither has my team. We've been holding off on doing anything because we wanted to speak with you first.'

Bart spoke. 'This is new, all of it. Not had a case like this before. The paper is wrapped in plastic but several times over. We probably should have noticed that, but because the dogs didn't pick anything up, we just thought someone was overzealous with their wrapping. You can actually extract quite a lot from the plastic, it seems. At least, that's what our preliminary online research has indicated. This is all making someone very rich. We just need to figure out who.'

Jayme interjected. 'However, we don't know if we are after Rainer or Mason at this stage. Which is where you come in, Tim. So, we want you to help our team meet the shipment as planned.' She waited as Tim thought it over.

'Why me? Why send me back in? It's not like I'm a detective.'

Jayme laughed. 'Yeah, we know. But you've done the groundwork with this. You know more than we do. We'd like to keep you involved - safely, of course.'

'Say nothing to anyone, though if you don't mind. We don't want this compromised,' added Bart.

Tim agreed, wondering how they would feel if they knew that he had already told Matt and Kate. In fact, he was on the spot a bit. Jayme and Bart didn't know that Matt and Kate were out looking for Mason at that very moment. He'd kept it to himself. They were all way in over their heads. That was a fact. He had warned Kate and Matt. It was up to them to make the right decision and not go after Mason. He was praying that they were doing the right thing over in Hong Kong.

• • •

MASON FINISHED his presentation and left the stage to an appreciative audience.

'Follow my lead,' Matt said to an apprehensive Kate. He stepped in front of David Mason.

'Mr Mason. Lovely to meet you. I'm Graham Bond, and this is Sarah Watkins. We're from Australia and really enjoyed your presentation. Do you have a few minutes?'

Mason had looked at both of them without a flicker of recognition. Matt was relieved. He wouldn't have been expecting to see them, so they were both out of context. Just another couple of interested investors attending the conference. Matt directed him into a small room near the fire escape.

'We have a few questions if that's okay in terms of timing with our future investments.'

'Sure.' Mason had replied with a friendly tone.

Once in the room, Matt shut the door. He looked around the room, checking that there were no windows open and that no-one was outside, looking in.

Mason looked at his watch and then at Matt. 'I don't want to be rude, but I have a plane to catch. I'm due back at my office in the States.'

'Sure,' said Matt, realising that he was planning on meeting the shipment. 'This won't take long.'

'Mason. We are here to do you a deal.' Kate just came out with it.

Matt looked at her, his eyebrows raised alarmingly. She had cut to the chase too fast without doing the groundwork. He hoped she hadn't scared him away.

Mason cocked his head to one side inquisitively.

'Sorry?' he asked. 'I do not do investment deals with clients, only advice. Sorry.'

'No. We want to do a deal with you.' Matt positioned

himself between Mason and the door. He indicated to Kate to do the same with the emergency exit door.

Mason noticed.

'What is going on?' he asked. 'Why am I in here?'

'We know about the drugs, Mason. We know how you export them from Hong Kong. We know about the paper, and we know about the plastic wrapping.'

Mason didn't move. 'I don't know what you mean. I have no idea what you are talking about. I am here to speak at the conference. That is it.'

He went to move forward towards the door.

Matt stopped him.

'Don't,' he said forcefully. 'You need to listen right now.'

TWENTY-NINE

BASKET WEAVING AND HELL

The woman sat in her chair, waiting for her patient to enter. She was hoping to stay positive this session and not let her client antagonize her. She had re-read the case notes the night before. Kate's case was complicated. There was a great deal to work through. So far, a pattern was emerging. Kate would take some steps forward, and then Kate would retreat. A few sessions were needed to find her again and bring her back. It went like that, backwards and forwards, and the motion tested the woman's patience and endurance.

This wasn't an inherently evil woman, despite what was in the notes. She had, in fact, been born very good. A child that was a ray of sunshine amongst a house full of darkness. She had been the hope for her parents' future. Kate's happiness and hope, however, had been tested and tried by a labyrinth of dysfunction. The woman believed that in Kate's predicament, the hope had literally been sucked out of her, leaving her lost and trapped in a void.

Could she blame her? Her job was never to lay blame but

rather to understand. To help her patient understand how actions were so closely related to consequences. Kate didn't seem to understand this ebb and flow. Kate understood things as black and white and seemed surprised when things went wrong, as if disassociated from her own choices. In Kate's world, there was no in-between with things. She used people and places as stepping stones. A way of getting from point A to point B, probably because she couldn't find her own way through life. Meandering would have been too haphazard for Kate and therefore too frightening for her.

This time, Kate had been stung. Hurt by the fall into the abyss between two points. She simply couldn't find the way out on her own. Thus, she supposed, it was her job to light a path forward for her. There was a knock at her door.

'Come in.' The woman tried to sound as positive as she could.

Kate entered, looking frail and tired. Her skin was pale, and there were hints of black circles under her eyes. She was already smoking a cigarette when she entered.

'How are you?' asked the woman, praying for a positive response.

'Same as,' replied a nonchalant Kate. 'Can't really complain.'

The woman waited. Her heart sank. It was going to be another battle. Not between her and Kate, but between Kate and herself.

'Did you do the exercises that I had suggested? The walking, mindfulness and the art?' asked the woman, hopefully.

'Yeah, I threw in some basket weaving as well,' said Kate, puffing smoke at her.

'How many baskets did you make?' asked the woman. 'I've heard that the record is ten in one day.'

Kate looked up. She hadn't been prepared for humour to

come her way. The rhythm of her attack on the woman momentarily slowed down. It broke the tension a bit. Just enough for the woman to speak a second time.

'You could bring some in and use them as ashtrays, perhaps?'

There was silence in the room.

'Why am I still here?' asked Kate.

'Because we need to get you into a better place, Kate. You know that, and I know that.'

'What if there is no better place? What if you're just flogging a dead horse?'

'I do not believe I am flogging a dead horse, Kate. I believe I am possibly trying to encourage an exhausted horse. A horse that has been carrying a burden for way too long. A horse that might like, for one day, to have the saddle undone and the burden taken off.'

Kate thought about herself as a horse. It wasn't a bad analogy. She imagined herself being born as a young foal. Then life had burdened her, one weight at a time. She had carried it all around with her, gradually getting more exhausted, and now here she was, collapsed by it all.

'You know there is no point, don't you?' Kate stated bluntly.

'There is a point, Kate. There is always a point.'

'Don't pretend.' Kate sounded angry. 'You remind me of someone. That nun that sang in the hills. Everything was a fucking platitude. Life isn't like that.'

'I'm not pretending, Kate.'

'I chose to do what I did. Don't you understand that? It was my choice. You can't just change the outcome using words. Words don't change anything. It's not like this can be fixed.' She stared at the woman with empty eyes. An expression that stated she was over life.

The woman stopped and took a deep breath. She was

trained to handle this, and she would. She would not give up on Kate. Not ever. She would work with her until she got her back on track. There would be no failure.

'Life can go fuck itself,' Kate said pedantically, blowing another puff of smoke towards the woman, 'and I really don't want to be rude… but you can too.'

JAYME MET Tim later that day in LA.

'So, from what we are learning, this type of drug smuggling isn't new. However, in this case, Mason or Rainer seems to have nailed it. It was notoriously hard to get the cocaine into plastic in previous smuggling attempts, and authorities would be alerted due to the appearance of tiny air bubbles in the plastic. Not, in this case, though, smooth as.'

'So, out of a matter of interest,' asked Tim, 'how do they get the cocaine out?'

'The extraction is fairly straightforward, so long as you know what you are doing that is. So, they make the plastic called polymethyl methacrylate, and they lace it with cocaine hydrochloride. In this case, they then created wrapping for the paper units. Once the plastic is no longer needed for the wrapping, the cocaine can be extracted using solvents such as petrol, benzene or acetone.'

'What about the finished product?' asked Tim.

'Is it any good? Hell yeah. They can get ninety-six per cent purity with this method.'

'Clever.' Tim nodded with approval. It was impressive science.

'Well, in this case, if you hadn't alerted us, we wouldn't have found it. Even the dogs can't sniff it when it's in the plastic, and if you can't see it, then you just don't know it's there.'

'So, what's the plan exactly?' Tim was a bit worried that they wanted him to stay involved.

'Well, we intercept the shipment and then wait for Mason, or Rainer depending on who shows up. We're fairly sure from what you have said that Mason is behind all of this. We'll send you in to warm him up and get him talking – you'll be wired, obviously. Once we think we have enough, we step in, seize the goods and hand it over to the police. They then take it from there.'

'So, my role in this from now on is like a mediator?'

'Right. Yeah. Spot on. I don't mind having you around either.' Jayme smiled at him.

Tim smiled back. Was Jayme flirting? 'One of your officers could do the same job?'

'Yeah, they could. Only we figured that you have a good sense of the back story, so we may as well leave you in there. So long as you do exactly what we say, that is. Can't have you getting injured.'

Tim immediately thought of Matt and Kate. He sent Kate another text.

'Need to discuss asap. This is urgent, guys. Did you get my voice message?'

There was no reply. Tim was getting worried. Either something had happened to Kate and Matt, or they were deliberately not getting back to him.

MASON FROZE ON THE SPOT.

'I would appreciate it if you would let me pass and exit the room.' Mason looked from Matt to Kate.

Matt did not move.

'You are not leaving this room, Mason,' he said sternly to him. 'Not until we have spoken to you.'

'Really? And says who? I will ask you one more time to get out of my way. Please.' Mason stared Matt down.

'No.' Matt said again. 'You need to listen carefully to what we are about to say Mason.' He raised his voice slightly.

Kate stepped forward.

'Sit,' she indicated towards a chair.

'What is this? What do you two want?' Mason looked around the room, looking for other exits.

'We want you to fucking well sit. Now just do it.' The gloves were off. Matt had changed tactics. He needed to sound more dominant with Mason.

Mason sat.

Kate thought quickly. 'We know about the drugs, Mason. All of it.'

Mason stared at the floor, not moving.

'The drugs Mason. We know about them. The paper you've been exporting from China to the US?' Matt sounded confident with his tone.

Mason kept staring at the floor.

'So, this is what is going to happen,' Kate said. 'You are going to tell us where Harry Rainer is and then leave here and disappear. Or we contact the police, and you can be arrested within a few minutes and go away for a very long time. How does that sound?'

Nothing.

Matt and Kate looked at each other. They hadn't expected silence.

'Why?' asked Mason, eventually.

'Why what?' asked Matt.

'Why should I believe you. What if I don't know anything about any drugs or where Harry Rainer is.'

'Well, we know that you do. Don't try and bluff Mason. We know everything, including the fact that you met him a few days ago.'

'I don't know what you are talking about. I'm leaving.'

'No, you're not,' said Matt standing in Mason's way.

'Get the fuck out of my way,' said Mason, his tone now having changed.

'No. Just sit down!' Kate was angry. She pushed him down into the chair. 'What you need to do, Mason, is to disappear. If you don't agree to do that, we phone the police, sending the authorities to your shipment. The one that arrived in San Fran. The one that you then have transferred to LA. Plus, we need to know where Harry Rainer is.'

Mason looked up at her.

'Yeah, you know the one.' She glared at him.

'No, I don't.' He shook his head.

Matt stepped forward.

'This isn't like twenty questions, Mason. How about I explain it to you in terms of choices. You leave here, and then you disappear. Or, the authorities can go collect your paper, and you go to jail.'

Mason looked at him. 'Why are you tipping me off?'

Neither Kate nor Matt replied.

Mason smiled. 'So, there is something you are hiding too? Something to do with Harry Rainer, perhaps?'

'No,' said Matt. 'We just don't like getting mud on us.'

Mason nodded his head. 'Kate Hemsworth and Matt Harmon. Australians living in London.'

Kate and Matt looked at each other.

Mason stood. 'Nice to meet you both, now get out of my way. You are amateur nothings to me. Not even a threat.'

'Where's Harry Rainer, by the way? What did you do to him?' asked Kate.

Mason made a dash for the emergency exit, which was now clear. Kate leapt after him.

'No, Kate, leave him. He knows what he has to do.'

'Over my dead body. I want him to tell us where the hell Harry Rainer is.'

'He heard us.' Matt grabbed Kate's arm, and she shook it off. 'He knows. Just leave it for now!'

She ran to the emergency door after Mason, taking the stairs two at a time.

Matt followed. 'Kate, don't follow him,' he shouted. 'Leave him to do as he was asked.'

'No!' shouted Kate. The blood was pumping through her. Pure adrenaline had supercharged her. This man was not going to get away and ruin her life. She needed to know where Harry Rainer was. Her career was over unless he did what she wanted. She was not going to let this happen. She needed to hear him say that he would do as she had asked. Mason was running away just as Ethan had, with no resolution.

Matt was right behind her.

'Kate, for FUCK's sake. Stop! Please.'

They got to the bottom floor, and Mason was in front of them. He was trapped as the emergency door was blocked from opening by a delivery truck that had stopped there for the conference. The timing was everything. Had the truck not arrived or had already left, Mason would have been able to exit the building. For the three minutes the driver needed to unload the goods, the exit was blocked. It was noisy too, as the engine was running.

They say in chaos theory that a tiny butterfly flapping its wings on one side of the world can impact everything that comes after. So, it was with the delivery truck. A duck had stepped out near a water crossing, resulting in the driver patiently watching it waddle across the road. Then a red light. The truck had arrived at its destination two minutes later than it should have arrived. The fact that it was there changed everything that came after.

Mason turned around and looked at them. 'You two aren't important to me. You are nothing. Inconsequential. As for Harry Rainer? I do not know where he is. Do you understand?'

Kate and Matt said nothing. Mason was holding a small handgun. He aimed it at the two of them.

'Now, how about the two of you do as I ask?'

Kate and Matt stared at the gun. They had not expected Mason to be armed at the conference. It seemed the least likely place to be carrying a gun.

'Now, we can do these two ways. I can kill both of you on the spot. Right now. Or you can walk the other way and forget that we had this conversation.'

'Fine,' said Matt. 'Kate, come on. We'll walk the other way.' He wanted to run from this. Matt turned to go. 'Kate,' he pleaded.

Kate didn't move. Something in her ignited. A rage. A searing hot rage started to bubble up, gaining momentum as it did. Her fight or flight mode exploded into action. She was no longer a helpless victim, being held hostage by other people's actions. She would not stand here and take this. She would fight. For the second time in her life, Kate Hemsworth would fight.

She was six. She had been in the bath, filling the little pink container up with water and had poured it over the edge of the bath. She wanted to see how much water the fluffy blue bath mat could absorb. Her seven-year-old brother had been sent in for his bath, and then mother had arrived. She noticed the wet bath mat and dragged her brother out of the bath. She was in a rage because the bath mat was wet. She hit and hit and hit him. He was screaming. Mother didn't stop. She was just hitting and hitting, dragging him by one arm along the carpet. Kate had leapt towards her mother, feeling how powerless and helpless her brother had been. She had been the one to wet the bath mat and not him.

Something in her had ignited, a rage that had been seething inside of her since her fifth birthday. She ran towards mother and screamed at her to stop. Her mother kept hitting. Kate snapped. She hit her mother repeatedly, screaming at her to stop, slapping her apron, legs, and arms. Anything to stop the screaming coming from her brother. Mother had thrown her off, but the attack had been enough for her to become perplexed at the behaviour of her normally quiet daughter. She stopped and walked off, leaving her brother sobbing on the floor.

Kate felt the same anger now, standing in front of Mason. She would fight back. She stepped forward quickly and extended her arm out to push the gun to one side. She threw all of her weight at Mason, who fell from the blow. There was a shot fired, and then Kate was falling. She heard Matt scream out to her, and then she fell onto the concrete with a thud. She hit her head then blackness enveloped her.

TIM PHONED KATE AGAIN. He got her message service. He called Matt and got his message service. Where the hell were they?

LOUISE WAS SITTING on her sofa. So far, the second episode in her series had been a bit more bloodthirsty. It appeared that sometimes it was better not to challenge criminals head-on. Sometimes there were more subtle ways of solving crimes that didn't put you in harm's way. She thought that was important and reflected on her decision to go and meet the criminal man. Perhaps in hindsight, it had been a bit silly. She stroked Mildred, who was purring loudly.

Kate was still in Hong Kong. Louise wondered whether she ought to phone her to discuss this new insight. After all, Kate might have been a bit headstrong to go over there and think that she could sort it out? She decided to watch one more episode before making any further decisions.

It was a moment when things could have gone two ways. If Louise hadn't decided to watch episode three, then she might not have chosen to do what she did next. A particular blood and guts episode where the hero had been murdered by the criminals was all it took. Louise reached for her phone as the credits were rolling.

'I'm doing the right thing,' she informed Mildred, and then dialled 999.

KATE CAME TO. Her head hurt and was throbbing. Her eyes tried to focus but couldn't. All she could see were shards of shapes in front of her. Where was she? She lay there. Vague memories were floating in and out of her head. She couldn't quite understand them because of the pain in her head. She was also cold. She felt around her and realized she was lying on concrete, and then ever so slowly, she remembered. Matt had been with her. There had been a gun. A shot. A scream. Was that her scream? No. It had been Matt's scream? No, it was her scream. Had she been shot? Mason had been there. Fear and panic enveloped her. Was she dead or alive?

'Matt,' she tried to call out. Her voice was weak though and small.

Silence.

'Matt. Help.'

Nothing.

Kate was terrified. Where was Matt? Had Mason taken him? He had taken him just like Harry? She lay on the concrete, trying to raise herself up on her elbows. Had she been shot? She felt over her body for blood, feeling wet on the back of her head. Had she been shot in the head? Was she in pain? She couldn't tell. She didn't know how long she had been there. It was dark, and there was silence outside as if everything had stopped at the conference.

'Matt. I need help,' she croaked hoarsely. She lay down again on the intensely cold floor. Her body started to shake uncontrollably.

Where had Mason taken Matt? She slipped back into darkness and then woke again. Her body felt like a wedge of ice. Solid. Unfeeling. She must be dead. She made a mental note to remember to inform people that when you died, you were still there. She wondered if her thoughts were making sense. She again raised herself up onto one elbow, peering into the darkness. Her eyes began to adjust to the dim light, and she began to make out shapes. There was something a few feet in front of her, a large shape on the floor. What was that? It was Mason. Matt had tackled Mason to the ground and had gone for help. She felt relief wash over her.

She started to crawl ever so slowly, her limbs not cooperating with her thoughts. She was crawling perhaps an inch at a time. Maybe the shape was Matt? If it was, then that was good. He could help her. Yes, it should be Matt and not Mason because if she crawled to Mason, he might try and shoot her again.

'Matt. Please. I need help.'

She reached out and felt material. Suit material on a leg. Moving her body further forward allowed her to reach up higher. A jacket, but it was wet. The floor must be damp, she thought. It didn't feel like Matt's jacket, though. More like the one Mason had been wearing. Had Matt shot Mason in the confusion as well? Maybe Matt had been carrying a gun too? That would have been clever. She hadn't predicted that

Mason would have brought a gun to the convention, and then, there it was.

This was Mason's body then. It wasn't moving, and she couldn't hear any groaning. Maybe he was lying still like she had been? She reached further, feeling a hand and then a wrist. It was colder than hers. Then was a watch. Feeling it, it felt like the one that Matt wore. What a coincidence, her mind told her. Mason and Matt having the same watch. Her mind shifted into a different place. Feel the hair it told her. Then you will know. She froze as still as she could. She remembered Mason's hair. Short, coarse, a neat style and black. Matt had curls, short sides and a longer front section.

If she stayed frozen, then time would also stand still. She held her breath, wanting to stay in that precise moment.

'Matt,' she asked in a small voice. 'Is that you? Are you hurt?'

No. She was being silly. Matt had shot Mason with his gun and had now gone for help. That's how this was going to play out. Matt had gone for help so that she would be saved. This was Mason. That's why he wasn't answering. If it were Matt, he would answer her. She inched her way forward to feel the hair of the body. Her fingers crawled up past the shirt buttons and then reached a chin. She gently felt the contour, but her fingers felt wet… what was that?

Her mind made the connection as she had felt those contours before, but she argued with it. Mason's face was angular too. Her mind told her it wasn't. She prayed out aloud as time started to speed up and the inevitable rushed forwards.

'Dear God, please let this not be Matt. It can't be.'

Panic started to well up inside of her.

'No, no, no, it can't be. It mustn't be.' She screamed. 'Matt! Please, Matt. Get up. Say something.'

She stopped and berated herself. She needed to pull

herself together. This was Mason, remember, she told herself. This was a good thing as he had pointed a gun at them both. Matt had gone for help. Check for a pulse. Feel the hair. Check the pulse and feel whether there are curls at the back of the neck. She had to remember to feel for the hair. Stay calm, she told herself and took some deep breaths, just like she had been taught to. The darkness made it hard to see, though. She reached into her pocket for her phone. It wasn't there. She needed it. It must have fallen out when she had tackled Mason.

Time breathed a sigh of relief. The inevitable could wait for a few more moments.

She crawled on her hands and knees back to where she thought she had been lying. Painstaking. Her knees hurt on the rough concrete. She reached out like a blind woman, grasping into the air and dragging her hands on the floor, trying to find the phone. Then her hand felt something cold, small and metal. Her phone. She put in her passcode and switched on the torchlight. This meant she had to be alive and not dead, she surmised. Turning around, she shone the light onto the crumpled mass she had felt. It would be Mason.

Time got ready for the reveal. This was the moment of truth. There would be no reversal and no pause. The consequences of Kate's actions would reveal themselves to her. The way in which she had decided not to tell the police about Harry Rainer and how she had invited Matt into her life for strategy. She had run after Mason, Matt screaming at her to stop and then she had launched herself towards Mason, and the gun had gone off.

The universe already knew what had happened, and some would say it was just fate about to expose itself to her. Some would say that Kate herself had caused it all by the actions she had chosen. Others would argue that no one deserved what Kate was about to see. She pointed the light onto the suit, and Matt's lifeless body filled her vision.

'NO!' she screamed. 'No! No! No! No! MATT!' Her voice screeched through the blackness of the stairwell. It was a razor-sharp scream that pierced the very fabric of time and space. The sort of scream that, if heard, is never interpreted as anything other than horrific. The universe already knew that when Kate had tackled Mason, some would say stupidly rather than courageously, he had fired the gun. When Kate's arm had hit his arm, it had fired the bullet's trajectory towards Matt. The bullet had hit him at approximately one hundred and twenty meters per second. Kate was slow in her catch up to find out what had happened, having been unconscious from a severe blow to her head for forty-three minutes.

'MATT!'

'SAY SOMETHING!'

'MATT!'

Lying on the concrete, still, cold and red, was Matt. He had been shot in the neck. A gaping hole instead of his skin. A hole blown into his carotid artery, allowing his life to seep out, pooling towards the wall. His eyes were still open, icy blue from the shock of feeling the bullet rip through his neck. He had then fallen backwards, smashing the back of his head into the concrete. He was dead. Matt Harmon was dead.

'NO! PLEASE MATT! PLEASE! PLEASE! PLEASE!'

Kate heard her own voice screaming in the blackness. Primitive screams that didn't quite sound like her, only she knew that they were her from the way they resonated through her. She repeatedly vomited, choking on the horror in front of her. Falling back onto the concrete, she screamed for Matt, willing the universe to bring him back so that she could warn him about the bullet. She banged on the door, her fists bleeding, needing help so urgently. She needed help to save Matt.

There was a bullet flying through the air, and if only she could warn him. Push him out of the way. She begged the universe to go back into time again and not lunge towards Mason. The universe, however, ignored her pleading.

A security guard who had been doing his routine shift around the convention centre heard the banging and the woman screaming. He knew that something catastrophic had taken place from the tone of the screams. He had followed the terrible sounds and had come across an equally terrible scene in the stairwell. Two individuals. One a woman, with blood on the back of her head, covered in blood, screaming and banging on the door and the other a male. Shot dead with a hole in his neck. He had bled out. Several litres of his blood had pooled at the wall. The scene made the security guard wretch. He hadn't seen a scene like that before. He also hadn't come across such profound distress. The woman was hysterical. Inconsolable. He called the police and an ambulance. He added, 'make that two.'

The police were there within minutes. Their notes said that the scene was 'chaotic and confronting'.

THIRTY

DECISIONS

The woman knew that her name was Kate but felt as if she were disembodied. She floated towards a staircase. She was in a house that looked vaguely familiar, as there was something about the swirling pattern on the green carpet that asked her to remember something. On the opposite side of the staircase, she could see a little girl. She estimated her age. Five? Six? She could see that the little girl was clutching a small white bag with red trim. There was a lot of noise though, and the air was filling with shouting and tension. A teenage boy stood halfway up the staircase, a little lost, she thought. She turned and saw two older people whom the woman knew instinctively to be his parents. They were furious, that much she could fathom.

Kate observed calmly, understanding the scene and that she was observing herself. These were her parents too, and the boy was her older brother. It was her fifth birthday. She observed the little girl standing there, pain etched into her face whilst adults raged at the world and against her older brother. He was being assaulted by verbal bullets. The noise made her head hurt. She reached back and felt wet and mattered hair. She was cold too and falling in and out of another place, one which was cold and dark. How was she floating near the staircase when she was also cold and lying down? There was a dark place and then this memory, swapping her sense of reality around. Where was she? Standing in an old memory? She had been watching it from a distance, and then all of a sudden, she had been suddenly immersed within it.

The older Kate floated slowly towards the younger version of herself, whom seemed frozen and overwhelmed herself. The shouting was horrific, with the two adults clearly raging against themselves, each other and invisible enemies. This wasn't about the boy, trying to defend himself on the stairs for having gone for a drink with his friends. This was about them and the anger that seethed from between their lips. There had been defiance which had clearly been interpreted as catastrophic.

Kate wrapped her invisible arms around the little girl. The small child couldn't see her older self, but she felt the woman's warmth. A small bird then appeared from somewhere. It chirped, and the older Kate recognised the song from long, long ago. A distant memory that revealed itself at that moment. The bird was important, but Kate didn't know why at first. Then she remembered. It was her job to show the child the bird and how to protect it. She carefully picked up the tiny bird and placed it delicately into the child's hands. A moment of warmth spread through her.

'Look after the little bird Kate. They live in nests so that they are protected. You will become the nest, and you must protect this little bird. Always, Kate. If things are horrible, then deepen and strengthen the nest.'

The little girl had turned her head to one side and had looked out of the window. She had heard the bird song but couldn't see a bird nor Kate. She seemed to have been the only one who had heard its chirping amongst the raging.

The older Kate knew that her job was complete. Little Kate would know how to protect the little bird. The memory began to thin out, then blur and then it was gone. There was something else now that she had to do? Something to do with someone else who needed her. The headache began to throb, and she felt wetness around the base of her neck. She was lost, though, in a blackness. She turned to her right and saw an area of brightness. Should she go towards it, she wondered?

It was as if she were suspended somewhere, not only in space but also with thought. Intentions were necessary, she knew at that moment. If she floated towards the light, then there was a suggestion of peace. She had always wanted peace, and part of her wanted to float towards it. There was something else, though, to her left that was asking for attention.

She was aware that she no longer needed breath and that the sound of silence was complete as if she were in a vacuum. She could go right or left but not up nor down. Her mind only gave her the two options. She must decide to go left or right. There was something to her left. An urgency. An urgency of what? She didn't know. Someone needed her, only she couldn't find them. Left. She needed to go left. The blackness got thicker, suffocating her and then there was nothing.

FELICITY WOKE SUDDENLY. She was sweating. It was early morning, and a faint light was hinting at daybreak through the curtains. She looked around her, trying to get her bearings. Her heart was racing, and she felt sick. She sat up in the new bed and put her bedside light on. What on earth was going on with her? What had happened to make her wake like that? She got out of bed and put her dressing gown on, making her way into her kitchen. There, she made herself a mug of hot chocolate and then went and sat back in bed, wrapping the doona around her. She was shaking but didn't know why. She gazed down at the new doona cover, which she was confident Matt would love. She smiled. She had bought blue, knowing that it was his favourite colour and if she had got it right, it was identical to the colour of his eyes.

THE CONSTABLES TOOK notes whilst Louise told them everything that she knew. The older man nodded and looked very sympathetic as Louise tried to summarise what she could remember. She had offered to get her journal, but the policeman had suggested that a simple verbal recount was enough at that time. He interrupted her a couple of times for clarification.

'So, you don't know where Harry Rainer is at this present moment?'

'No.'

'But you presume that he has been kidnapped?'

'Yes. I believe that he has been kidnapped because of the note.'

'A note?'

'Yes, the kidnapping note.'

The police officers had looked at each other at that point with a look of disbelief.

'So, Ms Hemsworth and Mr Harmon are in Hong Kong somewhere trying to find a kidnapped Harry Rainer? Mrs Hamilton, I don't wish to sound rude, but have you been drinking this evening?'

Louise's eyes widened at the thought that she was coming across as someone inebriated. 'Excuse me. I'm a lawyer. I happen to have an excellent mind and what I am telling you is the truth. No, I have not been drinking either.'

Mildred was impressed and settled herself more comfortably on the top of the bookcase so that she could observe the scene better.

It was decided that Louise should go to the police station to make a formal statement. Once realising that they were dealing with a sober lawyer, the police officers started listening to her with genuine interest.

'I need to phone Andrew as he should really be there with me.' Louise told them.

'Who is Andrew?' The younger policeman had asked.

'Well, he's Kate's personal assistant. He should really bring Rupert as well,' added Louise thinking hard. 'He knows a lot too.'

'Rupert?'

'That's Andrew's boyfriend.'

'I see,' said the older policeman. 'Anyone else?'

'Well, come to think of it,' added Louise. 'There's Felicity. That's Matt's girlfriend.'

The older policeman interrupted.

'So, Mr Harmon is away with Ms Hemsworth but has a girlfriend here in London?'

'Yes.'

'Anyone else we need to know about?'

'Yes. Then there is Tim. Now I don't know much about Tim, but I believe, from what Andrew has said, that he is with Matt and Kate.'

'How about you ask everyone to come down to the police station at their earliest convenience?'

'Certainly, I will.'

Louise then texted everyone and told them that her local police station was waiting for them all.

• • •

THE SECURITY GUARD held the screaming woman as he waited for the police and ambulance to arrive. She had eventually fainted. At least he hoped that's all it was. He had checked for a pulse that was faint and rapid. She had been inconsolable. The dead man lay there, staring. The blood had finished pouring out of him and was now coagulating. His skin was icy white, and his lips were going blue. The woman had initially screamed about how it was all her fault. The security guard didn't believe a word of it. The man had been shot, and there was no gun on the scene.

The woman had a nasty head injury. He grabbed the first aid box from the third floor and ran back to the scene. Applying basic first aid to the wound on the back of her head, he managed to stop the bleeding. He prayed for the sounds of sirens to fill the air so that he could run from the horror he had stumbled across.

Kate was rushed by ambulance to the hospital in severe shock. She had lost a massive amount of blood from a gaping head wound, and the race was on to save her.

Matt was taken by ambulance to the morgue. There he was stripped down, and an identification band was placed on his toe. Then he was placed into a cold room. His next of kin would also need to be notified.

EVERYONE MET up at the police station. They were all curious as to what was going on. They had texted Louise back asking what it was all about, but Louise had simply replied to them all 'see you soon.' Felicity had been relieved to have something to do other than sit on her bed and worry. She was still feeling out of sorts after her nightmare. Although, she had no idea why a woman from a rival law firm would want her down at a police station so late. It made no sense.

Andrew and Rupert had been soundly asleep when they got the text.

'Oh crap. They know.' Andrew sighed.

'Who knows Daff?'

'The police. They know everything. It's the only reason Louise would send a text like that.'

'Oh, fuck, daff.'

TIM and his team had positioned themselves ready for their sting. The cargo was waiting to be picked up. Tim had given up trying to contact Matt and Kate for the time being. This next part of the operation was important, and he didn't want distractions. He had complete faith that wherever and whatever Kat and Matt were doing, they were doing just fine. Otherwise, he would have been notified.

Tim was to be positioned near the office to identify Mason and get him talking. Typically, one of the officers would do this, but Tim had studied Mason's background. The plan was to allow the cargo to be signed for. That way, the person signing had accepted legal responsibility for the cargo. Then Tim would be sent in, get him talking to extract as much information as possible, and the team would swoop. Tim was to ensure that he asked about Rainer and the meeting at the port that had taken place between him and Mason. Wired ready, he waited. Small talk and the occasional joke were passed from one to the other. Then a sudden demand for silence on the airways. Their man was here. Tim looked up. Mason had caused all of them an incredible amount of problems. Now finally, he was to be stopped. Matt and Kate would be proud of him right now, that much he knew.

The truck pulled up, and a man got out on the passenger side. Was that Mason? Tim strained his head but couldn't see. It was a man. No, but not Mason. The driver wasn't someone he knew either, from what he could see. Then a second man got out. That must be him, thought Tim, but he couldn't see him fully with the truck door blocking his view. As soon as they had loaded the goods, then they would be signed for. He caught glimpses of the men operating forklifts to move the cargo. They were wearing caps which prevented him from seeing their faces clearly. Then it was done. The driver and one of the men got back into the truck as the other man started to walk forward to sign. The team sent the signal that Tim was to GO! As he stood up, something happened. The truck suddenly reversed and crashed through the boom gate. The man, supposedly signing, ran towards the central rail depot instead. A signal was sent for Tim to 'No Go!'

The operations team ran after the man and caught him. The truck, however, with the cargo, got away. Tim was waiting with Jayme, who was on the phone talking with the arrest team.

'They got your man.' She informed him. 'The truck almost made its way onto South 47. There's a Jim Acton and Charlie Pike on board. Know either of them?'

'No, sorry. Has Mason been caught? He was running.'

A few moments later, his radio crackled. 'They have Mason. He's in the reception area of the main building.'

Tim hurried into the reception area where Mason had been captured.

'Where is he?' asked Tim, looking around.

'Duh,' replied Jayme thinking he was joking. Then she looked at Tim's face. He was serious. 'The dude over near the window? David Mason. Yes?'

Tim stared at the man and then back at Jayme. He shook his head slowly. 'This man isn't David Mason,' replied Tim. 'That is Harry Rainer, and I have no idea who the other two guys are. Where's Mason?'

• • •

THE CROWD WERE at the police station asking lots of questions. Too many questions for the front counter officer.

'Please. If you could all be quiet for a moment, Senior Detective Andrew Mayweather will be with you all in a moment.'

They sat in a row like naughty school children waiting to see the headmaster.

Felicity texted Matt. 'OMG, at the police station. Have been asked in along with several other people. I will let you know asap re what for. Miss you xxx.'

'So,' asked Andrew Mayweather to Constable Francis Black. 'What have we got out in the waiting room?'

'You won't believe what you are about to hear. We've got fifty shades, a potential kidnapping, drug smuggling, Hong Kong, lawyers and a girlfriend who doesn't know that her boyfriend is cheating on her… plus all the stuff we don't yet know about.'

Andrew Mayweather raised his eyebrows.

'Christ,' he said, 'Brief me properly, then we had better get in there to sort this lot out.'

THE HOSPITAL IDENTIFIED THEIR VICTIMS. Matthew Harmon aged thirty-six. An Australian living in London. Divorced, no children, lawyer. Fatally shot in the neck. Next of kin is Felicity Sharpe, girlfriend according to the Metropolitan Police in London. The woman in Ward Three, now recovering from surgery, is a Kate Hemsworth, aged thirty-three. Australian living in London. Divorced, no children. Next of kin, Belinda and Graham Hemsworth of Stewart Town, Queensland, Australia.

Anna Chen was the hospital pastor. She was responsible for breaking the news to the next of kin that a loved one had passed away. She dialled Felicity Sharpe's mobile phone number as given to her by the hospital administration staff.

Felicity was sitting next to Andrew, waiting to be seen by the police, when her phone rang.

'Hello,' she said, not recognising the overseas number. She was about to launch into her marketing calls response. Although maybe Matt was phoning her from somewhere?

'Hello, may I speak with Felicity Sharpe, please?'

'Speaking,' she replied.

'Hello, Felicity. My name is Anna Chen. I'm the pastor at St George's Hospital here in Hong Kong. Have you got time to speak?'

Felicity felt sick. 'Why? Is Matt okay?' she asked quickly.

'I'm so sorry, Felicity. Have you got someone with you right now?'

'Yes.'

There was silence as Anna took in a breath. 'Matt was involved in an accident earlier today. He has passed away. I'm so sorry.'

Felicity dropped the phone onto the floor of the police station and stood up.

She turned to Andrew, her face grey, her eyes wide.

'Matt... he's dead.' She then let out a long, piercing scream.

Andrew Mayweather had just come to the front desk to ask the group into the interview room.

He turned to his colleague. 'Make that a catastrophe as well. It's going to be a long evening.'

Andrew and Rupert quickly leaned forward to break Felicity's fall.

Andrew turned to Rupert, his eyes wide. His heart sank. Matt was dead? Where the hell was Kate?

• • •

THE DOCTOR STOOD next to Kate's bed. His patient hadn't uttered a word since she had come around from the surgery. She was in deep shock. The wound on her head had been dressed and would heal nicely. Her MRI showed a slight bleed on the brain but nothing life-threatening. She was lucky that the security guard had found her when he had. Her blood loss had been their biggest concern.

The doctor was worried about her emotional state, however. Whatever she had witnessed had caused her a severe emotional injury. The police had repeatedly been asking to question her, and he had been able to stop them so far. However, at some point, Kate would need to be questioned.

'Ms Hemsworth. My name is Dr Huan. How are you feeling? Any better? We have your head wound under control, but I'm worried that you haven't spoken yet. Can you tell me what happened?'

Kate remained mute and unmoving.

'The police need to question you. They will do this by coming into the hospital room, and they will need to ask you a few questions.'

Nothing.

'Just do the best you can do, Ms Hemsworth, ok?'

The police visited, and Kate said nothing.

Then, on day seven, Kate spoke. 'I want to see Matt.'

The doctor saw this as a breakthrough. She had made a connection with them. This was good.

'Matt is dead, Ms Hemsworth,' the kind doctor had informed her gently.

'I know. I was there. I want to see his body.'

They wheeled Kate down to see Matt, explaining that people often looked quite different when they had passed on. Kate didn't say anything. They had placed Matt out nicely on a bed in a brightly painted, yellow room. They had placed plastic yellow roses in a vase on the table next to him. Kate saw the roses and smiled. Maybe Matt had bought them for her? He had always bought her flowers.

Her eyes moved up to the table. A man was lying on the top of it, asleep, she presumed. He looked a bit like Matt. He was lying still and idle, unusual for Matt, though. She looked at the sheet that had been placed over him, hiding everything from his chest down. It didn't rise and fall, indicating that the man was holding his breath. The nurse interrupted her thoughts.

'You can have as much time as you need with Matt,' she said kindly.

'Oh, is this Matt?' she asked, her eyes glazed and not understanding.

'Yes, darling. It is. He was shot, remember? He passed away, sweetheart.'

'Yeah, I knew that.'

She looked back at the man named Matt, not knowing what to say or do. She peered closely towards him, mostly out of morbid curiosity, as she had not been this close to a dead body. People often said that death made a person look peaceful… or serene. This Matt didn't look peaceful. He looked pissed off. The corners of his mouth were down-turned a bit, and there was a slight frown on his brow. His skin had gone a peculiar colour, and his lips and fingernails were blue. He wore a red cravat around his neck.

His neck? There had been something about a neck. Oh yes. She remembered. Matt had a hole in his neck from a bullet too. Maybe this was her Matt? She looked again. It could be, she supposed.

'Hi Matt,' she said.

The man didn't reply.

'It's okay. I would be pissed off too. I'm only saying that because you look pissed off.'

Silence.

'Well, this is fucked isn't it,' Kate said. 'I'm probably going to lose my job as well. First you, and now my career.' She laughed. 'There's nothing left, Matt. Absolutely nothing.'

In her mind, she wondered if she should confess to him that he had paid the ultimate price for being part of a strategy. She thought not. He was dead. He couldn't hear her anyway. Could he?

'Mason got away. That was my fault. I probably shouldn't have chased him and then lunged at him. I'm not sure that he intended to shoot you. It should have been me, Matt. But then he did. So that's why you are dead.'

Matt still said nothing. It irritated her that he didn't speak.

'Silence, hey. Yup, that's because you are dead. Hey, I need to hear your voice one last time. So that I can remember exactly what you sound like. Can you do that for me, Matt?'

He said nothing. He didn't even inhale as if trying to find the right words.

Maybe Matt really was dead? She reached out to touch him and then stopped. He would be cold. She didn't want to feel cold. She wondered if she needed to say more. Was there anything left to say? An apology perhaps for killing him? No. No need. He was dead.

She needed to check, though. Matt had always played practical jokes on her. She reached out to touch his face. It was cold, and his skin felt waxy, just like the texture of death. She flinched as she realised he was dead.

So Matt was really dead? Forever?

She sat and thought about forever. Matt would never inhale or utter another sound. Forever. Forever seemed so long.

'Matt. I think you must have died. It would have been better if this was swapped, I think. You sitting here, talking to me and me lying there. My future is going to be a living death, Matt. I've fucked up everything, and you are dead. Dead. Imagine how you would react, Matt, if I told you.'

He said nothing.

In the movies, people then leaned over, and they kissed the departed on the forehead. Kate didn't. She didn't want her lips touching death so closely like that. Absolute death needed to stay separate from her. Death was horrible. Matt looked horrible. He smelled like death too. God, death was horrible.

She started to panic. Final and forever seemed insurmountable at that moment.

'He shot you, Matt. He shot you. He hurt you. He killed you, and now you are dead. Because of me, Matt.'

She stared at the enormity of death. The finality of it. Where was Matt now? Trapped inside a dying body, screaming to get out? Or had Matt gone somewhere better? She doubted it. She should say something like 'rest in peace' or 'go and enjoy meeting your loved ones.' Kate didn't. She knew that Matt was just a corpse now. There was most likely no conscious thought, and he most certainly wasn't smiling down from heaven at her. If anything, he would be seeking revenge if there was an after-life, making her pay for her strategy and the deceit and incompetence that had seen his neck ripped apart.

Kate was moved to the mental health ward two days later. She had refused to speak to the police and simply repeated the same line over and over.

'I have a bird that I need to look after.'

They had searched the hotel room and her house looking for the bird that she kept referring to, and finding nothing had concluded that she was suffering a breakdown. She would need intensive mental health therapy to recover. Her mind had simply fragmented. Even Kate didn't know who she was anymore.

. . .

TIM TRIED to phone Kate again. He couldn't get through. Matt's phone didn't answer as well, going through to his message bank each time. He decided to phone through to Andrew instead, in case he knew anything. Just as Felicity had collapsed from the news about Matt, Andrew's phone rang.

'Hi. This is Andrew.' He was trying to prop Felicity up as Rupert fanned her with cold air.

'Andrew. Thank goodness. This is Tim. I've been working with Kate and Matt, as you are probably aware. I'm in LA at the moment.'

'Tim.' Andrew looked around at the chaotic scene.

Tim sounded rattled. 'Look, I've been trying to get hold of them for a bit, and neither of them are answering their phones. Have you been in contact lately? I've got some news.'

Andrew took a deep breath. 'I guess you haven't heard then?'

'Heard what?' asked Tim, his heart sinking.

'Matt is dead, Tim, and at this stage, I don't know where Kate is either.'

'Jesus, what?' Tim sat down, his heart pounding in his chest.

'I don't know the details. I don't even know how he died.' A hospital just phoned Felicity and dropped a bombshell.'

'Shit. Look, I've just met with the cargo. It was Harry Rainer who met the cargo and not David Mason. Mason is still out there, and we need to ensure that he doesn't go after Kate. Do you think it was Mason who killed Matt?'

'I don't know, Tim.'

Felicity had come round and was wailing. Andrew shook his head. It was all too much. For the first time since he was thirteen years old, he bent over and started to sob. Rupert gathered him up in his arms.

'Oh Andrew, please don't cry. I've got you.'

The detective stared at the group in the waiting room. Everybody was crying and trying to comfort each other. 'I think we need to bring them into the interview room and make a few cups of tea. This isn't a good look for the station,' he advised the constable on duty.

TIM TRAVELLED to LA International Airport. He needed to get straight back to Hong Kong. He felt partly responsible for all of this. Right now, though, he needed to find Kate. If Mason was still out there and Matt was dead, then Kate would be at risk. He phoned the police in Hong Kong. Why hadn't he insisted on speaking to them sooner?

THE LONDON POLICE listened as Louise took charge of the situation. She had been able to give them a detailed account of the entire, sad situation. From the beginning, Louise had noticed things, more than even she cared to admit. She was able to tell the policeman about Matt's visit to the office and how he and Kate had been quite active in there. Felicity had howled. She'd had no idea that Matt had been cheating on her with Kate.

'How could he?' she wailed. 'I hate him'. A moment later, she was crying, 'I loved him so much.'

Felicity called Nat, who drove like a madwoman to the police station to comfort her.

Louise explained about Kate's drinking, not that she thought it was terribly relevant, but just something that perhaps should be noted down.

The police had given her a book of identifying tattoos

from convicted criminals hoping that she could make a match. She did, in forty-eight seconds, by matching it to the one she had drawn in her diary. They sent someone to pick up the suspect immediately with sirens blaring. Louise was able to tell the policeman that Kate had been off work with influenza but hadn't really looked sick. She told them about the call that had come in from Hong Kong and how Kate had left a partial message on the office answering service. Again, some interesting background information.

The police were trying to put it all together.

'So, Daniel Parkes was really called Harry Rainer, then he was allegedly kidnapped?' they confirmed with Louise.

Andrew butted in.

'No. He wasn't kidnapped at all. He turned up in Los Angeles. Originally it was to do with the porn films.'

'So he made amateur...um... porn films with a Barry Evans, which is why he sought help in the first instance?'

'Yes,' said Rupert, who had been a silent witness to most of this journey. 'Only it wasn't actually about the films at all.'

'So… Barry Evans was posing as Greg. Although already married to Linda Evans, he had married Harry Rainer who introduced himself as Daniel Parkes to Kate?' The policeman was clearly trying to keep up.

'Yes,' said Louise.

'Kate thought he was Daniel Parkes. It was Matt who found the phone in Rainer's drawer when he was posing as a cleaner.' Andrew added that bit, suddenly remembering Kate telling him about it.

'So, this Mason individual… David Mason, otherwise known as Huang Fa Lee… he was supposed to pick up a cargo of cocaine that had been melted into some plastic wrapping. Only he didn't show up, but Harry Rainer did instead?'

'That's correct,' said Andrew, who had been filled in by Tim once he had been comforted by Rupert.

'Right,' said the policeman. 'Get me that Tim back on the phone.'

Andrew phoned Tim back.

'You're on speaker, Tim. London Metropolitan Police. Where are you now, Tim?'

'About to fly back to Hong Kong.'

'Do you know where Kate Hemsworth is?' asked the policeman.

'Yes, That's why I'm hurrying back. She's apparently in a hospital. She could be in danger, though. I've just spoken with them.'

'Do you believe that she might be in danger from David Mason?'

'Yes. The Hong Kong police told me that Matt was shot in the neck. One bullet wound. He bled out.'

Felicity was sobbing so loudly that the policeman had to suspend the phone call for a moment while she was taken out of the room by Nat.

'Get a cup of tea from the kitchen room. Just ask the constable for one,' he advised a bit more gently. This situation sounded horrific at best. 'The main priority now is to protect Kate Hemsworth as she appears to be a vital witness to a murder. I'll arrange an interview with the Hong Kong police when you get there, Tim.'

THE HONG KONG police informed Andrew Mayweather that Kate had been admitted into the hospital and later into the psychiatric unit for further treatment as she wasn't making a lot of sense. They asked if anyone knew about a pet bird? They agreed to protect Kate and allow Tim to see her once she was up to it.

. . .

MATT'S BODY was then flown to Australia for burial. His brother Simon gave a magnificent eulogy, and the firm sent several bouquets of red roses for the funeral. No one from the UK made it to the funeral, however, as work schedules were too busy for the long flight there and back.

Felicity was taken home by Nat, and she stayed for two weeks, helping her deal with Matt's death and his profound betrayal. She wasn't well enough to fly over for the funeral. She texted her ex-boyfriend Brad about Matt's death, and he promised to stop by in the next couple of days to touch base with her. Then she sold the new furniture and replaced it with items that wouldn't remind her of Matt and the future she had designed for them.

The Law Society in London quickly responded when Louise Hamilton informed them of what had happened at the firm. Such behaviour constituted misconduct, and Kate was struck off under the legislation. The Law Society were unsympathetic to a lawyer who failed to recognise their own limitations in such a serious situation. Louise was reprimanded as well and suspended for three months. She had thought that this was quite generous given her stupidity in getting herself involved in the first place. She channelled her newfound zest for life into getting herself a license to become a Private Investigator. In addition, she joined a ballroom dancing studio. In fact, Andrew Mayweather also did ballroom dancing at the same venue. The two of them enjoyed this coincidence. They perfected the tango and foxtrot.

There was no actual kidnapping in the first instance. There wasn't a criminal case to be investigated per se from that side of things.

Harry Rainer had staged the whole kidnapping in an

attempt to get rid of David Mason. By insinuating that Mason had kidnapped him, he had hoped to lead everyone to Mason's drug smuggling, which he had only recently discovered himself. It had been a stroke of luck that someone had delivered him a note when he had been visiting the San Francisco office weeks before, mistaking him for Mason. He hadn't intended anyone to get hurt and was devastated when he discovered that Matt had been shot dead.

Harry Rainer had acted out of pure stupidity. Instead of simply going to the police as he should have, he had staged it all so that David Mason would be investigated for kidnapping, even if no one had discovered the drugs.

Rainer had then approached Mason with a deal to just 'go away' and leave his business out of it all. Mason had started threatening him, and Rainer realised he was in over his head. Mason was using Rainer's name to export the drugs, and proving that he knew nothing about it all would be unconvincing.

Scared of what would happen if he went to the police, he had decided to engage the services of a legal team that might be clever enough to find the drug smuggling without implicating him. Rather than go and report it all himself and risk having Mason land the blame into his own lap, thus incriminating him in drug smuggling, he had concocted the story about the blackmail over the films. This was a story to get Kate hooked. If he then disappeared, she would be invested in finding him. He would lead her as close to Mason as he could.

Harry Rainer had told Kate to investigate Linda and Barry Evans in the hope that she was bright enough to find anomalies in her research. He bought a dummy phone and texted himself threats so that he could take them in to show Kate. He even left his mobile phone in the office for them to find and left it unlocked. He knew that an astute mind would see that the first phone call had come in, supposedly from David Mason. It wasn't his number at all, Rainer had changed the internal numbers on the company website predicting that they would do an online search. He had then fled the scene to make it look as if he had been kidnapped.

When Kate had organised to send the cease letter to Barry and Linda, Rainer organised for someone to pick the letter up from the receptionist, thus ensuring that it didn't ever get delivered to Barry and Linda. He'd even paid a gang member to drop off threatening notes to the firm to ensure that Kate was scared enough to continue investigating. He'd chosen a gang member that pointed to Mason's drug dealing, obvious because of the tattoo they wore on their hands.

MASON WAS clever enough to assume that Rainer would investigate the docks in Hong Kong and had confronted him there, seeing him leaving Eric Lee's office. He had wired himself and got enough out of Rainer to incriminate him. Rainer had clearly demonstrated in the conversation that he knew about the drugs. Mason had enough to sink him, especially given his name was on the export cargo. He was annoyed that Rainer had sussed out how he was smuggling. The railway customs process was slack compared to the wharf. Getting some of the drugs dropped off at San Fransisco and then taking the rest to Los Angeles had been easy. However, he knew that Rainer would fly on to LA to investigate the shipment coming in and so had decided not to meet it anyway. Matt and Kate were two steps behind. He was never going to meet the cargo in the first place.

Rainer however, had left the docks, now planning on killing Mason in LA. He would meet the cargo in Los Angeles before Mason got to it, and then he would kill Mason when he arrived. He had changed tact half-way through. If Mason was the only one who knew about the drugs, then he could kill him and take the profit? Then he would cover his tracks and stop all future imports. Hopefully, in the meantime, Kate and Matt would stop their investigation after having found a few dead ends. They certainly hadn't alerted anyone in his Hong Kong offices that he might be kidnapped, so he had to assume that they knew nothing.

'So, the whole fifty shades was simply a hook to get Kate interested?' Rupert was stroking Andrew's hair, his head resting on his lap.

'Yup,' said Andrew sighing.

'Crazy,' sighed Rupert. 'Insane situation. All of it.'

'Very,' said Andrew.

'Came at an enormous cost for Matt and Kate, though.'

'Yes. But if Kate had not been the sort of person who thought she could solve it all herself, it never would have turned out like it did. She should have gone to the police, and I should have encouraged her more. It's partly my fault Rupert.'

'Don't blame yourself, Andrew. You were just trying to protect your boss. That's what the court agreed upon, too.'

'Rainer got thirteen years, you know,' added Andrew. 'Harsh for someone trying to hide everything, don't you think?'

'I don't know. I wonder if Rainer was intending on taking the drugs for himself?'

'I suppose he could have been? He didn't go to the police, did he? He went and tried to pick up the cargo himself.'

'Who knows what he was hiding? Mason is lucky to be alive, I think. If Matt and Kate hadn't met him at the conference, I predict that Rainer was going to take him out in LA.'

'Do you think so?'

'Yeah. What do they call this sort of situation… a perfect

storm?' Rupert kissed Andrew on the head. 'You are going to be okay,' he murmured soothingly.

Andrew smiled. 'I'm thankful I have you in my life, Rupert. Seriously. I'm glad that what we say and what we do is soundly based on honesty. Look at what happens when you try to hide things.'

THIRTY-ONE

CURLS AT THE NAPE

The woman sat down, placed her file on the table and then opened it. Now was an opportunity to share Kate's case with her colleagues.

She took a deep breath and began. 'Kate has been in the ward now for six months. She was committed initially for three weeks and has spent the rest of the time here voluntarily. She was flown from Hong Kong to this facility where she has remained ever since.'

'This is your dissociative patient, Beatrice?' asked Paula, one of the other counsellors. 'The one who suffered the shooting trauma?'

'Yes, that's right. Just to go over the background again, briefly. Kate had a history of severe trauma as a child. Came from a fairly volatile and unsupportive family. I'd even call them destructive at times. She built up a strong defence mechanism as a result which dates back to when she was…' Beatrice looked through the notes. 'Five. The day her brother was thrown out of the family home. Her original birth personality, which we call 'Little Kate,' is locked away at the centre, essentially protected.' Beatrice demonstrated by cupping her hands together.

'So, the original personality that she was born with she calls Kate as well?' asked Michael, Head of Psychiatry.

'At this stage, she refers to it as a Little Kate at my suggestion. It's an analogous reference to a frail being. Something small and in need of protection. I called it Little Kate just to give continuity between the two of them. Then her first husband suddenly left, not giving her time to process the break, and she retreated further inwards. The death of her friend Matt, in such violent circumstances, has simply added further trauma to what was already a fragile predicament.'

'So, who are you dealing with during consults?' asked Paula, one of the other psychologists.

'Well, it's not a totally different character, rather a sub-section of the original one. It's Kate without little Kate. It's as if she locked away the fragile part of herself and left a machine to operate from within. A personality with little empathy or attachment capability.'

'You said though that the death of her friend had affected her though?' Michael had stopped taking his own notes and was looking at Beatrice over the top of his glasses, perched on the end of his nose.

'Yes, but not quite in the right way. It's more that she blames herself for Matt's death. They were lovers at the time too. He was having an affair with Kate, and I haven't yet worked out how serious the relationship was. She's more preoccupied with her reaction processes rather than with the fact that he lost his life.'

'Subtle, but important, I think?' Paula nodded and wrote something down.

'So, I'm confused. This woman was a lawyer, you say? How did she manage to hold down such a demanding interpersonal job?' asked Sandra, one of the younger members of the psychotherapy team.

'Well, it was easy for her. In a sense, law doesn't require attachment. It requires a stick adherence to logic. Kate could simply follow the rules. When you think about it, it was a logical career for her. She could fly solo, so to speak and push her way through. She didn't have to feel. She just had to remember the nuances of the law and the details of her clients.'

'Which ironically she didn't,' added Michael.

'Yes,' agreed Beatrice. 'Kate has elements of narcissism too. It was easy for her to have grandiose ideas. She truly believed that she could control this situation and was intelligent enough to figure it all out, obviously, at a terrible cost. She accepts from a literal sense that she is responsible. She also understands that her life as she knows it, is over.'

'So, where do you go from here?' asked Michael. 'That's quite a mess.'

'Kate doesn't want to leave. She feels that she has found a safe place for Little Kate. That makes sense when you think about it. We are providing medications to calm things down, and little Kate likes that. We are offering her nurture which she hasn't experienced before.'

'Perhaps if you concentrate on building Little Kate up, the two might be able to merge in the future?' asked Sandra.

'Exactly,' smiled Beatrice towards her younger colleague. 'By working with the fragile aspects of Kate's personality and giving them the nurture and stability that she has missed out on, we might be able to eventually merge the two of them back together again. I have to say, though, she's incredibly frustrating to work with. I'm sure there are some anti-social traits there too.'

'Well, it's an interesting case Beatrice,' said Michael. 'However, I agree that she needs to start including some references to leaving in her treatment plan. She can't stay here, forever.'

'Yes,' sighed Beatrice. 'I just wish I could make more positive progress with her. She spends a lot of time blowing smoke in my face and telling me to fuck off.'

The other counsellors shook their heads in sympathy.

BEATRICE SAT OPPOSITE KATE. Another therapy session. Another opportunity to help.

'Hi, Kate.'

Kate looked at her, not bothering to answer.

'How's the sobriety going?'

'Well, it's a bit forced, isn't it,' answered Kate sarcastically. She hadn't had a drink since arriving, which had been nothing short of hell on some days, despite being on numerous medications to soften the chaos around her.

'I'd actually like a drink occasionally. I'm not actually sober, am I? If it is forced, then it can't be sobriety.'

'I thought today we would look at 'Little Kate' and work with her. What do you think about that?' The counsellor had ignored her poke.

Kate rolled her eyes. Seriously? The woman was a pain in the arse. However, to stay in the mental hospital, she had to put up with this stupid therapy. There was no point in leaving. Her life as she knew it was over. Mason had ruined it all by shooting Matt. Rainer had ruined her life by walking into her office that day. What was the point in even going back out into the world when she had no world left to go back to? It wasn't like she would leave London and go do the thirteen-hour drive into the Australian Outback and have a happy family reunion.

'Tell me about Little Kate,' Beatrice asked her. 'What was it like to be Little Kate, growing up?'

'I've already told you. Fucked. Read your fucking notes.' She lit up a cigarette. She hadn't smoked before coming into the hospital, and now she did. She liked it. It helped take the edge off her forced sobriety. She didn't care about the health risks. Death would be welcome.

'Can you describe a typical day for Little Kate, perhaps? Help me to understand.' Beatrice smiled at her. It was that or go and hit her over the head with her file, which she knew wasn't appropriate.

Kate studied Beatrice's face. It was warm and one that generated kindness. It wasn't a hard face like her mother's had been. She had to admit that she felt safe in Beatrice's office. She could say what she wanted without fear of being screamed at for saying the wrong thing. When she was growing up, and throughout her adult life, she had constantly been second-guessing herself before saying anything. Her words had always been chosen so that they would not inflame or set off her mother's rage.

'Fine,' she decided on as a reply. She would do as she was asked just to get Beatrice off her back. 'A typical day, hey?'

'Okay, we can start with that.' Beatrice smiled. This was a huge step forward.

'Shouting. Fucking shouting. They hated each other, and yet they needed each other. You know why they needed each other?'

Beatrice shook her head. 'This is your parents?'

'So that they had someone to scream at.'

'Was there much screaming?'

Kate thought back. Always anger. Love then anger. Strange love. Not like with Ethan when she had felt safe. The love had felt dangerous. It was a currency that was given and taken. Give and take. There and gone.

'If you did what they said, they loved you. If you did anything they didn't like, they hated you. On. Off. Like a fucking switch. They hit too. Pow. There was no point to me. It wasn't me they wanted. They wanted to see themselves standing in front of them. I was irrelevant. I was a mirror, a reflection. So if I was reflecting on what they wanted from me, it was good. If I did anything to shatter the illusion, then it was game over.'

Beatrice nodded. This made sense.

'Cats. So many fucking cats. My mother had twenty-three of them. I had to feed them all. Just like all the kids she collected too. Only they were there, and then they were gone - except her favourites. She kept them encased in childhood. They still wear their hair in pigtails too. Nearly fucking thirty.'

She took a deep drawl of her cigarette and flicked the ash onto the floor.

'The others aren't dead like Matt though. Just sent away as soon as they did or said something wrong. So much fucking anger. They were always angry. I wasn't an angry person though...' she laughed. 'I was the one always trying to quell the fucking fires. I would do anything to just try to keep the peace. I always had a knot in my stomach...' her voice trailed off as she became lost in thought.

Beatrice allowed her a moment to reflect.

'How would you have described yourself, Kate?'

'I was kind and giving... too fragile to cope in a house that was an inferno. It was like two angry people had created a peaceful person. A plus A had created B. Do you get that? I wasn't like them. I didn't want to be like them. Not ever. It doesn't really matter now, though, does it? All this stuff? It seems irrelevant.' She shut down again. There was no point in trying to change the past.

'No. It's not. It's how you were shaped, Kate. Sometimes this can affect what we do later.'

Kate smoked another cigarette. She had clammed up

again. Talking about the past made her feel worse. It gave her a scared feeling. Like she didn't feel right.

'It's okay, Kate. We can do more of this another time.'

The counsellor could see that lowering the defences for Little Kate was a dangerous exercise. However, until they could keep uncovering the layers surrounding it and showing it that it was okay to come out, it would continue its hideaway.

MASON WAS BIDING HIS TIME. After killing Matt, he fled back to rural China and hid near his home town in the North West. He knew the police were looking for him. However, he had an extensive network of fellow gang members throughout China who were helping him. He would not suffer the indignity of an arrest. He had shot the stupid lawyer. He hadn't intended to, but the woman had lunged at him, and the gun had gone off. He was lucky that he had made it out of the conference area and into rural China before she had come to and had then raised the alarm.

He was pissed off that his drug business had been exposed by Rainer. Fucker. As soon as Rainer was out of jail, he would come after him. Thirteen years he would wait. Rainer would walk free, probably reformed too, he imagined. Maybe he would even find God in the jail. As soon as he was out, he would get revenge. The wait would be sweet.

'TELL me more about the relationship between your parents Kate.'

'Relationship? If that's what you want to call it. I remember anger mostly. Just uncontrollable rage. They thought that they owned us. That we would do exactly as they wanted. If we didn't, then they would rage at us. Screaming, hitting…' her voice tapered off.

'What did that feel like?'

Kate thought hard. There was a feeling somewhere. She could tell. She bit her lower lip. All she had to do was release it. Give it a name.

'Take your time, Kate.' This was a critical moment for Kate. She was finding a feeling and trying to identify it instead of pushing it further down.

Kate sat in the feeling. What was it? She closed her eyes and saw herself standing before them. The spit and rage was being unleashed from their mouths. She could feel their accusations hitting her, their words causing physical pain. Where was the pain? There was a place in her body close to her heart. That's where the pain was. It hurt. She connected her mind to the pain. She could numb the pain by using her mind. Closing off her mind, building a thickness. A wall. Their words hurt less. She could hear them now but not feel them. She could see their mouths opening and closing and the disappointment and anger firing towards her.

Kate looked up at the counsellor. Her eyes were now wide. There was a moment. Enlightenment. Beatrice saw it too. She put her pen down. Kate had made a connection and wanted to share it, perhaps?

There was silence. Was Kate going to trust the moment enough to share?

'I… I built up this protection like a wall. It eased the pain,' she whispered. She looked over at Beatrice. 'I get it now. I can feel it. It was painful… and the emotion was…'

She paused, looking out of the window at a nearby tree. A small bird was sitting on the branch. It looked at her, cocking its head to one side. Then it chirped.

At that moment, the sun streamed into the room as a ray

of light, landing on Kate's chest. She looked down at it and then whispered,

'Grief at knowing I wasn't really loved.'

Beatrice smiled. There was emotion and a name for it. Kate had connected with Little Kate. If Beatrice were wholly honest, she was also happy because Kate hadn't sworn at her for the first time since they had started the therapy.

KATE AND BEATRICE now both referred to Kate's younger personality as Little Kate. Gradually, over time, Little Kate started to stay in the space for a bit longer, understanding that it was safe to do so. Beatrice was sometimes very moved as Kate told her about her childhood. Clearly, this was a child born into a strange hell that would only have been understood by those inhabiting the same space.

Although Kate had made some abysmal choices that had resulted in the death of her friend, Beatrice wondered how much blame could truly be portioned towards Kate. Was she a victim of her own context? Some would argue yes and others no. Kate was a grown adult when she made those choices and therefore had to accept the consequences of her actions. She wondered how differently Kate's life would have turned out if she had been born into a different family? The court had concluded that Kate wasn't well enough to stand trial for anything. Her punishment was to be stuck off, and that would be the end of it all.

Beatrice had undertaken extensive research into epigenetics and the expression of genes. She wondered about Kate. Obviously, some unsavoury genes were flying around the family DNA. She wondered about Kate and how those had expressed themselves given her upbringing. In another family, Kate's temperament might have been nurtured rather than seen as an anomaly. Kate hadn't been born evil. She had been born whole. The problem had to do with her parents' own expectations around children. The children hadn't been brought into the family to be loved. They had been brought in to love their mother. This was a system destined to fail. As soon as the children could not pacify their mother's own internal disharmony, they were seen as failures and punished.

Kate's mother had no self-love and certainly no capacity to demonstrate what she couldn't feel for herself. Nor could her father. Their children therefore, grew up in an environment where they didn't know how to demonstrate love either. It was a vicious circle. They were raged at when they failed in their duty. Hit and stomped on for accentuating their own mother's distress. Their father was oblivious to the dynamic. All he saw was his wife's distress, and then he would try to seek revenge with the culprits, even if they were his own children. It was easier for him to hit to create silence than sit and listen to their emotional pain.

'KATE. Can we bring Little Kate out for a bit?'

'Yes.'

Little Kate was beginning to build up trust. She didn't get shouted at, and there was no more horror to witness around her. Kate liked Little Kate. She was funny.

'Kate, how about you show her your world?'

Kate pondered the suggestion. 'Sure.'

Progress was being made. Slowly. As the weeks progressed, Little Kate was staying out longer and longer. With that came a nicer, older Kate. A Kate who wasn't trying to hold on so tightly herself.

Beatrice was pleased with her client. It was slow progress, but they were moving forward. There was no need to ask Kate to leave the ward just yet. She was starting to help other patients settle in, and Little Kate showed her how nice it felt to help others without being told that she was doing it wrong.

Ethan and Fiona were discussed during sessions, and Kate understood that 'shit happens' in life. Sometimes people mess with you and hurt you. That's what happened there. It was different from what Litle Kate had experienced. Soon, Little Kate understood this and left it to older Kate to process the situation. Beatrice knew that they had yet to discuss Matt. Kate hadn't grieved yet for Matt. It was time to try with the help of Little Kate who could provide her with some comfort.

'Let's talk about Matt,' said Beatrice.

'Really? How about we don't.' Kate sounded panicked.

'Let's try Kate.'

Kate frowned. Matt seemed so unreal now. Like a bad dream.

'Tell me about your relationship with Matt.'

Kate thought back to Matt in Brisbane and how he had chased her.

'He used to give me white roses. Every month for ten months.' The memory made her smile.

'That's lovely. Sweet,' Beatrice said. 'So, how did you feel when you saw him again?'

Kate had learned to tap into her feelings. She would sit for a while, allowing the feeling to identify itself and then she could try to name it.

'I didn't want to get hurt. He would have left me.'

'The feeling though, Kate.'

Kate went deeper. 'I felt something for him. It was… respect, admiration… I don't know. I know that I didn't want to get hurt, though.'

'So, you were protecting yourself?'

'I guess?'

'Let me ask the same question to Little Kate.'

Little Kate knew the answer immediately.

'I felt deeply connected to Matt… but I didn't want to get hurt, so I pushed him away.'

Kate sat there thinking. The early times they'd had sex. She had primarily felt numb, deep down. Why? Was it because she had felt something for Matt but didn't dare to acknowledge it in case he turned on her and hated her too? After all, that's what she had been taught, even with Ethan. Every single person she had loved had turned on her. All she had ever wanted was to feel loved, and then Ethan had come along. It was as if she had found home.

She thought about Matt lying on the concrete. He had bled out meters from her. She had caused that gun to fire in his direction. She must have felt something for him, and when he had needed her, lying there bleeding, she had felt nothing. Lost in a void of her own. Unconscious to his needs.

'I felt lots,' said Little Kate. 'It was awful seeing him lying there so helpless.' Kate couldn't deal with death and endings. Little Kate confessed that she had hidden it from Kate.

Kate's dialogue became internal.

'I didn't want you to get hurt. I was protecting you. I knew that Ethan had given you the love you wanted. I saw your pain after he left.'

'So, you did this? You protected me all this time?'

'Yes.'

'By making me feel nothing?'

'I felt the feelings for you. To protect you. But I hid them from you.'

Kate stared at Beatrice, who knew that there had been a shift within her.

The tears were welling in Kate's eyes as she got a glimpse of what Little Kate had been hiding from her. So much pain and suffering. So much love for Matt and Ethan.

'What? What are you feeling right now, Kate?' Beatrice asked her gently.

'I... I think I loved Matt,' she spluttered. The tears fell from her eyes before running down her cheeks.

'I'm sorry, Kate,' said Little Kate, allowing the grief to release itself and subside. 'I just wanted to protect you.'

Kate stood next to Little Kate in her mind. A little girl gazing up at her, no more than five.

'You're just a little girl,' she said.

'Yes. I'm five. I got a bag on my birthday too.'

'I know. The white one with the red trim?'

'Yes, that one. How did you know?'

'I was there.'

The little girl thought hard. 'That was you?'

'Yes. That was me.'

'They made him go away,' said the little girl.

'They were wrong.'

'I missed him so much.'

'I miss Ethan too.'

'You miss Matt as well?' asked the little girl.

'Yes. Lots. Hey, I was thinking.'

'What about?' asked the little girl.

'Should we do the rest together?'

'I'd like that,' smiled the little girl.

'Tell me what is going on, Kate?' asked Beatrice gently.

Kate looked up at her, changed. Altered profoundly.

'You were just trying to protect me,' she said to Little Kate. 'I understand now.'

A RAY of sunshine landed on the small child's hand. Then it reached the older woman's hand. They moved their hands closer together, touched and then locked them.

'You put your arms around me. I remember feeling warm.' said the little girl.

'I did,' said Kate, nodding.

They held hands together for the first time since Kate had turned five. There was an unspoken promise between them. That they would now do this together. The small hand tightened onto the older woman's hand, and slowly, they merged into one. Hands that exchanged tenacity as well as empathy. Hands that could love, be loved and be generous and clever all at the same time. Little Kate had trusted Kate enough to go with her, and Kate had trusted that she could love Little Kate enough to nurture her. There be no more shouting or violence for Little Kate. She was free to live as she had been born to. Kate could walk forward as a whole woman. Ready to start again on her own terms.

Beatrice smiled. She had just witnessed something. She wasn't exactly sure what, but her patient had just done something quite remarkable, she was sure. She could tell because the energy had changed in the room for a fraction of a second, and the ray of sunshine was lighting up the room. Beatrice shivered and then had felt overwhelmingly warm.

At that precise moment, the universe saw this too. It made a slight change to the fabric of everything, and somewhere off the coast of Chile, a small bird flew for the first time from its nest and soared into the sky.

All was good.

CATHERINE, known as Kate to her close friends, closed the book just as her train pulled into the station. For four hours, she had read without so much as looking up. A story she had plucked from the station bookshop and yet one that had seemed strangely familiar. A book of fiction and yet so well written that she felt she had lived it herself. She looked out of the window and thought she saw Matt. She went to tap on the window and then stopped. Matt was dead, so it couldn't be him. Anyway, he was a character in her book. She smiled to herself. Then she wondered. Curls at the nape, just like the intelligent man in the bookshop. The man with the curls suddenly stopped walking. Kate took a deep breath. He turned. She knew a connection was about to be made.

Kate shut her eyes. She couldn't. She didn't want to know. It was time to walk into her new beginning and leave the past behind. She knew that if she looked, she would remember. What though? What would she remember? Did she need to remember something?

This question will always remain an anomaly. Whether it was a testimony to the writer in drawing her in so authentically or something else, will never be explained. Instead, Kate got up, leaving the book on the seat for the next person, put the empty bottle of sparkling water and the crisp packet into the bin and stepped off the train into her new life.

… and the little bird in Chile soared.

THE END.